The
SCENT
of
SAKE

The
SCENT
of
SAKE

Joyce Lebra

AVON

An Imprint of HarperCollins*Publishers*

HarperCollins books may be purchased for educational, business, or sales promotional use. For information please write: Special Markets Department, HarperCollins Publishers, 10 East 53rd Street, New York, NY 10022.

FIRST AVON PAPERBACK EDITION PUBLISHED 2009.

Designed by Diahann Sturge

Library of Congress Cataloging-in-Publication Data
Lebra-Chapman, Joyce, 1925–
   The scent of sake / Joyce Lebra.—1st ed.
      p. cm.
   ISBN 978-0-06-166237-9
1. Rice wines—Japan—History—Fiction.   2. Rice wines industry—Japan—History—Fiction.   3. Japan—History—19th century—Fiction.   I. Title.
   PR9499.3.L43S34   2009
   823—dc22   2008023674

09 10 11 12   OV/RRD   10 9 8 7 6 5 4 3 2 1

To those who preserve the tradition.

When Amaterasu came forth [from the dark cave]
the Plain of High Heaven in the
Central Land of the Reed Plains
. . . became light.

the *Kojiki*

The Characters

Kinzaemon IX
Hana, his wife
Rie, their daughter
Jihei, Rie's mukoyoshi
Fumi, Rie's daughter by Saburo Kato
Seisaburo, Rie and Jihei's son
O-Toki, Jihei's favorite geisha, mother of Yoshitaro
Yoshitaro, Jihei's son of O-Toki
Tama, Yoshitaro's wife
Teru, Jihei's daughter of O-Toki
Kazu, Jihei's daughter of O-Yumi
Eitaro, Fumi's mukoyoshi
O-Sada, Yoshitaro's geisha
Ume, daughter of Yoshitaro and O-Sada
Hirokichi, son of Fumi and Eitaro
Mie, daughter of Fumi and Eitaro
Mari, Seisaburo's wife
O-Haru, Sawaraya proprietress
Masami, O-Toki's lover
Goro, son of O-Toki and Masami
Nobuo, son of Seisaburo and Mari
Masako, daughter of Seisaburo and Mari
Naoko, Hirokichi's wife
Hana, daughter of Hirokichi and Naoko

Toji, brewmaster
Kin, banto, chief clerk
Shin'ichi, Kinnosuke, his successor
Nobu, wife of Kinnosuke
O-Natsu, faithful family servant
O-Yuki, maid
Mrs. Nakano, marriage go-between
Hirano, Seisaburo's banto
Buntaro, Hirano's son, Kinnosuke's successor
Yamaguchi, competing brewer
Yusuke, his banto

Chapter 1

It was a day Rie would never forget, the day her mother told her who her husband would be. That day she had knelt in the frigid courtyard scrubbing the wooden sake barrels, barrels so large they had to be lifted by ropes and pulleys. She gripped the big brush in both hands and scrubbed back and forth, back and forth until her muscles ached. She rubbed her blue-cold hands together and held them over her nose and mouth. Then she scratched under the cotton scarf that held back her long thick hair and shifted on the rush mat on which she was kneeling. As she did so, she glanced through the misty screen of her breath at the door of the brewery and inhaled the pungent, mildewy smell of yeast, the smell that permeated every corner of the drafty old wooden house and brewery buildings. Women were never to enter the forbidden door that gaped darkly before her.

"Let a woman enter the brewery and the sake will sour," the old ones always said. Her mother had warned her of this since childhood. But Rie relished the yeasty smell of brewing sake that hung in the air. She had always played near the door and the barrels as a child. As a little girl, she had waited, terrified, for the news that the sake had soured. It never had. Now that she was grown, now that she had her own secret opinions of what women could accomplish, she made it her duty to wash the barrels, a task she took on when she knew her father was not looking. As atonement.

This time he caught her. "Rie! Haven't I warned you to stay away from the brewery door? It's too dangerous to be so close to the *kura,* brewing building, and washing barrels is not your responsibility."

Rie looked up to see her father looming over her, frowning, hands thrust into the sleeves of the indigo work kimono he always wore. His white chicken-feather eyebrows were dusted with frost and seemed to stand erect in anger.

Understand me, she longed to say. *See me as doing my best for you and the house.* But she couldn't say it.

Rie stood and bowed, looking down at her feet. Her father, Kinzaemon IX, head of the House of Omura, was the one person in the world she most wanted to please. He represented all nine generations of the ancestors, a long line to which both he and now Rie owed *on,* the obligation that could never be repaid but toward which one must strive throughout one's life.

At first when her brother had died, so had all her father's hopes and dreams. But after weeks of grieving, he had uttered the portentous words that would change her life: "So now, Rie, the future of the Omura House rests with you. You alone are the one who will maintain the honor and prosperity of the house. Remember, this is a heavy responsibility."

Everyone knew that sake brewing was a man's world, and Kinzaemon could have brought a geisha's son into the house. But with the Kansai *chonin,* the merchants, they often preferred to adopt a husband for a daughter, an adult clerk who had proven his mettle and would be an asset to the family business. It was common practice among brewers, a good business strategy.

And she had felt it, felt the weight of the generations fall upon her, the hope her father had bestowed upon her. She could not bear his sad eyes or the way her mother got busy every time she neared so as not to let on that she had been crying. Rie had promised herself then that she would take this loss from their shoulders, this burden, and carry it as her own.

Now, as she washed the barrels, she pictured her little brother Toichi's large brown eyes, his sweet face. She should have been watching him closer, her father's only son. He had been her responsibility, and now he was gone. Her guilt was a burden she would bear the rest of her life, the result of her own carelessness and disregard of her responsibility to the house. As she finished scrubbing the last of the barrels all she got was blue-cold hands and a scolding from her father. "Yes, Father. But I do not want to leave this job to others. It's too important. And I'm not so near the door." She glanced up briefly, and looked down again.

"Get back to the kitchen!" Kinzaemon bellowed.

Rie was careful not to let her anger and disappointment show. She bowed, dropped the brush, and ran toward the door leading through the earthen corridor to the rooms of the house. The kitchen. That was the place of women. How unreasonable of her father to expect her to be only a confined "girl in a box."

Now she was the first and only child. The samurai knew what to do about barren wives who had only daughters. A mistress could always be found to provide an heir for the house. Still, the Kansai merchant houses found daughters useful. The midwives liked to announce with the birth of a daughter: "It's a girl, so the house will prosper." With a son you really had a gamble, true enough. You had to take what you got, and that could be a bright boy or a dull one. Her baby brother Toichi had been bright. Still, with a daughter, intelligent or not, you had a range of choices for an adopted husband for her. And for an important house like the Omuras, there were plenty of prospects, excellent ones.

With Toichi gone, it was imperative that Rie take an interest in the business, this she knew, to learn as much as she could from her imperious father and chief clerk, Kin. "Knowing about the brewery will help your husband in the future, the house. I want our brewery to be number one," her father had always said.

And so, as Rie glided rapidly along the pounded earthen corridor to the polished platform hallway and rooms of the house, she determined to fulfill her father's wish. As penance. But how, she wondered as she ran her hand along the dark brown woodwork that gleamed in the faint, frozen morning light? She turned and ran her hand along the sturdy aged cypress pillar that supported the house, the House of Omura, the house whose head she had so far disappointed. At nineteen, her arms could barely reach to embrace this post that had supported the house for nine generations. She walked more slowly to the kitchen door.

"Oh, there you are," said a smiling plump maid whose apple cheeks bespoke her country origins. O-Natsu held out a cup of tea to warm Rie's hands. "O-Josama," O-Natsu said, using the title reserved for the younger woman of the house, "your mother wants to see you. She is in her room waiting." She bowed again.

"Thank you, O-Natsu." Rie sipped tea and held the cup in both hands for a moment to warm them. She handed the cup back to O-Natsu, adjusted her scarf and apron, and walked along the chilly corridor and up the steep slippery wooden stairs to her mother's second-floor room.

"I have returned," she announced, kneeling outside the door.

"Come in," her mother's soft voice greeted her.

The strength concealed beneath Hana's voice was a source of wonder to Rie. She opened the sliding screen with both hands, bowed, and glanced at her mother's refined face, a face that did not reveal the manifold concerns behind it. A brewer's wife was responsible for the food, housing, clothing, health, and well-being of all the brewery workers. Rie entered the room on her knees and moved toward the hibachi to warm her hands. She looked down at her chapped red fingers and held them over the glowing coals, rubbing gently.

Her mother was sitting opposite Rie, her back to the paulownia dressing cabinet, sewing together sections of a kimono that had been taken apart for laundering. Her mother's room was a large eight-tatami room with a two-tatami dressing room adjacent. It was sparsely furnished according to Japanese sensibility: a low lacquerware table, the hibachi, the paulownia dressing cabinet, and *zabuton* completed the appointments. "Where have you been, Rie? Out in front of the kura again?"

Rie hesitated, bowing slightly. "Yes, Mother. I was washing barrels." She moved her back and wet feet closer to the warm coals and reached to pour tea for her mother and herself.

"You know, Rie, your father doesn't like you there. And so close to the kura. I've always felt we shouldn't be anywhere near the kura door. You know how great the danger of pollution is."

Hana snipped a thread and looked at her work critically. She had tried to show Rie the lock stitch, but Rie could not sew stitches as fine as her mother's and always felt awkward and inadequate when faced with a sewing task.

Rie put down her cup and poked at the hibachi coals with long metal chopsticks. "I know, Mother. But I'm not really so near the door. I must work there in order to wash the barrels. That's where the *kurabito* leave them when they're finished. And that's where the well is." She cringed, remembering the well. If she'd been closer that day, little Toichi wouldn't have fallen in. Rie was eight at the time, and Toichi had only been walking a few months. How was she to guess that he could have pulled himself up, fallen in. Gooseflesh crawled up her arms as she remembered. "I can't move the barrels, you know. And Toji-san has never complained."

"No, I don't suppose he would. He has always been so fond of you. He even let you play in the barrels as a little girl. He knows he can count on you to continue the traditions of our house. But you know the Ikedas lost their whole cellar last year when the sake went sour. And you must listen to Father. You must obey him."

Warmth crept up Rie's cheeks as she pressed her lips together and reached for a cup of tea, warming both hands and inhaling the comforting green tea fragrance.

"I know." She put down the cup and moved her hands back to the hibachi without speaking further. She knew better.

"Have another cup of tea, Rie." Her mother smiled ever so slightly.

Rie glanced again at her mother's face with its patrician Kyoto nose, the distinctive downward curve that marked aristocratic women from the old capital. It was known that someone in Hana's family had had a liaison with a Kyoto woman. Rie's mother had inherited the woman's best feature.

"Another thing, Rie. . . ."

Rie glanced again at her mother, and lowered her eyes. This must be why her mother had called her.

"You are close to twenty now, and it's high time we were serious about your marriage. And we have several good candidates. Your father and I are especially interested in the Okamoto son, Jihei. He has been apprenticed to the Ohara house, so we know he has had excellent training, and the reports we hear are good."

Jihei?

Rie looked up in alarm. She tried to remember what Jihei looked like. She knew he was one of the clerks who came on errands to the office.

"*Ah,* I remember now," she murmured, her heart sinking. She recalled a boy with a large nose and eyebrows that stood up straight like her father's. Not the handsomest of clerks by any means. Not as handsome as the Kato's third son, the son whose elegant bearing, fine chiseled features, and long fingers bespoke a certain sensitivity. On the day of Toichi's funeral, Saburo Kato had stood before her, murmured his apologies, then had looked up at her with such intense brown eyes that she knew then he shared her wound in some way. Understood it. Since then, she had noticed him more than once. *He* would be her husband, given a choice. But no choice would be given, of course.

"We have arranged the *o-miai* meeting for early next month. The Okamotos have been approaching us, and they are serious." Hana paused to turn a teacup around in her hand. "We don't want to delay too long or they will get discouraged and look elsewhere. We can have the wedding before summer."

"I see." Rie slowly put her cup down, her hand trembling.

"You know Father and I have your best interests at heart."

Rie sighed and tried to put Jihei's face out of her mind. Luckily, his face was very forgettable. Unluckily, she knew it was the interests of the house that mattered, not her own preferences.

Hana glanced at Rie's face before continuing. "Personal feelings have so little to do with marriage. Your father and I were fortunate. We grew fond of each other after we married. That is what you must hope for." She paused. "We know you understand. So we'll ask Mrs. Nakano to go ahead with the *o-miai* arrangements. We'll choose a good fortune day in May. I've always liked spring weddings. Summer is too hot."

Hana leaned forward slightly. "And you must try to be a good wife, Rie. Be compliant. Your feelings must not intrude." Hana put down her sewing and looked at Rie's face. "Women often find it necessary to 'kill the self.' Otherwise life becomes too difficult."

Kill the self. Isn't that what she'd done when her brother died? A sliver of guilt wedged inside her heart.

Her mother picked up her sewing again and bent over it. "And remember how fortunate you are. You won't have to live with a mother-in-law. Your husband is the one who will. He will have the bigger adjustment to make." She glanced again at Rie.

Rie put her hand over her mouth. She wondered how her mother had had to "kill the self." Was it the suffering at the loss of little Toichi? Remorse made her cheeks glow hot like the coals from the hibachi. "Yes, Mother." She bowed to her mother, excusing herself before leaving the room.

She walked slowly down the stairs and along the wooden walkway above the earthen floor, deliberately putting one slipper just in front of the other. She glided into the wooden *geta* and walked out to the gated garden. She opened the creaking weathered gate and stepped onto the large round stones toward a huge boulder. She leaned against it and gazed toward the koi pond.

Of course this was bound to happen. Once parents neared fifty, they were anxious to get the succession settled. Her marriage could not be postponed. Besides, her mother said she and Rie's father cared for each other, and she knew this to be true. Maybe the same would be true for Rie and her husband. At any rate, there was no choice. She would have to marry Jihei. She would have to forget Saburo Kato. Not that she could.

That night Rie sat musing in front of her dressing cabinet. "Kill the self," her mother had said. *How would it ever be possible to kill the self and still continue to live, to survive,* she wondered? She recalled the death a few years ago of one of the kurabito, something her mother had grieved long, almost as long as with Toichi, as it was her responsibility to ensure the health of all the workers in the brewery.

Rie gazed at her reflection, at the face she overheard someone in the office say belonged to a farm woman, something he had dared to say only when her father was not in the room. She sighed. Although her eyes were large and arresting, her teeth protruded slightly, there was no denying. She knew she was not a beauty, in the classical sense. She thought suddenly of the way her father banished her to the kitchen, wanted to keep her away from the business side of the brewery, especially transactions involving cash, something to which women of Kansai merchant houses had no access. How was she to fulfill her responsibility to the house if she wasn't allowed to be involved in the business of brewing? She sighed deeply and sat several minutes at the mirror before laying out the futon.

Arranged marriage was the way. She would not *kill the self*. She would find a way to survive.

The most elegant tearoom in Kobe was reserved for the formal meeting of the two families, with Mr. and Mrs. Nakano presiding as go-betweens. Rie bit her lip and held her breath as, attired in an elegant pale blue kimono of the finest silk, she entered the gold screened room behind her parents. She was able to see, even with her head properly bowed throughout the meeting, that she was right about Jihei. He did have a large nose and startling eyebrows. She continued to gaze at the lacquer plate before her as her parents and the Okamotos exchanged the perfunctory courtesies that sealed her fate. She sat perfectly still, her emotions tightly in check as she listened with a sinking feeling in the pit of her stomach.

A few days after the meeting the Omuras offered their formal proposal. The Okamotos accepted, and the last good fortune day in the May calendar was selected.

Rie spent the next days and weeks trying on the kimono she would own for the rest of her life. As she fingered the *kasuri,* silk and brocade fabrics, and counted the days, she wondered about the stranger her parents had selected as her husband. Would he be as boring as his face? Or would he surprise her? The wedding day approached, the day every woman knew was the most important day in her life. Then why did she have such a feeling of foreboding?

Chapter 2

Rie's wedding, her father told her, would be remembered in Kobe as a major event of the year 1825. He often talked to Rie about major events, unwittingly piquing her interest in matters supposedly of no concern to women. The shogunate and its neo-Confucian maxims was one of his favorite topics. The shogunate was in deep financial crisis, something her father discussed with fervor.

"What do we care for the Neo-Confucianism of the shoguns, this so-called philosophy that puts us at the bottom of society, below the samurai, the farmers, even the craftsmen? Empty words! Everyone knows we merchants hold the real wealth, that we are the arbiters of culture, not only in Kobe but everywhere."

Whatever the officials of the shogunate did, including the measures of Chief Councilor Mizuno, all had failed. He had tried to solve the financial crisis through a series of reforms: sumptuary edicts to curtail extravagance, restrictions on festivals and Noh and Kabuki performances, and limits on the activities of pawnbrokers. Nothing worked. As Kinzaemon said, it was the merchants, chonin, who held the real wealth. And of the merchants it was the sake brewers and pawnbrokers who were wealthiest. Most brewers of substance were pawnbrokers and moneylenders as well. If the country were to be saved, it would be houses like the Omuras that would save it.

It was natural, then, for the marriage of two major brewing houses to be viewed as an event of great importance. The engagement followed the o-miai, the formal meeting, and the wedding date was fixed. Mrs. Nakano, the most respected go-between in Kobe, was in her element. The plump, energetic brewer's wife boasted the news of the impending wedding to everyone she encountered, and she had without doubt the widest acquaintance in town. Soon the marriage was eagerly anticipated throughout the whole brewing community.

With the exception of Rie herself, of course.

The match was the talk of the May Brewers Association meeting. The meeting was attended, as usual, by a representative of each brewing house, generally the house head. The chief rival of the Omura House was there, Kikuji Yamaguchi, a bombastic man nearly as large as a sumo wrestler. His *obi* strained over his barrel stomach, and he surveyed the assembled brewers arrogantly. He swaggered and belched as he walked, and boasted loudly that Ogre-Killer would soon be the number one brand of sake in Japan. Kinzaemon overheard him say "*Huh!* She's marrying Jihei Okamoto. Some choice! What can he do for White Tiger? Well, so much the better for us!" Yamaguchi gloated. During the previous year he had succeeded in capturing ten percent of White Tiger's market, a serious blow in the competitive world of the brewers.

Kinzaemon, who had sunk into depression following Toichi's death, seemed discouraged by Yamaguchi's words. Rie knew this from a conversation she overheard while standing outside the office. He was speaking to Kin, she was sure. "This is a bad blow to us, to our position and honor. And he was insulting as well, talking about Rie's marriage to the Okamoto son." Listening, Rie felt her anger rising. *How dare Yamaguchi!* "We have lost part of our market to Yamaguchi too." She had to do something, somehow, to redeem the status of the house and to prove that the Omura House was superior to the Yamaguchi House.

Now, more than ever, marriage to Jihei would be crucial for the continuity and prosperity of the house, Rie knew. Kinzaemon had carefully chosen Jihei after a thorough investigation by Mrs. Nakano. The family of the groom, its reputation and standing, the training of the groom, the absence of contagious disease in the family—all these things had been weighed by Kinzaemon and his wife so that Yamaguchi could have nothing bad to say about the marriage. But everyone knew Yamaguchi was always bragging.

"Most unseemly for a man in his position. The other brewers should have enough sense not to take Yamaguchi's remarks seriously," Hana said one evening, seeking to comfort her husband.

Preparations for the wedding prompted a steady stream of vendors in the office and house of the Omuras: caterers for the reception, weavers and dyers from Nishijin in Kyoto, and seamstresses coming and going in a seemingly unending procession each day.

"Must we invite three hundred guests?" Rie asked. "All those return gifts will be such an expense."

Hana looked at Rie and smiled thoughtfully. "This is a modest list, Rie. You know it would be a bad oversight if we omitted even one of the major brewing houses. The list is critical. Besides, you are our only child and this is one of the most important events for our house."

But even Rie's mother had to admit the trousseau was impressive: three four-drawer aromatic cedar *tansu* chests with copper fittings, several sets of cotton and silk linens, and two dozen silk kimonos and brocade obis of every color, including formal black, sewn by the best Nishijin seamstresses.

Dressing the bride took all morning. Rie had to rise at dawn for a bath. Her mother and O-Natsu watched as two women unfolded the silk under-kimonos. They adjusted the sleeves and collars as Rie held out her arms for the many layered undergarments. She tried to stand patiently as the women worked, but her growing anxiety made it hard to stand still. Finally she lifted her arms so the outer kimono could be adjusted in place. The kimono was white silk with an exquisite design of pine, plum, and bamboo below knee level, signifying strength, courage, and harmony. The obi was adorned with a complimentary pattern outlined in gold thread. To Rie, tying the wide obi seemed to take forever. At the neck the collar was arranged so that the proper amount of under-kimono revealed the subtlest variations of white.

Rie's hair was piled into three sections over which was laid the wide white silk band to hide the bride's "devils' horns," symbolizing that a wife was never to display jealousy, whatever her husband chose to do. She doubted Jihei *could* make her jealous! Her face and neck were painted chalk white. Fitting for how she felt.

"But Mother, I feel twice as large as normal. I won't be able to move," Rie complained. She looked in the mirror that O-Natsu held for her and gasped. "I don't even look like myself," she mumbled.

"Don't worry, dear, you need only walk slowly, with very small steps. Remember to keep your knees together and bent and your toes pointed inward, won't you?" Her mother smiled and appraised Rie from every angle. "Very fine," she pronounced.

"You look beautiful," O-Natsu breathed.

The brief ceremony was presided over by a white-robed priest at the city's principal Shinto shrine. At the entrance of the shrine the bride and groom and family guests each took a sip of purifying water with a bamboo dipper from a tank engraved with the characters "cleanse the spirit." The ceremonial room was spare, the floorboards polished to a gleaming gloss, the only furnishing being the zabuton on which guests sat facing the priest and the bridal couple, whose parents sat closest to the bride and groom. The priest waved his paper wand over the bride and groom to invoke the blessing of the gods. Rie and Jihei exchanged the traditional three sips of sake from a black lacquer cup. Her head modestly bowed, Rie was nevertheless able to steal a nervous glance at Jihei. He was standing stiffly in his black wedding kimono, looking straight ahead. She wondered what he was thinking. Was he pleased with his bride? Or did he feel as she did? Rie had no clue to Jihei's feelings, other than his stiff, formal bearing, which was really fitting for the occasion. She would have to wait, she knew, for what lay ahead at night. She wanted to glance at his face, but forced herself to keep looking demurely down, as her mother had instructed.

The teahouse with the largest garden in the city was reserved for the reception. All the city's luminaries were present: shogunal commissioners, town officials, and representatives of each of the major brewing houses with their wives. Women paraded in their elegant kimonos and admired the azaleas while husbands gathered in clusters and discussed the significance of the adoption of the Okamoto second son as successor to the House of Omura. The bride and groom were toasted in the top grade of White Tiger and their virtues extolled by Mr. Nakano and the head of the Kobe Sake Brewers Association.

And so she was married. Jihei, this stranger, was her *husband*.

Standing in the reception line Rie caught her breath when she happened to glance up just as Saburo, the Kato third son, was passing. She looked directly into his arresting eyes, and smiled slightly before looking down. She thought she caught an answering smile as she murmured a greeting and bowed. He was so handsome! And she felt drawn to him, there was no question. Her emotions were in turmoil as she recalled his sympathetic reassurance at little Toichi's funeral, the way he had caught her elbow when she felt faint. The strength he'd somehow transferred to her in that small gesture. She would never forget it, or him. She wondered if negotiations were under way for the marriage of this man she found so appealing. Her shoulders tensed and she pressed her hands more tightly together. Her thoughts lingered on Saburo Kato during the rest of the reception as she stood beside her new husband.

Rie tensed as Kinzaemon turned to look at her. She made sure her head was modestly bowed, her hands folded in front of her as guests congratulated Jihei at her side. Rie knew that for Kinzaemon the marriage was the culmination of a successful negotiation to ensure the future of the house. But for Rie it felt like a death sentence.

When they returned to the Omura House following the reception it was late evening. Rie's mother helped her out of her obi. "O-Natsu will help you with your kimono, Rie."

Rie's parents vacated the second floor room for the newlyweds and moved downstairs to Rie's former room. Hana said, "The stairs are becoming too much for us, dear. We'd rather you had the room."

"Only if it's really difficult for you, Mother," Rie had demurred.

Rie put on the kimono especially selected for the wedding night, trembling as she did, beads of sweat forming on her brow. Jihei had already been shown to their quarters, but had drunk so much that he stumbled on the stairs. Rie heard him grumbling, his speech slurred, as he staggered around the room bumping into the *shoji. Please be so drunk that you fall asleep the moment you lie down*, she prayed.

As Rie walked up the stairs, she hesitated. The stairway and her mother's room above were so familiar, but tonight they seemed strange, almost forbidding. She put her hands on the yellow plaster walls on either side of the stairway for reassurance, for support on this portentous night.

When she entered the anteroom she saw that Jihei was already recumbent on the futon, eyes closed, his breath smelling of sake even from where she stood. Had her prayers been answered? She entered the room slowly, sat at the dressing table and took down her hair, glancing at Jihei's reflection in the mirror as she combed the glossy locks. When she could delay no longer she went to the futon that had been laid out beside Jihei's and quietly slipped under the covers. She breathed as lightly as possible, hoping that Jihei was already asleep. It seemed an eternity that she lay there wakeful, apprehensive. This man beside her on the futon was a complete stranger.

Some time during the night, she could not say just when, Jihei came to her abruptly, grunting and sweating, without saying anything, without a word that might have shown consideration for her. The shock of his sharp, piercing thrusts caused her to gasp and struggle to stifle a cry of pain. When he stopped, she tried to move but was pinned by Jihei's moist, slack body. *Disgusting!* She lay wakeful, barely able to breathe, the pain between her thighs acute as she listened to Jihei's heavy breathing. A single tear fell. Was this what their life together would be like? If she'd had a dagger, she would have cut her throat now rather than face this nightly humiliation. She thought of Kato, of the tenderness he'd shown her at her brother's funeral. Now she would forever be locked away with a man who would control her destiny. No, she could not think about it. Her mother was right. To survive, one must kill the self.

She closed her eyes, then opened them, determined to get as far away from this man as possible. Finally she was able to edge out from under him. Despite the ache in her heart and the sense of violation, she knew she would have to be with her husband in this way to bear an heir for the house. She bit her lip and tried to sleep, but the pain and sense of outrage made it impossible.

She rolled gingerly out of the futon, drew her kimono around her, and, picking up her padded wrapper, glanced at her still-sleeping husband. She slid open the shoji, then crept quietly down the stairs and along the drafty dark corridor past the kitchen to the bathroom. As she dropped her kimono into the wicker basket in the dressing room, she wrinkled her nose in distaste when she noticed bloodstains. Shivering, she entered the room where the wooden tub stood. Scooping up the tepid water still standing from the evening's baths, she sloshed bucket after bucket over her body until every trace of blood, dried perspiration, and sticky fluids was washed away. Then she wrapped both kimonos around herself and walked softly toward the inner office. She entered and sat in the silent darkness at the main working table. She breathed in slowly. The comforting aroma of musty ledgers mingled with the hint of yeast that never left the house. For the next several minutes, the tears fell in earnest. She listened to her muffled sobs, saw her breath in the dim, wintry light.

As she was busy feeling sorry for herself, a barrel on the floor bearing the White Tiger logo caught her eye, the brand name under which the Omura sake had been sold for nine generations. She gazed at the leaping white beast, talisman of all those ancestors before her father. Of Toichi, had he lived. Something swept over her, stronger than feeling.

Whatever was necessary to ensure the birth of an heir she would do, *must* do, for the house. That was not only her obligation, but her atonement for the lapse that had ended her brother's life. Yes, she would fulfill her obligation, but the inner office here, the core of the brewery, this she would make her own sphere, a place to forget that other life with Jihei. Here she would work for the house, do her best for White Tiger and for her father. Just how she would accomplish this she was not sure. But she would do it. She would work to redeem herself to her father and position herself to defeat the braggart Yamaguchi, the White Tiger enemy. Kinzaemon would come to know that she was indispensable to the business, far more than "a girl in a box." She would find a way into the business, maybe through Kin, the chief clerk. She knew he was fond of her and had been since she was a small child. He had given her clues about the business from time to time. Sniffling, she rested her arms on the table, then glanced at the White Tiger logo again.

"I will do this, and Father will know," she murmured.

Chapter 3

As soon as her eyes opened, Rie extricated herself from her futon, rose, and folded it away in the wall cupboard. She turned to glance at her husband. He showed no sign of waking. Relieved, Rie opened the shoji and quickly changed in the dressing room. She knew her mother would be expecting her to prepare her husband's first breakfast in his new home, and she padded rapidly down the slippery stairway.

Jihei appeared in the breakfast room several minutes later, and as soon as he had eaten the rice, miso soup, and pickles Rie placed before him, he rose abruptly and followed Kinzaemon into the office. Wasn't he able to speak, to acknowledge her at all?

Rie wanted to erase her memories of the night before, of Jihei's body on hers, his breath smelling of sake. She shuddered at the memory, and forced her attention to brewery concerns. Even as a child she had taken an interest in her father's business, and now she felt a greater urgency. He would be retiring soon, and with him Kin. They had been looking for a successor. But before a decision was made about who would succeed Kin, she needed to find out what they were planning, especially in regard to Jihei. Curious to see Kin's reaction to Jihei, but also mindful of Yamaguchi's evaluation of her new husband, she slid quietly along the corridor toward the inner office and peered cautiously around the shoji that stood open. Her father's back was to her, she was relieved to see.

Kinzaemon had taken Jihei into the office to introduce him to Kin, chief clerk and manager of the entire White Tiger operation. A spare spidery figure of a man, prominent front teeth barely covered by his lips, Kin had been with the family business almost as long as Kinzaemon. He was consulted in any major decision. Close in age to Kinzaemon and equally dedicated to family traditions, Kin nevertheless also had more of an eye to the future. Each autumn he insisted on projecting White Tiger's markets three years in advance.

Rie had been watching her father and had noticed how tired he seemed lately, how depressed he'd become as he neared retirement. Always he'd dreamed of a son to carry on the family business, to help him create the dynasty that he'd envisioned long ago. Her shoulders slumped as a familiar weight rested on them. She was more determined than ever to make her father's dream a reality.

"This is Jihei Okamoto, Rie's new husband and my successor," Kinzaemon said. "Now we have a man to succeed me." Rie bit her lip as she heard this.

Kin bowed lower than Jihei, as was appropriate. "Good." He nodded to Kinzaemon and Jihei.

Rie backed quickly out of sight but lingered to hear more. A man to succeed made her father happy, of course. She expected it of her father and was glad that it pleased him, but for her the union had been an outrage that even now left her feeling unclean. Her throat tightened at the memory as she ducked farther out of sight. She did not wish to be seen by her husband, or by

Kin either. She would have to catch Kin sometime alone and talk to both him and Jihei about increasing market share. There was nothing to prevent her from going to the office in the evening after her father had left.

She heard Kin open the ledgers and begin to relate a summary of White Tiger's main suppliers, customers, and sales routes to Jihei. She tried to remember everything Kin said. "In this ledger here you see all our suppliers of Yamada Nishiki rice, *koji* mold, and yeast. And in this one here are all our major customers." As Kin talked, Rie heard the shoji to the outer office open and the men's voices grow fainter. She moved along the corridor toward the outer office so as not to miss any of the valuable summaries of White Tiger's operations.

Rie brought a flask of heated sake to the bridal room that evening and turned to Jihei, her hands shaking as she handed him his drink. She needed to prepare for the future growth of the business, but she could only do so if her husband was in concurrence with her wishes. She took a steadying breath before launching in.

"You know you will be house head as soon as Father retires," she said hesitantly. "And it isn't far off now. He is fifty. So is Kin, therefore we may have a double retirement."

"That would be a problem if they both retired at the same time, wouldn't it?" Jihei asked. He pulled at his bristling eyebrows.

"Oh, we're sure to find someone to apprentice with Kin before that happens, maybe one of the boys from Tamba. Anyway, Father and Kin will soon be on the lookout among the brewing houses."

Jihei picked up a small cup, and Rie leaned over to pour for him.

"Maybe we should be looking now," Jihei offered.

"Yes, I've started looking myself."

Jihei worked at his eyebrows again and shifted uneasily. "I wonder if the daughters of other houses are as active as you."

"Well, I'm an only child and have always loved brewing, even when I was little." She smiled, tentatively.

Jihei leaned back and drained a second cup. "I was trained as a child too, but then it was always my elder brother who would succeed, so there wasn't the same pressure on me. Still, my father always said there was sake running in our veins, not blood," Jihei said, smiling at his joke.

"Yes, we all felt that way," Rie responded, beginning to relax in his presence. Maybe last night was an aberration, and tonight would go better. She hoped so. And yet she couldn't bring herself to think of it.

When Rie drew their futon from the cupboard for the night she deliberately placed hers as far from Jihei's as possible. After they had lain on their separate futon for a few minutes Jihei slid out of his and moved over to Rie. He lifted her quilt and began to move closer.

"*Uh!*" She grabbed the futon tightly around herself. "Let's wait until we both feel ready," she said more gently. She knew she couldn't continue this way, that she would have to relent, and soon, but the thought of his breath, his clumsy moves, put an ache in her chest. Rie guessed that the reason he didn't insist was that he felt a stranger in the house, his position as a *mukoyoshi* without much power as he saw it.

To his credit, Jihei moved back to his futon, picked up a flask of sake from his tray, and drained it without a cup. With a sigh of relief, she heard Jihei slump back onto his futon. *Saved. For tonight at least.*

A few days later Rie overheard her father and Jihei talking at the dinner table. She paused beyond the shoji to listen, a sake flask in her hand. As Kinzaemon aged, his quick timing and nose for business had gradually diminished. Although her father loved her, she knew he didn't put the same faith in her as he would have in a son, but she had promised herself that one day she would make her father proud. Be the son he couldn't have. She knew that if they didn't act quickly, Yamaguchi would soon own a much larger share of the market and she could not allow that, she decided, as she held her breath so as not to be heard. She couldn't wait for Jihei to learn the business. For years she'd been watching and listening in silence, learning so that one day she could act. Now was the time.

"Yes," Kinzaemon was saying in his heavy, husky voice. "Our shipments to Edo are doing well, very well."

Rie entered the room and poured sake for her father and husband.

Jihei made no response to Kinzaemon other than to pick up his sake cup and drain it. Well, *she* would have a lot to say were she in Jihei's position! She put down the flask and glided back through the corridor to the inner office, where Kin still sat bent over a ponderous ledger. He worked later than anyone else, even her father.

"*Ah*, excuse me, Kin-san. May I disturb you for a moment?" Rie bowed and sat down on the tatami opposite Kin.

He looked up. "Good evening, O-Josama." He smiled, his teeth protruding over his lower lip. "Yes, what is it?"

"You know it's difficult for me to speak with Father of any business matter," she began.

"Yes, it seems so, doesn't it? Well, you know, most men in Nada don't want women entering the business side or handling cash."

"But I have an idea, Kin-san." Rie picked up a writing brush and twirled it between her fingers before continuing. It was important to appear nonchalant. "Our shipping to the Edo market has been going well, hasn't it?"

Kin nodded. "Yes, perhaps better than we anticipated."

"Wouldn't this be a good time, then, to expand our shipments to Edo, to try to sell, say another twenty percent in that growing market? Can't we take advantage of it and recover the ten percent of our market we lost to Yamaguchi?" Rie stopped to look intently at Kin.

He sucked in his breath, folded his arms, leaned back against the wall, and closed his eyes. For several minutes he said nothing.

Rie inhaled her favorite yeasty aroma and waited. Would he listen to the merits of her idea or dismiss what she said just because she was a woman, or because he knew her father didn't want her intruding in business decisions? She kept her eyes on Kin's face. *Come on, come on. Agree!*

At length he opened his eyes and looked at Rie. He nodded. "Yes, maybe so. Yamaguchi has caused us a loss. But twenty percent . . . I wonder if your father would agree?"

"Oh, if you agree, then I know you could persuade him. He always follows your opinion, values your judgment so highly."

Kin sucked in his breath again. "Well, now, it isn't only your father. I'd also have to convince your husband, Rie. It might be difficult."

Rie tapped the handle of the brush on the table. "I don't think my husband will object to something you suggest, Kin-san, with your experience, especially if you convince Father." She leaned forward. "You will talk to Father, won't you?"

"It may be difficult, Rie." He glanced at her eager face.

She bowed. "Please, Kin-san."

"Well, then, all right. I'll try." He rubbed his face.

"Thank you so much. I'll come again tomorrow evening after Father has left the office." Rie smiled as she bowed out of the room. Kin could be her ally.

The following evening Rie again took a sake flask to the dining room where her father sat with Jihei. She paused beyond the shoji to listen to their conversation, hoping to glean something that would help her learn more about the business, as well as about Jihei.

"You know both Kato and Yamaguchi have increased their Edo shipments in the past two months," Kinzaemon said. "It might be a good time to raise our shipments twenty percent."

Good work, Kin. Rie smiled, peered cautiously into the room, and glanced at Jihei.

He pulled at his collar uncomfortably. "But twenty percent? Isn't that quite risky? Shouldn't we start more gradually, say five percent?"

Kinzaemon paused. "Well, as Kin says, we have to watch Kato and especially Yamaguchi. Perhaps Kin is right. The market in Edo looks very good. You know the samurai there love their sake as much as anyone. And they have more leisure time than we do."

Jihei shifted on his zabuton. He snorted. "*Leisure!* We don't know the meaning of the word." He reached for his cup. "And we don't want to do anything to jeopardize our local sales, do we? They're secure." He pulled at his eyebrows.

Fool! Rie thought, trying to contain her anger.

"Kin assures me they will remain secure." Her father folded his arms and leaned back, his eyes closed.

Rie kicked at the wall. So Jihei would resist any forward move by White Tiger. How could he be a worthy successor to the house with so little business acumen? What would become of her father's dream? The dream she'd vowed to uphold. She closed her eyes and forced herself to think. She would somehow have to intervene, so that her father wouldn't realize he had made a poor choice in Jihei. That Jihei could not be worthy of the house Rie had no doubt now. And that he had been a poor choice for a husband, she was certain. No love was growing between them as her mother had hoped, only an uneasy alliance. She thought of Saburo and felt an unnamed yearning so strong it almost made her stagger. No. She could not give in to weakness right now. She straightened her obi before entering the room to pour sake for the men. And to listen, closely.

In the ensuing months White Tiger did begin to increase its sales to Edo, reaching a total rise of twenty percent.

"You were right, Kin-san," Rie overheard her father say in the inner office one day. "The risk was well worth it."

She peered in around the shoji, equal bursts of pride and relief inside her.

Kin bowed. "Now we are moving up to Yamaguchi in our Edo shipping."

Rie smiled to herself and walked back to the kitchen. *She'd been right! Now she knew she had what it took to make her father's dream a reality.* Later in the evening she found a chance to slip into the inner office when she knew her father and Jihei were dining.

"Good evening, Kin-san." Rie bowed as she entered the room.

"*Ah,* O-Josama." Kin beamed. "The increase in our shipping to Edo has succeeded."

"You didn't tell Father that I spoke with you, did you?"

"No. I believe he thought it was my idea."

"Thank you, Kin-san. I knew I could count on you." Rie nodded slightly, but inside she was dancing. "This is a big step for White Tiger." Rie was so pleased that even the thought of her inept husband couldn't subdue her good mood.

After her experience of the wedding night, Rie had shuddered at the thought of a repetition, but knew there was no choice if she were to fulfill her major obligation and produce an heir for the house. For many nights over the next weeks and months she forced herself to succumb to Jihei's drunken groping and thrusting, wishing it were Saburo instead of this horrid man who disgusted her. She imagined Saburo soft, tender, those intense brown eyes watching hers . . . unlike Jihei, who didn't seem to notice whether or not she responded, caring only for himself. Rie wondered how other women felt, endured, to produce an heir, but she had no sisters to enlighten her. Each time Jihei touched her, she closed her eyes and forced back tears as she imagined herself in a faraway place. When she extricated herself, she slipped down the stairs, along the dark corridor and into the o-furo room, where she washed herself vigorously, then stopped in the outer office to sit and breathe deeply, glancing at the White Tiger logo on a barrel. This became her regular ablution ritual. Thus she kept her spirit intact and enabled herself to survive the distasteful nighttime ventures.

One night as Rie was dressing and washing herself she heard slippers slapping toward the *o-furo* room. The shoji opened and her mother stood there.

"Ri-chan, are you all right?" her mother asked, frowning.

"Yes, Mother, I'm just washing."

Her mother stepped into the dressing room and looked at her hesitantly before speaking. "We know you are trying to do your duty, dear. And, well . . . your father and I appreciate it. It will be so important for the house."

"I know," Rie murmured softly, yet feeling a tightness in her chest as she thought of what it was costing her.

"Sleep well, dear," her mother said, bowing slightly as she left.

So long as her parents understood, Rie would continue, would endure, until she became pregnant. She prayed it would happen soon, that she would be relieved of the unpleasant but pressing duty. In the meantime, she would continue to think of Saburo. No one could control her feeling for him.

One morning a few months following the wedding Rie did not feel her normal self. She lingered in her room later than usual.

Jihei had already gone downstairs. She heard O-Natsu's voice outside the shoji.

"Good morning. May I come in?"

"Yes, O-Natsu."

O-Natsu stepped in with a tea tray, which she set down on the tatami in front of Rie. "You did not come to breakfast, so I wondered, are you all right?"

"There may be something wrong. I don't feel like eating."

O-Natsu paused and glanced at Rie's eyes, a sign of pregnancy, so the midwives had told her. "I wonder, could you be pregnant?"

"Oh, I thought of that, O-Natsu. I skipped the last two months." She had kept that to herself, until she was sure. Today she *knew*. She smiled for O-Natsu's benefit.

"Shall I call your mother?"

"I guess so, thank you."

"Meanwhile, try to sip some tea. I'll bring up some rice gruel."

Rie nodded, unenthusiastically. She picked up a teacup, then set it down. If she really were pregnant, she would have succeeded in her duty to the house. Her parents would be delighted. She would be relieved of further responsibility toward Jihei at night. Why did she not feel happy, then? She heard steps on the stairs, and her mother and O-Natsu entered. O-Natsu set a tray with a bowl of rice gruel and chopsticks in front of Rie.

Hana sat on the zabuton next to the hibachi and looked intently into Rie's face. "How do you feel, dear? I know you have missed a month, or is it two? And O-Natsu tells me your eyes indicate pregnancy. Let me see." Her mother gazed at her intently. "Can you eat some rice gruel?"

Rie looked down at the food and put a hand on her stomach. "I don't really feel like eating, Mother."

"I know, dear, but you must eat. I'll send O-Natsu to the old herbalist to get something for you."

There was no doubt that Rie was pregnant. That evening Rie and her mother joined Kinzaemon and Jihei around the table. It was Hana's prerogative to make the announcement to her husband and Jihei.

Hana put down her chopsticks and straightened. "We have an important announcement for the future of the house." She paused and looked from Kinzaemon to Jihei, then she continued. "Rie is going to have a child, an heir for the house."

Rie excitedly awaited her father's reaction.

Kinzaemon smiled broadly. "That's wonderful, Rie. A most important child. And you must be especially careful of your health now."

She smiled back.

"Yes, Father. I have always been quite healthy." Rie knew her father would hope for a boy, but she herself would welcome a girl.

"I have sent O-Natsu for some powders from the herbalist, the same ones I used," Hana said.

Jihei nodded but said nothing, Rie noted. He pulled at his eyebrows and reached for a sake flask. Jihei rarely had anything to say or reacted to what she did or said.

In succeeding days Rie noticed that her father spoke less about Yamaguchi, and the depression that had lowered his spirit seemed to have lifted. His step became sprightlier, and there was a general air of well-being in the household. O-Natsu and Rie's mother were continuously solicitous of Rie, and her mother cautioned her to slow down, to leave more responsibilities to others.

Hana purchased several sets of clothing and wrappers for the baby. She insisted on sewing tiny kimonos of her favorite cotton patterns. One afternoon she took out some baby clothes she had saved from her own son who had died. She fingered them lovingly as she showed them to Rie. Rie smiled and nodded, touching the clothes. Her beloved Toichi. How she missed him still. And now the clothes reminded her of her duty—her duty that she was fulfilling.

Late one afternoon three months later, Rie felt a gripping pain in her abdomen. She hurried to the lavatory, feeling weak and perspiring heavily. O-Natsu saw her hurrying to the lavatory and followed her. Rie opened the shoji quickly and stepped inside, squatting over the hole in the floor. A sharp pain stabbed at her. She huddled over and felt something slipping out and heard a splash below. *No,* she screamed silently. *No! No!* She looked down and saw that her legs were covered with blood. She could not stifle an anguished wail. She stood weakly, her hand clutching the wall for support. The shoji opened, and O-Natsu stepped in with towels and rags, which she handed to Rie.

"I've lost the heir," she moaned. "I've failed the house."

Chapter 4

Gloom pervaded the house following the loss of Rie's baby. Her father and mother tried to be sympathetic toward Rie, but they were also depressed. O-Natsu tried to cheer Rie, but she could not be consoled. Jihei, as usual, had nothing to say about the loss of the heir.

One night as Rie was preparing for bed she wondered where Jihei was, hoping to avoid him somehow. He was nowhere to be found, nor did he return that night until long after Rie was asleep. She was relieved, but still wondered. Where was he? Two nights later the same thing happened.

Rie tried to broach the subject indirectly one day when they were alone upstairs. Jihei shifted uneasily and tugged at his ear as she spoke.

"You remember I mentioned when you came into the house that Father has not been as active as he was, because of his health. Perhaps you should spend more time here in the evening, get a firmer grasp of the financial side." She tapped her fan against her shoulder and glanced at Jihei, who was turning his teacup around in his hands, admiring it closely.

"This is a fine cup. Is it old Shino?" he asked.

Rie frowned, ignoring his question. "I think Kin would like to see you in the office more, in the evening. You know he spends long hours here."

Jihei sighed. "Yes, he never seems to stop. Well, you know, between you and Father and Kin, it seems everything gets decided. I sometimes wonder where I fit in, where I should focus my attention." He twirled his eyebrows. "Of course I work here every day with Father and Kin."

How lazy he was! She wouldn't mind twirling *him* by those eyebrows. "A brewer's work is never done, day or night. That's what Mother always says. Father hasn't said anything to Mother or me about retiring, but I can see him slowing down. We don't know when he'll decide the time has come to step down. It's a big decision. But when he does you'll have final authority in everything. You want to be prepared to take charge. Father felt you had the experience for it, coming from the Okamoto House."

Jihei put down his cup. "Of course we were never this big. But I feel I'm as much a brewer as anyone, after so many generations." He smiled tentatively at Rie.

Rie put a hand over her mouth to stop herself from cackling. Did he really believe that? "Yes, of course we all do. I can't remember a time when I wasn't surrounded by barrels or inhaling anything but the smell of yeast. And the sound of the kurabito singing in the kura has always given me a sense of well-being. So then you understand, don't you?"

Jihei bowed slightly and murmured in response to Rie's spoken and unspoken questions.

Late that night Rie lay alone on her futon. She had left the shutters open because she enjoyed watching the moonlight filter into the room, casting mysterious shadows from carvings on the lintel above onto the sliding screens. She listened to the haunting flute of the blind masseuse who walked by each night at the hour of the boar. The fire watcher went by too, clacking his wooden sticks together to warn residents to be careful to put out their stoves and lamps before they went to sleep.

It was, she supposed, too much to expect that she would have strong feelings for Jihei, or he for her. Rie turned and moved out of her futon. She realized she felt no fondness for her husband, none at all. She went to the open window and looked out into the stone and gravel garden, gray stones on gray pebbles, gleaming in the moonlight. She gazed at the full moon, and looked at the shadows that ghosted through the garden. No sound broke the stillness. She moved her hand over her face.

Her mother's response to most problems was, "Can't you try to endure, Rie?" Her mother was an authority on endurance.

Rie closed the wooden outer shutters and lay down on her futon. Where Jihei was at this hour of night she could only imagine. It dawned on her that she could not count on her husband for anything, that the future of the house rested with her alone.

She turned and closed her eyes.

One blustery evening Jihei managed to once again elude Rie and other family members on the pretext of an errand. He hailed a ricksha at the corner bridge. As he stepped up into the seat he said, "The Sawaraya," and the ricksha puller made off down the road at a run. The Sawaraya was one of the more elegant teahouses where patrons could ask that their favorite geisha be called for an evening's entertainment. Jihei had sent a clerk ahead to make sure that O-Toki would be called from her *okiya* this evening. A cold drizzle began and Jihei drew the collar of his gray cloak closer around his ears. He peered into the darkness as the ricksha drew into the brighter entertainment quarter of the city. The rain could not dampen his spirits as he took in the lively activity of the district, listened to the voices of gesticulating, shouting hawkers, and watched brilliantly kimonoed geisha fluttering through narrow lanes to their evening's assignations. He alighted quickly at the carved wooden gate, handed coins to the puller, and announced himself at the entrance hidden from the street behind a high wooden wall.

He heard footsteps scurrying toward the front entrance.

"Yes! Yes! Please come in!" O-Haru, the ample, faultlessly groomed owner, greeted Jihei effusively and bowed again and again. "Ah, Master! Welcome! How pleased O-Toki will be to see you this evening!"

Jihei felt a sense of relief as he appraised the most fashionable house in the whole district. Raku ware stood on the cabinet that held guests' getas. Above the shoji, beyond the entrance, was a cryptomeria carving that extended the length of the shoji leading to the reception room. An *ikebana* arrangement of three white lilies in a flat obsidian vase was visible on a corner cabinet. The aroma of freshly polished wood assailed him.

Jihei slipped out of his geta and stepped from the stone entryway up to the highly polished cedar floor. O-Haru leaned over to place slippers in front of his feet, then swished down the long corridor, motioning Jihei to follow. Up the slippery wooden stairway she led him along the plaster-walled corridor, down another hall and around a corner to the most exclusive private tatami room at the rear of the house. She opened the sliding screen and ushered him to the low table at the center of the room, indicating the seat of honor that backed to the tokonoma alcove, adorned with another ikebana arrangement of the season's yellow chrysanthemums in an oblong white vase. She opened the shutters that looked out on the koi pond and garden, lit so it glittered like a flight of fireflies.

"Won't you have a bath while you wait?" she invited. "O-Toki will be here shortly."

Jihei acknowledged her invitation, and O-Haru hurried out. He inhaled the distinctive mown-grass aroma of fresh tatami and turned to admire the white crackleware vase holding the chrysanthemums, above which hung a kakemono of a misty Chinese landscape. If there was one thing Jihei appreciated, besides O-Toki, it was fine pottery. He sighed, felt his senses quicken. Again he heard the sound of slippers rapidly slapping toward the room. A maid entered with towels and a house yukata and bowed as she held the robe for Jihei to change.

"Please come to the private bath downstairs. This way, you know." She bowed gracefully and swayed as she guided Jihei down the back stairway, polished until it was slippery, opened the door to the steamy outer room and placed towels in a straw basket, then slipped out. Jihei shrugged off his yukata and dropped it carelessly over a basket, opened the sliding door to the bath and entered. Immediately he was enveloped in a warm earthy mist so damp that everything in the room dripped. He sat on the small wooden stool to wash and rinse at the tap, then put his toes gingerly into the bath. The water was close to boiling, and his foot soon resembled a lobster. He inched himself slowly into the steaming water, slapped a hot towel on top of his head, closed his eyes and sighed.

A bath at the Sawaraya was so much more relaxing than one at home, with Kinzaemon preceding him, maids hovering about, and Rie following him, dropping hints about this business deal or that one. He felt eternally on inspection, judged. He had to be cautious at home, always on guard. The house was growing more and more oppressive. It was like a cage, a trap that brooked no escape. They had no appreciation for his talents. He felt overshadowed by Kinzaemon and Kin, with Rie ever ready to catch him in an error of some kind. What a woman to have as a wife! But what could he do about her? The Sawaraya was his refuge. Here they treated him with the respect befitting the heir to the

Omura House, one of the largest and most prestigious in the city.

"Excuse me!" The mellifluous voice of O-Toki wafted into the room. Jihei opened his eyes and saw her emerge like a vision through the vapor, a young woman whose impeccable grooming and stark white face and neck only enhanced the sinuous eroticism that she exuded. He smiled.

O-Toki knelt at the edge of the tub, tied up the sleeves of her kimono, and began to massage Jihei's shoulders. He moved them in appreciation.

"*Ah!* Your wonderful touch!"

"You have a lot of tension in your neck and shoulders. You must have had a difficult day." She continued kneading his shoulders and arms.

"What day isn't difficult at White Tiger? But I can forget it here, can't I?"

O-Toki moved her hands down Jihei's back and around to his stomach, just below the navel. *Ah.* And Rie was so unresponsive, even resistant. Hardly what a man needed.

"Of course you know you can."

She stopped with a final thrust toward his groin, then rose and handed Jihei a dry towel.

"Excuse me. I'm going to bring sake to your room. I'll be right there."

As O-Toki left, Jihei emerged from the tub, dried himself in the outer room, and put on the geometrically patterned blue-and-white cotton yukata. He swaggered back to the room and stood a few moments gazing down at the stone garden. He enjoyed the hollow sound of the bamboo dipper as it emptied of water, filled, then emptied again in endless motion. O-Toki's returning footsteps prompted him to take his seat at the table.

She entered bearing a black lacquer tray with a heated sake bottle and two small cups. She knelt and placed the tray on the table, every gesture part of the well-rehearsed tableau Jihei knew so well. Then, hands before her on the tatami, she bowed her head to her hands. Raising her head, she greeted Jihei formally.

"Welcome, Master! How good to see you!" Again she bowed. With both hands she handed Jihei a small cup, then filled it with White Tiger as she smiled and bowed again.

"I have a special treat for you tonight."

Jihei downed the sake in a single gulp. "A special treat? A surprise? Something to eat?" Some delectable concoction?"

O-Toki laughed. "Yes, all of those."

"Well, then?"

O-Toki smiled enchantingly. "A surprise can't be rushed if you really want to relish it."

"Oh, I see you mean to keep me in suspense, right?"

O-Toki's smile became more coquettish. "Of course. That's the only way to really enjoy a surprise. But I guarantee you will be very pleased, maybe even happy."

She filled his cup again. After emptying it he handed a cup in return to O-Toki and filled it. She sipped delicately, glancing at Jihei between sips.

He leaned forward. "*Ah*, you said happy. Now that sounds most promising!"

Jihei admired the way O-Toki's peach-flowered kimono and collar revealed an enticing amount of flesh at the nape of her neck, the most erotic part of a woman's anatomy.

"You must be hungry after your bath. Please excuse me while I bring your food."

"Your sense of timing, O-Toki! I'm more interested in happiness. That is much rarer than food, in my experience."

"Well, there is no reason you can't have both, is there? I'll be right back." She smiled as she glided from the room.

Jihei continued to sip slowly, his face reddening as he anticipated O-Toki's touch again. Then he rose and went back to the window overlooking the garden. He hummed a drinking song off-key, then turned back and sat down heavily at the table.

O-Toki returned with a large tray on which were numerous small dishes, followed by a maid with more items. O-Toki set these out on the table one by one, each arranged like an ikebana exhibit with a tidbit of fish or vegetable on it. She bowed and looked at Jihei expectantly.

"You really know how to tantalize a man, don't you?"

O-Toki's hand did not muffle her throaty laugh. She focused her attention on serving food and sake rather than responding. She picked up a delicate mountain mushroom and held it out toward Jihei on a pair of lacquer chopsticks.

"Here, try this." She popped the choice morsel into his mouth.

"You're right. Delicious!" He grinned, food and juice dripping down his chin.

When Jihei finished eating he sighed, belched, and picked his teeth with a toothpick from a small red lacquer box O-Toki opened and offered him. He leaned back as O-Toki continued to pour sake for him. His face was by now bright red from the hot bath, hot sake, and hot food. He loosened his yukata. O-Toki reached over to fan him with a gold-leaf fan.

"*Ah!* This is always the best time of day, or night. I feel so good!"

"Are you happy?"

"As nearly as is possible in this life."

"You sound philosophical. And speaking of night, I was hoping you would stay tonight. It has been a while." She smiled and bowed.

Bemused, Jihei asked, "Is this a bribe? No surprise unless I agree?"

O-Toki tittered. "Well, I do have a surprise, as I said."

Jihei always enjoyed the repartee, something O-Toki, like all geishas, was skilled at as a qualification. "And will it take all night?" he asked.

"Well, part of it anyway." O-Toki relaxed, leaning on one hand.

"You are always so persuasive." Jihei smiled.

O-Toki straightened, as though sensing she had won. "Your wife won't expect you?" It was a question she did not ordinarily ask of customers, but with Jihei, who was, after all, her patron . . .

"I doubt she'll even notice my absence. Her mind is always on sake, producing, not drinking." Jihei's speech was becoming slurred and his yukata fell open further. They both laughed. "She's always trying to stick her nose into the business, to influence decisions, increase our production. I'll stop her the next time she tries to influence a business decision. You know women can't manage a business."

O-Toki glanced at Jihei and opened her mouth but said nothing. She rose, went to the storage cupboard, and brought out the futon. She cleared the table rapidly, moved it to the side of the room, set the tray out in the hall, and closed the wooden shutters for the night. Jihei fell back on the tatami, his head resting on the futon. When O-Toki tried to arrange the futon, Jihei grabbed her.

"Oh! How can I manage the futon?" she cried in mock distress.

"I think we'll manage together very well. We always seem to."

O-Toki fell into Jihei's embrace. He moved her onto the futon and fumbled with her kimono. She undid her obi and kimono and Jihei moved over her, grunting.

"Is this the surprise?" Jihei whispered in her ear.

"Who is surprised?" she laughed.

Jihei thrust her thighs apart and moved abruptly, then moments later rolled off, turned over, his back toward O-Toki. Soon he was snoring.

Toward morning Jihei stirred, sat up and looked at O-Toki, who awoke slowly and yawned.

"Actually, the surprise is something I must tell you," she said, rubbing her eyes and sitting up.

"*Ah*, at last."

She looked at Jihei and hesitated. "I'm pregnant with your child."

Fear mingled with excitement at the prospect as Jihei leaned toward O-Toki, looking at her intently. "Really?" he cried. "My first child! A son for the Omura House!" He caressed her abdomen. "When is it due? My wife shows no sign, after she lost our child. I was beginning to wonder if I would ever have one."

"In six months' time. And what makes you think it's a son?" she asked. "What if it's a daughter?"

"Then there will be rejoicing in the Omura House, an adopted husband for another generation. Merchant houses always welcome a daughter, you know."

"But if you acknowledge the baby, I'll lose him. I can't give up my own baby!"

"You won't, I promise," Jihei said, putting a hand on her arm. "You'll be able to see his wedding. I'll tell you whatever you want to know about him. And you know, as first son he will succeed me and have a great future in our house." He did not need to add, far better than he would have here in the water world of geisha houses.

When Jihei returned home in the early morning hours he was relieved to find that Rie had already left their room. He lay down on the futon and closed his eyes. He knew he would have to tell her soon. It was a conversation he dreaded.

Chapter 5

Several seasons had passed, and Rie had yet to become pregnant. Instead, she poured herself into her work. Early one evening, Hana sat in her room sewing while Rie hunched over an account book on the other side of the hibachi.

"You know that's not really your responsibility, Rie. Father and Kin may be annoyed if they discover the ledger missing from the office."

"Mother, I always keep track of accounts now. Kin realizes that I need to know where we stand. And he says our finances have improved since I have been following them and making suggestions. Father doesn't need to know." She smiled proudly.

"Well, it isn't expected of a woman, you know, even here in Nada. Women don't handle the cash. It's always been that way. And Father and Jihei could do it, with Kin." She paused and held up her work to examine the fine embroidery with a crane pattern, symbol of longevity.

Rie rested her hands on the ledger and looked at her mother.

"You didn't have an adopted husband, Mother. And I'm not actually handling cash. Kin does that. And Father. So no need to object if I'm helping the house."

Hana said nothing further, no doubt glad that Rie had begun to take an interest in the house, after her tragic miscarriage.

They were interrupted by a high-pitched voice beyond the shoji.

"Excuse me!"

The shoji opened and O-Natsu entered, bowing. For a moment she said nothing as she glanced at Rie and her mother. Then she acknowledged Hana's gesture and sat on her haunches, smoothing her kimono under her.

"Yes, O-Natsu, what is it?" Hana asked.

"I have some news, Oku-san," she said, using the title befitting the female head of the household.

"So you've been gossiping again?"

O-Natsu's apple cheeks grew redder. "Well, I thought you should know. . . ." She glanced at Rie, then back at Hana and looked down.

"I was talking with a maid in the market today, who knows one of the Sawaraya maids."

"Tell us!" Hana said, speaking sharply.

O-Natsu looked at the floor and took a deep breath. "They say Rie's husband is friendly with a geisha, O-Toki, and that she is going to have a child." On the verge of tears, O-Natsu put her hands to her face.

Rie and Hana both looked at O-Natsu. Rie's mouth opened and she frowned.

Hana gasped. "Are you certain, O-Natsu?"

"I'm told there is no doubt. She is due in a few weeks." O-Natsu looked down again and bowed apologetically.

"Thank you, O-Natsu," Hana said, more gently. "You may be excused now."

O-Natsu bowed and left the room, glancing at Rie as she left.

With a sharp intake of breath, Rie looked down at her clenched fists and avoided her mother's gaze for several minutes. Shame burned her cheeks as she thought of her husband with the geisha and a child together, so soon after her own miscarriage! Anger quickly suffused shame.

"Well, Rie, I'm afraid this may be the result of your constant involvement in the affairs of the house. Maybe you are intimidating Jihei. As I've said, a mukoyoshi often feels a stranger in his new home. You know, his position is not so different from a bride's."

The rebuke sent a flush of warmth through Rie, but she was silent, stealing a glance at her mother to try to detect any sign of emotion. She pressed her clenched fists against the edge of the table and rocked back and forth.

"Yes, Mother . . . but he is from a brewing house too. What we do is no mystery to him." Her voice rose slightly. "And I know our family traditions better than he does, so I've tried to help him ever since we were married. This is what you and Father trained me to do, isn't it?"

Her mother's tone softened. "Maybe you should leave any advice to Father and Kin. It may be difficult for Jihei to accept suggestions from a woman."

Rie was silent. Her mother was often right when it came to understanding human beings and why they behave as they do. But Rie had a sense of foreboding, and the gloom that had blanketed her since first hearing about Jihei's indiscretion returned. If she couldn't bear a child, it meant the geisha's son or daughter might be the successor to the house. The thought sent a chill racing through her.

"Try to be more gentle, Rie."

Rie leaned back from the table and frowned. "I'll try, Mother . . ."

Then, as if to reaffirm her own thoughts, her mother said, "If you don't become pregnant soon we may have to bring the child into the house, especially if it's a boy."

Rie bent over her hands, her mouth open, feeling the pressure of her mother's words. She would have to lie with that disgusting fool every night. "But Father hasn't retired, and when he does my husband will succeed. Why do we need to think of another generation now?" She rested her forehead on one hand, elbow on the table.

"Please, Rie." Her mother looked admonishingly at Rie's unfeminine gesture.

Rie took her elbow off the table.

"It's always well to be prepared in advance in case something should happen to Father. We need to think ahead, for continuity of the house. It's just as important as looking after the family altar and ancestral graves. I know you realize that, Rie. And Father will want to retire before long. He would like to see things more settled. It would set his mind at rest if there were an heir."

Rie sat forward and poured tea for her mother and herself, her hand trembling. Then she excused herself and went out to the garden, her oasis for silence and thought. Still shaken by the news, she leaned against her favorite rock and gazed at the koi swimming lazily in the pond. She knew she would have to try to become pregnant again, as soon as possible. Her honor as daughter of the house depended upon it. She sighed, her lips pursed together tightly. For several minutes she sat in silence, willing away the words she'd heard, wishing she could undo the last twenty minutes. Then coming to a decision, she lifted her chin and returned to her mother's room. She announced her presence, and entered properly on her knees.

"Mother, wouldn't a geisha object to giving up her child?"

"Those women don't. She knows the child will have a better chance in life here in a house of substance than out there in the water world, especially if it's a boy."

Rie sighed and slumped. "Jihei spends so much time out at night, Mother. I don't know what to do." Unbelievable. Now she actually *wanted* Jihei home at night to force himself on her so she could get pregnant. But how could she keep him from going out?

"I've never told you this before, Ri-chan." Hana put down her sewing and looked at Rie. "But your father had a child by a geisha too."

What? Rie put a hand to her mouth to stifle a cry.

"But since you were already in the *koseki* register, we didn't have to bring the geisha's son in. I was fortunate. It's more difficult for you, having this geisha's child the firstborn. But I know you want to have a child, Rie, as soon as possible. It's so sad that you lost your first." She picked up her sewing again as if to end the conversation.

Rie frowned. "Yes, but what should I do?"

"Try to make yourself more attractive, Rie. Pay attention to your grooming. Cook one of his favorite dishes some evening." She glanced at Rie.

"Oh. . ." Rie put her hands on the table and looked at them critically. The thought of enticing Jihei made her sick to her stomach.

"Put on your best kasuri kimono some night . . . and here." Hana turned to the dressing table behind her, a piece made of polished paulownia wood with carving around the mirror, her favorite antique.

"Here, dear." Her mother held out a small red round lacquer box with a plum blossom design on the cover. "This is a special perfume cream my mother gave me. It's from Kyoto. We can't find it here in Kobe. They say it gives a woman special powers with a man, makes her irresistible." Hana smiled but with an underlying steel that belied the gesture. She opened the lid and held the box under Rie's nose. Not accustomed to using scents, Rie inhaled the aroma, heavier and spicier than anything she had ever smelled.

"Try a bit tonight, dear. It may help."

Lure that vile man to her body. Repulsive! But it was what she had to do.

"Thank you, Mother. I'll try . . ." Her mother gave her a stern look and she quickly amended her words to "I'll do as you say." She cautiously reached for the box and slipped it into her sleeve. She wrinkled her nose at the inevitable prospect.

Late in the afternoon Rie made certain that Jihei was still in the office. She walked over to where he was working and spoke to him softly, out of earshot of her father, Kin and the clerks.

"You know, tonight we'll be having fresh mackerel cooked with miso the way you like it, and sesame tofu. And I thought we could try some of the special sake Toji has been experimenting with." She smiled at Jihei, she hoped enticingly. "Your bath will be ready soon."

Jihei looked at Rie and nodded. "All right." Was he such a dolt he thought nothing of her sudden change of personality?

Rie shook her head as she checked the bath to be sure it was heating and hurried to the kitchen to instruct the cook to prepare the special dishes for the evening. She set aside three bottles of the highest grade of sake. Upstairs she pulled out the tansu drawers holding her kasuri kimonos. She fingered several before selecting a lighter shade of indigo with a larger pattern than she generally wore. She slid her mother's perfume box into her sleeve and took out the kasuri she had selected.

While her father and Jihei were bathing, Rie went again to the kitchen to ask O-Natsu to heat the sake. Jihei and her father retuned from the bath, their skin still moist and flushed, their moods relaxed.

When Rie and her mother were seated with their husbands Rie poured, first for her father, then for her husband.

"This is the special sake that Toji has brewed this year. I thought we could enjoy some with our mackerel this evening." She looked at her mother, who urged her to continue, then turned toward Jihei, caught his eye, and smiled as she poured for him.

"Mother, why don't you have a taste too?" She held the bottle and a cup toward her mother.

"Just a sip, dear." Her mother held up her tiny cup delicately to Rie.

Rie turned back to Jihei. "How do you like it?"

"Here, try some yourself," Jihei said, holding out a warmed flask toward her cup.

She inhaled the yeasty bouquet and savored a sip. "*Mmm. Wonderful!* We should be able to market it at top price."

Her mother sighed and cast a warning glance at Rie not to talk business, but her father, oblivious to the interchange said, "Yes, Rie, I think you're right. It's something new. I haven't tasted anything quite like it before."

Rie smiled inwardly at this sign of approval from her father.

With a nod to Rie, Hana excused herself to prepare her bath and retire early, but Kinzaemon and Jihei continued to enjoy their evening sake. Rie excused herself as well for a quick bath, then hurried up the stairs and lit a lamp in the anteroom. Light from the lamp sputtered and flickered through the wooden carving above the screens, and shadow cranes drifted into the bedroom. She took out the futons and laid them side by side. In the dressing room she took out her mother's Kyoto perfume and applied some behind her ears, neck, and wrists. She smoothed her kimono and obi and surveyed the room quickly. Satisfied, she returned to join her father and Jihei. She paused outside the room and adjusted the collar of her kimono so that a bit more of the nape of her neck showed than was proper. As she entered the room she glanced at Jihei to see how red his face was. It would not do to wait too long. Seated at the table again, she turned her back toward Jihei and lingered over the sake flasks and cups.

She turned back toward Jihei and forced a smile. "I can take a flask upstairs if you like."

"Yes, I'd like to have another sip, a nightcap."

As Rie rose with the sake tray she saw out of the corner of her eye that Jihei was rising to follow her. She could feel his gaze on the nape of her neck as she glided toward the stairway. That the plan worked should have excited her, but it only sent a shiver of apprehension running through her.

In their room upstairs Rie placed the sake tray carefully next to Jihei's futon and water glass. She turned her back toward Jihei and untied her obi. Before she got any further she felt Jihei's arms around her and his face pressed against the nape of her neck.

She stiffened but then forced herself to relax to his touch. She knew Jihei would not leave tonight. She prayed that she would conceive a child, that she would not have to spend many nights this way. For the next half hour she set her mind free and pretended that it was Saburo who touched her, Saburo whose child she would bear.

Over the next few weeks Rie looked for signs that she was pregnant. She examined her body and waited impatiently. When no sign appeared, she despaired. This must be how empresses had felt over the centuries when they failed to produce an heir and instead the son of one of the concubines was brought into the palace in line to the throne. Kinzaemon also was deeply concerned about an heir to provide continuity for the house.

One day when Rie was passing by her father's office, she heard her father and Jihei talking in the inner office, and peered in to see them seated at the low table strewn with ledgers, facing each other.

Kinzaemon ran his hand through his bushy hair. "I heard a rumor the other day," he began.

"Yes?" Jihei moved the abacus nervously.

"I'm told that the geisha O-Toki at the Sawaraya is bearing your child. Is it true?"

Jihei cleared his throat. "Actually, yes. A son has been born, just four weeks ago." He moved his hand across an eyebrow.

Rie stifled a gasp, and absentmindedly rubbed her barren stomach.

Kinzaemon straightened his bulky frame and pulled his kimono more closely around him. "I see." He paused. "A son, is it? And are you sure he is yours?"

"Yes, he is my son."

"And does Rie know about this?"

"I believe she may have heard."

Kinzaemon glanced at Jihei, whose face had reddened noticeably. "Have you seen the child? Is he normal, healthy?"

"Yes, I have, and he seems very healthy . . . eats well. . ." Jihei stopped, uncertainly.

"Of course the house needs a successor," Kinzaemon said. "And Rie has not borne a child yet. Well, then, shall we bring the child into the house? Recognize him as your legitimate heir?" He paused and sighed. "I never did that. My wife insisted that Rie and her husband succeed us. And I didn't wish to bring in an outside child by a geisha." Kinzaemon pulled at his ear and drew the corners of his mouth down. "Of course Rie may not be entirely pleased about it. But she always understands that the interests of the house come first. That was fundamental in our teaching as she grew up."

Rie fought back tears as she rushed off, feeling every bit as disemboweled as a samurai who had committed seppuku.

The following evening when Rie took sake to the dining room she found her father sitting alone.

"Oh, Rie, come in." Her father beckoned toward the seat opposite him.

Rie seated herself and poured for her father. Although she had slept little the night before, she managed a weak smile.

"I want to let you know, Rie, that we plan to bring your husband's son into the house, since there's no sign of your producing an heir." He sipped and glanced at Rie as if to gauge her reaction.

She set the flask down abruptly and looked at her hands, which were shaking. "But Father, what more can I do?" Her voice rose higher than usual.

Her father sighed. "*Uh* . . . do you know the child's name?"

She had heard the rumors whispered by the servants, who had gleaned bits and pieces at the marketplace, each piece of news cutting her more deeply than the last. "I believe it's Yoshitaro. My husband hasn't spoken about the baby, but I think he is four weeks old now."

Kinzaemon cleared his throat. "Then it will be time to bring him in soon. We'll have Jihei go and take care of the formalities at the Sawaraya. We can send O-Natsu with him to carry the baby. I'm glad you understand, Rie." He put down his cup and exhaled loudly.

She bit her lip so hard she tasted blood. Yes, her parents were always sure to mention her understanding. She felt a sense of desperation overcome her. She slumped on the zabuton and when her father left the room she felt tears starting. She rocked back and forth, overcome, desolate, that her father had now deserted her.

Chapter 6

Rie's mother supervised preparations for the arrival of the infant, assisted by O-Natsu. They arranged for a wet nurse to come in, a young neighbor named Masa who had a baby of her own. Rie despaired and took no interest in the preparations.

"Rie, you know Kin is really looking forward to having another generation here, for continuity of the house," her mother commented. "We all are. He'll inhale the smell of sake as soon as he's drinking milk here. And once there's a baby in the house, who knows, you may become pregnant," Hana added, as if to console her. "It sometimes happens that way. Did that perfume help, dear?"

She thought of all the nights she had to lure Jihei to her futon.

"Yes, Mother. But I'm not pregnant yet."

Although distressed about the baby, Rie was pleased to see the nursery prepared near the kitchen, away from her room. Wasn't it presumptuous of Jihei to have named the child Yoshitaro, "the good first son"?

On a morning when Yoshitaro was four months old, Jihei and O-Natsu took a ricksha to the Sawaraya, where the transfer was scheduled to occur. O-Haru and O-Toki came to the entrance and ushered them into the formal parlor just beyond the entryway. Jihei and O-Natsu sat opposite O-Haru and O-Toki. A maid brought tea, and after they were served, a second maid carried Yoshitaro in and sat at the end of the table holding the squirming infant. Jihei noticed O-Toki's flawless grooming but avoided eye contact. He was still embarrassed by his errand.

He bowed. "The Omura House is grateful to you," he said stiffly. "Yoshitaro will be recognized as eldest son of the house, my heir. Before long I will succeed. And he will be raised well, trained to become a good brewer."

Jihei bowed again and raised in both hands an envelope which he handed across the table to O-Toki. "You need not be concerned for his welfare," he said. Kinzaemon had told Jihei exactly how much to include in the envelope.

O-Toki held the envelope in both hands above the level of her head, bowing so low that her face was concealed. But her voice revealed the strain. "I have no words to thank you adequately."

"We are grateful for your continued patronage," O-Haru said as she and O-Toki bowed in unison.

A maid entered carrying a large *furoshiki* of baby clothing and set it on the floor in front of O-Natsu.

Jihei and O-Natsu rose and bowed stiffly. Jihei tried to ignore what he knew was O-Toki's pain. When O-Natsu took the baby in her arms, he began to scream. For just one brief flicker, the mask of the geisha wavered but she quickly held it in check. Jihei picked up the bundle of clothing, carefully avoiding all eye contact.

They left the Sawaraya amid more formal bowing and caught a waiting ricksha. Yoshitaro yelled all the way to the Omura entrance, where he was greeted by Hana, the wet nurse Masa, and Rie, who scowled at the screaming infant as O-Natsu handed him to Masa.

That evening the baby was brought for inspection before Kinzaemon and Hana. Rie and Jihei sat at one side of the table, Rie's parents on the other. Even as Rie's heart was breaking, she made sure that no expression was visible on her face. As she watched her mother undress the baby while the wet nurse held him, she burned with shame. Once again she had let down her family and the house. Then and there she determined that one way or another she would redeem herself, but how?

Yet first things first. It was necessary to confirm that Yoshitaro was a baby boy, normal in all respects. Hana held him toward Kinzaemon, who looked the infant up and down and nodded. She then took each of the baby's hands and feet in turn and shook them gently to test his reflexes. She wrapped him up again.

"Thank you, Masa," Hana said. "You may take him now." She handed over the wiggling infant. Masa stood holding him for another moment to listen to Kinzaemon's verdict.

"He seems a fine, healthy boy, yes. We'll make him into a first-rate brewer." He glanced at Jihei and nodded.

Rie looked around the table at her father, her mother, her husband, these her closest family members, none of whom seemed concerned for her feelings. She did not speak, nor did Jihei. Her mouth tightened. She glanced with distaste at the squirming infant, curdled milk dribbling down his chin onto his wrapper. This puking flesh, creature of her husband's infidelity, would remain here under her nose, an eternal reminder of his geisha's bloodline. A hard knot of rage gripped her stomach at the betrayal of those she loved most. Her fists clenched. She felt her nails press into her palms. She rose abruptly, excused herself, and left the room. As she passed the pillar she stopped and pounded her fists against it.

She walked quickly out the door nearest the garden, opened the gate, and went to her rock. It had grown dark and she could not see the koi in the pond. She leaned heavily against the rock, so often a source of comfort. Tonight there was no comfort anywhere. There was no moon. She could not stop the flood of tears rolling down her face. She bit her lip and reached in her obi for a handkerchief. Not only had she failed to produce an heir, her most important responsibility, but here under her eyes was this geisha's child, this product of Jihei's philandering installed as heir, as the future Kinzaemon XI. She felt as though her life had ended. Her goal of working for the house, her father, proving once and for all that she could be responsible, that she was worthy of her father's love by producing a successor to the Omura line, was beyond her reach. She bowed her head and could not stop sobbing. She sat there ignoring the passage of time. Then she felt black anger overcome her, a wild fury the likes of which she had never felt before.

Chapter 7

The morning after the baby's arrival Rie rose even earlier than usual, determined to be the first one up in the family. Hard work seemed the best antidote to the outrage she felt at the illegitimate infant Jihei had brought into the house. She felt energized, determined to somehow redress this betrayal. She walked through the chilly corridors to see to preparations for breakfast. O-Natsu was already there, supervising the kitchen maids. Rie paused. She noticed a small boy with protruding front teeth boiling rice in a huge black cauldron, his thin form completely enveloped in steam. She watched him for several minutes, and then approached O-Natsu.

"Good morning, O-Natsu," she said softly. "Who is the boy boiling the rice?"

O-Natsu bowed. "Oh, good morning. He came with the workers from Tamba this year. His name is Shin'ichi. He's thirteen, almost fourteen." O-Natsu looked at Rie inquisitively and turned back to the stove.

Rie, always alert for good workers, walked over to the boy and watched his fast, efficient work.

"Very good, Shin'ichi. You seem to like to work." She smiled.

The boy bowed rapidly three times. "I have always wanted to work in a brewery, Madam. And this year Toji-san allowed me to come." He bowed again and gave a toothy smile.

"I see." Rie paused. "Well, how would you like to do errands for us in the office?"

Shin'ichi put his hands stiffly at his sides and bowed repeatedly. "Oh, yes, Madam, very much."

"Well then, Shin'ichi, please come to the office tomorrow morning early. We will find someone else to cook the rice." This conscientious boy might prove important in the house's future with Kin facing retirement.

The thin figure continued bowing as Rie nodded, then turned and left the kitchen.

O-Natsu walked over to Shin'ichi. "You have attracted Oku-san's favor." She looked directly at him. "See that you don't disappoint her. She will treat you fairly."

"Oh, I will never disappoint her," he replied. He bowed again.

That evening Rie opened the door of the inner office and found Kin sitting alone, as she hoped.

"Excuse me, may I come in?" she asked softly. She had long been thinking of ways to help the house. A solid idea had formed over the past week.

"Yes, do." Kin beckoned toward the seat opposite him.

"Kin-san," Rie began, seating herself, I have an idea, two suggestions, for our business." She smiled.

Kin nodded. "Yes?"

"They will help White Tiger, I'm certain."

"Well, what is it? Your suggestion about our Edo shipments was useful." He looked at Rie.

"Can't we expand our moneylending and gold-silver exchange?

That way we can counter any risk in increasing production and shipments to Edo." She tapped the table with her fan.

Kin nodded and scratched his cheek. "You may be right. Yes, far less risk in moneylending, gold-silver exchange too. They are traditionally safe, and we always get a faster return on the financial side. More secure too. I'll take it up with your father and husband."

Rie nodded. "You know my husband seems much more cautious in business than you or Father. Or than I am." She bit her lip. She knew Kin understood.

"That's the survival strategy of smaller houses, O-Josama. They can't afford the risks we can. It's often written in their house rules: 'take no unnecessary risks.'"

"Is that so?" She sipped a cup of tea pensively. "And another thing. A boy is boiling rice in the kitchen. He seems so capable I would like you to consider using him in the office."

"We could try him out. How old is he? Why don't you bring him to the office tomorrow? I'll give him a task, and if he does it well I'll recommend him to your father."

"Thank you, Kin-san. He must be thirteen. Yes, I'll bring him in early." She smiled. Kin was even more receptive than she had hoped. Pragmatism . . . that was the key to approaching him.

Early the next morning Rie met a smiling, bowing Shin'ichi at the kitchen door, before anyone had started work.

"Good morning, Madam," he said in his high piping voice when Rie greeted him.

"Yes, Shin'ichi. Good. Come, we will go to the office and you will meet our *banto*, Kin. I believe he has a job for you this morning." She motioned for him to follow.

Shin'ichi bobbed up and down three times and trailed Rie, who slid open the door to the inner office.

"Good morning, Kin-san. Here we are." She glanced through

the door to the outer office where barrels of sake were stacked at one side of the room from floor to ceiling. Near the front entrance was a low table on which stood three small barrels and rows of tasting cups to entice customers.

Kin bowed smartly and, noting her glance toward the door to the outer office, he closed it and turned to Rie and Shin'ichi. Shin'ichi shivered and thrust his hands into his sleeves but stood respectfully back from the hibachi.

"How is your rheumatism this morning, Kin-san?" Rie inquired.

"We have to expect it in winter." He rubbed his hands together briskly.

"Well, I never hear you complain." Rie motioned Shin'ichi to her side.

"Here is Shin'ichi, the boy I mentioned," she said.

Kin looked at the smartly bowing boy. His hawk eyes took in Shin'ichi's erect posture, alert eyes, respectful manner.

"Good. Yes, we can use someone who is not afraid of work, an extra hand. Well, Shin'ichi, you can begin by picking up an order of yeast this morning at the Hayashi place. Here, this is how to find it." Kin sketched a map on a small piece of rice paper and handed it to Shin'ichi, who looked at it closely, then slipped it into his sleeve.

"It will take you most of the morning to get there and back. You can take the cart outside the number one kura," Kin instructed. He walked back through the corridor and out to the street, Rie and Shin'ichi behind him.

He slid open the front entrance and ducked under the hanging *noren* banner bearing the White Tiger logo.

"Here. You know how to pull one of these, don't you?" Kin indicated the wooden cart.

Rie watched Shin'ichi nod, adjust his straw sandals, then maneuver between the two handlebars. He picked them up and started off down the road at a run, bowing to Rie and Kinzaemon as he left.

"I hope you'll be pleased with his work, Kin-san. Be strict with him as you always are. Father won't object, will he?"

"Not if he does his work well," Kin said.

Rie had a hunch that Shin'ichi, young though he was, might prove more capable than any of the clerks working under Kin, and she followed her instinct in matters of business.

Rie walked to her mother's room early one evening several months later. Sounds of the baby playing in the room, mingled with voices, caused Rie to pause outside the shoji. She recognized Jihei's and her mother's voices.

"Excuse me," Rie called.

"Yes," her mother replied. "Come in, Rie."

Rie found her mother and Jihei playing with Yoshitaro, who was crawling back and forth between them, chortling. All three were enjoying themselves. Upon seeing them together, Rie suddenly felt dizzy as if she couldn't breathe.

"Come, Rie. Come and play with Yoshitaro," her mother invited, smiling. "My first grandchild," she said in musical tones. Hana clapped her hands rhythmically and laughed.

No blood relation, Rie wanted to say as she fought down the pain in her chest.

Yoshitaro crawled to Hana, then turned and crawled back to Jihei, fell on his lap, and squealed, never stopping his continual motion. He sat up and clutched Jihei, who helped him to stand. The baby kept one hand on Jihei's shoulder and began to take halting steps around him.

"Oh, look! His first steps!" Hana cried.

Rie looked at Yoshitaro's face next to Jihei's and saw unmistakable hints of the same large nose and long eyebrows.

"He does resemble his father," Rie said finally. She tried to think of something more to say about the baby. "We can start taking him into the office soon," she managed.

Her mother laughed softly. "Not yet, Rie. He's just a baby. But of course he can learn words, gradually." She smiled and nodded at him.

"He is learning now, just look at him. He's bright," Jihei said, taking obvious pleasure in the child.

Hana clapped her hands and began reciting a nursery rhyme: "Momotaro, Momotaro, Momotaro. . ." Yoshitaro stumbled back to Hana and fell. She picked him up and hugged him. "Yes, that's the way," she cooed.

Rie sighed, looked at her mother, and stood. "Good night, Mother." She nodded, not quite a bow, toward Jihei and left the room. She walked slowly up the stairs to her room, dressed for bed, and took out the futon. As she sat in front of her mirror combing her thick hair she choked back a sob and wiped away tears forming in her eyes. She sighed and lay down. She wondered if she would ever have a child of her own, if someday she could find a way to remove the geisha's bloodline from the house.

The next morning when Rie went down to breakfast her mother looked at her and saw how dejected she was. Ri-chan, why don't you and cousin Sunao go to the chrysanthemum festival this morning? I used to enjoy them so. It would be good for you to get out of the house a bit, go on a nice excursion with Sunao."

Rie looked at her teacup, then picked it up and sipped before answering. Sunao, daughter of Kinzaemon's younger brother living nearby, was really Rie's only friend and roughly her age. Rie put a finger on her mouth thoughtfully, then glanced at her mother. "All right, Mother, I'll have one of the maids go over to Sunao's and tell her I'll meet her at the exhibition grounds."

"Finish your breakfast, dear."

Rie nodded as she quickly ate some rice and miso soup. She went upstairs and picked out one of her finer kimonos. O-Natsu helped tie the obi, a chore Rie always found onerous. She asked one of the clerks in the outer office to find a ricksha and hummed as she walked out the entrance near the number one kura to wait for the ricksha.

As soon as she stepped up on the ricksha seat she felt some of the same elation she experienced whenever she had an opportunity to leave the confines of the house. Jihei's oppressive needs, her frustration at his inability in business, and his nightly demands lifted. She looked right and left, enjoying the sight of the rows of large wooden kura that lined the road and the breath of coastal salt air as they jogged along.

At the park she quickly found Sunao and they smiled and bowed in greeting, then walked together beside the rows of chrysanthemums. Anyone who saw them would no doubt take particular notice of two young women in elegant kimonos, Rie knew, but she was so intent on finally having a conversation with an intimate friend she could trust that she was oblivious to all else.

"Sunao, I haven't become pregnant yet. I don't know what more I can do. And now it's too late. You know a geisha's child has been brought in as heir. It's just intolerable!" Rie grabbed Sunao's arm.

"I heard, Ri-chan. It must be dreadful! I can't imagine."

"You are so fortunate, Sunao, having a child with no difficulty."

"I know this troubles you, Ri-chan, and I'm so sorry. Maybe an herbalist can help. They seem to have powders with magical properties."

Rie looked around at the crowd, individuals and couples, all apparently enjoying themselves, all seeming so carefree. As her glance passed over the crowd, it stopped. Saburo!

"Sunao, aren't they the Kato brothers over there at the end of that row?"

Sunao followed Rie's gaze. "Oh, I guess so. I saw all three at the Akita wedding recently. Shall we speak to them?"

Rie paused, her heart racing, but not wanting to appear overly interested, even with Sunao. After all, as a married woman, that would not do. "If you want to, Sunao," Rie said, affecting nonchalance.

The two walked toward the Kato brothers, admiring chrysanthemums as they went. Rie hesitated, waited until Sunao spoke first. Both bowed at the same time. Rie took in Saburo's fine chiseled features, his above-average height, his elegant bearing, a contrast to his stockier older brother who lacked his fine features and refined manner.

"Kato-sama, how are you?" Sunao asked sweetly.

The elder brother replied, "Omura-san, how nice to see you." Both men bowed slightly.

Rie summoned her voice. "I trust your family is well?" She glanced at the elder brother, then briefly at Saburo, smiling and bowing, her heart fluttering in her chest like a caged sparrow.

The Kato brothers murmured thanks, Saburo briefly catching her eye and then looking away.

"A lovely exhibit, isn't it? Please greet your family for us." Sunao took Rie's arm and they bowed and walked away.

Out of the corner of her eye Rie glanced again at Saburo before turning away and caught him doing the same. Sunao and Rie continued through the exhibit, admiring the variation in colors, sizes, and textures of flowers as they went.

As Rie and her cousin found separate rickshas to return, Sunao remarked, "Aren't those Kato men handsome, Ri-chan?"

Rie smiled and waved as she agreed and climbed into her ricksha to head back to the Omura House. She thought again of Saburo's kindness so long ago, of the surprise warmth of his touch at a time when she needed it most. And here he was again, just as she was being shunted aside for another woman's child. A lump formed in her throat. It occurred to her that she would like to see Saburo Kato again. Yes, she would like very much to see him again. And from the look on his face, the feeling was mutual. But she was a married woman. How in the world could she ever manage such an improper thing?

Chapter 8

Rie still relished the memory of the outing with Sunao to the annual chrysanthemum exhibit. Seeing Saburo had supplied welcome relief from the stifling atmosphere of the house, now that the geisha's child had created even greater tension than normal between her and Jihei. How she longed to bring a child of her own into the house. However, with each passing day, the distance between her and Jihei had grown until they spent little time together, inside the bed or out. As her dreams had faded for fulfilling her father's hopes, killing her *self* and enduring her life had become harder. Her one experience of pleasure in the past year had been her recent outing. She smiled again, thinking of the chrysanthemum exhibit and Saburo.

"It was wonderful, Mother. I wish you could have seen it. So many gorgeous varieties on display this year," Rie said as she sat with her mother at breakfast some days later.

"Yes, dear, I know I would have enjoyed it. I just didn't seem to have the energy this time. I guess I'm feeling my age."

Rie glanced at her mother sharply. "Sometimes I think you're working too hard, Mother. You know I can take more of the responsibility for the kurabito now. There are so many things to remember. I ordered some of those new rubber tabi for them."

"Yes, dear, I appreciate it."

"And you should eat more, Mother. You need more than rice and pickles."

Her mother smiled. "You know how much I enjoy these *nara-zuke*, made with the sake lees." Her mother picked up a pickle and delicately brought her chopsticks to her mouth. "I feel a meal isn't complete without them, even breakfast. And we have always believed rice is what makes the meal. Rice is sacred, you must remember."

Rie sipped her miso soup. "Sunao said she would enjoy going to the special ikebana exhibit that's on now, if we could go together. I think I'll see if she wants to go tomorrow."

"Yes, do, Ri-chan. I think going to the chrysanthemum show did you a lot of good, and this isn't our busiest season."

There was an entirely different reason that Rie wanted to go to the exhibit. A *very* attractive reason. She smiled, holding the secret close to her heart.

The next morning Rie dressed in one of her favorite kimono, even managing the cumbersome obi herself. She caught O-Natsu in the corridor. "O-Natsu, would you tell Mother I have gone to the ikebana exhibit with Sunao?"

O-Natsu nodded. "Shall I call a ricksha for you?"

"There's no need. I know where they wait in the next street."

O-Natsu frowned. "Is it all right, finding one by yourself?"

"Of course." Rie laughed, went to the door to find her geta, and let herself out.

No one need know that Sunao was not accompanying her this time. Rie did not want to worry her mother, but today's was a special outing. She had heard the Kato brothers mention the ikebana exhibit. What Rie would risk for just a long look at Saburo.

Minutes later, as she stepped up into the ricksha she felt a sense of anticipation, almost as if she had grown several years younger, so carefree was her mood. It was always exhilarating to see the large wooden kura lining the main road. She alighted at the exhibition hall, handed coins to the puller, and said she would be looking for him later if he were still there.

Inside the hall the lines were long, and polite chatter about the exquisite arrangements floated on the air. The kimonos of the women were especially elegant, and Rie felt suddenly abashed. She knew Sunao's taste in kimono was superior to hers. Perhaps she should have brought Sunao along after all.

If truth be told, Rie did not appreciate ikebana as much as her mother or Sunao. Somehow she preferred to see plants and flowers in a more natural setting, as in the garden at home. She knew that even there, in her favorite private place, the gardener always pruned in a prescribed way. Nothing grew wild unless one went into some out-of-the-way rural area, something Rie seldom had an opportunity to do.

She turned her attention to an exhibit of her favorite flowers, wisteria, and stopped to admire the arrangements, some in flat obsidian containers, others in white or celadon vases of ingenious shapes, of subtle, impeccable taste. She noted most were in the prescribed three-part placement of flowers and greenery. She tried to remember a few of the most striking designs, thinking perhaps she might try her hand at them. Such fine art was not something that usually occupied her time in the workday of the busy brewery, but she knew it would please her mother. As she paused, a voice at her elbow interrupted her reverie.

"Omura-san, we meet again amid flowers."

Her heart raced. There in front of her was Saburo Kato. More handsome than ever.

"Yes, what a pleasant surprise," Rie managed to say, bowing and smiling. She felt her heartbeat accelerate.

"Shall we look at the prize winners?" Saburo asked.

Rie smiled and nodded, temporarily speechless at her good fortune. She could barely take her eyes off him.

As they walked, Saburo slowed so that they were walking abreast rather than with Rie three paces behind.

"I heard about the inappropriate remarks made by Yamaguchi at your wedding," he said, glancing at Rie. "My father said it was too arrogant, and coming from the president of the Brewers Association. I hope your father was not upset by the insult to your house."

He understood. Here was a man who understood her *and* her family. She paused. "Thank you, Kato-sama, for your understanding, but I fear my father was annoyed and a bit depressed." She looked directly into Kato's eyes, the man she had always found so attractive. She felt their connection in her inner being, a connection she had never felt with anyone else. And to her surprise she felt no awkwardness in talking with him. Rie felt her spirit soaring, dancing in the air.

His glance rested on Rie's face. "Well, I doubt that he will be reelected. Shall we work together to see that he is not? Of course I am not the heir, but my father and brothers listen to me. I know that you are heir . . . your husband . . ."

She longed to touch him, to feel the protection of his embrace for just a moment.

"Ah, Kato-sama, that would be wonderful. I must be returning home now, but I feel we shall meet again." She knew they would. And that she must not linger today. She bowed.

"Yes, it will be my hope, Omura-san. I look forward to it." He smiled and bowed in return, his eyes lingering longer than what was necessary and sending a warm tingle racing through her. What it took to leave his company, to tear herself away from him.

With one last look at Saburo, Rie hurried out to the ricksha. It was more than she could have hoped, not only meeting him but knowing he cared for her and her house, that they had a common antagonist, and especially that he wanted to see her again. He felt what she did, she was certain. She smiled and hummed all the way to the Omura entrance.

Rie arrived home in a mood of elation. She nearly ran up the slippery stairs to change into her work kimono before joining her mother for lunch. "It was such a special exhibit, Mother," she remarked as she sat at the table where her mother was looking at her food. Rie was hungry and did not notice immediately that her mother was not eating. Rie put down her chopsticks.

"What's the matter, Mother? Don't you feel well?"

"Oh, it's nothing. Just a stomach upset, I imagine. Don't worry."

"Are you sure, Mother?"

Her mother nodded, so Rie excused herself and left for the storeroom, her favorite workplace, and not off-limits to her. She was eager to be alone with her memories of Saburo, of his plan. *Their* plan.

Late in the afternoon she went to her mother's room to see how she was doing. Hana was lying on her futon, her eyes closed. Rie saw that the hibachi coals had gone out. She touched her mother's hands.

"Mother, how are you feeling?" she asked softly.

"Oh, Rie. . ." Hana opened her eyes and struggled to speak. "I am not well." She closed her eyes again.

"Has anyone sent for the herbalist?"

Hana shook her head. Rie relit the hibachi and reached to touch her mother's forehead. A shot of alarm raced through her. Her mother was burning up.

"I see you are in pain, Mother," she said, hiding the panic from her voice. "I'm going to send someone now."

"Oh . . ." Her mother only frowned.

Rie rushed to the kitchen and asked O-Natsu's assistant to go for the herbalist.

"Run! Right now! You know where he lives? Bring him back with you as soon as possible," she ordered.

Rie ran to the inner office and opened the shoji abruptly, without announcing herself.

Her father, Jihei, and a customer looked up, startled. She stood in the doorway.

"It's Mother. She's having abdominal pain. I've sent for the herbalist."

"Oh, I'll come." Her father frowned and rose to follow Rie along the earthen corridor to the step leading to the family rooms.

"I'm afraid it's serious, Father." *Please let me be wrong. Let her be all right.*

Her father gasped. "Good that you called for the herbalist, Rie. Let's see what he has to say."

They entered Hana's room. The light creeping in through the shoji dimly lit Hana's pallid face. O-Natsu had propped up Hana's head and was holding a bowl of rice gruel to her mouth. Hana shook her head, and O-Natsu set the bowl on a tray.

"She won't eat," O-Natsu said, anxiously. She bowed herself out.

Rie and her father sat on either side of Hana's futon and watched her face intently.

The old wizened herbalist arrived with a brown pouch filled with potions and powders tied to his obi. He knelt beside Hana's futon and felt her pulse and pressure points on her arms and legs.

"Hmm," he murmured.

He took from his pouch two powders and measured them into folded papers, which he handed to Rie.

"She must take these with hot water three times each day, beginning now. Send for me tomorrow if she isn't better."

Rie's father followed the herbalist to the door, questioning him as he left.

Rie took the powders and held one packet to her mother's mouth, a cup of tea in the other hand. She raised her mother's head.

"Please open your mouth, Mother. You must take this." *Do not leave me! You must not go. Please.*

Her mother took a small sip.

"One more, Mother. Here." Rie held the second packet of powder to her mother's mouth. *Please work. Please!*

Hana groaned and shook her head. Her eyes moved slowly toward Rie and then to her husband, who had reentered the room and sat near his wife.

"I know," she said feebly, "my time has come." She struggled to continue. "I have had a good life. I am ready."

Kinzaemon dropped his head to his chest, hands clenched in his lap.

"No, Mother, please!" Rie pleaded. She continued to hold the powder to her mother's mouth, but Hana simply closed her eyes.

Rie glanced at her father from time to time as they both sat in consternation at Hana's side. In the evening Rie looked at her father. "Go to bed, Father, and have something to eat. I'll stay here with her."

Her father shook his head. "I want to be with her now."

Hours passed. During the night Rie glanced at her father and saw that he was dozing where he sat, head resting on his chest. Jihei came in and sat for a while, then left. O-Natsu crept in with tea to see if Rie or Kinzaemon wished to be relieved. Rie whispered no.

Alone with her late-night thoughts, tears ran down Rie's cheeks. No one could replace her mother. Rie's father was fond of her, relied on her for the future of the house, she knew. But her mother understood her as only a woman can. She had a tender-hearted way with a woman's problems. Rie sobbed softly as she gazed at her mother's white hands crossed over her chest, hands that had so often held fine needlework with invisible stitches, hands that had nurtured Rie ever since her earliest memories. Now the hands lay so still. Rie watched the futon rise and fall almost imperceptibly with her mother's breathing and felt her own breaths match her mother's, as if to lend her mother her own life force.

At the first faint light of dawn filtering in through the shoji, Rie started at a sound from her mother's futon. She reached toward the futon. Her mother moved as if to sit up but fell back, her eyes and mouth open. Rie touched her hands and felt her pulse. *No. No. No!*

"Father!" Rie reached a hand to her sleeping father's arm. "I think Mother's gone." She sobbed, a hand over her mouth.

The cremation was a most painful experience for Rie, reminding her once again of Toichi, of her failing the house, failing to produce an heir. When would she ever get it right, she wondered, as she sat with her father, shuddering and sobbing as she picked each bone from the ashes with chopsticks? She looked at the cluster of bones, all that remained of her mother. There was the skull that had underlain the delicate features and patrician nose. Rie glanced at her father's devastated face and squirmed as she decided to save him this most painful part of the final devotion. She picked up the skull and separated it from the ashes. When she finished she closed her eyes and imagined her mother's patrician face bent over the needlework she was so fond of. Imagined her sitting in her room in front of her carved paulownia dressing table. For several moments Rie held the vision before opening her eyes to attend to the rest of her difficult task.

The funeral ceremony was a sad, solemn affair, the large room lined with black-clad mourners and priests intoning their droning mantras. Saburo was there too, his heart reaching out to her even across a crowded room. She had heard that he had lost his mother at an early age and had never fully recovered from the loss. She sneaked a glance at him and bowed quickly as his glance locked with hers.

Only once before had Rie experienced such complete and utter grief: the day her brother had fallen into the well. The day she hadn't taken her responsibility seriously. Now, once again, she had failed in her duty. Her mother had not lived to see the grandchild of her blood. It was too late. Watching her father's drawn face, Rie tried to conceal her own desolation. Numbness overtook her, a closing off of all aspects of her normal daily life. For several days she had energy only to sit with her father or in the garden, silent to the world around her.

Though she had never seen her parents demonstrate their affection for each other, she knew it was there, a deep, abiding bond. Her father grew increasingly dispirited in the days and weeks to follow. Added to her own bereavement, Rie felt the heavy weight of an even greater responsibility. Soon it would be up to her and Jihei to maintain the business and tradition of the house. She knew this meant the weight lay squarely on her shoulders, since Jihei had demonstrated so little ability. What kind of support could she count on?

One morning soon after the funeral Rie knelt at the Butsudan altar to light incense and to offer rice before the tablets of her mother and ancestors. Her father entered the room, she could sense without turning. She placed an incense stick in the powdery ash, lit it, bowed and clapped her hands to attract the attention of the gods.

"*Ah,* Rie," her father said behind her when she had finished.

"It's so important to keep our communication with the ances-tors, the Buddhas, just as we see to the continuity of the house with our heirs. And Rie, your mother was fond of plum wine. Why don't you serve her a cup each morning with the rice? She'll be pleased."

"Yes, Father, I'll do that." She glanced at the new tablet on which her mother's posthumous name was inscribed. A fresh stab of grief overtook her.

"I was gratified that all the major brewers sent family members to attend the funeral. It shows our standing here. You know you need to keep a record of the donation each house made. Then we can return the same amount, with interest, when they have their funerals. Mother always kept strict records."

Rie took a deep breath. "Yes, Father, I have them now. Don't worry." Rie took a rice paper pamphlet from a small wooden cabinet near the Butsudan and pushed it toward her father, seated next to her. "I've entered all the donations."

"Very good, Rie. And the kurabito too. Mother was always so attentive to their needs. This will be your responsibility from now on."

"I know, Father, that's why they have been content here and come back year after year from Tamba. I'll take care of them."

Kinzaemon pushed his bushy hair off his forehead and nodded.

Rie sat at the Butsudan long after her father left the room. Now the enormity of the obligation resting on her shoulders made her catch her breath: the on to her father and nine genera-tions of ancestors, and the burden of the important business of the Omura House, one of the largest in the most ancient and respected industry in all Japan. Soon her father would retire, and the entire responsibility would rest with her. The reality of Yoshi-taro, the new heir and the bloodline of the geisha, in the main house sent a wave of agony through her. He was a reminder of everyone she had failed. In the tragedy of her mother's death, she had temporarily forgotten about him. Although her father had been understanding about bringing the child into the house, she could see in his eyes that he had hoped for a child of his own blood. She buried her face in her hands. The time had come to turn her attention now to this intolerable situation.

Chapter 9

Rie opened the wooden shutters and looked out at the garden from her upper-story room early one morning. The wintry landscape, in the garden and compound, out on the streets, wherever she looked, was defined by a narrow spectrum of color from brown to gray. In the house she insisted that flowers in red and yellow be displayed to counter the gray monotony that had taken hold since her mother's death. She still hoped for a child, but as the months passed, she had given up on the idea that she would ever have one with Jihei. There must be another way, but how? The glimmer of an idea rose inside her. Something unthinkable. So unthinkable she put it from her mind immediately.

She reluctantly admitted that she was beginning to enjoy the bursts of vibrant energy from Yoshitaro to enliven the somber atmosphere of winter that came with this period of mourning. She regretted that as a married woman she was required to appear in black at weddings and funerals, generally her only occasions beyond the brewery. In the house she wore kimonos of indigo-dyed kasuri fabrics.

When she opened the wooden shutters of her room in the morning and looked at the garden, she watched for the plum blossoms that heralded the beginning of February, and the pink and fuchsia azaleas, harbingers of early spring and the end of the brewing season, precursors of the cherry blossoms. In muggy summertime, the cicadas competed in a buzzing humming chorus that increased in volume with the temperature. In autumn, yellow chrysanthemums reminded her that the brewing season was beginning again. The life of the garden thus marked the seasons of Rie's days following her mother's passing.

Of course, there would be no meeting with Saburo. Perhaps in some future time. In the meantime, just thinking of him consoled her. During the summer months after the brewing was finished, the workload in the brewery abated. The kurabito went home to their farms in Tamba, where they worked in the rice paddies. Apart from selling and shipping sake, the focus shifted to moneylending and gold-and-silver exchange. Because the Tokugawa shoguns had fallen on hard times and their economic condition was reflected in the lives of their daimyo vassals, the samurai were impoverished, forced into the grip of moneylenders. Some of them tried to eke out a living in craft occupations, making umbrellas or fans.

"The samurai are parasites, leeches on us, Father," Rie said, unconsciously echoing her father's sentiments. "It's we merchants who produce the real wealth."

"Quite right, Rie," her father agreed. "They mouth their Confucian maxims and look down on us, but they are completely dependent on us economically."

The House of Omura, like most merchant houses in Kobe and Osaka, benefited from the penury of the samurai class, which depended on the cash and services of the merchants.

Every summer when the days were particularly hot and humid, the Bunraku puppet troupe came from its Osaka headquarters to perform one or two of Chikamatsu's masterpieces for the merchant audiences of Kobe.

Rie turned to Jihei one morning. "Why don't we take Sunao to Bunraku this Saturday? Her husband is away in Edo. I think we can spare the time, and she would enjoy it. Father would too." Rie did not mention that she would also enjoy the outing.

"Not a bad idea," Jihei replied. "Yes, I'd enjoy it too. We can all go."

The Omuras had reserved seats in one of the best sections in the packed theater. Just as Rie, her father, and Sunao were following Jihei inside, he was shouldered aside by a huge figure Rie at first took to be a sumo wrestler.

"Move aside, Omura! Let me pass!"

Rie watched as Jihei struggled to catch his balance. She glanced up in time to see the fat, arrogant face of Kikuji Yamaguchi, and Jihei straightening his collar and brushing off his kimono.

"Incredible effrontery!" he said to Rie, loud enough for anyone nearby to hear. "Who does he think he is?"

"He thinks he's the most important person in Nada," Rie replied. "We'll show him." She gave Yamaguchi a withering glance.

Geishas butterflied in, tittering, long-sleeved hands covering their mouths. They timed their entrance to attract the attention of the entire audience just before the lamps were extinguished.

Rie watched Jihei out of the corner of her eye as he scanned the geisha section and settled on an individual. It must be O-Toki, Rie decided, noticing a geisha with mask-white makeup wearing an apricot kimono that blatantly displayed the nape of her neck. Perhaps that kind of makeup and dress did excite men, as intended. As she watched, the geisha turned toward them, then quickly covered her face with a fluttering fan and turned away. Humiliation bubbled up inside Rie at the thought that she was still barren.

The lamps were snuffed out, and the purple curtain billowed upward on Chikamatsu's perennial favorite, *The Love Suicide at Amijima*, portraying a triangle in which the hero is caught between his duty to his family and his passion for the alluring courtesan. The nasal twanging of the *samisen* accompaniment helped to transport the audience to the magic world of the unfolding drama. As the play advanced toward its climax, the puppets raised their eyebrows, waved their arms, shrieked and wailed in an agony of frustration and despair.

Then came the denouement: the anguished hero committed suicide with his mistress, a lovers' suicide. Rie could hear men clearing their throats and shifting in their seats. When the lamps were relit, she noticed tears glistening on Jihei's cheeks, and several men around them weeping. She smiled ruefully. Chikamatsu was in truth the master playwright. He had so accurately evoked the two separate worlds of Japan, the world of the family and the world of the geisha, the water world where wives never ventured. It was obvious where the sympathies of the men in the audience lay: with the hero and the geisha, not with his wife and children who were left behind.

"What a master Chikamatsu was," Sunao said to Rie as they rode home in a ricksha together.

"And did you notice all the men in the audience weeping?" Rie asked. "We are supposed to sympathize with the hero and the geisha, not the wife and family at home," she added with a wry smile.

"Isn't that the way with most of his plays," Sunao asked rhetorically.

Work at White Tiger continued as if the Bunraku expedition had not occurred. Kobe was home to all the largest breweries in

Japan, and competition among them for the Edo market, key to the success of any large brewery, was fierce. Thousands of other brewers scattered throughout the countryside did not enter the Edo market but brewed wherever farmers had a rice surplus and sold locally to loyal clientele.

Rie stood eavesdropping beyond the office one morning, as she often did. "Yamaguchi tried to contract one of the cask ships we've been using, to monopolize the whole ship," Kin said to Kinzaemon and Jihei. "He offered a price higher than the going rate, but the shipper was wary because of his long connection with us. The man just has no scruples."

"Well, it's good that we're in time with this year's shipment to Edo," Jihei said.

"Especially since we contracted the two extra ships to handle expansion this year," Kinzaemon agreed.

Kin scratched his head. "But I'd like to see our gold-and-silver exchange expanded further. Always less risk that way, as Rie says."

Kinzaemon rubbed his chin. "That's what we've always believed. Yes, we could raise it five, maybe ten percent."

"Perhaps as much as fifteen, or twenty," Kin said.

They heard someone running toward the door and looked up. Kinnosuke, as Shin'ichi was now called since he had become Kin's apprentice, entered out of breath and bowed twice.

"There's a messenger from the shipping contractor in the outer office. He's very agitated," he blurted out. He bowed twice.

Rie backed out of sight, but strained to hear. She moved down the hall toward the outer office. "Have him come in," Kinzaemon said. "No, let's go, Kin and Jihei." Kinzaemon struggled up from the tatami and the three walked quickly to the outer office.

"*Ah*, Hayami-san," Kinzaemon said to the bowing official. "What brings you here?"

Hayami bowed again. "Very sorry to say, Sir. There has been

a shipwreck on the way to Edo. One of the ships with part of your shipment has been lost." He bowed again. "It was that dangerous shoal near Nagoya." He wiped perspiration from his face with a towel from his sleeve and sighed.

"Oh! Oh!" Kinzaemon groaned. He pulled at his ear and glanced at Kin.

"It wasn't our whole consignment, was it?" Kin asked, frowning. "We were using five ships."

"Yes, I think one fifth of your total," Hayami agreed.

"How will we repay our loans this year?" Jihei asked, rubbing his eyebrows.

"We'll give you a discount on your next year's shipment," Hayami said. "Fifteen percent. We have no words to apologize adequately." He bowed continuously.

"Yes, we'll need a discount for next year," said Kin. "Let's look at the figures." Kin and Kinnosuke moved to the section of the office where Kin kept the ledgers. Hayami followed them.

Kinzaemon and Jihei walked back to the inner office. Kinzaemon sat heavily and sighed.

"What a disaster," Jihei said, pulling at his eyebrows.

Listening, Rie frowned, pondering what she could do or suggest. She bit her lip, tapped her chin with her fan.

"Brewing is a risky enterprise, as we all know," Kinzaemon sighed. "This is why we need an equal business in moneylending and gold-and-silver exchange. Without that cushion we might be out of business this year, relying on the two-year wait for the return from our brewing investment." He ran his hand through his hair.

Rie's voice came from the hallway, and she hurried into the office. "This is terrible!" She moved a hand up and down her arm. "What do we do now, Father?"

"We haven't lost our whole shipment, Rie. Please ask for some tea for us."

Kin came back into the room with Kinnosuke and stood facing Kinzaemon and Rie.

"It's a loss of one-fifth of the year's shipment," he said in a thin voice. "I'm making arrangements to increase our gold-and-silver exchange ten percent over last year. It will be a struggle to make it till next fall."

Jihei rubbed his hands over his eyebrows. "Other brewers must have lost too," he said.

Rie turned to Hayami. "What about Yamaguchi? Was he using this ship too?"

"I don't believe so, no," Hayami replied.

"Then I wonder," Rie said, "was it really an accident, or another case of Yamaguchi's treachery?"

They sat in fraught silence around the table. Monsoon rains pelted against the roof and added to the gloom inside.

Chapter 10

With the death of Hana, the atmosphere and relationships in the house altered. Rie and her father spent more time together, especially in the evenings when Jihei was away. Rie, still protective of her father and wishing to spare him the disappointment of Jihei's lack of commitment, often made excuses for her absent husband as she sat companionably with her father after dinner. They had weathered the storm of the lost shipments, but only through careful planning and tight control of their finances, no thanks to Jihei who once again was out spending her father's money.

"Father, I believe Jihei said he was going to a gathering of other brewers, trying to keep up with the latest news, especially now that you are no longer attending the Brewers Association meetings." Of course Rie doubted Jihei was doing any such thing. More likely, he was spending time at the Sawaraya with that geisha. "I also need to know what is happening with the business, Father. We don't want Yamaguchi to take advantage of us, now that it's known you may retire soon."

Kinzaemon sighed. "Yes, that's so, Rie. And of course Kin is almost my age, so he may retire soon too. It would be a problem if we both retired at once, a big problem."

Rie sorrowed to see her father looking older, seeming less resilient after his wife's passing.

"Kin told me that he would be able to continue for a while even after you retire. And you know Shin'ichi is doing exceptionally well. Kin says we are fortunate to have him. I believe Kin feels Kinnosuke may be able to succeed him one day." Rie smiled and poured sake as her father held out his cup. "I think Kinnosuke is about fifteen now."

"You did well, Ri-chan, to recognize his ability even as a young boy."

Rie nodded and bowed slightly at her father's compliment. She relished the increased opportunity for her father's companionship, time he had normally spent with Hana while she was alive.

Early one morning several weeks later, as Rie dressed before going down to breakfast, she sat before the mirror on her mother's paulownia dressing cabinet. Her thoughts turned to Yoshitaro, now walking and making his way into the office. More than once Rie heard Kinnosuke giving him bits of information about the business. Rie did not think this inappropriate. Still, the reality of the geisha's bloodline in the house rankled, never leaving her consciousness for long. What could she do? There was no altering the fact that Yoshitaro was heir, that after Jihei he would become Kinzaemon XI.

This morning as she sat before the mirror she thought of Saburo Kato and their meeting at the ikebana exhibit the morning before her mother died. The tragedy had pushed all thought of their discussion from her mind. Earlier in the week, Rie had received a note of remembrance from Saburo on the anniversary of her mother's death. He had reiterated a desire to work together to prevent Yamaguchi's reelection, and their mutual hope to meet again. Something in the way he'd penned his note had made her think that perhaps he had more in mind.

Was Saburo's talk of working together against Yamaguchi perhaps just his way of forming a bond with her? She hoped so, even though they both wanted to defeat Yamaguchi. She pictured in her imagination meeting Saburo at night, alone. She would make it happen, make it possible to be with him so that she might bear his child, a child growing of love, a child without the blood of a geisha. A child that might someday make it possible to expel the geisha bloodline from the Omura House. She had always felt she belonged with Saburo, not with her dolt of a husband. She would do it.

The idea she hadn't dared let surface so many months ago now blossomed. She pictured his caring brown eyes and pondered for several minutes. Then with a tingle of anticipation and renewed excitement in her step, she went to a tansu and opened a secret drawer where she kept some cash. She took out several coins and placed them in a pouch of finest silk. She inserted the pouch into the sleeve of her kimono and hurried down to breakfast. O-Natsu and others would notice if she delayed too long.

She ate a perfunctory breakfast alone. Her father and Jihei were already in the office, and it was not often they spent time together at this busy hour. She hurried back upstairs, took a brush and inkstone from a tansu drawer, added a bit of water to the inkstone, and quickly rubbed the inkstick back and forth until the ink was of proper consistency. She knew her calligraphy was not highly skilled, but she carefully wrote a few lines on the best rice paper, folded the note, sealed it with wax, and thrust it into her sleeve. She was proud that she could write and use the abacus, skills not common to every woman in brewing families. She went back to the secret drawer, took out a few more coins, and placed them in another small silk pouch. She touched her kimono sleeve to make certain the pouches and note would not slip out, and went downstairs.

In the corridor Rie asked one of the maids to send O-Natsu to her room with tea.

A few minutes later O-Natsu entered on her knees with a tea tray and set it on the tatami in front of Rie. She looked at Rie expectantly.

"Thank you, O-Natsu. I have a very big task for you. It is a great responsibility for the house."

O-Natsu's eyes widened. She bowed. "Whatever O-Josama requires."

She knew she could trust O-Natsu. Discretion was paramount. "Well, O-Natsu, I wonder if you have some relatives in a nice house not too far away who may be having financial difficulties, and who are completely trustworthy?"

O-Natsu paused, biting her lip. "Yes, O-Josama, they live not far from here."

"What I want you to do is to go to your relatives tonight. Ask them if they would make their house available two nights from tonight from midnight until dawn. If they agree, give them this money." Rie handed the larger pouch to O-Natsu with both hands. "But tell them they must remain absolutely silent about this, on pain of death. And they must not be there those hours from midnight until dawn." Rie studied O-Natsu closely as she spoke.

O-Natsu gasped. "Are you . . . do you intend to go out at night alone?"

"Yes, O-Natsu, but you must tell no one. This is between us. And do you know the chief servant at the Kato residence?"

"I do, yes."

"And is she completely trustworthy?"

"She is my good friend, and I trust her."

"All right, O-Natsu. Then give your friend this packet of money for her help, and ask that she give this note to the Kato third son, Saburo, to no one else in the house. Tell her she must speak to no one, or there may be consequences. This is a very big responsibility, O-Natsu. Do you understand you must also speak to no one about it?"

O-Natsu nodded and bowed deeply.

"Will you please repeat what I asked you to do?"

Rie sat intently while O-Natsu repeated the instructions.

"Very good. Now when dusk falls this afternoon, please go on your errands, and let me know when you have completed them."

"Certainly, O-Josama. I will do exactly as you say." O-Natsu thrust the bags and note into her sleeve, bowed, and left the room.

Rie smiled and sighed. She looked in the mirror, adjusted her hair, then took out the container of her mother's Kyoto perfume, opened it, and inhaled. She tried to imagine what it would be like to be with Saburo Kato. How would she manage to leave the house at night without being seen, to find a ricksha and make it to the house O-Natsu had indicated? More important, would Saburo really come to the house to meet her?

For the rest of the day and the day following, Rie went about her chores with a distracted air, thoughts of Saburo, his reaction to the note, filling her with anticipation.

Chapter 11

Rie awoke early. She sat up abruptly as she realized it was two days since she had sent O-Natsu on her secret errand. To her immense relief and great pleasure, she caught her breath, as the following morning she opened Saburo's note in reply. Her hands trembled as she read his words. Saburo agreed to the rendezvous. She had never felt so elated. She dressed quickly and sat at her mirror combing her hair. How was she to effect her escape from the Omura House and reach her destination by midnight for her rendezvous with Saburo Kato? She would have to go in disguise, cover her face, pretend she was a low-ranking servant.

Although she knew she could never provide the heir for the house, she wanted a child of her father's blood, a child who would carry on the Omura bloodline. Carry the heart and soul of her parents. Besides, loneliness had been a constant companion. She knew she could never love Jihei, nor he love her, and all her attempts at seduction had ended in failure either because he was too drunk or because he hadn't come home at all. Lately she would lie awake at night, remembering Saburo's eyes, his lips, and the gentleness in his voice. She was in love with Saburo. Deeply in love. And he had given her enough subtle clues that he felt the same. She just hoped that they didn't get caught. She knew the penalty for a woman would be severe, probably even death. Of course there was no penalty for a man, whether married or not. Saburo was not married, and there would be no danger for him, even if he were.

Downstairs, she ate a quick breakfast. When O-Natsu brought in tea and miso soup, Rie saw her opportunity. "O-Natsu, can you find some old clothes that I can use . . . later?" She did not want to be more specific in case one of the maids happened to be listening. Walls and shoji were so thin.

O-Natsu, always quick to guess Rie's meaning, understood. "Yes, I'll find something suitable. You need not be concerned." She nodded and bowed.

Breakfast finished, Rie hurried to the Butsudan to pray to the ancestors, to burn an incense stick, to leave rice and a tiny cup of plum wine for her mother. She sat unmoving for several minutes before the altar, folded hands raised to her chin as she prayed, entrusted her mission to the ancestors. They would surely be listening.

She walked briskly to the storeroom to inventory supplies for the kurabito. She worked to ensure that they were as content with her management of their health and well-being as they had been when her mother was alive.

Next she went to Yoshi's room, where he was playing with an abacus Kinnosuke had given him. At two, her father said it was time he began to learn skills that would be useful later.

"Good morning, Yoshi." She smiled, pleased to see him with

the abacus. "Shall we have a lesson in writing today? You did so well starting with *hiragana* the other day." Rie sat next to Yoshi and took a pad of paper from her sleeve.

Yoshi nodded and opened a cabinet where his inkstone and stick were kept.

Rie poured a small amount of water on the inkstone.

"I can do it, Okaa-san." He reached for the inkstick and began to rub it back and forth on the stone.

Each time he called her "Mother" she had stifled a comment. The first time she had wanted to say "I'm not your mother," but of course she didn't. She needed to treat Yoshi as if she were, and she did her best to behave that way. Yoshi after all had not chosen his parents. He was not responsible for Jihei's action. Besides, he was eager to please, and she had to admit he was an appealing child. In any case, she had learned to adjust her behavior when it had no relationship to her feelings. Was that what her mother had meant when she told Rie women had to "kill the self"?

Yoshi continued busily rubbing the inkstick.

"Very good, Yoshi. I think that's enough." She pushed two sheets of rice paper in front of him. "Now, do you think you can write '*sa, shi, su, se, so*' for me?"

Yoshi dipped his brush into the ink and awkwardly wrote the crude syllables, then sat back proudly and looked at Rie.

"That's good, Yoshi, yes. And you remember how I told you to hold your brush so it points straight up and down?"

Yoshi nodded and did his best to hold the brush properly.

Rie spent some minutes this way each morning instructing Yoshi. She found that she began to take satisfaction in watching his improvement and childish enthusiasm. It helped alleviate some of the pain of not having borne an heir herself.

The day seemed to Rie to be passing impossibly slow. She filled the afternoon hours with as many tasks as possible, impatiently hurrying from one to the next. Toward the dinner hour O-Natsu brought a bundle of old clothes to Rie's room.

"I hope these will do," she said as she laid them in front of Rie.

Rie held up the tunic and long scarf and fingered them. "These should be perfect, O-Natsu." Rie wound the scarf over her neck and arranged it so that it covered her face, leaving an opening for her eyes.

"Yes, you look like a poor peon." O-Natsu giggled.

Rie smiled broadly and removed the scarf. "At dinner this evening I'll tell my father and husband that I am tired and will go upstairs early."

"Do you want me to help you leave tonight?" O-Natsu scratched her face.

Rie pondered. "Maybe when it is twenty minutes before midnight you could make certain no one is awake, and that my husband is not here. Let me know. That would be a help. Yes, thank you." It was likely that Jihei would not be around, but she needed to make certain.

When O-Natsu left, Rie sat thinking. She and Saburo Kato had so many things in common. She had never forgotten his sympathy when little Toichi had drowned and he had realized her responsibility. And now they both wanted to prevent Yamaguchi's reelection. They even had similar taste in flowers, so important an indication of a man's sensitivity. And she knew Saburo was as dedicated to the Kato house as she was to hers. He appeared to Rie to have strength of character, something she admired in a man, something so lacking in Jihei. But this was not the time to think of Jihei.

He was nowhere to be seen in the evening, Rie was pleased to see. She dressed in her room for the adventure, making sure her mother's perfume was secure in her sleeve. She sat alone in anticipation.

Late in the evening she heard O-Natsu's voice beyond the shoji. "It's time."

Rie opened the shoji and followed O-Natsu down the stairs, both walking as quietly as possible. O-Natsu led the way to the door closest the storeroom and opened the outer gate. Rie peered out and saw a ricksha standing at the corner. She turned to O-Natsu. "Be sure to meet me here at the gate just before dawn," she whispered.

She quickly hailed the ricksha, adjusting the scarf over her face, and instructed the puller where to take her. As the ricksha jogged toward her destination, Rie reached into her sleeve and applied the crème parfum liberally to her neck and wrists. She didn't care if she used it all.

As they neared the house, Rie saw another ricksha standing not far from the gate. She felt a thrill go through her. Saburo was already there as he had said he would be. She alighted and went through the gate to the front shoji. "I'm here," she said, not so loudly that a nearby neighbor might hear.

Saburo was at the door to meet her as she stepped inside. He wore his ordinary kimono, as he had not wanted to attract suspicion either, and his oval face bore an expression of tenderness that she had never seen on Jihei. Rie stood directly before him, unable to hide her excitement or her nervousness, as she fidgeted with the hem of her tunic. Saburo smiled and raised his hands to her face. For a moment they gazed into each other's eyes. Neither knew exactly what to do, what to say. But then Saburo drew her to him and embraced her gently, kissing her face, neck, lips. Trembling, Rie clung to him tightly, then more tightly still.

"I knew when I saw you at the ikebana exhibit that you had a place in my heart," he murmured. "I knew from the first time I saw you."

She nodded, hearing the truth in his words. "I felt the same," Rie said, breathlessly, remembering the day of her brother's funeral, Saburo's gentleness even then. "Just the same." She felt tears start, but they were tears unlike others.

"As you know, my mother died when I was a child, so I understood your deep loss at the death of your mother. And I remember about your little brother." He ran a finger along her chin. "I was so happy that you responded to my note." He pressed his cheek against hers.

Saburo held her from him so he could look at her. "The heart has its own song," he said, smiling broadly.

Rie felt her whole being smile joyfully. Until now, she hadn't realized how deprived her life had become with Jihei, how lonely she'd been. "*Ah* . . . You would have been a poet in the Old Capital." Her mother had once told her of the poet lovers in the Old Imperial Court, of the beautiful poems they wrote for the women they courted.

"You would have sat behind a screen listening to my poems."

"And I would have chosen your poems above all others," Rie replied. She had never felt such harmony and peace. She glanced quickly at the tea tray and futon thoughtfully laid out by O-Natsu's relatives. "I'm glad we have no screen now." She had her arms around Saburo's neck.

"We need none." He led Rie toward the futon and pulled off her tunic, kissing her shoulder, caressing her neck with his tongue.

Soon there was not only no screen between them, but nothing else.

Rie felt something in her being released, becoming free. For the first time in her life it seemed there was no separation between her feelings and her behavior. She felt totally new, so new. They lay on the futon, light from the candle revealing the secrets of each other's bodies.

Saburo met Rie with a tender passion that caused her wonder. This was how it was meant to be, she was sure. For the next few minutes, the next few hours, there was nothing for Rie or Saburo but each other.

Some time later, still in the afterglow of love, Rie started. "Have the crickets become silent?"

Saburo pulled away and raised his head. "Perhaps so."

Rie sat up. "Oh! I must get back before dawn. No one must see me."

"Wait!" he said, drawing her to him. "Why did you come here?"

She knew that he was asking about Jihei, but she only shook her head.

He lifted her chin, forcing her to look him in the eye.

"He has others," she said, lowering her eyes to his lips, unable to look at him directly.

"And the child?"

"Hers," she said, feeling the burn of shame.

"Oh," he said, lifting her chin again. The sympathy she saw in his eyes was too much and a tear trickled down her cheek. "Then maybe we shall have our child of love."

His words were too much to bear. She closed her eyes, knowing she must leave but wanting to savor the gentleness of his touch. Without it, she would shrivel up and die as surely as cherry blossoms on the third day.

"I must go," she finally said.

Saburo touched Rie's back, caressed her shoulders. "I know. Something like this . . ." His voice caught.

Rie sensed he meant to say they might never have this time together again, this timeless time. She longed to tell him they *would* meet again, she would make sure of it, but she did not know if they ever could. They rose and dressed quickly.

"We never spoke of Yamaguchi," Rie said.

They both laughed and held hands.

Rie walked to the door, Saburo behind her. They embraced,

then Rie pulled away. She reached for the shoji, and Saburo touched her face.

As Rie moved to leave, Saburo took from a pouch tied to his waist a small tortoiseshell hair ornament and handed it to Rie. "This belonged to my mother. I would like you to have it to remember me."

Rie took it and held it closely. "I need nothing to remember you by. But I shall cherish this always." She kissed him, and reached into her simple obi for a small ivory netsuke which she handed to Saburo. "This was in my grandfather's collection." She had kept it on her always as a cherished memento of her grandfather. "Please keep it with you."

Saburo smiled and put it in an inner pocket. "I will wear it close to my heart so it will never forget its song."

They clung to each other, then Rie broke away.

"Please be careful, Rie. Shall I find you a ricksha?"

"There's no need." She pulled the shawl over her face. "One should be waiting." She peered out the gate. "I see one at the corner." She turned, embraced Saburo, and stepped out quickly. She glanced back, and saw Saburo watching. Then with immense sorrow, she stepped up into the ricksha to return to her life, to the Omura House.

Chapter 12

Rie alighted from the ricksha beyond the house, so as not to awaken the family, and walked as quietly as possible on her wooden geta. She noticed the first hint of dawn above the kura rooftops as she went to the gate.

"O-Natsu," she said softly.

The gate opened and O-Natsu looked at Rie inquisitively.

Rie smiled. That was all O-Natsu was getting out of her. "Is my husband here?"

"No, and I have laid out your futon."

"Thank you, O-Natsu, I'll take a brief rest."

Rie removed her geta and crept upstairs. She discarded the peon's clothes, lay down, and remembered every moment of her rendezvous with Saburo. Then she slept more peacefully than she had in years.

Not long after, she awoke and knew by the birdsong in the garden that the day had already begun. She wished she could remain at leisure to savor her memories, but it was not possible.

Yoshi would miss his lessons, and Kin and her father would notice if she did not stop in the inner office to learn the day's plan.

Why was it, she wondered, that society prohibited what she felt in her inner being was right and expected only what her instinct told her was not right? She arose, dressed quickly, and went downstairs to attend to her obligations, her responsibilities, her many duties. During every spare moment, though, she would allow herself to remember. Her private life was hers to keep. She walked into the garden and sat on her favorite rock, stealing a few precious moments to silently thank the gods.

Over the next few days Rie realized something she had never known was possible: her body, her physical being, felt happy, satisfied. She relished the sensation and cherished the memories of a night she knew would remain in her heart as long as she lived. She smiled inwardly every time she thought of Saburo, and she thought of him now each morning when she arose, each night as she retired.

A few weeks later Rie felt the familiar lack of hunger, the slight nausea that had signaled her first pregnancy. O-Natsu agreed that she was indeed pregnant. Rie recalled her failure to produce an heir and prayed that this time she would bear a child, Saburo Kato's child, for it was surely his. Then she realized that this meant she would also once more have to endure the indignity of sleeping with Jihei. This would require some effort and endurance on her part, since Jihei was so seldom home at night. Normally she was relieved at his absence, but this time his presence was required. Rie resented not being able to simply revel in her secret, instead having to plan something so distasteful. She could not discuss so intimate a matter even with O-Natsu, who perhaps might have guessed, and certainly not with Sunao, who would be shocked and also disapproving of her departure from propriety. She puzzled over the problem for several days, knowing that the time to act was limited. The sense of urgency informed her days as she hurried through her normal tasks. Fortunately she was able to eat enough so that her father did not notice anything amiss. Her mother might have taken note.

Two days later, in the afternoon, when Rie was in the kitchen talking to O-Yuki, a maid who worked under O-Natsu, shouting erupted from the area of the storeroom.

"Kaji! Kaji! Fire! Fire!"

Smoke billowed along the corridor toward the inner office and main rooms of the house. Her father, Kin, Jihei, O-Natsu, everyone seemed to be running in all directions. Rie covered her face with her sleeve. Through the smoke she glimpsed O-Natsu and several clerks scurrying through the corridor carrying buckets of water.

"O-Natsu!" she shouted. "Where's the fire?"

"The storeroom and number one kura," O-Natsu gasped.

Rie ran into the courtyard and grabbed a bucket from one of the maids. In the compound a line of clerks pushed hoses along toward the kura. Kin and Kinnosuke were working buckets at the well. Her father, Jihei, and Toji were directing the work, all shouting at once.

Rie looked up in horror as orange tongues licked above the number one kura and storeroom, dangerously close to the inner office. Kin ran back to move ledgers to the outer office, and Rie ran after him to help. Black smoke belching from the brewery billowed over the neighborhood, and neighbors came running to join the sweating, smoke-blackened firefighters. Rie's coughing mixed with sobs as she saw flames leap from the storeroom toward the inner office. She and Kin worked frantically to move all the records to safety.

The smoke and flames drew the city's two competing guilds of firefighters, who converged on the scene simultaneously with their carts and clanging bells. Bannermen from each guild slammed their ladders against the kura wall and clambered to the roof. The man who reached the rooftop first held his banner high with a shout of triumph signaling his men to go into action against the flames.

For the rest of the day the men battled the raging furnace until flames began to subside, to spit and hiss.

Rie ran to the kitchen. "O-Natsu, quickly. We need to prepare food for the men, at least forty of them." O-Natsu, O-Yuki, and two other maids rapidly chopped vegetables, prepared miso and rice, then brought out the best pickles and barrels of White Tiger.

The exhausted, blackened men sat in groups in the still standing number three kura, eating the hastily prepared meal and drinking sake.

Rie watched her father go around the groups of men and thank them for saving the brewery. Would it be his last official act as head of the house, she wondered? She felt a deep sadness overtake her.

All that remained of the number one kura, storeroom, and inner office were charred, hissing coals and ash. Men coughed under the acrid smoke that draped a shroud over the buildings and still rose in the darkened sky.

Spent and speechless, Rie put a hand on her father's arm. She didn't know how she had the strength to fight the tears that threatened.

"We're all exhausted, Ri-chan," he said, returning the pressure of her hand. "We'll talk tomorrow about what we need to do. Now we all need sleep."

Rie caught Yoshitaro in the hall chattering excitedly with the nursery maid, describing the spectacle. This was his future—*their* future—and so much had been destroyed.

Ashes smoldered through the night. Later, as she lay on her futon, unable to sleep, she knew it would be days, weeks, before the smell of smoke left the house. The damage was something they would be paying for for months, more than a year. And how had the fire started?

Fire was a serious hazard. Everyone knew that arson was punishable by death. At night fire watchers walked the streets of the town clacking their wooden sticks together to warn people to be careful, to put out stoves and lamps before they slept. Rie had enjoyed the hollow sound of wood striking wood as she prepared for the night at the hour of the boar. But the sound that meant all was well in the neighborhood would now take on a terrifying meaning for her and everyone in the house.

No one could have started the fire deliberately. The cause would have to be unearthed. Large barrels filled with water were kept atop the kura roofs, a precaution Rie's grandfather had introduced, one generally employed only by temples. Rie tried to put these thoughts from her mind as she tossed on her futon. She touched her abdomen, remembering how precious it had become. Then she saw Jihei enter the room and nestle into his futon, one of the rare times he had stayed home.

This was her chance. She moved closer to Jihei, for once not redolent of sake, but of smoke. She touched his futon, opened it, and murmured, "Anata, wasn't it terrible? How will we ever recover?" She could never address him by his proper name, instead using the word all wives used for their husbands: Anata. Jihei murmured indistinctly, then reached for her, touched her where Saburo had touched her not that long ago. She closed her eyes and imagined herself again in the house of O-Natsu's relatives, with the man who would always remain her lover. When it was over, she felt sick and dirty. She pushed his heavy sleeping form off her, then quickly washed and returned to her own futon, where she willed away all memory of Jihei's repulsive touch. *Saburo*, she thought before finally drifting to sleep, hand on her belly.

The next morning Kinzaemon, Kin, Kinnosuke, Jihei, Rie, Toji, and three junior clerks assembled in the outer office, which reeked so heavily of smoke that it was impossible not to cough. Rie had never seen her father look so despondent, so frail, as he sought to reassure them in a faltering voice.

"The fire has been a catastrophe. We have been fortunate that in nine generations this is the first fire at White Tiger. Thank you all for your efforts in putting it out." He paused to brush the hair back from his forehead. "We are fortunate that the other two kura are still standing. We can produce part of this year's quota in those two." He sighed and glanced around at the faces of the others. "We will begin rebuilding the office, the storeroom, and number one kura starting tomorrow. This is a financial blow, a big one. But if we were a smaller operation we would be totally destroyed. Now we need to ascertain the cause."

Kinzaemon paused and looked around the room again. No one spoke.

"Fortunately Kin and Rie moved our records of nine generations, our ledgers, to the outer office. Otherwise we would have lost it all." He glanced at Rie, and she felt a glow of pleasure at her father's recognition.

Kinzaemon sighed, looked down, then seemed to straighten. "What remains is the tradition and honor of the house, the reputation of White Tiger for excellence. This we have not lost."

Rie felt tears beginning as she heard her father speak of the honor, the reputation, of White Tiger. She looked around the circle of men whose fates were so intimately connected, caught a certain squaring of the shoulders, a firming of the jaw as each responded to her father's words. She felt a surge of energy and hoped she herself would one day be able to inspire the men as her father did.

"Father, I wonder if the water barrels on the roofs were full," she asked sharply.

All eyes turned to Toji, the brewmaster in charge of everything relating to the kuras.

Rie looked at the face that had always reminded her of one of the country entertainers who walked in troupes from village to village during the summer. His eyebrows formed a perfect triangle with his eyes, lending his face an expression that made Rie feel he was about to tell a joke. But there was no mirth in the room this morning.

Toji bowed low, his fists clenched in his lap.

"I learned this morning that one of our kurabito vanished during the night. It was Norio, one of the younger men. We don't know if it had any connection with the fire." Toji bowed after each sentence.

"Very strange," said Kin.

"Yes, most suspicious," Jihei agreed, pulling at his eyebrows.

Kinzaemon nodded. "In any case, we'll have the construction people here tomorrow to make bids on the rebuilding. We need to start with the inner office and storage area, and of course the kurabito quarters above. They can't sleep in the kura many more nights."

Rie rose to go to Yoshi and to give instructions to the maids about removing bedding and clothing from all the cupboards so that things could air. As she opened the shoji to leave, the worker in charge of the koji room bowed and entered the office.

He faced Kinzaemon, bowing again. "They have just found Norio's body at the bottom of a cliff at Mount Rokko. He apparently killed himself in the night, jumped off the cliff. One of the kurabito says Norio was smoking one of those Nagasaki pipes in their room. It must have caught the tatami on fire. That's why the storeroom burned first." He bowed to Kinzaemon and Toji.

Toji knelt and bowed to the floor in front of Kinzaemon. "I have no words to apologize adequately," he said, and bowed again three times, his eyes squeezed tight against his tears.

"It seems he chose his own punishment," said Kinzaemon. "He knew what would have befallen him when he was found."

"He left a wife and three children in Tamba," said Toji.

Kinzaemon turned to Kin. "Send his widow money each year on the anniversary of his death, starting today."

Kin nodded.

Amazed by her father's compassion and sense of tradition, Rie sighed and looked at his ashen, ravaged face.

Chapter 13

The construction on the storeroom and number one kura went ahead as scheduled, with the work on the inner office a bit behind. Meanwhile, they used the outer office for all the administrative work of the brewery. One morning, soon after the fire, the office shoji rattled open and Toji entered abruptly, bowing to Kinzaemon, Kin, and Jihei.

"Sorry to interrupt. He paused to catch his breath. Hiroki, one of the kurabito, says that just before the fire broke out he saw someone from the Yamaguchi brewery lurking behind the number one kura. He called out, but the man disappeared. He didn't think much about it at the time, but now he thinks Yamaguchi may have been behind the fire, not Norio." He bowed repeatedly and looked from Kinzaemon to Kin.

Kinzaemon frowned. "Unspeakable! Then Norio's suicide . . . but he thought he was responsible. And Yamaguchi was behind it. Norio's death must be avenged. Yamaguchi must be punished." He put his elbows on the table and held his head with both hands.

Kin bowed. "We won't forget it, Master."

Kinzaemon raised his head and looked at Toji, then at Kin. "I'll talk to Hiroki, and Kin, you talk to Norio's widow when you go to Tamba. Let her know . . . no, perhaps it would be better not to distress her further with the knowledge that his death was unnecessary." He sighed.

Rie could see her father declining as the reconstruction proceeded. The fire, which in earlier years he might have taken in stride, exacted a toll from which he could not readily recover. Rie saw in his face signs of a fatigue that was as much spiritual as physical. She knew the fire had amplified the bereavement he felt over losing Hana not long ago. His resilience eroded, his normally optimistic view of life dimmed. It saddened Rie to see, and it increased her determination to bring down Yamaguchi, the cause of so much destruction.

Not long after the fire, Rie decided it was time to announce that she was pregnant. She told her father that this time she felt the child would be born safely. She hoped this would lighten his mood.

"Rie, that's wonderful," her father said as she sat with him. Jihei was not present, but Rie had already told him. Jihei, of course, thought the child was his and showed as much pleasure as he ever did at anything in the house. "*Ah,* is that so?" Jihei had said when she told him. "That will be good for the house." For once Rie did not see him pulling at his eyebrows. "I'll be glad to have a second child, maybe another son," he added. Rie smiled, but not because of Jihei's pleasure.

"I've chosen the name Fumi, Father, as I feel it will be a girl. And I want a name that portends intelligence, a connection with letters. I would be surprised if she is not an intelligent child."

Kinzaemon beamed, and Rie was pleased to see his depression lift. She brought her hand to her swelling belly and thought of Saburo. How she wished she could share the news with him.

Rie left her father to look through the cupboards in her bedroom for the baby clothing her mother had prepared during her former pregnancy. She also found the clothing she knew her mother had kept for Toichi. These items she wrapped and put away. She did not want the tragic association of Toichi's clothes to affect Fumi. Rie anticipated motherhood in a way she had not thought possible. She took time away from the management of the brewery but did not worry about the lack of attention. The baby she sensed would in some way help the house as much as the work she did in the brewery. She launched into the preparations for Fumi's birth with the same zeal and energy she devoted to other aspects of the family enterprise. She knew Fumi and her future husband would never succeed to the main line, but somehow, some day, Fumi would play a role, of this she was certain. Thinking of her mother, Rie began to sense for the first time her own place in the eternal cycle of death balanced by the birth of new life.

When the day approached, the day she had awaited for nine long months, Rie called for O-Natsu. Rie had been forced to curtail her busy schedule and had to spend more time resting. But she was glad to do so. She did not want to risk losing this baby.

"O-Natsu, please go for the midwife. I know the baby is on her way. Please hurry!"

O-Natsu rushed down the stairs and sent O-Yuki to be with Rie until the midwife arrived.

The midwife was the most experienced in the neighborhood and arrived with all her birthing materials. She examined Rie carefully.

"Yes, the baby is coming. Take deep breaths. Don't worry.

This is a normal birth," she proclaimed. She issued directions to O-Natsu, who was helping.

Rie was glad that Jihei was not there that morning to say to her: "*Yamato damashii*. Don't cry out," as he was likely to do. The midwife had told her this is what some men said as their wives were giving birth. Without him there, she felt free to groan and cry as the baby made her way into the world.

Rie heard the words she wanted to hear. "It's a girl, so the house will prosper," the midwife pronounced. Rie smiled in spite of her discomfort and reached for the baby when the midwife had cleaned her. It was a blessing that the baby was a girl, since there would be little possibility that she would resemble Saburo so closely as to arouse suspicion.

"Fumi," Rie whispered, and put her arms around her baby.

For the next days and months Rie was totally engrossed in her new role, completely happy, more than happy at the secret of Fumi's birth. O-Natsu was the only other person in the house who guessed. Rie did not call Masa, the wet nurse, but fed Fumi herself.

Rie spent less time on the business of the brewery, but after two months she began to take part of each day to attend to matters in the office and new storeroom. When she was away from Fumi, Rie made certain that O-Natsu was in charge of her.

The kurabito quarters above the storeroom had been rebuilt, and Rie had to see to re-supplying clothing and other necessities for the kurabito. This remained her responsibility in addition to caring for Fumi and for attending to Yoshi's lessons. Rie found her days more than full and also satisfying. She was fulfilling her role and responsibility to the house in all respects.

Rie was pleased to see her father showing affection for his new grandchild, as much as he had shown toward Yoshitaro, even though Fumi would have no place in the main house. In the evening after dinner he often held Fumi on his lap. Even Yoshi was curious about the new baby and wanted to hold her. He had tried once to lift her. This Rie forbade as it raised painful memories of her own lapse with Toichi. Rie became a most watchful mother.

Several months later, as Rie held Fumi after dinner and sat with her father, O-Natsu's voice came from beyond the shoji.

"Excuse me, may I come in?"

"Of course," Kinzaemon replied.

O-Natsu entered slowly, reluctantly, it seemed to Rie. She looked up. "Yes, O-Natsu?"

"Well, I was in the market this morning," she began, then paused, looking first at Rie, then at Kinzaemon.

Rie smiled to hide her uneasiness. "Gossiping again?"

"I was talking to one of the maids who knows people at the Kitaya. She says the geisha O-Yumi has had a child, a girl. They believe she is your husband's child."

Rie gasped. "What! What does he think he's doing, spawning children all over town?" She hugged Fumi closely.

"I believe the problem is that he's not thinking," Kinzaemon replied, pulling at his ear.

"What shall we do, Father? Try to ignore it? Or give my husband a stern talk? Perhaps it should come from you." Rie put a hand over her mouth, aghast at this latest outrage by Jihei.

Rie handed Fumi to her father, touched the column as she passed, and went out to the garden, to her rock, her refuge.

She put her hands on her face and swayed back and forth for several minutes. Just when she was so happy with Fumi, her own special child, whose father was the most important man in her life, Jihei had to destroy her sense of well-being, her chance for happiness. What could she do? How could she recover from yet another assault?

Chapter 14

Rie awoke the next morning still angry about this new woman, O-Yumi's child by Jihei, wondering as she had most of the night what action, if any, the house should take about this other child. As she went about her work during the day she kept thinking, pondering. There must be a way to turn this disaster around, to find some way out of this new cloud that had blown into their lives. In the evening she was glad that Jihei was not present because she had an idea.

"Father," Rie began, and paused. She took a deep breath. "You know that Jihei has had another child by a geisha. I've been thinking all day about what we should do."

"Yes, Rie, so have I." Kinzaemon ran a hand through his bushy hair and over his face. "I haven't decided yet what we should do about this disgrace, if anything. Of course the child is not really our responsibility, though if Jihei's philandering becomes public, then it will affect our reputation, inevitably."

"I'm wondering, Father," Rie said as she patted Fumi on her

lap, "what if we took in this child as we have Yoshi, though of course she wouldn't inherit or be heir. Couldn't we raise her as our own, then send her out, marry her into another brewing family? That way we'd be expanding our connections, our enterprise."

"Hmm." Kinzaemon took a sip of sake, then closed his eyes for a moment. "That's an interesting idea, Rie, one I haven't really heard of before among brewing houses, though perhaps it happens without becoming public." He folded his hands on the table in front of him and frowned.

"Well, in fact, Father, if Jihei spawns another child or two we could bring more than one into the house. Just think of the *do-zokudan* we could create!" The dynasty her father had always dreamed of began to take shape in her imagination. "It's rather exciting, don't you think?" Rie sat straight, inspired by her own idea. "Of course it would mean more work for me, for the maids, for all of us. But if it expands our enterprise, then we would be able to hire more help. Besides, it would be a better life for the children than in the water world." Rie relished the idea of being able to redeem herself in her father's eyes, to fulfill some of her duty to the house, to enlarge the White Tiger enterprise.

"Let me think about it tonight, Rie." He looked at Rie and reached for Fumi, who went to her grandfather whenever she saw him. She reached for his eyebrows, fascinated. "Sometimes I think you'll be as good a brewer as anyone in the whole district," Kinzaemon said, smiling.

Rie bowed, unable to conceal her pleasure at her father's compliment. She stood and held out her hands. "I'll take Fumi to bed with me, Father. It's her bedtime. Sleep well." She smiled and glanced at her father as he sat motionless, his hands still folded on the table.

The next morning Rie went to the breakfast table early to speak with her father before Jihei arrived from nightly activities.

"Good morning, Father." She handed Fumi to O-Natsu for feeding in the kitchen.

"And what do you think of my suggestion of last evening? I know you have given it some careful consideration." She picked up a bowl of miso soup and sipped.

"Yes, I have, Ri-chan," Her father did not often use this term of affection. "And I like the idea. Yes, let's see if the child is healthy, normal, then we can take her in. I doubt the geisha will object." Kinzaemon continued eating his rice and plum pickle.

"So shall we ask my husband about the baby's health when he arrives?"

"I'll do that, Rie. You won't have to. Then if the infant appears normal, I'll ask him to make arrangements to adopt her, just as he did with Yoshi."

"He may wonder at our motivation. We don't have to explain it to him, do we, Father?" Rie looked at him expectantly.

"There's no need," her father replied.

Rie would enjoy this small pleasure, not explaining to Jihei, keeping him off balance a little.

One afternoon, a few months later, as Rie was caring for Fumi and Yoshi, O-Natsu came into the children's room.

"Look, O-Natsu," Rie said. "Don't they play well together?" Rie was no longer so worried about Yoshi picking up Fumi, but she still warned him always to be careful of his little sister.

"Yes," O-Natsu agreed. "It's good to see." She paused and bowed, her hands crossed formally in front of her.

Rie looked up. "Is something on your mind, O-Natsu?

O-Natsu bowed again before speaking. "It seems, I was told in the market, that another geisha is pregnant by your husband, O-Toki. She believes it will be another girl." O-Natsu pursed her lips and nearly closed her eyes, so close to tears. She had not heard of Rie's plans for bringing more children into the house and what it might portend. And as much as it angered Rie to know, she would not let his infidelities consume her.

Rie exhaled loudly. *"Huh!"* She paused and turned to Yoshi.

"Yoshi, will you go to Kinnosuke in the office and ask if he has any errands for you?"

Yoshi left the room, eager to go about his favorite activity, helping Kinnosuke.

"I didn't want Yoshi to hear the details. But my husband will give the house a bad reputation in the water world at this rate." She paused. "Don't worry, O-Natsu, my father and I have a plan to deal with this situation, a plan that will help the house in the long run."

Rie stepped into the office and asked her father to join her at the Butsudan, the place where the most intimate details of the family were often discussed, before the ancestors. She followed her father to the main room, noting that he had become more stooped than she had realized. She placed a zabuton in front of the altar for her father and joined him.

Rie bowed slightly toward the Butsudan, then to her father. "Father, O-Natsu has just told me that O-Toki, Yoshi's mother, is also due to have a daughter by my husband. Now there will be two girls that we might bring into the house. I think perhaps we should do so as soon as possible, to avoid news of this scandalous behavior being spread widely around town." She looked at her father inquisitively.

"All right, Rie. I'll speak to Jihei this afternoon and have him go to both places and make arrangements to bring them here as soon as the babies are ready. Yes, his behavior is quite outrageous." He ran his hand over his face.

"And perhaps he will be embarrassed enough to remain at home this evening. I would like to speak to him as well, maybe before you do. Yes, would you wait until tomorrow morning, please?" Rie wanted to embarrass Jihei, if it were in fact possible.

"I have never heard of such behavior in another brewing house. I feel shame," her father said.

She prayed her father wouldn't fall into melancholy as he was apt to since Toichi's death, then his wife's. "We'll turn this disaster into an advantage for the house, Father. I feel certain of it."

That evening Jihei did in fact retire at home for a change. When he entered the bedroom Rie was still up, seated before her mirror, arranging her long luxuriant hair.

Rie spoke as Jihei was lying on his futon, hands behind his head. "I hear that you have fathered two more children with geishas, at the Sawaraya and Kitaya, she said, turning slightly to look at him.

Jihei's face flushed beyond the effects of the sake. He turned so that his back was toward Rie, his face hidden from the glimmer of the lamps. "That is true, yes," he mumbled.

"We want to adopt them," Rie stated firmly. She looked at his reflection in her mirror.

"We . . . we do?" he stammered and turned toward her.

Rie enjoyed Jihei's consternation. She glanced in the mirror again. She wanted to make him wonder. It was a small pleasure she allowed herself in their unsatisfactory relationship.

"Father and I think it would be wise to have three or more children, in case anything should happen to Yoshitaro." Rie continued combing her hair.

"What could happen?" he stuttered. "There's no question about his succession, is there?"

"No question now. It's settled with him. But I've noticed that he isn't the most robust child, haven't you? We never know, no matter how careful we are about a child's health." She stopped, thinking suddenly of Toichi. She had not wanted to bring up her own painful memory just at this point. She only wanted Jihei to worry about Yoshi, though there was no threat to his health. She also wanted to make him wonder about the motive for adopting his two illegitimate daughters.

"So, I believe Father wants you to go to meet the two geishas, to ascertain if the babies are perfectly healthy and normal, then to arrange for their adoption, as you did with Yoshi."

Jihei sat up, frowned, and rested his head in his hands. "I'm not sure that they will want to give up their daughters." He rubbed his face.

"You will persuade them, then. They will realize that their lives will be far better than if they were raised in an okiya. And of course they will be compensated, and their daughters well cared for here."

Jihei groaned and lay back on his futon. Rie smiled and slept well, thinking of the future expansion of the Omura House. Her father's dream.

Chapter 15

The memory of the night Masami became her lover O-Toki would cherish always in some secret recesses of her heart. Only O-Haru of the Sawaraya would know, she who could so well divine anyone's deepest emotion. Masami had asked for O-Toki at the Sawaraya twice before that night, and she had served sake and played the *samisen* for him and his two friends. As she filled the three small cups she took in the features that set Masami apart from his friends: the finely chiseled chin, the skin that seemed almost luminous, the wavy hair, and the compelling black eyes that seemed to penetrate her inner being.

The fabric of her life was woven of men, so many that she thought she was immune to them, until Masami. And the irony was that she should feel this passion for Masami, a man without the worldly position and wealth of the Omuras. Masami was a cooper's son, an honest enough profession, but one that could never aspire to the status of a large brewer. After his first two visits, O-Toki found herself waiting for his next visit as breathlessly as a sixteen-year-old for her first lover. When he appeared alone, and asked for her again, the force of O-Toki's passion surprised even herself.

The next day and the days following, O-Toki found herself anticipating Masami's next visit, regretting that he was not free to come more often. For Jihei she felt only the sense of obligation toward a principal patron. When she became pregnant again, O-Toki knew the child was Masami's, not Jihei's.

It was O-Haru who first noticed the physical changes. She and O-Toki had become friends, something difficult at O-Toki's okiya, where competition so often precluded friendship. O-Toki sat with O-Haru one morning as they manicured their nails. It was a time for confidences.

"Let me see your eyes," O-Haru said.

"Why?" O-Toki asked, looking up at O-Haru.

"Yes," O-Haru began, "I can always tell when a woman is pregnant by looking at her eyes, even before the other signs. You are pregnant, O-Toki. I'm certain."

To O-Toki's dismay, O-Haru was right, as always. As the weeks passed and it became more difficult to conceal her condition, O-Toki had to make a decision . . . two decisions. She spoke with O-Haru again.

"What about Masami? Have you told him you are expecting?" O-Haru asked.

O-Toki stroked her stomach, sadness enveloping her. "He knows I am pregnant and that the child is his. He thinks he is my only patron. But he is in no position to recognize the baby," she said, trying to hide the bitterness she felt. "He is about to be married and won't have much to inherit. He isn't the first son. So he won't be concerned with the child's welfare. He knows I can support her. I say 'her' because I feel the baby will be a girl."

"So you plan to keep the child?"

"I have no plans for an abortion. But no, I won't raise her," she said sadly.

O-Haru raised her eyebrows. "Why not?"

"I let my son go to the Omura House because he'll inherit a powerful house. A boy born here in the water world has such meager prospects." She paused to arrange her hair, and cringed as she glanced at her mirror. What would happen when her beauty faded? Where would she go, she wondered with a sigh? At least her children would be cared for. "Now there's also a reason to give up my daughter, though it pains me more than I can say. Two reasons, or maybe three. I don't want her to grow up here, to do what I do. I want Jihei to adopt her. And as an Omura daughter she'll have a good life and a chance for a respectable marriage. And a third reason: it will give me great satisfaction to tell Jihei she is his child when I know she is really Masami's." O-Toki smiled and pulled her comb through her high coiffure.

O-Haru nodded. "Ah, O-Toki, I've always known you were clever. It's the only kind of power we really have, isn't it, the ability to dissemble? And if I've learned anything working in the water world all my life, it's that nothing is what it seems. There's what we see on the surface but something else beneath it, something quite different, which may possibly be the truth." O-Haru paused and glanced at O-Toki. "But will the Omuras want a geisha's daughter when they already have an heir?"

"What Jihei tells me makes me think his wife and her father are willing. They have recognized a girl from another house, the Kitaya I believe. Jihei has been busy here in the quarter, it seems."

O-Haru pursed her lips and frowned. "That's strange, isn't it? Not that he frequents more than one house, but that the Omuras want to recognize the daughter of a geisha. A son I can understand, since the house had no children of its own. But the daughter of a geisha stays with her mother. And doesn't Jihei also have a daughter? Daughters are useful to us in old age. The patron gives something toward raising her but does not recognize her. *Hmm.* It's an unusual situation, something I haven't encountered before." O-Haru smoothed her hair slowly.

"In any case, I won't need to discuss the baby's future with Jihei until after she is born."

One evening Jihei went on his errand to the Kitaya to see O-Yumi. She was a woman taller and more mature in years and figure than O-Toki. She also seemed genuinely fond of Jihei. He wondered. *Perhaps the fact that she is getting on in years, starting to lose her youthful bloom, makes her so attentive, almost anxious.* Of course, geishas were all attentive, Jihei knew, but with O-Yumi her devotion seemed to surpass the simple training they all received in serving a man's moods and needs, especially in the case of a patron. Still, it was becoming difficult financially to be the patron of two women, since Rie was keeping such close track of finances now, but Kin gave him a small sum on the side each month, the secret "navel savings" fund that did not enter the ledgers. After all, it was expected that a man of substance would have a woman other than his wife. And Kin was pleased to have Yoshitaro in the house. He knew the importance of maintaining the continuity of house head for White Tiger, and he was after all a man himself.

As soon as Jihei arrived at the Kitaya, O-Yumi hurried to the entrance and greeted him enthusiastically.

"Oh, Master, welcome. I'm so happy to see you."

She led him to the room they regarded as their own. The house was not as lavish as the Sawaraya, but Jihei felt the atmosphere was warmer, less commercial and imposing. And more intimate, as soon became apparent when O-Yumi helped him to undress and put on a house yukata, preparing him for a bath.

"I'll join you in a few minutes," she promised.

The bath was a small private one, not generally intended for guests. Jihei enjoyed the intimacy and inhaled the fragrance of citron left from New Year's that gave the steamy room a lemony aroma. As he waited he mused. *I married according to my parents' wishes and produced an heir for the Omura House. Now I've earned this. A man needs something for himself. But how do I persuade O-Yumi to give up Kazu?*

When O-Yumi joined Jihei she disrobed, washed, rinsed, and stepped into the bath. She embraced him without hesitation. He decided to speak before he lost his nerve.

"How is Ka-chan today?" he asked, releasing O-Yumi's arms from around his neck and looking into her face.

O-Yumi laughed. "She is growing fatter every day, such a joy. I'm so glad I decided against an abortion."

"So am I," Jihei said, pausing. "Actually, the Omura House would like to adopt her." He pursed his lips and frowned, aware that O-Yumi would protest.

"No! I can't give up my daughter! She is mine. She will comfort and support me in my old age. No geisha wants to give up a daughter. I can't." She began to sob.

"But O-Yumi, you won't really be giving her up, you know. You will be able to come to special events . . . her marriage, to watch. And you know she will have a good life and good prospects for marriage being brought up as an Omura daughter. We will care for her well." He refrained from saying "better than you could."

"What will happen to me when I can no longer work, without her to help?" She was biting her nails in distress.

He put his arms around O-Yumi and tried to comfort her as

she continued to sob. "You need never worry. I will always make certain you are cared for. Please, O-Yumi. You know we will do our best for her."

O-Yumi put her hands to her face. *"Uh . . . huh . . ."*

"All right, then, I'll come for her tomorrow. Don't worry, please. We will take care of you, *both* of you."

As Jihei left the Kitaya, O-Yumi followed him to the door, her face red from crying. She bowed but said nothing.

Chapter 16

The day after Jihei's visit to O-Yumi, he was sent on an errand to the Kitaya with O-Natsu to help as they had done when Yoshitaro was brought home. The difference was of course that Kazu would not become head of the house. Rie knew the sum Kinzaemon instructed Jihei to give O-Yumi was not as large as what was given to O-Toki for Yoshi. At the same time, Kinzaemon told Rie that taking the daughter of a geisha also meant a continuing financial obligation to the geisha. Rie was not happy about the financial arrangements, though she welcomed the daughter for her future value to the house. She knew that when Jihei frequented geishas it was a financial loss to the house, and this she found hard to accept. She felt it was a difficult balance.

Both Yoshi and Fumi were curious about the new baby in the house. They spent time in the children's room talking to her, petting her, kissing her. Rie was pleased to see them playing well together. Yoshi had begun trying to teach words to Fumi, even to teach her to write kana. Rie could see Yoshi becoming an asset even as a young boy. Perhaps he would become a far better house head than Jihei one day. Anyone would.

It was time for the end of brewing season celebration, one of the big events of the year, a grand affair to which well over a hundred guests were invited: heads of major brewing houses, coopers, suppliers, officials, and shogunal commissioners. No expense was spared in the preparations. The maids spent days cleaning, and the kurabito made preparations to serve the highest quality of the year's cellar. A large leaf ball was hung out at the entrance of the brewery, next to the White Tiger *noren* banner to announce to customers that the first sake of the season was ready. It was the one occasion when several geishas were called to serve the guests. Rie sat with her father and Jihei as they planned the event. "Oh, by the way," her father commented, "I hear that the Katos are marrying off their third son. They announced his engagement at the last meeting of the Brewers Association."

Rie froze, stopped looking through the guest list. She felt a knife had slashed through her heart. She could not expect him to remain alone forever, and his family would not allow it, at any rate. Still, her heart seemed to have shriveled at the news, and she hadn't slept well since. She would not want to see his wedding. It would be too painful to watch. Jihei could represent the family and she would make an excuse. For once, she had no desire to see her beloved.

"Which geishas should we call this year?" Kinzaemon asked as he went over the long lists of guests.

"How about calling someone from the okiya that serve the Kitaya and Sawaraya this time?" Rie asked, grateful to think about something other than Saburo.

Jihei looked up, startled and embarrassed. She knew he wanted to ask why they should mention these two establishments, the ones he frequented, but he couldn't without loss of face.

"A good idea, Rie," her father replied. "We can ask the madam in charge of each to furnish two or three names."

Rie smiled and Jihei pulled at his eyebrows.

Unlike weddings and funerals, this was a celebration to which only men were invited, generally heads of houses. Rie was disappointed that Saburo Kato would not be included, as he was third son. Except for Fumi, the light of her life, she often felt lonely and wished she could experience just one more sweet moment like the one she and Saburo had shared when Fumi was conceived. Now, with the impending marriage, she truly knew what it meant to "kill the self," she realized, as she forced her attention to the upcoming celebration.

On the day selected, the shoji were removed to create a huge main room. Several rows of lacquer tables were arrayed in the room, one small table for each guest. On each table were sake cups and small plates containing choice morsels of beans and dried fish to accompany the tasting of the best brew.

The guests arrived in a flurry of festivity as finely groomed geishas flitted through the rows with flasks of sake, kneeling to pour for each guest. Since there were no women invited, it was necessary for geishas to serve the guests. Rie was not able to appear openly, but peered into the room without being seen herself. She thought she could pick out O-Yumi, whom she knew was Kazu's mother, but O-Toki she could not pick out.

Kinzaemon gave the welcoming speech, urging the guests to enjoy the year's cellar. The event lasted three or four hours, and by the time the last guests had departed, everyone in the house was exhausted. Kin had taken care of financial arrangements for the geishas, and everyone else had performed their proper duties for the occasion.

When it was over, Rie came into the room to hear her father's assessment of the event.

"I think it went well," Kinzaemon said. "Even Yamaguchi behaved." It had been impossible to avoid inviting the president of the Brewers Association, though Rie had hoped they could omit him from the list for this event.

"I heard quite a few favorable comments about the taste of the brew this year," Jihei said. "And I heard a few people wondering about our recipe, which of course we don't share."

Kinzaemon smiled and nodded.

"I wish I could have been in the room," Rie said, hiding the longing from her voice. But as in everything to do with the brewery, she knew this was an all-male custom that would not change.

Six months later O-Toki gave birth to a baby girl she named Teru. During the later months of O-Toki's pregnancy she had not been at the Sawaraya, and it had been some time since Jihei had seen her. He was sent on the same mission that had taken him to O-Yumi and for the same purpose, since this was Rie's plan now. Jihei did not relish this visit, especially after bringing Kazu into the house. For him the visit was a disappointment, without the bath and sensual gratification he expected with O-Toki, a slight, he felt certain. When he mentioned Teru, O-Toki asked, "Would you like to see her?" As O-Toki poured sake for Jihei he noticed an undercurrent of tension. He longed for nothing more than to rise and leave, but how could he refuse to see the baby, his own child?

A maid brought in the infant and handed her to O-Toki. She held her out toward Jihei, who took one of the baby's tiny hands in his but did not offer to hold her. Only a girl, after all.

"I think she has your forehead and eyes, don't you?" O-Toki said pointedly, as she kissed the baby. "I have named her Teru."

"It's hard to tell who they look like when they're so small," Jihei said.

The baby cried, and O-Toki opened her kimono to feed her.

"You probably want to raise her yourself," Jihei began, awkwardly.

"It's usual with a girl, isn't it?" O-Toki replied, innocently enough. Still, he thought he caught a gleam in her eye that made him uneasy. "She will be a comfort to me in my old age. She will care for me when I'm too old to work."

"You know you need not worry about your old age, O-Toki. That is my responsibility, as I've told you before." Certain that O-Toki wanted to keep the baby, Jihei wondered how to broach the official reason for his visit.

"Actually, the Omura House would like to adopt her, to have a sister for Yoshitaro."

O-Toki rocked the baby before speaking, her jaw tight. She clutched Teru to her. "Why do you need my daughter, our daughter? Don't you have enough children? Won't Yoshi succeed you?"

Jihei gazed at the sake cup in his hand. "It's true that the succession is settled. But you know, for a large house one or two children don't always guarantee security of succession. What if something should happen to Yoshi? My father feels that we need more children. I understand how you feel about Teru." He glanced at the baby. "It may be hard to give her up, but she will have a good life with us, a good marriage. I realize it will be a different life from what she would have with you." He reached over and touched O-Toki on the arm. "So will it be all right then if I come for Teru in a month's time?"

"If you are going to insist, what can I say?" O-Toki kissed the baby, then looked directly into Jihei's eyes, a rare challenge. Then she dropped her chin abruptly, as was fitting. "But you must promise me regular reports, and I would like to be able to see her."

"You will surely be able to see her marriage, and perhaps see her on other occasions as well."

O-Toki smiled at him through tears glistening in her eyes. Then she hugged Teru closely and whispered a farewell.

Jihei felt relieved as he said good-bye and left for home. He still did not understand why it was necessary to bring in another girl.

Chapter 17

For the next two years, Rie and Jihei called an uneasy truce. One evening, when Kinzaemon had retired early and the children were all in bed, Rie and Jihei sat at the dining table together, something that seldom happened. Rie was pouring sake for Jihei, thinking instead of Saburo Kato and his new wife. Their marriage had sent her into a spiraling depression that had lasted days, but Fumi, their love child, had soon pulled her out of it. The marriage had only tightened her bond with her child, whom she loved with a fierceness she'd never thought possible, even more so since it was her one link to Saburo, a reminder of the love they had shared. Whenever she looked at her precious Fumi she was reminded of her love for Saburo. She knew her feeling for Fumi outweighed what she felt for any of the other children, but she should take care not to make her preference too obvious. It would not be fair to the others, who had not chosen their parents.

Jihei disrupted her musing. "Why don't you drink some of our sake? How can you make decisions about White Tiger when you refuse to enjoy it? Are you unable to drink our own product?"

"No, of course not. Yes, I can drink." Annoyed at his challenge, she held out her cup, and Jihei filled it. She drank the cup down and held it out again.

"Good." Jihei smiled. "That's more like it. You'll soon become a judge of our cellar, the grades of our brew."

Rie held out her cup again. How presumptous of Jihei to assume he was a better judge of White Tiger sake. She lost count after a few cups, unaccustomed as she was to drinking more than a single cup of three sips. It was not really expected of a woman, unless she worked in the water world.

At length Jihei held up a flask and said, "One more? A nightcap?"

Rie felt dizzy. "Oh . . . maybe not," she managed to say. She rose to stand, but stumbled against the table for support.

Jihei smiled. "I'll help you upstairs." He took her arm and assisted her as they wove unsteadily toward the stairs and made their way up, one labored step at a time.

Rie fumbled for a futon and collapsed on it, unable to dress for bed.

Jihei disrobed and moved over Rie without hesitation. "No!" Rie moaned, struggling to prevent him from going further, but Jihei persisted. She had not slept with him since it was necessary after becoming pregnant with Fumi, and she was not at her normal strength. "No!" she grunted again. Feeling angry and violated, she panted and pushed but then collapsed under his weight as he spread her kimono and her legs roughly apart. As she flailed against him, he thrust himself on her, into her, moving vigorously until he abruptly slackened, and lay inert.

Rie was unable to move, not fully aware what had happened, and unable to go downstairs for her ablution ritual. She slept fitfully.

When she awoke in the morning she found herself still in her work kimono, her clothing disarrayed and her body feeling soiled, unclean. She remembered little of the previous night. Then she felt her clothing and realized what had happened. She sat up and rubbed her aching head. Jihei was not in the room. For a few minutes she sat breathing rapidly in anger. Jihei had found a way to exact revenge for her bringing the children into the house. Furious, she got up, dressed, and walked down the stairs toward the bath, not speaking to any of the maids. She went into the bathroom and washed vigorously with the tepid water left from the previous night's baths, trying to remove the disgusting evidence of Jihei's violation.

She went into breakfast alone, wishing there were some way she could erase what had happened from her thoughts, her body.

O-Natsu came in with miso soup and rice. "Are you all right?"

"Yes, O-Natsu." Rie had no desire for conversation. "Please see that the children are doing their lessons."

O-Natsu bowed and left the room, guessing Rie's mood.

Rie drank more than her usual two cups of tea, trying to heal the pain in her head. When she finished, she walked down the corridor to the door to the courtyard, put on geta, and went to the empty barrels. She picked up a bucket, filled it at the well, set it down, and reached for a brush. She scrubbed at a barrel with all her strength, her anger adding to her energy, until she finally put down the brush and sighed, wiping tears from her eyes. How many times in one lifetime must one kill the self?

O-Natsu, concerned about Rie, had gone along the corridor to the door to the courtyard and stood there watching. O-Yuki came up behind her and looked out.

"You can tell how angry she is when she goes out to scrub the barrels, especially if she's not talking," O-Natsu said.

"I wonder why she's so angry?" O-Yuki asked.

"Who knows? Maybe we'll find out later, maybe we won't.

Just watch and wait." They walked back to the kitchen and their day's chores.

By afternoon Rie had recovered enough to go to the nursery, where she found O-Natsu and O-Yuki playing with the three girls. Rie entered and joined them on the tatami. O-Yuki was tossing a red ball to the three children in turn. She was younger than O-Natsu, hardly more than a child herself, and was especially fond of playing with them.

O-Natsu and O-Yuki nodded and bowed as Rie sat down.

"The house has become a lively nursery." O-Natsu laughed, hoping to improve Rie's mood.

Rie caught hold of Fumi, stopping her irrepressible motion, and held her. "Even at this age you can tell how bright Fumi is, can't you?" Rie smiled at Fumi's obsidian eyes, so reminiscent of Saburo's. Fumi helped to erase memories of the painful night. And of Saburo's marriage.

"Well, I have to admit, she does seem more precocious than Kazu or Teru," O-Natsu said. "But I try to treat them all alike."

"I want to give Fumi special training," Rie remarked when she knew Kazu and Teru would not understand.

"Of course all the girls will marry into brewing families, won't they?" O-Natsu asked. "But I guess it's far too early to ask."

"Yes, Kazu and Teru will go as brides to brewing families, but . . ." Rie took out a tortoiseshell comb from her hair, paused, and replaced it.

"How about Fumi?" O-Yuki asked.

"Let's wait and see about her," Rie responded, still arranging her hair with one hand, the other holding Fumi.

O-Natsu leaned forward, both hands on the tatami. "Won't she marry a brewer too?"

"Oh, yes. I have an idea, but we need to wait. It's too early to talk about it." Rie put Fumi down, rose, and left the room.

When she was out of earshot, O-Yuki turned to O-Natsu. "I never know what she's thinking," she said.

"I don't either," O-Natsu admitted. "But you can be sure she's planning something. Always."

Several evenings later Rie, carrying Fumi on her back, paused outside the shoji to her father's room.

"Father, may I come in?"

"Yes, Rie, please do. I'm sitting here alone."

Was there a slightly different, almost purposeful, note in her father's hoarse voice?

"Have you had your sake yet, Father?" Rie asked and put Fumi down. Rie sat opposite her father. She felt his attitude toward her soften, especially at this hour of the evening.

Her father cleared his throat. "Yes, I still have some here. Will you join me?"

"Just one sip, to keep you company." She held the three-sip cup out, and her father filled it. Rie smiled as Fumi walked toward her grandfather with her arms out, and he reached and took her on his lap.

"Father, I have an idea . . . for the house." She refrained from using the term *business,* though of course they were connected, identical.

"What now, Ri-chan?"

"Well, I know it's way too soon to speak of this, but you've noticed, haven't you, how bright Fumi is? Brighter than Yoshi, really."

"She is your child. Of course she's bright." He looked at Rie inquisitively.

Rie felt warmed, embraced by her father's affection. "When she's old enough to marry, I want her to have a mukoyoshi, a very good one. I want to set her and her husband up as a *bunke* rather than have her marry out as a bride to another family."

Kinzaemon ran his hands through his hair twice. Rie noticed that though still thick, his hair had gone completely silver since her mother died. *I wish I could talk to you about Mother,* she thought, Hana's sweet face coming to mind.

"Oh? And then?"

"Well," Rie said carefully, "in a bunke, her child could come back to the main house either as heir or his bride, depending on Yoshitaro's eldest child. It would be an ideal combination for the house, Father, don't you think?"

"Thinking so far ahead, Ri-chan. And Yoshi is not a stupid child." He pulled at his ear.

"I know, and I'm glad he enjoys the work, even at his age. But I think with a child of Fumi's . . . a daughter. . . . And of course I'd want to find the best person in Kobe as her husband." Rie took out her comb and turned it over in her hands.

"It would cause a few raised eyebrows, wouldn't it, if you adopted a husband for her when we already have an heir?"

She reinserted her comb. "Raised eyebrows are not my main concern, Father."

"I'm aware of that, Rie. It's only that we need to consider the opinions and feelings of others in Kobe if we are to do business with them successfully. You know what they always say about the peg that sticks up. It gets pounded down. But it's possible what you suggest may work to our advantage. Let's wait a few years though, quite a few years." He chuckled. "Of course we need to plan in business. And I can see that you are a planner." He smiled, his eyes wrinkling to slits.

Rie reached for her father's hand and gave a gentle squeeze. Sometimes she felt that her father did understand her. Fumi squirmed back to Rie and began to cry.

"She's tired, aren't you?" Rie said, picking her up and kissing her. "I'll take her to bed. Sleep well, Father." *I love you,* she added silently as she carried her daughter to her room.

One morning several weeks later, Rie arose with a sinking feeling. She recognized the signs: the lack of appetite, the slight nausea, and missing a month already. She put her hands to her face, aghast. She knew she was pregnant again, with Jihei's child, the child of the agonizing night when she had drunk so much sake and Jihei had violated her. She would have to bear a child of Jihei's, bring his blood into the family again. This was no happy occasion. She sat alone, tears streaming down her face.

Chapter 18

Eighteen thirty-seven was an eventful year in the Omura household. Rie had her second child, a son whom she named Seisaburo. A son to be sure, but he evoked mixed feelings in Rie, feelings she could not share with her father. He was of Jihei's seed, not Saburo's. For her, Jihei's shadow loomed over the child. Rie was relieved to see none of Jihei's features visible on Seisaburo's face. For that she was most grateful. But she felt none of the sense of fulfillment she had felt with Fumi's birth. Her chief regret remained that Fumi had not been firstborn, before O-Toki's son, or that her initial pregnancy had failed. Seisaburo, already a year old, showed early signs of being precocious, Rie had to admit. Yoshi was now nine, Fumi was already six, Kazu five, and Teru four. The girls were having their lessons separately from Yoshitaro.

Yoshitaro's succession, though not imminent, still rankled, a festering sore that would never heal. Her father was of course pleased to have a grandson born of Rie. Even Jihei was pleased.

Kinzaemon spent a great deal of time with his grandchildren, and in turn they provided him comfort in his old age. Although he was affectionate with all of them, Rie sometimes thought she saw her father display a special feeling toward her own children.

One afternoon Rie sat with her father after lunch. Jihei and several of the children were present as well.

"He seems a fine, healthy boy, Rie," her father said, holding Seisaburo.

Teru grabbed the baby's blanket and tried to kiss him. "Let me see!" she cried and took the infant's hand.

"Be careful of your baby brother," Rie cautioned.

"Second son," Jihei said. "No question about Yoshi's succession."

Defensive, wasn't he? She had noticed how possessive Jihei was about Yoshi and his position in the house.

"A brewing house can't have too many children," said Kinzaemon. "They will all help the house, help our enterprise."

"They're all capable children," said Rie. "And look at Fumi. She learns so fast."

She smiled at her beautiful daughter.

"So does Yoshi. Always helping Kinno," Jihei rejoined.

"I know Kin is pleased at how well Yoshi is advancing," Kinzaemon said. "And speaking of Kin, I heard him say something about retiring too, soon after me. He'd like to hand over the main responsibility to Kinno. Our operation is growing so fast."

Rie glanced at her father, a sense of sudden loss overcoming her. "Our old customers will surely miss you, Father. You've worked with many of them nearly forty years, and Grandfather worked with their parents."

"Oh, our connections with some of our suppliers and customers go back several generations, many more than two." Kinzaemon nodded and picked up his teacup.

Jihei's face reddened. "I've had ten years to get to know them.

I think they're used to dealing with me. And Kinno can do many of the transactions Kin does now."

Rie looked at the baby. "Yes, I've watched Kinno work, not only carrying out orders, but taking charge in an emergency, when something goes wrong. We're lucky to have him to succeed Kin. He's good with customers, and he has a sense of timing too."

"We Nada brewers have always been the best business people. They say some of those small brewers in the north make the finest sake, but they don't know how to sell beyond their local districts," Kinzaemon said.

"Small brewers always say they're more interested in quality than quantity," Jihei said. "That was my family's philosophy. They don't really want to expand. They think it would affect quality." He pouted.

Rie frowned. "There's nothing wrong with our quality. We produce both quality and quantity. Toji is always experimenting, making improvements." She glared at Jihei.

Kinzaemon nodded slowly. "We have to balance tradition with trying to improve. Sometimes that means doing something new, making some alteration in our production, or trying for an expanded sales route."

"And timing, Father," said Rie. "We have to constantly watch our competition. We can't relax our attention, especially with Yamaguchi. He's so sly."

"Some day White Tiger will be number one, yes Rie?"

Rie nodded, determined to fulfill her father's dream.

"Well, I'm happy you have a son, Rie. We'll leave you. Jihei and I need to get back to the office."

After the men left, Rie pondered. She no longer worried that Jihei spent less time at home in the evening. The problem was the effect of his profligate ways on the reputation of the house. She had noticed that his face was becoming bloated and flushed as its normal state, and that he smelled of sake even during the day. She knew just what to do.

That evening she was alone with her father after dinner. The perfect time for discussion. She turned to him. "I'm afraid Jihei's drinking is becoming a problem, Father. I haven't said anything to him about it. But the smell never leaves him, and his face is becoming so red and bloated." She held her hands over the hibachi.

"Yes, I've noticed, Rie. It's a concern, especially with my retirement coming soon. But so long as he does his work I don't know what we can say. I've seen this happen often in heirs to family businesses. I think it's the family pressures that make them drink. I'll try to speak to him, think of a way to broach the issue."

"It can't be good for his health either." Rie frowned. "Let's hope Yoshi doesn't follow his example. I hope he takes after you instead." She let the words linger in the air for a moment, then glanced at her father. She knew he understood.

Kinzaemon mumbled as he shuffled toward the office the next morning. He opened the shoji and saw Jihei sitting at one end of the office alone. Kinno's voice could be heard talking to customers in the outer office.

"*Ah,* Jihei." Kinzaemon settled himself at the table opposite his son-in-law.

"How are you this morning, Father?"

"Well, I have a concern." He placed both hands on the table. "A difficult matter."

Jihei pushed a cup of tea across the table and looked at Kinzaemon, who straightened his collar before speaking.

"I have noticed, Jihei, that of late you have been drinking more than usual." He paused.

Jihei began pulling at his eyebrows and looked down.

"I'm afraid it's being noticed by others, our business associ-ates. When this happens it can endanger our reputation, our busi-ness. And our house."

"Oh, I don't drink more than any other brewer. A man needs some relaxation in this work. I'm here in the office all day, ask Kinno. And surely I have provided enough children for the house." He glanced at Kinzaemon, then looked down at his hands.

"It's not lack of heirs that concerns me. But Yoshi is only nine and it will be several years before he can succeed. In the mean-time you will represent the Omura House and White Tiger to the world. And frankly, I've been delaying retirement because I see what's happening to you."

Jihei's eyebrows drew together in a deep frown. He was breath-ing heavily and struggled to speak.

Kinzaemon paused.

"I was selected for this position, and I have done my best for White Tiger. I have worked hard." His face was a moue.

Kinzaemon's expression was intent. "I know you spend nearly every evening at the Sawaraya. I urge you to curb your drinking. You have let it get out of hand. You owe it to the house." Kin-zaemon looked at Jihei, then placed his hands on the table and pushed to his feet. "Don't forget your obligation," he said as he turned and left.

Jihei put his hands to his face, resting his elbows on the table. *Huh!* Obligation, obligation! This was all he'd heard ever since he had married into this family. Being a mukoyoshi was something no one could envy, no matter how wealthy and important his adoptive house. It was suffocating, this network of relationships and obligations that entwined around him, an intricate spider's web. There was no escape, no relief, other than the Sawaraya or Kitaya, a geisha's understanding ways. Of course he needed his sake in the evening. He shook his head and his mouth pulled down at the corners. Kinzaemon was imagining something that was not there. Probably Rie had told him to speak to Jihei. She had never tried to understand him. He would get back at her somehow.

Chapter 19

Kinzaemon's retirement in the spring of 1841 was a major event in Kobe brewing circles. For forty years he had shepherded White Tiger through the precarious cycles of the brewing business. He was highly esteemed by all members of the Brewers Association. There was hardly a brewer for whom he had not done some personal favor over the course of the years. That a formal ceremony should mark his retirement and the passing of the mantle to Jihei as Kinzaemon X seemed only fitting. White Tiger was among the largest breweries in all Japan; the status and prestige that accompanied brewing in even the smallest hamlet was many times magnified in a brewery the size of White Tiger.

The ceremony was held in the spring. Kinzaemon insisted that no brewer be slighted, and this meant a long list. Extra help was hired for the occasion. Shoji partitions were removed to make a grand, enormous room. Unfortunately, as the younger son, Saburo would not be among the participants. Rie's heart saddened at the thought. Over the years, she had often thought of contacting him, telling him about Fumi, but the risk was too great, so she had grieved in silence, mourning his loss as she had her mother and Toichi before her.

On the day of the ceremony Rie opened the wooden shutters and looked out at the garden. Early morning dew shimmering on the azaleas reminded her that it was spring and that the brewing was finished. As she gazed out she felt a sense of melancholy, a sadness that it was her father's final day as Kinzaemon IX.

The activity began immediately. Everyone put on a formal kimono, lacquer tables were set in rows, and O-Yuki chased children and attempted to keep them clean and out from underfoot. Food was served with the best brew. Yoshitaro and Jihei sat on either side of Kinzaemon, Rie next to Jihei. Kin, Kinnosuke, Toji, the kurabito and clerks, all were included, with guests from breweries, officials, and customers. Seating in relation to Kinzaemon was according to status.

Lengthy formal speeches were made, as with a wedding or funeral. Kinzaemon spoke first. He bowed and cleared his throat.

"Forty years have passed since I succeeded to headship of the Omura House. During all those years you have granted us the favor of your support and cooperation. For that we are eternally grateful."

Rie detected a hoarseness as her father struggled to keep his emotions under tight control. He asked for the continued patronage of customers and suppliers during the headship of Jihei, now Kinzaemon X. Finally, he prayed for the benison of the gods on the house. As Rie listened, her affection and admiration for her father congealed in a lump in her throat. When he finished he was greeted on all sides by raised cups and shouts of "Banzai!"

Rie felt apprehensive as Jihei rose to speak next. She knew he could never equal her father in business or as a man, even in a speech.

"I am eternally grateful for being chosen to the headship of the Omura House. I will do my best to continue the leadership and long tradition of this house in the production of fine sake." Perspiration glistened on his face as he continued. "I will always strive to ensure that the next generation continues the venerable traditions of White Tiger."

His words were beginning to slur. Rie wished he would stop. Had he been drinking before this important occasion?

Before finishing he asked for the continued efforts of Toji and the kurabito in maintaining the White Tiger quality, and of Kin and the clerks in selling to Edo and elsewhere. When he stopped, cries of "Banzai" and the raising of cups followed. Rie detected less enthusiasm than for her father's words.

Kin spoke next, of his service of forty years, during which the house had survived fire, shipwreck, and other crises. He mentioned his own retirement, but promised to visit the office when Kinnosuke took over. Rie noticed Kinnosuke looking down modestly.

Toji spoke last, his honest, simple face the picture of loyalty and dedication. Rie felt as moved by Toji's words as by her father's. The skill of Toji and his workers from Tamba was in the last analysis what ensured the quality of White Tiger. He vowed to do his best to maintain its excellence. Rie was thankful she was keeping her eyes downcast, for she could feel tears beginning. Her gratitude for Toji's loyalty was mingled with a sense of poignancy that her father had reached this advanced life passage. She recalled clearly her father's words to her as a child, that one day the future of the house would rest on her shoulders. Now the enormous responsibility did. But with Jihei holding the reins of the house, she knew it would be harder than ever to ensure the house's success.

The next day Jihei poked his head through the kitchen door, where Rie was instructing the cooks on the day's meals. "Rie, Father wants you in the office," he said.

"I'll be right there." The meal plans completed, she hurried to the office, where her father, Kin, Jihei, and Toji were assembled. Each held a tasting cup.

"It's one of the finest sakes I've ever tasted," said Kin. He held the cup to his nose, twirled it twice, took a sip, and spat into the spittoon. "There's something special about this Yamaguchi sake from Nishinomiya. Here, compare it with this from the main brewery in Nada."

Rie held out a cup. "Let me try it."

Toji poured from a small barrel. Rie inhaled the aroma, sipped the Nishinomiya sake, then tried the Nada brew again.

"How could the two be so different?" Rie asked.

"I don't think they changed the recipe," said Toji.

"It has to be one of three things," Kinzaemon said. "The water, the yeast, or the mold. One of the three is definitely different."

Kinnosuke entered the room, and Kin gave him samples of the two sakes. Kinno nodded and looked at Kin and Toji.

"The difference is obvious," Kinzaemon said. He looked at Kinno. "Go to the Yamaguchi main office. Buy more of each. And see if you can learn why they're different. You know some of the clerks there."

Kinnosuke nodded. "Yes, I've been dealing with them these last few years, but you know they guard their secrets, we all do. Well, I do know one of the girls working there. Maybe I can learn something from her. She may tell me, if she knows."

"Don't delay, Kinno. But do your inquiring discretely," Rie warned.

He bowed as he left. "I'll be back as soon as possible."

Speculation continued in the office as Rie excused herself and went to attend to the children's lessons. In the afternoon her curiosity about the Nishiomiya sake brought her back to the office, where Kin and her father were still pondering the problem. She was about to leave for the kitchen when Kinnosuke's voice came from the outer office.

"I bought more sake," he said, "and I got some information from Nobu. We talked where no one could hear us."

Rie rested her fan under her chin and studied Kinno's face. She thought she detected a special sense of longing when he spoke of Nobu. Well, he was of an age to marry, and it might do well to have access to what was going on at Yamaguchi's.

"Listen!" Kinno could hardly contain his excitement. "She says their toji discovered a new well near their Nishinomiya kura. They used the water from that well for brewing this year. That's why it tastes different from their Nada sake." He straightened, bowed, and grinned.

"Amazing!" said Kinzaemon. "Let's call Toji." One of the clerks ran out of the office.

"We need to get some of that water immediately to try a test batch, even though it's late in the season," Kin said.

Toji entered the office, bowed, and looked at Kinzaemon, then at Kin.

"Taste this, Toji-san." Kinzaemon held out a cup. "Kinno says Yamaguchi found a well near their Nishinomiya kura and used this water for the brew. If we got some of the water could we do a test run this late?"

"We could try a small test and use ice to keep it cold when the weather turns too warm."

"Are they selling the water?" Rie asked.

Jihei scratched his head. "Selling it?"

"Maybe I can get a sample," Kinnosuke said.

Rie tapped her fan against her shoulder. "I wonder if we need a test when we know it's the water that makes the difference. Maybe we should focus on getting access to the well so we can use it for next year's brewing. Then maybe we could sell some to other brewers."

Jihei looked puzzled. "If it's so good, why would Yamaguchi

sell any? And what would other brewers think if we started selling Yamaguchi's water?"

"They'd think we're getting ahead," Rie retorted. Did her husband know *anything*?

Her father smiled, and Kin and Kinnosuke chuckled.

Jihei glowered. "How could we accomplish that? Why would Yamaguchi sell, to us especially?"

"Offer a good price," Rie replied, "and do it right away before any other brewer thinks of it." She paused and straightened. "No! Just a minute. We can't go to Yamaguchi directly, you're right. Send Jihei's cousin Yunoki, or his chief clerk. The family has a heavy obligation to us. They can't refuse. And Yamaguchi won't remember their connection to us. We'll pay for getting access to the well and for purchase. They aren't likely to refuse. They're in financial need. I hear one of their clerks took a lot of cash and vanished." She smiled and hooked both thumbs in her obi. "It's a question of timing."

"This would be a bold move, wouldn't it?" Jihei protested.

Rie sighed and looked at her father, then at Kin.

"We'll be first, I'm certain," Kin said. "That will give us a big advantage. We need to find out who makes decisions there now, with Yamaguchi aging. It may be their chief clerk, Yusuke. I've known him for years."

Rie's voice rose. "Try for a big purchase. If necessary we could mix some of the water with our own well water, do some testing." She took out her comb and fingered it.

"We need to find out the water table of the well too," Toji said.

Rie wished she could go to the Yunoki brewery herself. She sighed. "Kin-san, can you go early tomorrow and talk with Yunoki? Take Jihei with you. Have Yunoki offer Yamaguchi a big loan and then try to negotiate a purchase and access. What do you say, Father?" She ignored Jihei.

Kinzaemon ran his hands through his hair. "Yes, Rie, we should go tomorrow."

"Aren't we moving too fast?" Jihei protested again.

Rie sighed again, louder this time. "Not to move tomorrow would be too slow. We'd lose our advantage."

Kin nodded.

Jihei glared at her. Rie reserved her satisfied smile for herself.

Over the next few months the reputation of the Nishinomiya well, which became known as "Shrine Water," spread among brewers of Kobe and beyond. At a meeting of the Brewers Association, brewer Ikeda said, "This Shrine Water is amazing. Just the right quality of minerals for top grade sake. And you know, Yunoki moved right away and got access to the spring. I hear they're selling the water."

"Damned aggressive!" growled old Yamaguchi. "I don't know why Yusuke allowed it, and I don't know how that small a brewery got the funds. I wish he had consulted with me first."

"Quite a coup," Kin said to Rie later. "It's good you insisted that we move when we did. The demand for Shrine Water is growing; the price has soared."

"I've never done anything that gave me this much satisfaction," Rie said, cradling her elbows and smiling at Kin and her father.

Jihei just glowered at Rie, who had ignored whatever he said, dismissed him. Now Rie worried that he would try to get back at her. But how, that was the question.

Chapter 20

"Can you believe it, Father?" Rie asked as she sat with her elderly parent later that evening, her thoughts turning to family. "Yoshi is thirteen, Fumi is ten, Kazu and Teru eight and nine. Even Sei is nearly six. They're growing so fast. I suppose the next time I notice, they'll be old enough to marry." She nodded at her father, and noticed that his silver hair had thinned and the lines had deepened around his eyes.

"It means we're aging just as fast, Ri-chan. It's over ten years since Mother died. Nothing in life ever remains the same. Everything keeps changing." He set the book he'd had in his hand down.

"Yes, it seems so. I'm glad we were able to act as go-betweens for Kinno and Nobu. It's a good connection for us. We can keep better track of Yamaguchi now with Nobu here as Kinno's wife. And I'm glad I was able to find a house for them nearby. So convenient for him."

"You know, Yoshi went to his first Brewers Association the

other night with Jihei. Yoshi tells me that the brewers were talking about you and Kinno as an unbeatable combination, almost like watching Kabuki." Her father chuckled. "Selling Shrine Water took them all by surprise when they realized we were behind it." He chuckled again.

"Yes." Rie smiled. She couldn't be more delighted. "It has worked out well."

She put her hand on the calendar. "It's New Year's next Sunday, Father. I think I'll take the children to the temple after breakfast. It can't hurt to have people see the girls looking their best. It will help when it comes time to arrange their marriages if other families have seen them growing up. And they'll enjoy the outing, whether or not my husband goes with us." She just prayed she didn't run into Saburo and his wife for fear of her re-action, seeing them together for the first time. But she knew she would have to face them eventually. Her joy at seeing Saburo's face would outweigh her heartache at seeing him with his wife. She hoped so, anyway.

Fortunately, New Year's was the busiest time of year in any household and kept her in motion so that she didn't have time to think. Not only was it necessary to clear all debts from the year just ending, but gifts had to be prepared for regular customers and suppliers. The house was given a thorough cleaning, deco-rations of pine and bamboo were placed at the main entrance, and ceremonial lacquerware cups and trays were unpacked and cleaned. Toji brewed a traditional sweet sake to serve callers, but work in the brewery halted for five days so that the kurabito could return home for the holiday.

Three days before the holiday the children gathered around the large stone mortar and pestle near the well as Kin and Jihei pounded the rice into *mochi*. Kin held the hammer-shaped pestle high while Jihei quickly thrust his hand into a water bucket then back into the glutinous rice and water mass before Kin slammed the pestle down on the mortar again. Mochi pounding was a ritual Rie had loved to watch, even as a child. She felt mesmerized by the rhythmic thudding as Kin wielded the pestle. Mochi pounding reminded Rie that it was time to take stock of White Tiger's progress over the preceding year. Her musing was interrupted by Yoshi's voice and she turned to watch the two.

"Let me try," he begged his father.

Jihei stopped and looked at him. "You'll have to be really fast, Yoshi. Move your hands quickly after you turn."

"I will." When Yoshi stepped up to the mortar, Kin slowed his strokes. Yoshi struggled to keep pace until Rie noticed that he was tiring. Jihei soon replaced him. That he was stronger than a thirteen-year-old was the only accomplishment Rie could think of since marrying him.

For several days the kitchen maids worked, preparing the festive foods that would be served New Year's morning and also shared with visitors who came to pay their respects that day and the three days following. Long noodles symbolizing longevity were cooked for the New Year's Eve meal, and even Jihei remained at home with the family that night.

In the morning Rie wished her father felicitations and saw the pride on the faces of the boys as they stood for inspection in their black kimono wraps and brightly colored obis. They sat behind her as she lit incense and poured New Year's sake before her mother's name tablet at the altar already decorated with piles of mochi cakes, tangerines, and bamboo stalks. Then the children were allowed to open their gifts, brightly colored kites for the boys and for the girls a complete set of formal dolls for Girls' Day.

New Year's breakfast was the most elaborate meal of the year: soup with mochi and beautifully arranged morsels of fish cake, pickles, and vegetables in artfully cut shapes and colors, served in small exquisite dishes on individual lacquer tables.

"We're all going to the temple this morning, to pay our respects," Rie said while they were finishing breakfast. "You know this is our family temple, where our family grave is located." She patted Sei's shoulder. "You may come this year, Sei, and bring your paddles."

The children's holiday spirits were contagious, and even Jihei seemed agreeable. "Yes, I'll go with you," he said to Rie, "but I need to be back early to help Father greet the callers."

Rie and the girls walked slightly behind Jihei and the boys as the family strolled like peacocks in their finery through the pine tree-lined temple walkways. She bowed and smiled at neighbors and was careful to speak to brewers as they passed.

Her worries about meeting Saburo and his wife soon faded as she saw brewer after brewer and none was Saburo. She had thought that perhaps she would avoid him after all when suddenly she recognized Saburo Kato and his wife coming toward her. She started, her heart pounding. *Saburo, my own heart!* She should have been the one beside him. They had not been able to arrange a meeting since the night they spent together, the most important of Rie's life. Memories of that precious time crowded in as she attempted to keep her emotions in check and to greet the couple formally.

"Happy New Year," she said, smiling and bowing, her heart breaking. "So wonderful to see your family." She saw three sons, one a striking replica of his father, and a lump formed in her throat. Saburo was still as handsome as he was then, even distinguished now with graying temples, a reminder that they were approaching middle age.

"You're looking well, Mrs. Omura," he said.

How she had missed him. She wanted to embrace him, not walk formally past, but she merely smiled and said, "The boys are helping with brewing already."

"Is that so?" Mrs. Kato bowed. "Already? And your girls are so pretty."

Wasn't it annoying that Mrs. Kato was glancing at Teru, not Fumi? Well, maybe the Katos would consider Teru as a bride for one of their sons. Perhaps even Kazu for another son. Of course for Fumi it was out of the question, something Fumi would never know.

As they walked past, Rie glanced quickly back, and caught Saburo doing the same. Rie felt tantalized, drawn to him as always, but knew a tryst such as the one they had shared was unlikely to happen again, especially now that he was also married. Besides, her family and business responsibilities were now so heavy. She did not have even the smallest chance at the liberty she had taken then.

She let herself steal one last look at him.

At the temple entrance Rie pushed away her thoughts of Saburo, clapped her hands to attract the notice of the gods, then stood silently and offered a prayer for the welfare of the house and brewery. She dropped coins into the offertory box and lit an incense stick. The girls begged for amulets being sold by the priests, and Rie bought three.

When they returned home Rie found her father still greeting callers, visitors below her father in age and status. Each guest was offered a cup or two of ceremonial sake and a package of mochi to take home. Rie thought her father was looking especially tired after the long day, his face haggard and gray. His younger brother had come with his wife, son-in-law, and daughter Sunao, Rie's friend. They chatted and exchanged family news.

Rie glanced at her father. "He looks so exhausted, Sunao. I'm worried about him." She rested her hand on Sunao's arm and frowned at her father's ashen face.

"He does look older than last year," Sunao agreed.

"He stays in his room a lot now, but he especially wanted to come out today and greet people. But uncle is looking well, and you always look so fashionable." Rie scrutinized her cousin's glowing complexion and flawless kimono and obi.

"Yes, Father is what, seven years younger? He still works hard," Sunao said.

"The children could all have played together."

"Yes, maybe next year." Sunao glanced around the room at the children.

"Who does Teru look like?" Sunao asked.

"I'm not sure," Rie answered, her face flushing beneath her cousin's scrutiny. "You know she and Kazu came from distant relatives on Mother's side. They're from the country, both of them." Rie was relieved she could come up with a plausible explanation in a hurry. "I'm sorry we don't have a chance to get together more often," she said as she bade good-bye to Sunao and her parents. "I wish you could come by sometimes. We could go to the flower show next year."

Rie turned back to the room where guests continued to call and mingle in the room around Kinzaemon and Jihei. Maids scurried in still bearing carafes and sweets. Sei began to cry and throw himself on the floor.

"Fumi, would you please take Sei to bed?" Rie said. "And Yoshi, you can go and play cards with the girls now."

Rie saw that the noise and confusion were fatiguing her father. He sat stooped and suddenly silent. Rie and Jihei sat with each set of guests who came to offer greetings until the last visitor departed and darkness was whispering into the room.

Rie hurried over to her father, who was slumped over his tray.

"Father, are you all right?" She put her hand on his shoulder.

"Oh," he murmured feebly and looked up at Rie.

Jihei quickly joined Rie and put his arms around Kinzaemon's shoulders. "Can you get up, Father?"

"Are you in pain?" Rie's voice rose.

Kinzaemon struggled to move his legs as if to rise. "Rie . . . no," he gasped for breath. "There's . . . something I must . . .

tell you." He moved forward slightly, then slumped over on the tatami.

"Father!" Rie gasped and reached for his wrist and pulse. His arm went limp.

"No!" Rie put her hands to her head and rocked back and forth. "No!"

Jihei cradled Kinzaemon's head on his lap and looked at Rie, disbelief on his face.

Rie had spent the day thinking of her children and had neglected her father, the most important person in the world. Now he was dead.

After the initial shock of her father's death Rie felt bereft, totally abandoned. She mourned for days and weeks following the funeral, a ceremony attended by every brewer in the city. The morning after the funeral she sat at the Butsudan weeping, offering sake and rice before the tablet newly inscribed with her father's posthumous name. For nearly eleven years following her mother's death he had been her solace, her support in every major crisis. Now she had just Jihei and the children. She felt utterly alone. There seemed no way to assuage her grief. She alternated between numbness and sorrow. For days she wandered through the garden and rooms of the house that seemed colder now than ever, often ending up in her father's room, as if she half expected to find him there.

One evening, the hour after dinner when she had so often enjoyed her father's companionship, she opened his cupboard and took out his kimonos, piling them on the tatami. She picked up one of the finest formal kimonos, held it to her face and inhaled the camphor aroma mingled with the slightly woodsy scent she associated with her father. Tears ran down her cheeks and she let them fall freely. No, she would give none of the kimonos to Jihei.

He did not deserve anything her father had worn. One or two could go to Yoshi, and some to Sei when he was old enough.

O-Natsu became more attentive to Rie than usual and now seemed to Rie the only individual who really understood her. Rie drew closer to Fumi too, a sensitive child nearly eleven, and the bond between them strengthened. As the darkest days of Rie's mourning passed, she again turned to the office for comfort. Working with Kinnosuke began to provide a semblance of normalcy. Kin retired soon after her father died, and she sorely missed his wisdom and experience in the double loss.

Before Kin left he told her what her father wanted to tell her before he died: how proud he was of her, and that he wanted to give her the family seal. Kin handed Rie the seal Kinzaemon had entrusted to him the night before he died, asking that he give it to Rie with his special blessing.

Rie took the seal with both hands, held it to her head, then her heart, and inserted it in her obi. Two tears coursed down her face as she did so.

Rie felt a catch in her throat, an emotion that rendered her nearly speechless. Her father, for whom she had worked so long, had recognized, after all, what she had done. She stuttered. "Thank you for telling me, Kin-san. Thank you." She bowed low.

Jihei showed signs of taking his responsibilities more seriously, but he continued his heavy drinking. While he worked in the office, it was to Kinnosuke and Kin, on his occasional visits, that Rie turned when a serious problem demanded attention. Yoshi as a young teenager became a real presence in the office, now formally ranked as apprentice, although it was understood that he would succeed Jihei. Her father's death made it palpably clear to Rie that the future of the Omura enterprise rested with Kinnosuke and Yoshitaro. And herself.

Chapter 21

After the chance meeting with Saburo and his wife, and the death of her beloved father, Rie poured herself into the business as never before. For the next five years, everything seemed to be going well. Then one day Rie saw Kinnosuke come running past her into the office, his gown flapping and fluttering in the breeze. She quickly followed him.

"Toji is worried about the sake," Kinnosuke said to Yoshitaro and Rie, frowning. "He's been sampling it."

"He's on his way here now," said Yoshitaro in a voice breaking lower.

Toji rushed into the office and knelt on the tatami. He bowed abjectly.

"The sake has gone bad! It's terrible! I've tried three barrels. They're all the same." His head remained bowed.

"No!" Rie cried. "It's not possible!"

"I have no words to apologize adequately," he said, bowing to Rie.

"Let's go and see," said Kinno. He and Yoshi followed Toji briskly out of the room and along the corridor toward the number one kura. Rie followed and stood beyond the door to the kura. She shifted impatiently from one foot to the other as she waited for the men to emerge.

"What a calamity," she said half to herself, half to Yoshi who stood with her. What will we do? Yoshi, go and ask them to bring samples from all three kura to the office."

He nodded and disappeared through the kura door. Rie walked back to the office and sat at the work table. Minutes later the men reappeared with several flasks. Kinno and Toji were shaking their heads.

"Well?" Rie asked, her heart pounding.

The men put the flasks and cups on the table. Each man poured from the separate flasks, swirled the sake in their mouths briefly and spat into spittoons. All three were frowning.

Jihei stumbled into the room and looked at the three.

"What's wrong?" he asked.

"Taste this," said Kinno.

Jihei picked up a cup. "Awful!" he said with a grimace and spat.

"Let me taste," said Rie. She sipped and spat samples from each flask. "A disaster," she said, frowning.

"This is the first time this has happened in all the years I've been here," Toji said.

"It happened to Kato many years ago, others too. If one or two barrels from one kura are bad, chances are the whole cellar is ruined."

"We have to recognize it's a total loss," Kinno said. He slumped.

"We'll have to discard it all," Toji agreed.

"All of it? All three kura? Nothing to be done?" Jihei picked at his eyebrows.

"How did it happen?" Rie asked, tapping her fan on the table.

"We've never had this kind of thing happen before. I've always been so careful to wash the barrels and trained the girls to do likewise. I wonder if I could have missed something? But I keep a close watch."

"Now, don't blame yourself," said Kinno. "You just never know when this is going to hit a brewery. Who knows why? It's happened to many others. Hardly anyone has escaped."

"I wonder if Yamaguchi had something to do with this?" Rie said, frowning.

"It's possible," Kinno said. "Yoshi, bring the ledger books for this year, please."

Yoshi staggered under three heavy ledgers. Rie watched intently as Kinno opened them to the pages of the year's expenses and income. Kinnosuke began working with the abacus.

The room was tense and silent for several minutes except for the rapid clicking of the wooden counters.

"We'll have huge debts with a loss of this magnitude," Kinno said finally. "We'll have to rely on sales of Shrine Water, plus our income from gold-silver exchange and moneylending to survive until next year. I'm not sure if we can make it." He sighed, leaned back, and looked at Rie and Jihei.

No. No! This couldn't be happening. Her father had trusted the house to her. She would not fail him. Rie let out a puff of the cheeks. "We must diversify even more. We have to now in order to survive." She put down her fan and pulled the comb from her hair.

"You're right, no question," said Kinno. "We'll lose customers as it is, we're bound to." He bit his lip.

"What do you suggest?" Jihei wondered.

Did the head of the house have no ideas of his own? Disgraceful.

"How about buying from several small brewers who have little or no brand recognition beyond their local areas?" Kinno asked.

"Excellent idea, Kinno!" Rie cried. "Yes, we could sell in our barrels under our label, using sake blended from several small brewers. It would be a new product that way." She tapped her fan on the table.

"Could we do that?" Jihei bounced up and down on his heels in a petulant manner.

"Why not?" Rie asked. "Who would object? Shogunal commissioners like White Tiger as well as anyone."

Yoshi looked back and forth from Rie to Kinno with his mouth open.

This was how he'd learn. It was how she had learned—by listening to her father and Kin as a child.

Several streets away, Kikuji Yamaguchi sat, elbows on his table, issuing orders and going through ledgers. He belched.

Yusuke, his aging clerk, sidled up to him with a crablike gait. "Have you heard, Master? White Tiger's brew has turned sour, all of it!" He smiled and looked at Yamaguchi expectantly.

"So!" roared Yamaguchi. "Omura's sake has gone bad! And we didn't have to do anything. Excellent. This is our chance to capture their customers, their whole market. They'll be helpless. Good, Yusuke," he bellowed.

"Master?"

"Start working on Omura's customers. Get the list at the Brewers Association, can you?"

"I think so, but . . ." Yusuke took three steps backward.

"Don't hesitate." Yamaguchi's jowls trembled as he spoke. "Divert thirty percent from our regular customers to Omura's regular clients. Promise our regular customers more next season, and buy up all you can from smaller brewers."

Yusuke nodded.

"And have three clerks assist you. Get started today. No delay!" he barked.

Several mornings later Kinno approached Rie in the inner office. "Oku-san, I heard some news about Yamaguchi."

Rie looked up quizzically. "What?"

"I hear he's trying to move into our markets, to take over our customers. He has heard about our sake disaster."

"A devil! He's a devil!" Rie frowned darkly.

Kinno scratched his head. "How are we going to stop him?"

No one answered.

Late that morning Rie walked out into the garden as the sun broke faintly through the clouds and caressed the azaleas. She strolled slowly, head down, her hands behind her back in unconscious imitation of her father's walking posture. She halted at the stone and sat. Resting her chin on her hand, she gazed pensively at the pond.

She looked around the garden for a moment, and her eye fixed on the time-haunted fences that enclosed the carefully manicured space. She felt transported to the temple garden, far from the brewery. A sense of timeless peace pervaded her being, and she silently thanked her ancestors for creating this oasis of tranquility. As she looked around, her eyes rested on the clump of bamboo whose leaves rustled in the breeze. Bamboo, a favorite kimono pattern, symbol of adaptability, of bending with shifting circumstances.

As she mused, her father's voice came to her: "A major setback always offers a major challenge, an inevitable part of doing business." She looked back at the bamboo and listened as the leaves whispered softly. Her gaze shifted upward, above the vine-covered fences to the roofs. Her eye traveled along the rooftops over the office and two-story section of the house and beyond, to the towering roofs of the three kuras. The kuras, the kuras! She slapped her knees, rose, and walked back into the office.

Yoshi was working at one end of the room.

"Yoshi, can you find your father and Kinno?" she asked. "I want to talk to them."

"I can find Kinno, but I don't know about Father."

"Please ask Kinno to come to the office, then."

Yoshi nodded and left.

Minutes later the shoji slid open and Kinno and Yoshi entered. They looked at her expectantly as they sat.

Rie sat perfectly straight. "You know that each time we have had a crisis in the past we have survived because we found a solution other than brewing. That is how we survived. Brewing is the work given us by our ancestors and we must continue it, no question." She paused and looked up as Jihei walked into the room.

She ignored the supposed head of the house.

"Now we need another solution. Selling the sake of small brewers under our own label will not be enough, now that Yamaguchi is moving into our markets. We must look elsewhere. We need something new." She paused and took a deep breath. "I have a question for you, Kinno-san." She tapped her fan on the table. "Do you know of a small brewer in Nada or anywhere in Kobe who is forced to close his brewery this year?"

Kinno scratched his chin. "Let's see. I think Yanagihara in East Nada . . . I heard something about them. They had a shipwreck and it finished them." He looked at Rie.

Jihei frowned at her. *Frown all you want,* she thought.

She continued. "If it's true that Yanagihara has had to stop, then I propose that we buy his brewery, his kura, and sell it at a higher price. If he had to stop he won't be able to bargain over the price."

Jihei's mouth hung open. "Are you talking about buying and selling kura, dealing in kura? Whoever heard—"

Rie tapped her fan again. "That's just the point. If no one else is doing it, it will be our chance. What do you think, Kinno-san?"

He sucked in his breath in a hiss. "A new idea. Interesting. It might work. *Hmm*." He scratched his chin. "Let me think a bit." He leaned forward. "As a matter of fact, I hear the Ozawas are having a difficult year; had to cut back on production. I have an idea we might be able to buy one of their kura too."

Rie nodded and smiled at Kinno. "Good."

Jihei frowned. "You're always pushing to be first in everything. I thought a brewer's task is to brew good sake and not worry about anything else, except maybe lending money."

"That doesn't work on our scale here in Nada," Rie said, stating the obvious. Why didn't Jihei understand this by now? "We have to be always on the lookout for something new as well as trying to improve our quality. Otherwise we'd be relegated to second or third class, if we survive at all." She shook her head. "Do you follow what we're discussing, Yoshi?"

"I think so." He nodded.

"All right, Kinno and Yoshi. Our credit is good. See what you can do about the Yanagihara and Ozawa kura. Let's start on it tomorrow."

Jihei frowned and walked out of the office.

Some head.

She had led the house out of this crisis.

Two weeks later Rie sat with Yoshi and Kinno in the office.

"I was right," said Kinno, nodding and placing his hands on the table. "Yanagihara had stopped brewing. He was receptive to selling. I hesitated to make an offer, but Yoshi helped convince me. We had to raise our price a bit. So now we own the Ozawa kura in East Nada and the Yanagihara kura."

"Excellent, Kinno and Yoshi." Rie slapped her fan on the table.

Just then the shoji opened and Jihei walked in. "I heard what you were saying," he said, his speech slurred. "I think it's too fast. We should proceed one kura at a time."

Yoshi stole a glance at his father, then looked down. "I felt sorry for Yanagihara, having to stop after so many generations," he said.

"It's all right to feel sympathy for someone, Yoshi," Rie said, "and natural. But please remember that such emotions should not intrude when you are doing a business negotiation. Your head must rule, not your heart." She rested a hand on his arm. "But you succeeded. Congratulations." She felt Jihei's glare. He was too drunk to sustain it, though. What an embarrassment he was.

Kinno's eyes crinkled in appreciation, his mouth shaping a toothy grin. "I think we should sell one kura now and keep the other for next winter, when we may be able to increase our production."

"Very well," Rie agreed. "And Kinno and Yoshi, I want you to start giving Sei small jobs in the afternoon. Remember, Yoshi, you were following Kinno everywhere when you were five. That's how you learned so well." She beamed at him. "Teach Sei to do just as you did."

Late one afternoon Rie stopped outside the boys' room. The tutor had left, and she hoped to learn what he was teaching them, especially Yoshi.

"Yoshi," she called as she slid the shoji open and entered the room.

The boys sat at the low table with papers and copy sheets. Sei was painstakingly copying syllables with a brush. Yoshi was reading aloud from a book printed on rice paper. They bowed to Rie.

"Continue, please. What are you reading, Yoshi?"

"Sensei left me these two books." He pushed them across the table.

"*The Way to Wealth,* by Saikaku," Rie read aloud. "Yes, a good lesson, Yoshi. Saikaku says here what a merchant needs is frugality, persistence, a ready mind for figures, mastery of the abacus, a pleasant manner, honesty, and imagination. Just what Grandfather and I have been teaching you. We must keep this so Sei can read it when he's old enough." She read on. "It is not plum, cherry, pine, and maple trees that people desire most around their houses, but gold and silver, rice and hard cash."

Rie burst out laughing, covering her mouth with the book. The boys grinned.

"Of course we value gold and silver, *and* hard cash. But we also enjoy the plum and cherry blossoms in the garden too. And the other book, Yoshi?"

She picked it up and read, *"The Man Who Spent His Life in Love."* Then she turned to Yoshi. "Have you read this one?"

"Not yet."

"Well, let me read it first. I'm not sure it's suitable." She slipped the book into her sleeve, rose, and went to the door. "Continue. We'll have dinner soon."

Rie retired early, intending to read Yoshi's lesson book. She set the lamp next to her futon and pulled out the story. She read aloud to herself the words of one of the characters in the story. "'Many years ago it was observed that a father slaves, his son idles, and the grandson begs.' *Ho!*" she exclaimed aloud. She read the story of the rakish, profligate son who spent his time and money in the entertainment quarter where he squandered the money so painstakingly accumulated by his father. This was a good lesson for Yoshi . . . and for Jihei. She would ask the tutor if he had any more of these stories. She finished the book and decided to leave it on Jihei's seat in the office where he was sure to see it.

Chapter 22

Rie walked to the courtyard one morning and looked at her three daughters standing in front of the barrels in their indigo *mompei* work pants, slapping each other and giggling in their high-pitched voices. Rie tied her sleeves back and walked up to them.

"Talking won't get the barrels clean, girls. Come on, pick up the brushes. I want to see how you're doing. You too, Teru. You're old enough. Watch your sisters. You've washed your hands and feet? And remember, stay away from the kura."

"Yes, Mother," all three replied at once. They bowed quickly and picked up the large brushes next to the hose.

"Get to the back of the barrel first, the bottom. You'll need this small ladder to reach," Rie said. "I know some brewers just run water through the barrels, but that isn't enough. We don't want a repeat of last year's sake."

"But it's so cold, Mother." Fumi shivered and rubbed her hands together. "My hands are freezing."

"I know. Cold weather is what makes good sake. You can stop when you're too cold and warm your hands. Like this." Rie held her hands over her nose and mouth. "And after a while your back gets tired. But there are three of you. I used to do it all alone, so you'll each do only a third of the work."

"But we have more barrels now. We produce more," Kazu said.

"Yes, you're right." Rie laughed. "Use the ladder, Kazu. You'll need it to reach the bottom, there at the side. And Teru, use some force. That's right, Fumi. And it helps to sing. It takes your mind off the cold."

Rie began to hum a rhythmic folk tune and clapped her hands in time to their brush strokes. They all began to sing.

"You'll get to enjoy it after a while, when you realize how important it is for the sake, and for the success of the house."

"You always talk about the house, Mother," sixteen-year-old Fumi said.

"Yes, it's the most important thing in the world, Fumi. In whatever we do we need to think of the house."

Rie mused as she watched the girls. Kazu was already fifteen, taller than average and a capable, responsible model for her younger sister. Teru was obviously attractive and must be watched closely so that she did not behave like a geisha. Rie felt a twinge of guilt that she had given Fumi more attention than her sisters. She turned and walked to the inner office, allowing herself only the briefest of thoughts of Fumi's real father.

Rie opened the wooden shutters one morning and looked out into the garden. The maple leaves were reddening, yellow chrysanthemum buds were ready to burst, and the cicadas had fallen silent. Could summer have come and gone so quickly? Even when the autumn foliage was at its most brilliant, Rie always felt a faint twinge of melancholy at the cold gray winter to come. Of course that was the weather that produced good sake, the colder the better. It also brought on O-Natsu's painful rheumatism and everyone's sniffling noses the whole winter through. And there had not been time to go to Bunraku this summer, regretfully.

The autumn colors in the garden also reminded Rie that it was time to prepare for the start of another brewing season. She prayed that the previous year's disaster would not be repeated. Maids cleaned the kurabitos' room to prepare for their arrival from their farms. Jihei must call the priest for the start of season ritual, a Shinto observance performed in the kura. Rie and the girls were not allowed to witness it. Rie had O-Natsu and O-Yuki ready the fruit and mochi plates to set on the white-draped table at the entrance to the number one kura. Ropes hung with white folded paper amulets were strung above the entrance to each kura. In her father's time Rie knew prayers were said each morning before the Shinto god shelf. Now the ceremony was performed just once annually, though Toji said a prayer himself each morning. Sake brewing required the help of the gods.

The purple-robed priest in his pointed black cap arrived the morning of the ceremony and was greeted by Jihei, Yoshi, Toji, and Kinnosuke. Kin returned for the occasion. The wooden shutters of the main room were open so Rie and the girls could witness the ceremony from a distance as they were not allowed in the kura. Jihei, Yoshitaro, Kinnosuke, Toji, and the kurabito stood in a row in front of the main kura. The priest held his white paper wand in both hands and shook it several times at the entrance to each kura before entering the main kura. He stood at the ceremonial table inside the entrance. The women were silent as they listened to him intone solemn prayers to the god of sake for the success of the season's brew.

Completion of the ritual was the signal for everyone to spring into action. Huge baskets of rice were carried inside the brewery for polishing with the wooden waterwheel. Then the rice was steamed in the huge black cauldron. Next, rice was inoculated with koji mold to produce sweet saccharified rice that would turn all the rice to sugar, while yeast was simultaneously introduced and the process of fermentation begun. The whole operation was the province of Toji and the kurabito.

Rie, forever outside the kura, relied on the sounds and smells as the brewing progressed. She heard the kurabito sing as they worked and knew when the fermentation began by the pungent yeasty smell of something growing that wafted from the kura through the courtyard and permeated the house. When the sake was filtered, Rie was next after Toji and Kinnosuke to judge the brew. Jihei did not always bother to be present.

With the brewing in full swing, White Tiger expanded production in the newly acquired fourth kura. Seisaburo, at age nine, was now an apprentice in the office under his elder brother's and Kinnosuke's supervision. Rie was gratified to see the brothers working together but at the same time distressed that Jihei was becoming increasingly ineffectual as head of the house. He seldom did anything on his own initiative. Planning and decision making were done by Rie and Kinnosuke with Yoshitaro, and, where the kura was concerned, by Toji. Jihei was usually absent during the days *and* evenings, which only relieved Rie. Old Kin came less often, but when he did he never failed to inquire about the sale of Shrine Water. On his latest visit he asked Kinnosuke about the sale of the Ozawa kura.

"We got seventy for it, Kin-san," Kinnosuke told him. "We sold it to Sugiyama. They had a fire in their kura and would have had to stop. They were glad to get it. It enabled them to stay in production this year."

"A good price, yes. Very good," Kin said. "Oku-san must have been happy." Only a few yellowed teeth showed when he grinned.

"Yes, I was pleased," Rie said and leaned toward him. "I can see your rheumatism is troubling you." She glanced at the gnarled, swollen joints on his fingers. "But please come back whenever you feel well enough. It's good for the boys to see you here. Sei was so young when his grandfather died. Your visits are important to us now."

Kin slurped his tea appreciatively and smiled until his eyes vanished in slits. "I'm glad that Toji is still here," he said in his faint, raspy voice. "Yes, I'll come whenever the rheumatism isn't too bad. Brewing is my life." He looked down at his hands.

"As a matter of fact, there is something I wanted to discuss with you," Rie said. "I need your wisdom and experience. You know how lax the authorities have become in enforcing the kabu license regulations." She took out her comb and twirled it in her hands.

"Yes. There's not much the commissioners can do here in Kansai any longer. The shoguns are on shaky ground now, no longer able to control anything, despite their efforts. The whole samurai class is indebted to the merchants. I just wonder what's going to become of these Tokugawa shoguns."

"Well, this is my point, Kin-san. They can't enforce the regulations. They can't dictate the amount we produce. I heard Kinno-san say something about buying or renting additional kabu so we could increase our production. You know he is negotiating to buy two more kura, the old Kuribayashi kura in Nishinomiya. That will put us closer to the Shrine Water. And we'll need more kabu. What do you think? Do you see any risk in buying up more shares, a lot more?"

"I can't foresee any risk. The commissioners can't move against us." He paused to sip his tea. "Yes, I know people have been buying and selling shares. Kinno-san mentioned it. He really is keeping on top of things, isn't he?"

Rie refilled his cup, and he warmed his hands on it.

"We couldn't have done better in our choice of your successor. Not that anyone could ever fill your place." She looked at the old man's lined, sunken face and felt a twinge of nostalgia.

"Well, I've seen you two working together and it's often difficult to say which of you gets an idea first. You two are of the same mind." He grinned toothlessly and chortled deep in his throat. "There's not another pair like you in all Kobe. It's something to watch. Of course you received the best training from your father."

The compliment delighted her.

"Oh, I learned from you too, Kin-san, especially in those years when Father didn't want me near the business."

Kinnosuke walked in and joined them.

"Kinno-san," Rie said, smiling at him.

He looked up and bowed briskly.

"How many more barrels are we using than last season?"

"Ten more, with the new kura."

"And each time we add a kura we'll need that many more barrels?"

"Yes, that's true," he said, and nodded.

"Then shouldn't we think about hiring a cooper and setting him up here instead of buying barrels from outside?" Rie asked as she pulled out her tortoiseshell comb and reinserted it.

"I can make inquiries. I know the Setookas. They might be receptive. They own an old cooperage, and have several sons, so they'll need to send out the younger ones. We've always bought some barrels from them. Setooka comes by at this time of year when he thinks we may need some."

"Good. See what you can do there. We need a cooper and an apprentice or two."

Several months later a coopers' shed was built next to the

number three kura, and Masami Setooka's son Goro and his younger brother Kasumi were installed as apprentice barrel makers. All the barrels used in White Tiger were now made on the premises, an economy in production costs.

Rie sat in the parlor one morning renewing a flower arrangement and replacing the rice and plum wine offerings on the family altar. The wooden shutters were open toward the courtyard, affording a view out toward the coopers' shed. At one side of the entrance, wood for making barrels was stacked. At the other side of the door stood Goro, a boy with strikingly fine features. Rie recalled his father's face, the way O-Toki had lingered before him at the end of season celebration years earlier. Not surprising that Goro had inherited a handsome face. But who was the girl talking with him so earnestly, her back toward the house? Rie watched until the girl turned to walk back toward the house. It was Teru, now fourteen and the most beautiful of the Omura daughters. She was smiling to herself as she approached the house, teapot in hand. She walked like a geisha, seductively.

Annoyed, Rie rose and slid open the door to the corridor just as Teru entered from the courtyard.

"Teru, please come in here. I need to talk to you." Rie turned abruptly and walked back into the room. She sat before the Butsudan and indicated a zabuton for Teru.

"Teru, what were you doing over there at the cooper's shed just now?"

"Oh, I was just taking them some tea. It was time for their morning tea."

"And why did you think this was your job and not the kitchen maids'?"

"Oh . . . *uh* . . . they were busy, Mother." Teru looked down and shifted uneasily on the zabuton.

"It wasn't because you wanted to talk to Goro?" Rie persisted.

Teru blushed. "*Uh* . . . well, he does seem nice."

"And what have I taught you about talking with the men, the workers, Teru?"

Teru was silent, her face red, her head still bowed.

"I'm waiting, Teru."

Teru spoke in a voice barely above a whisper. "That we shouldn't."

"Please remember that, Teru. I don't want to have to speak to you again about it. And another thing: who taught you to walk like that?"

"Like what, Mother?" Teru looked up, frowning.

"As if you wanted to attract some man's attention."

"I'm just walking, the same as you and Kazu."

"Not exactly the same. Remember to keep your toes pointed in and your knees slightly bent. You must be more circumspect. Remember who you are." Rie paused. She noted O-Toki pausing several times in front of Masami at a ceremony and guessed that he, not Jihei, was Teru's father.

"As an Omura daughter you will have a good marriage to another brewing house, but you must safeguard your virtue and the honor of the house. Talking carelessly with our workers can endanger our reputation. It is simply not acceptable behavior. I am sorry to have to remind you of this."

Teru's head was still bowed, and Rie saw that she was pouting.

"You may be excused now. Go and finish your abacus lesson."

"Yes, Mother." Teru rose and left the room quickly, without bowing.

Rie sat with her thoughts. She hoped she was being fair with Teru, not venting her old anger about Jihei's mistresses' children. She sighed and had a flash of memory of her own mother and her feelings toward her. She hoped Kazu and Teru felt toward her as Fumi did. Strange, it did not seem like half a lifetime ago that she had sat in this same room with her mother. Teru's beauty was a potential danger as well as an asset to the house. Was there a hint of insolence in her manner? She would bear watching now until her marriage could be arranged. And it must be arranged soon, perhaps as early as the next year, after Fumi and Kazu were married.

Chapter 23

"Yoshi, you're nineteen now," Jihei said to his son one day as they worked in the inner office. Jihei looked around to make sure they were alone. "There are things you need to learn, things other than brewing. I want you to come with me this evening."

Yoshitaro looked up. "Where are we going?" he asked.

"Somewhere you've never been before. It will be a surprise, a pleasant one. But you're not to tell your mother. Do you understand?"

"Yes, Father."

"We won't have dinner at home this evening. I'll tell your mother that we're going to a Bunraku performance, just you and I. We'll leave after dark."

Jihei had spoken to O-Toki the previous week.

"Yoshi has had his nineteenth birthday. I want him to have his initiation here. Do you have a suitable geisha? Someone with real beauty and experience, a bit older than he but not so old that he'll be put off. What do you think?"

O-Toki smiled. "Yes, it's time. I know he's nineteen. I thought of him on his birthday. A mother does, you know." She raised her eyebrows but continued looking down.

"Do you have someone in mind?"

"I've been thinking about it, actually. Yes, I think O-Sada would be perfect. She's a beauty and much in demand. She has a patron so she's experienced. Her patron needn't know. I'll arrange it with O-Sada."

"I'll bring him a week from tonight. We'll want to have a bath and a meal. He and I can bathe and eat together, but after that. . . ."

"I understand. O-Sada will be very sensitive."

"Will she know you're his mother?" Jihei asked. "You know, Yoshi still doesn't know. He thinks my wife is his mother."

"I'll let her know everything she needs to know, you can be sure." O-Toki did not elaborate.

"Let's go, Yoshi. I had a ricksha called. He's waiting out beyond the number three kura."

Jihei glanced at his son and was pleased that he had taken special care with his appearance. They looked strikingly alike, Jihei had to concede, only that Yoshitaro was slighter of build. And with his bushy hair and slim figure he might almost be mistaken for an artist or actor, the type that would attract women. Yoshitaro seemed to have caught his father's sense of adventure, Jihei thought as they rode to the Sawaraya. Yoshitaro turned to look at the hawkers, the lights, the scurrying geisha as the ricksha rocked along the bumpy roads.

At the entrance O-Toki and a younger geisha greeted them, a woman whose striking eyes gave her an air of intelligence it was difficult to conceal even with her geisha's makeup and bright kimono. Yoshitaro followed his father and the geisha along the corridors, stumbling as he watched O-Sada and looking curiously at his surroundings. *Good that he especially noticed O-Sada,* Jihei thought.

Seated with his son in the back room always reserved for him, Jihei looked around the room and relished the thought that they were a family—he, O-Toki, and their son, the first time the three had been together since Yoshitaro's infancy.

"So wonderful that you have brought your son this evening," O-Toki said as she and O-Sada bowed deeply. O-Toki looked at Yoshitaro intently, then glanced down and bowed.

A maid brought in a tea tray, the evening's preliminary. O-Sada poured two small cups and set them before Jihei and Yoshitaro.

"And you will want a bath before you dine. O-Sada will show you to the bath when you have changed." She indicated the house yukata and the women left the room.

Yoshitaro glanced at Jihei, who nodded and rose. They changed into the blue-and-white printed yukata and slid open the shoji. O-Sada motioned for them to follow her. Jihei glanced at Yoshitaro and saw that he was watching O-Sada walk with her small swaying steps. In the bath anteroom O-Sada handed towels to Jihei and Yoshitaro and withdrew as they removed the cotton robes and entered the steaming bathroom. Jihei tried to reassure his son as they soaped and rinsed. "It's the same as at home, Yoshi. We always bathe before dinner here too. Nothing unusual."

They stepped into the vaporous steamy tub. Jihei slapped a hot towel on top of his head and sighed.

"Relax, Yoshi. We're here to forget the pressures of work."

The door slid open and O-Toki and O-Sada advanced through the mist and knelt behind Jihei and Yoshitaro.

O-Sada smiled at Yoshitaro and asked in a soft voice, "May I massage your back?"

Yoshitaro covered his groin with his hands.

Jihei smiled. "Don't worry, Yoshi, she's seen men before."

O-Toki glanced at Yoshitaro, then quickly focused on Jihei's back.

For the next few moments the only sound was water splashing as the women ran their hands around Jihei's and Yoshitaro's backs. Jihei watched O-Sada's hands move up and down Yoshitaro's arms and around to his stomach. Jihei closed his eyes and exhaled loudly.

"A wonderful way to relax, isn't it, Yoshi?" He opened one eye.

Yoshitaro nodded but didn't speak. Jihei saw Yoshitaro's eyes following O-Sada's hands in their exploratory tour of his body.

After a few minutes O-Toki rose and said, "We'll see to your dinner." She motioned O-Sada to follow her.

After the women left, Yoshitaro said, "Do they always come into the bath and massage you?"

"Usually, yes," Jihei answered. "It's part of the whole evening."

"What else?" Yoshitaro asked.

"We'll have dinner and a drink and then . . . we'll see. . . ."

Yoshitaro frowned slightly but said nothing more.

The meal was the Sawaraya's best fare, Jihei could see as tray after tray of small, beautifully arranged dishes was set before them. Most striking was a miniature ship covered with enticing pieces of fresh sliced sashimi.

"Have a drink, Yoshi. It's White Tiger," Jihei said, laughing.

O-Sada held out a flask.

"I think you're old enough to have more than a taste." Jihei winked at O-Toki.

Yoshitaro's face reddened as he sipped his second cup. Jihei drank steadily as the meal progressed. Tastefully cut melon appeared as the final course.

O-Toki and O-Sada sat attentively as maids cleared away the trays.

Jihei half lay on his side, elbow resting on the tatami.

"Let's stay the night, Yoshi. I'm too relaxed to move," Jihei said.

"Will it be all right at home?" Yoshitaro asked with a slight frown.

"Don't worry, Yoshi. Just relax," Jihei said.

O-Toki took Yoshitaro's arm. "Come. I'll show you to your room," she murmured.

"My room?" Yoshitaro asked. "Don't I stay with my father?"

"He'll be nearby. It's all right," O-Toki said gently.

Yoshitaro looked back at Jihei's prone form as he left the room with O-Toki.

Jihei closed his eyes. He heard the shoji slide open again some time later.

"O-Sada is with him in the next room," O-Toki whispered. "I think she'll stay with him most of the night."

"It's a big step for him," Jihei mumbled. "I'm glad he's here with me, and you."

O-Toki yawned. "*Ah,* what happened about your plan to cut back on your wife's production increase?" She glanced at Jihei.

"Oh, it worked better than I thought. Actually I thought only one kura would go sour, but all three did. The whole cellar was spoiled. Couldn't be helped." He closed his eyes and smiled at the thought of his successful revenge against Rie.

"Oh, I'm sorry." O-Toki put an arm across Jihei's chest.

He embraced O-Toki. "Sake brewing isn't the only thing in life."

Some time during the night Jihei was awakened by sounds coming from the next room. He listened closely, aware that Yoshitaro's initiation had begun.

Before dawn Jihei rolled over and sat up. O-Toki was still asleep next to him. He put a hand on her arm. "O-Toki," he said softly. "Wake Yoshi. We need to get back."

O-Toki sat up, pulled her kimono around her and put on her obi. She shuffled out the door. Jihei could hear her calling, "Excuse me," and Yoshitaro's muffled reply mingled with O-Sada's voice.

Jihei dressed quickly and stepped into the corridor. Yoshitaro emerged, hair disheveled, his face a study in confusion.

"Let's wash quickly and leave, Yoshi. We want to get back before breakfast."

Jihei led the way through the corridor to the washbasins. They splashed cold water over their faces and wet down their hair.

"Why didn't you tell me, Father?" Yoshitaro asked.

"Some things a man learns best by experience, Yoshi."

"I mean why didn't you tell me that Mother is not my real mother, that O-Toki is my mother?" He looked at Jihei accusingly.

Jihei paused, his jaw clenched as he hazarded a fierce glance at O-Toki. He gave her one last look, then adjusted his collar and said, "We'll talk about it on the way home, Yoshi,"

As they stood at the entrance waiting for the ricksha, O-Toki looked at Jihei, then put a hand on Yoshitaro's arm and said softly, "Yes, Yoshi, I am your mother."

Yoshitaro looked at her, and Jihei once again felt a stab of anger at O-Toki when he realized his son was about to cry.

"It's all right, Yoshi," O-Toki said.

O-Sada took out Yoshitaro's sandals and bowed to him. "Please grace our humble house with your presence again," she said without looking up.

"It's like this, Yoshi," Jihei said after they were seated in the swaying ricksha. "I'm also adopted, you know. Your mother's— my wife's—parents adopted me as her husband. So I was selected especially to continue the Omura House and brewing White Tiger. And she and I, her parents and I, adopted you so that you can continue after me. You are my real son."

He was greeted by angry silence.

"And my wife also regards you as her son and treats you as her son. She and I have raised you, so we really are your parents. We care for you and want you to continue the traditions of the house, as she has always told you. Please don't regard her any differently. The experience you had last night is something completely separate. It has nothing to do with the house, or with marriage. It was about individual human emotions."

"But O-Sada said that is where I was born," Yoshitaro insisted.

"Yes, it is true that you were born there. But you are a member of the Omura House, and after I'm gone you will be the most important member of the house. Don't forget that, Yoshi."

Jihei sat back, exhausted from his predawn exertions. They were silent the rest of the way home. Jihei listened to the creaking of the racketing ricksha on the bumpy road.

He alighted at the rear entrance of White Tiger, between the number one and two kura and left Yoshitaro to fend for himself at the main entrance to the corridor between the storage area and the number one kura.

Just as Yoshitaro entered the corridor the door slid open from the storage room and Rie stood frowning at him.

Yoshitaro bowed, his face suddenly flushed. "*Uh* . . . good morning, Mother."

"I see," Rie said, her mouth an angry line. "So the Bunraku performance lasted all night. Well, I hope you enjoyed the performance."

Yoshitaro bowed again, not looking up. "*Uh,* yes, Mother."

"And your father?"

"I believe he's gone to the kura."

"Most likely, yes," Rie replied. The kura was Jihei's usual escape. "Well, I know Kinnosuke has work for you this morning."

Rie turned and reentered the storage room, sliding the shoji shut with a bang. She stood for a moment resting her trembling hands on the table where she had been working. She scowled, and her angry breath came in rapid gasps. This was the way it had always been with men. Now Jihei was training Yoshitaro to follow in his footsteps, spending on geishas time and valuable money earned by the efforts of herself and the kurabito. Jihei always said geisha entertainment was necessary for business negotiations, but business negotiations never produced babies. When her rage subsided she walked rapidly out through the corridor to the barrels in front of the number one kura. She lifted a small barrel of water from the well to place it beside a huge barrel, tied back her sleeves, knelt, and picked up a brush. She tied a scarf over her hair and attacked the barrel with savage energy.

O-Natsu and O-Yuki came to peer out from the main corridor next to the storeroom.

"You can always tell how angry she is by the way she washes the barrels," O-Natsu said in a low voice. "She's furious because Yoshi didn't return last night. He was out with his father."

"Well, what can she do? It was bound to happen sooner or later. Still, she can't be pleased about it. No woman is," O-Yuki said, "except the geishas." She raised an eyebrow and looked at O-Natsu.

"I'm not even sure about them," O-Natsu said.

Rie scrubbed until her hands were raw and chilled, her fury abated. Then, exhausted by emotion and exertion, she went to her room to change clothes and comb her hair.

Later, she decided to speak to the girls in their room before dinner.

"Kazu, Teru," she called and slid open the shoji to their room. Now sixteen and fifteen, the girls were able to read simple stories and do sums. Fumi was elsewhere. Kazu was a bright, active girl, and Teru had already attracted attention with her sultry beauty. When Rie entered the room the girls were lying on their stomachs on the futon giggling, a book in front of them. They turned and sat up simultaneously as Rie entered the room.

"It's nearly dinnertime," Rie began. She glanced at the book. "What is it you're reading? May I see?" She knelt and took the book on her lap.

"Oh, you're reading Saikaku. "*Five Women Who Loved Love*," she read aloud. "Yes, I read it myself just recently. I hope you have understood what Saikaku is telling us? These five women did not know how to behave properly, to control their emotions. They led lives of reckless abandon, and where did it lead them? They ended in tragedy, in disgrace and death by execution or suicide."

She knotted her fist, knowing only too well the consequences if one was not vigilant.

"I've told you often you must be very careful not to meet with any boy alone before you are married. And some of the girls in the stories were no older than you. I hope you'll read all five of these stories carefully and think about them."

If she could not control the nightly exploits of the men in the family, Rie was determined to protect the girls, to give proper guidance until she was able to arrange their marriages.

Chapter 24

One morning Rie walked out to the garden for a breath of fresh air, needing relief from the stifling humidity that always hung over the city just before the monsoon rains broke. Only here could she find solitude and respite from the burdens of business, the luxury of time to reflect. She was pleased that Seisaburo showed signs of real ability when it came to the brewing business, but she needed to turn from thoughts of her youngest son to the eldest. Yoshitaro, heir to the house, had just celebrated his twenty-first birthday and had been visiting the geisha O-Sada more than she deemed necessary. The thought that Jihei had orchestrated their meeting still burned. And she had been doubly annoyed to learn that O-Toki had told their son that he was adopted. She fanned herself, her anger boiling over every time she thought of how it had put a wedge in her relationship with Yoshi these last two years. But be that as it may, the time had come to think of his marriage, and to do more than think of it. She started at the realization that she herself was beyond forty.

For a merchant class family, marriage was a matter of momentous import. The selection of a spouse for the head of the house would inevitably affect the business and welfare of the entire house, beneficially if the selection was made wisely, adversely if adequate care was not taken. Yoshitaro was just one among many things to consider in the plan of arranging the marriage. Choice of a spouse depended on many factors, least among them the emotional preferences of the two individuals. And yet, it had made her parents' relationship much smoother to have some common ground from which to work, unlike with her and Jihei.

Rie fanned herself with her sandalwood fan and watched as her three daughters entered the garden and strolled single file from one end of the garden to the other and back. Their wooden geta struck a rhythm on the stone steps.

It was time to speak to Mrs. Nakano, the ample matron who had negotiated her marriage to Jihei, a woman who delighted in arranging other people's lives.

Rie's thoughts were interrupted by the girls' singing. She glanced at each of them: Fumi, now nearly nineteen and as energetic as herself; Kazu, a tall, willowy eighteen; and Teru, seventeen, with a hint of a geisha's sensuality in her every gesture. Marriage was not so far off for any of them, and Mrs. Nakano's good offices would be required repeatedly over the next few years, for the boys as well as the girls. Rie closed her fan and tapped her knee with it in time to the folk song the girls were singing. Fumi was actually of marriage age already, but Yoshitaro had to be married first.

Rie still smarted at the memory of Jihei taking Yoshi to the Sawaraya. She wished Seisaburo could be spared the experience, but some patterns of male behavior were so deeply ingrained that there was nothing she could do to alter them. She needed to assure that her daughters behaved properly before marriage.

What she must do, no matter what, was to safeguard the interests of the house. This was becoming increasingly difficult to do, what with Jihei's heavy drinking. He was no longer functioning effectively as house head even where formalities were concerned. Rie saw to it that Yoshitaro always accompanied his father whenever a negotiation or meeting was involved. It was simply not safe to leave matters to Jihei alone. Within the house everyone now realized that for all practical purposes Yoshitaro was head of the house.

"What happened at the Brewers Association meeting last evening?" Rie asked Yoshitaro one morning when they were alone. "Did you speak for your father?"

"I did, Mother. It was all right. Father nodded as I spoke. I managed to acquire ten more shares. The Sumidas were willing to sell. They've been having difficulties for some time."

"Good, Yoshi. I'm glad. Now you can see the danger of all that drinking. I know you go to the Sawaraya," she said, fearful that any mention of it would drive a further wedge between them, and yet knowing that he might very well be on the same path as his father if she didn't. "But drinking to excess is ruinous. If it weren't for you we'd be in bad shape now, even with Kinnosuke's management. Appearances are important. People notice. And your father's condition could destroy us, without your efforts. The whole house rests on your shoulders now, Yoshi. This is a heavy responsibility. I'm grateful that you are able to carry on." She smiled at Yoshitaro, who straightened and adjusted the collar of his kimono.

Rie gazed at his face, the face that so vividly reflected his father's, even to the eyebrows. Yoshitaro did not share his father's nervous habit of pulling his eyebrows, a habit that had always given her a vague unease, a sense that Jihei was not quite up to the responsibilities he was being called on to assume. Yoshitaro seemed to take after Kinnosuke's brusque but efficient mannerisms. It was natural enough, since Yoshitaro had been trained not by his father but by Kinnosuke, and by herself.

Rie picked up the teapot and poured for Yoshitaro.

"You know, Yoshi, I don't know how much longer your father can keep up even the appearance of being house head. It's such a worry." She sighed and sipped her tea. "He's really too young to retire, you know. My father was over sixty when he retired, a bit later than usual, to be sure. But your father is only forty-nine. He has a while to go before he can retire respectably. But he may have to retire next year. I know you'll do your best until then, Yoshi. Every public appearance counts where our house's reputation is concerned."

"I know, Mother. I'm aware of it. I'm doing my best to cover for Father at the Brewers Association."

Rie nodded. "Another thing, Yoshi. I was going to talk to you about this before I became so concerned about your father. Now that you're nearly twenty-two and really acting house head, it's time we thought about your marriage. And we need to do more than think about it. I'll speak to Mrs. Nakano soon. You know she arranged my marriage to your father." Rie removed her comb from her hair and reinserted it. She reached for the teapot and poured again for Yoshitaro.

He frowned. "Already, Mother? Can't we wait a year or two?"

His bond with O-Sada must be greater than she'd feared. She must put a stop to it, soon. "Not really, Yoshi. Fumi is almost nineteen, and we can't wait much longer for her either. Your father and I want to see your marriage settled first. It's most important for the house, far more than the girls' marriages."

Yoshitaro pursed his lips and sighed.

"I'm so glad we had this chance to talk, Yoshi. We're both always too busy or we aren't alone. All right, then. Mrs. Nakano will be very circumspect. She'll help us make the best possible choice for you, so you needn't worry."

Yoshitaro put down his cup, rose, and bowed before leaving the room, yet she couldn't help but notice the slightest bit of curtness in his bow.

* * *

Rie put on one of her better kimonos, a formal silk. She must appear properly, if not elegantly attired for her meeting with Mrs. Nakano, who was due to arrive at any minute. Rie hurried down the stairs and instructed O-Yuki to serve tea and the choicest cakes from the Kadatoya as soon as Mrs. Nakano arrived. She glanced into the reception room to make sure that a tasteful vase and ikebana arrangement had been placed in the tokonoma alcove.

Rie trusted that Mrs. Nakano kept in mind all the factors that needed to be considered in the choice of a spouse for a large house like the Omuras, including the presence or absence of contagious or hereditary disease in a family. Only after painstaking investigation by the go-between and due consideration by both families could the go-between arrange the preliminary meeting, the o-miai. After the date was fixed for the meeting, great finesse was needed by the go-between to see that neither party lost face should negotiations not proceed further. To agree to the formal meeting was proof that both sides were serious.

Rie went to the entrance herself to greet Mrs. Nakano. Rie bowed low, crossed hands pressed on her thighs.

"How wonderful to see you again after so long," Rie said. "We are so grateful that you were able to spare time from your busy schedule to visit our humble house."

Both women bowed as Rie ushered her plump visitor into the drawing room and indicated the seat of honor backing against the tokonoma.

"And how is your family, Mrs. Omura?" Mrs. Nakano asked.

"They are all well, thank you, growing faster than I can keep track." Rie laughed, her hand politely over her mouth.

O-Yuki brought in a tray with green tea and small cakes.

"And how old is your eldest son, Yoshitaro, now?" Mrs. Nakano inquired pointedly, her body inclining forward at each utterance.

"He is twenty-two," Rie replied, bowing.

Mrs. Nakano bowed in return. "Then I know you want to consider his marriage."

Rie pushed a lacquer plate with two delicate peach-shaped cakes closer to Mrs. Nakano and bowed even further. "We rely on you." There was no need to be more specific with Mrs. Nakano.

She nodded and put her round white hands to her brocade obi as if to adjust it, though no adjustment was necessary. "Of course your house will want a bride from one of the best families in Kobe. You know the Sawada family, I'm sure. The eldest daughter is fortunately just now of marriage age, and so beautiful. She is nineteen."

"Yes, I have seen her," Rie replied. "But her house does not brew, do they? Aren't they rice wholesalers?" She smiled and dipped her head slightly. It would not do to appear too forceful in rejecting a suggestion from Mrs. Nakano.

"Yes, that is true," Mrs. Nakano replied. "But that would also be useful for your business, to have a marriage connection with a rice dealer, wouldn't it?" Mrs. Nakano picked up her cup and sipped delicately.

"For the eldest son of the main house we really need a bride who knows brewing, who was raised in a brewing house, who can care for the live-in workers during brewing. That is the first requirement for our eldest son's bride." Rie gestured again toward the peach-shaped cakes on Mrs. Nakano's plate.

"*Ah*, I see." Mrs. Nakano paused to cut a minute sliver of cake with a small ivory pick. "Well, I wasn't going to mention it, but you know the Tamiya family, the Nishinomiya brewer. Their daughter Tama is also of the right age. But I'm afraid she is not as beautiful as the Sawada daughter." Mrs. Nakano bowed and looked at the untouched slice of cake.

Rie stiffened. "What about ability? Is she capable?"

"They say both she and her brother are very bright, very well raised. She is older than her brother, so I believe they wish to see her settled first. I feel confident that they would be happy to have a marriage alliance with your house."

"You say her name is Tama? And her age?"

"She is just three years younger than Yoshitaro."

"Tama. Let us hope she turns out to be a real jewel for our house," she added under her breath. "It is possible, yes, that she may be a suitable bride for our house. Please begin the inquiry. I'll inform my husband and Yoshitaro. If your investigation proves positive, and the Tamiyas agree, we can have the o-miai soon. And if she appears suitable, I would like an autumn wedding. But I am being too hasty. We must wait for your report and see if the Tamiyas are willing." She smiled politely.

Mrs. Nakano bowed. "Rest assured that I will do my best." She paused to admire the arrangement in the tokonoma behind her. "And I am gratified to see your house doing so well since your own marriage, now so many years ago."

Rie bowed. "Thanks to you," she said, careful to hide her true feelings about Jihei behind a mask of politeness. She showed Mrs. Nakano to the door. "We are so grateful to you for your help over the years."

After dinner that evening Rie sat with Jihei and Yoshitaro at a small table while the other children sat at a table nearby. Jihei was drinking and Yoshitaro also had a sake cup but drank sparingly, Rie was relieved to see. She cleared her throat and adjusted her comb.

"You know, Yoshi, as I mentioned earlier, we can't postpone your marriage any longer. Mrs. Nakano came this afternoon with a very suitable suggestion. The Tamiya house, you know, the Nishinomiya brewers? Their daughter is the right age. She also mentioned the Sawada daughter, but you know they don't brew."

Yoshitaro brightened. "The Sawada daughter! A real beauty.

And I've also seen the Tamiya daughter. Nothing to look at." He wrinkled his nose. "I prefer the Sawada daughter."

Rie took her fan from her obi and turned to face Yoshitaro. "As you know, Yoshi, where the house and succession are concerned, family and economic considerations are uppermost. The Sawada family are not brewers, the Tamiyas are. Your bride must come from a brewing house." She looked at Jihei, who pulled at his eyebrows and looked at Rie, then back at Yoshitaro.

Jihei cleared his throat. "Yes, Yoshi. As I've told you, individual preferences are a private matter. They aren't concerned with marriage. I believe the Tamiya daughter would be a good match for us. A good house." He glanced at Rie again.

"What's her name?" Yoshitaro asked, frowning.

Rie's tone became more conciliatory. "It's Tama, 'jewel.' She's three years younger than you, just right. So we'll ask Mrs. Nakano to go ahead with arrangements for the o-miai meeting. Then if they agree we can set the wedding date four months from now. That will give us time to make all the arrangements for a fall wedding. It will be quite a big affair."

Yoshitaro sighed and rested his chin on a hand.

"You understand, don't you, Yoshi?" Rie asked.

"I guess so," Yoshitaro mumbled, looking down, his lips pressed together.

"It's best, Yoshi," Jihei said, downing a cup of sake. "And it's not as if you were going out as a mukoyoshi. You'll be here in your own house."

Yoshitaro looked at his father, a mukoyoshi.

The afternoon chosen for the o-miai arrived. The two families met in a private room in one of Kobe's best establishments. Carved cryptomeria cranes marched along the tops of gilt screens that enclosed the room. The famous two-hundred-year-old garden was revealed beyond the open shutters. Stone steps led along a pathway to a curved bridge over a koi pond and beyond, to banks of green shrubbery so that the eye never encountered a barrier.

Ranged on one side of the lacquer table were Mr. and Mrs. Tamiya and Tama, on the other side, Jihei, Rie, and Yoshitaro, with Mr. and Mrs. Nakano at one end of the table facing the garden. Although the two families were acquainted, the importance of the occasion lent it an ambience of formality and restraint.

Yoshitaro sat stiffly, looking straight ahead and bowing as he replied briefly to Mr. and Mrs. Tamiya's questions.

"And how many years have you been helping your father in the business?" Mr. Tamiya asked.

"Nearly sixteen years," Yoshitaro replied.

"*Ah,* is that so? So long, and you are so young," Mrs. Tamiya breathed.

Jihei smoothed his eyebrows. "He has been helping me since he was a small boy of five, even earlier," he said. "He has a natural aptitude for it."

Rie saw Yoshitaro steal a glance at Tama, who was modestly looking down at the table. She did not raise her eyes to look at Yoshitaro, Rie noticed. Remarkable self-control, such a valuable asset, and it reflected good breeding. She appeared healthy, if not robust. *Good working and child-bearing material,* Rie thought.

"And I understand that Tama knows the abacus and has helped in the office," Rie remarked, smiling and bowing.

Tama bowed but did not look up or speak.

"Yes, she is better at the abacus than I am." Mrs. Tamiya put her hand over her mouth and giggled politely, bowing.

Rie's gaze shifted to Tama's mother, often a portent of a daughter's older age. Mrs. Tamiya appeared in good health and had an appealing calmness of manner, verging on refinement.

The sipping of tea was an incidental but necessary part of the occasion, which ended with more formal bows and glances of mutual appreciation by Rie and Mrs. Tamiya.

Mrs. Nakano tactfully brought the meeting to an end. "We are both so happy that you were able to meet on this occasion." She did not mention any commitment on either side.

Rie wanted to proceed as soon as possible. "It's very apparent that Tama has had good training," she said that evening as she sat with Jihei and Yoshitaro at dinner.

"A good brewing house," Jihei said. "I see no objection."

Yoshitaro frowned. "Such a flat face and large mouth."

Rie impatiently replaced her comb. "Let's agree on the Tamiya daughter. We can't decide on a superficial basis in a matter so vital to the house, Yoshi. Your father and I have explained all this to you. Please try to understand."

"Your personal preferences are a private matter, Yoshi," Jihei said. "Where human feelings are concerned you can do as I do." Jihei spilled sake on the table as he reached to pour for his son.

Rie had the urge to slap her husband's face.

"Even her name is propitious: Tama, 'jewel.'" Rie said, attempting to recover her dignity. "I expect to hear from Mrs. Nakano in a few days."

But she could see the glint of fire in Yoshi's eyes and knew that the matter was far from settled in his mind.

Chapter 25

Rie reeled from the news that had just now reached her ears, but which must have been buzzing through the geisha houses for these last two years. How could she have been so blind, she wondered as she went in search of Jihei?

"I must speak with you. Now!" Rie commanded when she caught him in the chilly corridor outside the inner office. "Come to the reception room."

Rie turned abruptly and stalked to the door of the parlor. In a single movement she slid open the door and slipped off her slippers. She hurried into the room and pulled out a zabuton in front of the Butsudan for herself, then slapped a second cushion onto the tatami opposite her. Jihei stumbled into the room after her and slumped onto the zabuton. He glanced uneasily at Rie's frowning face.

She took out her hairpin and began to twirl it rapidly in both hands on her lap.

"Now I know your true colors at last," she snapped. She leaned forward. "I understand that it was you who ruined our sake. It has become the talk of the geisha houses, I hear." Rie's words split the air in staccato syllables. "What were you thinking, trying to ruin our house? It wasn't enough that you were drinking yourself into idiocy." She breathed rapidly and tried to loosen her obi.

Jihei gasped and reddened, swaying on his zabuton. "But . . . I. . . ."

"You are no longer head of the house. You have brought us dishonor and disgrace, nearly caused our financial ruin. As of now Yoshitaro is head of the house. I do not wish to see you in the house again. Get out!" She spat out the icy words in controlled cadences, then turned to face the Butsudan.

Jihei gasped and blinked, staggered to his feet, and wove back and forth to the door. He slid the shoji open with a bang and stumbled along the corridor, bumping the walls on either side as he headed out the door next to the number one kura.

Rie leaned over and covered her face with her hands. Her breath came in racking sobs, and she reached into her obi for a handkerchief and wiped the tears from her face. She heard Jihei slam the outer door shut. She rose, straightened her obi, and went back into the corridor toward the stairway.

O-Natsu stood at the other end of the hallway wringing her hands. "Can I do anything?" she asked in a hushed voice.

"No, O-Natsu. I am going upstairs. I don't wish to be disturbed. Oh, yes, please see to the children's dinner."

She stomped rapidly up the stairs to her room, went to the window, and sat looking down into the garden. How could she save the house from this unprecedented disaster?

Stunned and desperate, Jihei stumbled along the road in the dark. It was unheard of. How could Rie evict him from his own home? He was still house head. She had no power, no authority. He could not go to the Sawaraya now. O-Toki must have been talking to someone about what he had told her, about the sake souring. Not like her to reveal a confidence. But she must have told someone, maybe O-Haru. O-Haru was a gossip. Where to turn? He paused, swaying in the gloom of the street. His eye caught a red lantern down by the bridge, and he began to stumble toward it. He could get a drink there. They would know him, though it was not a place he frequented. Everyone in this part of Nada knew him. Where was he to go? His mouth felt so dry. He pushed toward the lantern, then bent to duck under the noren and opened the squeaking sliding door.

"Please come in!" came a thin high voice.

Jihei saw a serving girl behind the low counter. She wore a rough kimono and had round red cheeks and was clearly far below the status of geisha.

Jihei didn't hazard her another glance. He slumped down on a stool at the single counter. "Sake!" he grunted.

"Yes." She nodded and turned to get a heated flask and single cup.

"Hurry!" he growled.

"Yes, sir." The girl turned and placed the flask and cup in front of Jihei. She poured quickly before Jihei had a chance to pick up the cup properly. He emptied the cup and poured himself another. Then another. He glanced around furtively and saw that he was the only customer. When the flask was empty he mumbled, "More!"

The girl removed the empty bottle and placed a full one in front of Jihei, pouring the first cup for him. He continued to drink. What could he do? Surely Rie could not have been serious. She had no right, no authority. He was head of the house. He began to nod and sway on the stool. His eyes closed.

"Sorry, sir," came the girl's voice after he had emptied several flasks. "We are closing now. You will have to leave."

Jihei's head had sagged to his chest.

She prodded Jihei on the shoulder. "We are closed now," she said insistently. "Please leave."

"Oh," Jihei groaned. He tried to stand but instead fell off the stool. He reached for the counter to raise himself but slumped back onto the floor. The girl bent to help him up. Jihei leaned against her and reached for her breasts. She brushed his hand off, opened the door, and pushed him out, quickly sliding the door shut behind him.

Jihei lurched into the street and slammed against the rough wooden wall. He gripped his stomach, leaned over, and retched. He wiped his mouth with his kimono sleeve and took a few halting steps away from the wall. He fell and sat immobile, his head down. Then he moved his hands along the ground trying to rise. How could his wife do this to him? And she had never been a real wife, not like O-Toki. But how could he go to O-Toki now? He thrust himself onto all fours and reached for a lamppost to try to stand. He began to shuffle along the road toward the bridge, halting and swaying every few steps, groaning with each breath. He retched again, and stumbled further. As he arrived at one end of the bridge he reached toward the railing for support. He slipped in the mud, missed the railing, and slid down the steep muddy embankment. His arms flailed frantically as he splashed into the black river below and disappeared.

Chapter 26

Rie came to breakfast with her children the next morning. She said little beyond "Good morning, Yoshi."

Before breakfast was finished, Kinnosuke rushed into the dining room out of breath. "Oku-san!" He glanced at Yoshitaro. "Master has been found in the river. He drowned in the night." He gasped in quick sharp breaths and bowed.

Rie glared at Kinnosuke and placed both hands on the table, even as her heart raced. Could he not have told her privately first? She closed her eyes for a moment, her tirade from last night so fresh in her mind. What had she done? "I see." She pushed up from the table. "Come, Yoshi, to the office." She walked purposefully down the corridor followed by Yoshitaro and Kinnosuke. The girls who had been sitting at the table began to weep loudly as Rie made her way to the office.

Rie sat at the table and motioned Yoshitaro and Kinnosuke to join her.

"Just as we've formalized arrangements for your wedding, your father. . . ." She put her hand to her forehead. There was no need to tell the children that she had sent Jihei away or that he was responsible for the sake failure two years earlier. O-Natsu knew, but she would keep quiet.

"What do we do now?" Yoshitaro asked, biting his lip, sorrow written in the lines of his face.

"Of course you succeed now automatically. And you and Kinno need to make the funeral arrangements."

"Why did you push him so hard?" Yoshi looked at Rie accusingly. "That's what drove him to drink as he did. He didn't see any role for himself here, with you making the decisions all along. He felt frustrated. That's why he drank so much, and it only got worse."

Rie glared at Yoshi. "Are you accusing me of being responsible for what he did, Yoshi?"

"I see a connection."

Rie felt her anger rising out of control. "It was your father who caused our sake to sour. He ruined it deliberately! He was destroying our house." She instantly deflated. She hadn't meant to tell him, to hurt him further.

Yoshi stood up, hands on his hips. "I don't believe you. He couldn't have done that." He left the room abruptly.

Rie let out a deep, sobering breath.

That evening Jihei's body lay on the futon in the parlor. The shutters had been closed and the smell of stale sake and death pervaded the room.

Rie paused at the doorway and looked at the lifeless form of the man by whom she had had a child. She arranged zabuton around the futon, and the family seated themselves for the wake. She turned to Yoshitaro next to her.

"It can't be helped, Yoshi," she said softly. "We'll have to postpone the wedding until the year of mourning is over. If only he had not drunk so heavily. All the weddings will be delayed a year." She paused and looked at Yoshitaro.

He nodded, but it was a brusque nod filled with silent anger and accusation.

Silence enveloped the family. Lamplight flickered against the shoji. Kazu, Teru, and Fumi dabbed at tear-filled eyes.

"Sei, go to bed," Rie said, her hand gentle on his shoulder.

Seisaburo stumbled to his feet. He was about to open the shoji when another hand did so from outside.

Kinnosuke knelt at the edge of the tatami and bowed toward Rie and Yoshitaro.

Rie nodded to him and motioned for him to sit opposite her. She looked over at Kinnosuke and bowed slightly to the man she had trained since childhood, a man now so vital to the house and totally dedicated to Yoshitaro. She sighed and looked back at Jihei's corpse. Fumi leaned against Rie, who put an arm around her daughter. Strange that she felt so little for this man she had sent away; mainly relief. No, perhaps not so strange. Hatred had been the real bond between them. And yet she knew that hatred had now created a rift between herself and Yoshi, one she must find a way to overcome.

Early the next morning Rie went down to the kitchen and looked out over the vaulted rooftops. The first light of dawn was just yellowing the sky. Alone in the kitchen, she lit a fire to heat water for tea. O-Natsu and O-Yuki would be in soon. She turned and walked slowly out into the garden. Nothing stirred. No sound was audible. She sat on her favorite rock and rubbed the back of her neck and shoulders. She realized that she had sat at Jihei's deathbed without shedding a single tear. Now her shoulders began to shake and she began sobbing as she released her anguish. Not for the loss of Jihei, for whom she had trouble concealing her distaste. His drinking was just the most obvious of his weaknesses. What she felt was rather a poignant sense that so much of her own life had passed, and relief that he would no longer embarrass or dishonor the house. And finally, sadness for the breach in her relationship with Yoshi. She walked back into the house, paused at the pillar and moved her hands over it thoughtfully.

The children and the business, the house, were still her reason for being. She must find a way to mend her fences with Yoshi. With a last shuddering sigh she walked into the office to ask that a notice be posted over the entrance announcing the funeral.

Rie sat next to Yoshitaro at the head of two long lines of black-kimonoed brewers and their wives. Three Buddhist priests intoned their deep monotonous mantras, rising and falling in sonorous unison. Incense hung heavy in the air and lamps flickered against the shoji and glanced off the elaborate gilt Butsudan. Rie sat absolutely upright looking straight ahead, her face impassive. Out of the corner of her eye she saw that Yoshitaro sat equally immobile at her side and that none of the other four children ranged below him was shedding a tear. Rie felt a sense of family pride as she surreptitiously eyed the five children she had raised so carefully. Her marriage had not been a total loss. It had enabled her to add these five children to the house.

Then a reassuring thought came to her. Now it would never become known that she had banished Jihei from the Omura House, something she really had no authority to do, but Jihei had been too drunk to argue. A huge scandal would have erupted if the news had leaked out. She took a deep breath and pressed her lips together, a twinge of guilt accompanying the relief she felt. If Jihei had not died as he had, that one moment of anger could have very well cost them everything her father had worked his whole lifetime to achieve. She shivered at the thought.

Rie watched with pride as Yoshitaro stood and spoke briefly, thanking all for attending his father's funeral and asking formally for the cooperation of the brewers as he assumed the headship of the Omura House and of White Tiger.

After sake was served, Yoshitaro moved toward the entrance

to greet each departing mourner. He overheard Yamaguchi and another speaking as they shuffled toward the door.

"What difference will it make if Yoshitaro is in charge instead of Jihei, anyway?" Yamaguchi said gruffly. "Kinnosuke is far more powerful than Jihei was or his son could ever be."

Yoshitaro did not catch the other guest's reply, but he felt a smoldering anger, nonetheless. As he reached the door Yoshitaro was conscious that his mother was at his side, bowing and joining her words to his as each brewer passed through the door. He knew she was trying to win him over, but he also knew he wasn't ready to make peace. Too much had happened between them.

Later that evening as the family sat together Rie turned to Yoshitaro. She raised a sake flask for him as he held out his cup. Then she picked up a cup, raised it, and toasted him saying, "Now, Yoshi, this is your time." She said no more but rose and went upstairs alone.

Fumi, sobbing, jumped up and ran after her.

Yoshitaro looked around at his glum brother and two weeping sisters. He thought of the comment by the departing Yamaguchi and once again felt the smoldering anger. Of course his mother and Kinnosuke made the decisions. It was natural enough since she had been born in the house. It was moreover necessary, especially since his father had taken to drinking so heavily. What he knew about brewing he had learned from his mother and Kinnosuke. He shifted uneasily in his seat as he remembered his postponed wedding and the bride his parents had selected for him, Tama. Well versed she might be in brewing and even intelligent enough, but Yoshitaro found her flat face plain and unappealing. His affections belonged to O-Sada.

He rose and addressed his siblings, his first act as official house head. "You'd better go to bed. It's been a long, difficult day."

He walked along the corridor, then out through the door next to the number one kura. He hailed a passing ricksha and said abruptly as he climbed in, "The Sawaraya."

At the entrance it was O-Toki herself who greeted Yoshitaro.

"Ah, it is you, my son!" she exclaimed, bowing. "You must be worn out. O-Sada is here. She thought you might come. She will join you in a bit."

O-Toki led the way upstairs to the back room, the one always reserved for his father, Yoshitaro noted.

O-Toki bowed. "Please be seated. I'll be back presently."

Moments later Yoshitaro heard O-Toki's voice again and looked at her more closely as she entered. His natural mother. She knelt, bowed, and poured ceremonial green tea.

Yoshitaro bowed and raised the cup to his lips: "I did not see you at the funeral," he said.

"I was there, in the back room. I could not stay away." She paused and blotted her glistening eyes. "Your father was the most important person in the world to me. He was good to me. He would be so proud of you, to see the way you are taking hold. You will be an illustrious Kinzaemon XI." She bowed again, then moved back to the shoji.

Yoshitaro bowed in acknowledgment of his mother's words—words that contradicted what Yamaguchi had said.

O-Toki rose. "Now I know you will want to spend some time with O-Sada. She will be here shortly." She bowed herself out of the room.

His mother. His *mothers*.

I really have two mothers, my natural mother here in the Sawaraya and Rie, virtual head of one of the most powerful houses in all Kobe. One dedicated to business, the other to pleasure. Many would consider it fortunate, but tonight he felt only pain. Still, he could move with ease between the two worlds, more easily even than his father. A lump formed in his throat. His father had never felt at home in the Omura House. He'd always moved in Mother's shadow. He was far more at ease here at the Sawaraya, but that in the end was his downfall. He lost himself, killed by the very sake they brewed. It was a fate he had no wish to share. Now, he had no choice but to marry Tama, but O-Sada would be his real life partner, just as O-Toki had been his father's. From this day forward, for the rest of his life, he would never take another drink. He would only pretend to drink ceremonial sake.

I will not share my father's fate.

Yoshitaro's musing was interrupted by O-Sada, who entered with a tray of sake and two cups. She bowed and smiled sympathetically before pouring a cup for him.

"You have had a most arduous day. I hope you will be able to relax now. Perhaps a hot bath will help."

Yoshitaro nodded and looked at the beautiful, intelligent face of the woman he had grown to love. He rose and followed O-Sada's swaying figure down to the steaming bath.

Several days later, as Yoshi sat at his desk in the office, Kinnosuke turned to him.

"Master, we need the seal to affix to this document," he said as he put the finishing touches on the paper.

"I'll get it. I think Mother has it." Yoshi walked to the storeroom where Rie was working.

"Mother, we need the seal in the office for the document Kinno is working on."

"Yes, Yoshi, I'm coming. I will affix it."

Yoshi frowned as they walked to the office. "But I'm house head now. I need the seal for official business."

"I have made final decisions since my father died, and I will continue to do so."

"But. . . ." Yoshi shook his head and clenched his hands.

"This is the way it is, Yoshi."

Chapter 27

"Come in, O-Natsu. Join me in a cup of tea?"
Rie called when she heard O-Natsu's voice beyond the shoji.

O-Natsu bowed as she entered, smiled, and seated herself opposite Rie. She poured for Rie, then for herself. It had been a year of many changes, least of which was the one Rie'd seen in Yoshi since his father's death. The seal had been a sore point, and he had not failed to let her know it each time a document needed to be signed. She had tolerated his anger, even understood it, but for the sake of the house, she knew she must maintain control. Yoshi didn't have the business acumen necessary to run an operation the size of theirs, and until he did, she could not trust him with it.

"You know, O-Natsu," Rie said, "we two are the only ones who have been in the house this long. Over forty years."

O-Natsu laughed. "Yes, that's so, isn't it?"

"And now that the year of mourning is approaching the end, I want to see Yoshi married as soon as possible. It is unfortunate that it had to be postponed so long, all the marriages." She took her folding fan from her obi and fanned herself slowly.

O-Natsu smiled again. "It will be good to have some activity in the house again. The year has been quiet, hasn't it? Of course we all needed time to mourn the master."

For several minutes the only sound to break the silence between them was the sipping of tea. Conversation was unnecessary to their companionship. Especially false conversation.

At length O-Natsu set her cup down and broke the silence. "Yes, didn't you have some discussion with Mrs. Nakano about the girls as well before the master passed away?"

"Oh, yes, she has them in mind. There will be offers, I am sure, soon after Yoshi's wedding, no doubt." Rie looked at her cup thoughtfully. "Then there will be Fumi, then Kazu and Teru. And of course, finally Sei."

Rie pulled a delicate long-stemmed pipe from her sleeve, filled it from a small pouch in her obi, and lit it, a prerogative of her age and status. Tobacco had entered the country through the Dutch enclave on Deshima Island, and smoking small pipes had caught on with older women as well as men.

O-Natsu, as though sensing Rie's relaxed mood, also took out her pipe.

Rie nodded. After three short puffs she turned her pipe over on a small raku ware ashtray. "It's important that Yoshi's wife be from a good brewing house." She smiled and nodded.

O-Natsu also tapped her pipe and set it on the ashtray. "I know you have special plans for Fumi and Sei."

"I don't want to overwhelm her with too many marriage arrangements all at once. But I have a plan for Fumi. Sei too. Actually I have something special in mind for Teru as well."

O-Natsu refilled her pipe, then waited for Rie to speak.

"I'll ask Mrs. Nakano to contact the Tamiyas and set the date for the wedding for two weeks after the end of the year of mourning. No need to postpone it longer." She paused to pour tea for O-Natsu and herself. "I'm going to let Yoshi and Tama have the upstairs room. My parents did that for me when I was married, remember? I'll be glad to be back in my old room, close to the garden. It's the first thing I see when I get up in the morning."

"I know," O-Natsu nodded. "Well, I imagine the Tamiyas will be glad to see the wedding over too. The delay can't have been comfortable for them either."

The wedding day was fixed after consulting the calendar, avoiding the unlucky days and selecting one of the most auspicious.

"I've always felt April was the best month for a wedding, especially for a brewing house, at the end of the season. We can turn our whole attention to the occasion," Rie said to her children gathered for an early breakfast on the appointed day. "The cherry blossoms have just come out. Very auspicious for a wedding. Let's all get dressed now. Girls, help each other with your obis."

"I never can get mine right, Mother," said Fumi.

"Kazu will help you. Just be glad you're not the bride, Fumi. It will take two hours to get her dressed," Rie said, patting Fumi on the back.

Fumi wrinkled her nose and walked with an exaggerated swaying after her sisters.

Rickshas were lined up at the main gate waiting to take the family to the Shinto shrine.

Rie stood with O-Natsu as the children emerged for the ride to the shrine. Yoshitaro came first, walking stiffly in his formal black kimono.

"Doesn't he look distinguished!" O-Natsu said loudly enough for the ricksha pullers to hear.

Yoshitaro stepped up into the first ricksha with Rie, who was dressed in the formal black worn by wives and widows alike. To Rie's disappointment, he carefully avoided her eyes. She knew in the long run that this was the right thing and he would thank her later, but she felt an unease recalling his adamant opposition to the thought of marrying Tama, whom he found so unattractive. Rie disliked the idea of imposing an unhappy marriage, perhaps similar to her own. Yet she felt Tama would add strength to the house. That had to take precedence.

Kazu and Teru looked fashionably elegant in their apricot and sea green kimonos. Even Fumi managed to look beautiful in a light blue kimono with a crane pattern at the hem and a beige under kimono and obi. The girls needed to appear at their best to any prospective groom's family. Seisaburo also looked formal as he stepped into the third ricksha.

"Kinno-san and O-Natsu, please take the fourth ricksha," Rie said, and smiled as the runners pulled out into the street.

During the Shinto ceremony Rie scrutinized Tama and found she looked the perfect bride: white silk kimono and brocade obi, face and neck completely whitened, her hair and "devils' horns" covered with the traditional white silk band. No fault could Rie find with Tama's mincing steps, her downcast eyes, her measured bows to each guest present. Even though Tama was not the most beautiful woman, Rie found her more than acceptable. She watched every move as Yoshitaro and Tama exchanged sips from the shallow red lacquer cup. Despite his mixed feelings, Yoshitaro played his role well.

Rie was pleased that every brewer invited appeared for the reception, an assemblage as large as for Jihei's funeral. Yoshitaro's wedding was also a celebration of his status as Kinzaemon XI of the House of Omura. The glittering occasion was proof of the prosperity and reputation of White Tiger and one of the largest affairs of the year 1852. It was now up to Yoshi to adjust to this bride about whom he was less than enthusiastic.

Rie had no firsthand familiarity with the experience of a bride going into a groom's house, no acquaintance with the traditional terrorizing of a bride by a mother-in-law or critical scrutiny by a groom's sisters. Marriage, the abrupt beginning of the most intimate possible relationship, was a harsh test of the mettle of any bride. Rie had been spared what Tama faced: the severity of having to marry into a whole house full of strangers. She did share with Tama what all brides faced: marriage to a total stranger.

What Rie knew above all was that she was responsible for initiating this young bride into the traditions of the Omura House and her role in the White Tiger enterprise. The fact that the house and the business were inextricably linked was why Rie had insisted that Yoshitaro's bride be from a brewing house. Rie did not intend any deviation from the custom that the bride should be the first to rise in the morning and the last to retire at night, the last in the family to enter the bath and the last to eat at the table. For a bride, eating cold rice was an adage that reflected harsh reality.

The morning following the wedding Rie opened the shutters facing the garden and glanced up toward the room she had given Yoshitaro and his bride. The sun had not yet reached the second floor shutters. Just then Rie saw a feminine hand open the wooden shutters and withdraw. Then Rie heard slippers slap quickly down the stairs and head toward the kitchen.

When Rie entered the kitchen, Tama, in a work kimono with sleeves tied back, bowed to the floor three times.

"Oh," said Rie, surprised at Tama's alacrity.

"Please accept my humble efforts to learn and conform to the traditions of the Omura House," Tama said breathlessly.

"Yes, good morning, Tama," Rie replied, nodding.

"I am eager to learn. I shall do my best," Tama repeated.

"Yes, Tama." Rie nodded. "You may help O-Natsu and O-Yuki with breakfast. Please begin by preparing the rice this morning."

Tama bowed again and rose. She took a deep breath and straightened the cotton scarf covering her hair. She turned toward the big rice cauldron.

O-Natsu and O-Yuki exchanged glances without speaking.

It was no small task Rie had given Tama. To be able to cook rice to the exact fluffy palatable consistency was the first test of any woman, a requirement that, if unfulfilled, could send a bride away in disgrace. The proportion of water to rice had to be precise. The word *rice* was synonymous with the word for "meal" or "dinner." All rice served was to be consumed to the last grain. To waste rice was unconscionable. Moreover, rice was sacred, of the gods. In addition, in the Omura household rice was the critical source of the family's livelihood, the raw material of White Tiger.

Rie joined Yoshitaro and his siblings, who were gathered at the dining table for breakfast. She looked expectantly toward the kitchen. Tama entered bearing a tray with a large wooden Kamakura serving bowl. She knelt at the table and bowed toward Rie, who handed Tama the wooden serving paddle symbolic of the status of wife of the house head. Tama held the paddle with both hands above her head and bowed again. Then, lifting the lid of the serving bowl she took the wooden ladle, filled the first bowl, set it on a tray and, hands trembling, held it out toward Rie. The five brothers and sisters all fixed their eyes on their mother's face. Tension enveloped the room.

With her chopsticks Rie brought a few grains to her mouth, then paused.

"Well, Tama, perhaps just a bit less water."

Rie was instantly sorry at the slight, but it was a necessary one, of course.

Kazu and Teru looked down quickly.

Tama bowed again, biting her lip. "Oh, I have no adequate words of apology," she said.

"You may serve the others now, Tama," Rie replied.

O-Natsu and O-Yuki brought in the pickled plums, miso soup, and tea.

"When you are finished serving breakfast, Tama, you may come to the parlor."

Tama bowed. "Certainly."

Tama filled each rice bowl, placed it on a tray and handed it to a family member, first Yoshitaro, then his brother, then his sisters in order of age. This task finished, she hurried to the kitchen for a hastily eaten bowl of rice with pickles.

Rie finished her breakfast and went to sit before the Butsudan to wait for Tama.

Rie had heard enough stories from O-Natsu about cruel mothers-in-law intimidating frightened, helpless brides, making of them abject slaves. Intelligence was a quality Rie valued, and when she found it in Tama she decided it could be used for the welfare of the house, to foster a daughter-in-law who would work hard and willingly. This same quality Rie had discovered in the small boy who was now her chief clerk, Kinnosuke. Tama would be an ally in her plans for the future of the house, as dedicated to the reputation of White Tiger as she herself. Yoshitaro was O-Toki's son, as Rie had never forgotten and Yoshi had made clearer over the last few years, and while Tama was now his wife, Rie hoped to forge with her a close bond. Tama, on the other hand, had no connection with the Sawaraya. Therefore she was a potential ally. Rie would let Tama know now that while Yoshitaro was formally house head, the representative of White Tiger to the world, in reality it was she, Rie, who had the final word in all important decisions. This was how it was with everything, wasn't it, the *tatemae* appearance and the *honne* reality? A perceptive woman like Tama was certain to recognize the difference.

Rie heard footsteps along the corridor, a pause, then Tama's voice excusing herself as she opened the shoji, bowed properly, and entered the room kneeling.

"Come here, Tama, to the Butsudan."

Tama did as bidden.

Rie turned to face her. "You know that your position as wife of the house head is a most important one," she began, with a nod to acknowledge Tama's bow. "You were selected with utmost care for this role. You are aware, I am sure, that you will be first in the family to rise in the morning and last to retire?"

Tama bowed again, but did not speak, eyes downcast.

"As a person entering the house from outside, you will need to learn the customs of our house as rapidly as possible. I will teach you what you need to know."

"I am unworthy of such an honor, but I will make every effort to justify your faith in me."

"First, please direct your attention to the Butsudan."

Tama bowed toward the altar.

"Here you see the tablets of my mother and father. I offer rice and sake to them each morning, also the plum wine which my mother enjoyed. If I am too busy you will assume this duty, and eventually it will be yours alone. And you will also learn about observing their death anniversaries as the time arises." Rie paused and glanced from the Butsudan to Tama.

"Now, to start with, you need not spend too much time with your husband." Rie knew this might only alienate Yoshi, but duty came first. It was a fact that Yoshi would have to learn.

Tama did not respond, but Rie thought she noticed a slight tightening of Tama's mouth.

"You know the work of the wife of the house head is never finished," Rie continued, "so you must be ever vigilant and alert to any possible problem in the house."

"Most certainly," Tama replied, always ending each statement with a corresponding bow.

"You must take charge, for example, of the scouring of the barrels," Rie said, tapping her folded fan on her lap. "The girls all know how to do this—Fumi, Kazu, Teru. But the responsibility is now yours to see that this critical task is always done thoroughly.

The girls will be going out as brides before long, and it is only proper that you see to this matter."

Rie rose. "The workers are your primary responsibility, both the kitchen workers and the kurabito. You need to see that they are well fed and clothed and cared for when they are ill. Without them we could not maintain the reputation of White Tiger. When the kurabito are content, as they are now, they will continue to come back to us year after year."

Tama bowed. "That is what my mother always said also."

Rie looked at Tama and nodded.

"We can go to the kitchen now. You have already met O-Natsu. She is in a special category, like a family member because she has been here so long. You will meet the kitchen helpers."

Rie led the way along the earthen corridor to the kitchen where two maids were scrubbing vegetables. Here are Michi and Shizu."

Tama bowed slightly to acknowledge the two bowing girls.

"They are the main workers in the kitchen. They prepare the food for the family as well as for the kurabito. You will see that the rice is always properly prepared."

Rie saw a flush rising from Tama's neck to her face. In the corridor they met O-Yuki vigorously flourishing a feather duster.

"And O-Yuki keeps our rooms clean." Rie smiled and turned along the corridor toward the storeroom. "Come, Tama, while the men are gone, I want to show you the kurabito quarters, though of course in the future you cannot go in there, since they are men."

Rie climbed the long steep ladder leading from the storeroom to the large tatami room above, a room lined on two sides by built-in cupboards.

"You will get to know our Toji. He has been here several decades, his father and grandfather before him. He is getting on in years now and is training his son to succeed him. He takes great pride in maintaining the quality of White Tiger."

Tama bowed toward Rie. "Such an honorable tradition, my father always said."

"Yes, let's go down now. Be careful." Rie continued her instruction as they descended the wooden ladder slowly.

"Be sure their clothing is clean at all times and that they are in good health. We have nineteen men here now. You will get to know their names and faces. Here is where they have their meals." Rie pointed to a tatami room off the storeroom. "And I have started to teach some of them to read in the evening, when there is time. You may want to take this over later."

Rie noticed a faint smile on Tama's face.

"Come, we will return to the parlor. You may ask O-Natsu to bring us tea," Rie said.

Rie and Tama sat at the low table in the parlor where the instruction had begun.

"So you see what your main responsibilities are, don't you, Tama?"

Tama bowed.

Rie replaced the comb in her hair.

"I am told you are a good worker. You will need to be. It is no small responsibility, being the wife of the head of the Omura House. I was born here, unlike you, so I was raised with our customs. But you need to learn them all. You can always come to me. I will guide you in the proper course."

"I will do my utmost for the house," Tama replied, bowing so that her forehead reached the tatami.

Rie smiled with satisfaction as she glanced at her bowing daughter-in-law. Then she paused, because she knew that Tama, as Yoshi's wife, meant trouble. For Rie was quite certain she hadn't heard the last out of Yoshi about Tama and the marriage.

Chapter 28

"I have no intention of allowing any of the girls to marry a farmer, which is what the kurabito are most of the year," Rie said to Yoshitaro. "You know I caught Teru talking to Goro twice." Rie tapped her fan on the table.

Yoshi had been surly ever since the wedding. Try as she might to appease him, he had not settled in well with Tama. Rie feared that the two might end up like herself and Jihei. She hoped not, but for now she needed to focus on finding husbands for Fumi and Kazu. Then she would deal with Tama and Yoshi.

"Well, I know you will be careful to watch them, Mother," Yoshitaro replied, employing the barest hint of sarcasm that Rie was determined to overlook.

Because of the house's indebtedness to Mrs. Nakano, both for the arranging of Yoshitaro's marriage and for asking her good offices with Fumi and Kazu, Rie dressed with special care for her meeting with Nada's most sought after go-between.

Rie heard O-Natsu welcome Mrs. Nakano and hurried to the

parlor. Rie leaned into a full bow. "Our house is forever grateful for your assistance in Yoshitaro's marriage." She smiled and motioned Mrs. Nakano to the zabuton backing to the tokonoma.

O-Natsu brought in the finest grade of Shizuoka green tea. As Rie looked at Mrs. Nakano's dark green kimono and obi she realized she needed more help from Sunao in the selection of her own kimono.

"And how are your other children?" Mrs. Nakano inquired.

Rie bowed. "Thank you. As you know, since Yoshitaro's wedding had to be postponed due to my husband's passing, Fumi and Kazu have now both reached the age for marriage."

Mrs. Nakano had not inquired about their health as was customary in an arrangement such as this. She bowed abruptly, then quickly adjusted her plump hands on her lap. "Does this mean that you want two husbands for your daughters, two at the same time?" Her voice rose higher than normal.

"Well, they would not be married in the same ceremony, but I feel they should both be settled this year." Rie smiled, bowed low, and pushed a plate of two delicate plum-shaped cakes closer to Mrs. Nakano.

Mrs. Nakano looked at the exquisite cakes. "It may be difficult to find two brewers' sons of the right age this year, for autumn weddings," she said, no longer smiling.

Rie sat straighter. "In that case we may be satisfied with a wholesaler for one of them, or a shipper. A house related to our business in some way."

"How old are Fumi and Kazu now?" Mrs. Nakano asked.

"Fumi is twenty, and Kazu will soon be nineteen. Just the right ages," Rie replied, smiling and bowing.

"I haven't seen them lately, but I recall at Yoshitaro's wedding they were attractive, especially Teru, if I may say so."

Rie bowed, at the same time pressing her lips tighter together at the praise given O-Toki's daughter. "We need not arrange Teru's marriage for another year or so."

"Let me see," Mrs. Nakano began. She lifted her teacup and paused. "Well, there is a wholesaler here in Nada whose son is the right age, the Nagata family. And, oh yes, the Kawano family has a son of that age as well. They are in yeast production."

"Yes, I know both families." Rie bowed. "You can be sure that Kazu has had strict training. She's accustomed to hard work, and will have the best of trousseaus."

"I am certain," Mrs. Nakano said.

"We would be grateful if you obtain complete information on the Nagatas. Then we can go ahead with the o-miai soon, if they are agreeable. Yes, I would like autumn weddings for Fumi and Kazu, before the brewing begins." She paused and bowed again. "Now for Fumi there is a special requirement. I plan to adopt a mukoyoshi for her, train him here, and send them out in a bunke branch, closely connected to the main house."

Mrs. Nakano hesitated. "A mukoyoshi? But you already have Yoshitaro as house head."

Rie bowed. "I am sorry to trouble you with this special requirement. Of course we hope to find the most excellent clerk in all Kansai. I have heard that the Ikeda family has a second son who is very skilled."

Mrs. Nakano cleared her throat. "I will see what I can learn about the Ikeda son."

"We are eternally obligated," Rie said, bowing lower than usual as she saw Mrs. Nakano to the door. Rie bit her lip, remembering Mrs. Nakano's slight shift in manner at the mukoyoshi matter. It would not do to alienate this woman on whom the house relied so heavily. Perhaps it would help to give an extra generous go-between fee for Fumi's marriage arrangement.

Rie was pleased but not surprised that both the Ikedas and Nagatas agreed to Mrs. Nakano's request for the o-miai meetings, then for the weddings of the two girls. Lucky days were selected for Fumi's wedding in early September and for Kazu's in early November.

Fumi was less than enthusiastic when Rie broached the topic of her marriage. "Not yet, Mother." She puffed out her cheeks.

Bold girl.

"You know you won't really be leaving the house. We'll find a skilled mukoyoshi for you, train him here, then send you out in a branch house. You'll stay close to the main house that way." She smiled.

"But how can you do that when Yoshi is house head?"

"It won't affect his position, you'll see. And when you have a child, he or she might be able to succeed Yoshi."

Fumi's eyes widened. "Really? I'm not sure Yoshi will like the idea. Isn't it unheard of?"

Rie laughed, enjoying Fumi's spirited argument. "I'm going to speak to him, don't worry." Rie was sure she would not enjoy *Yoshi's* spirited argument.

At dinner that evening, Rie had her chance to discuss the matter with Yoshi when the others had left the table.

"Yoshi, you know I think I'd like to keep Fumi here close to the business. I'd hate to see her leave as a bride to another house. I'd rather find a mukoyishi for her, train him here, then send them out in a branch house, close to us."

Yoshi's face reddened. "A mukoyoshi! What would his position be here? I'm house head, and I have no intention of retiring. I don't see what. . . ."

"Calm down, Yoshi. Of course your position is secure. We'll make it clear Fumi's husband will not remain here. He won't be entered in our koseki." Rie leaned over and poured tea for Yoshi. "You can see that this will help the house, can't you?"

"Well, maybe," he said with an edge of bitterness to his voice. "But why not send Sei out in a branch?"

Rie smiled. "Exactly what I have in mind."

Rie continued her plans for the two weddings of Fumi and Kazu. "This way we can order all the kimono, linens, and chests for both at the same time," Rie said to her daughters. "These kimonos will last the rest of your lives," she added. "And we will give you a sum of cash, Kazu, in the event of divorce by your groom's family, though of course we don't anticipate that. You know a samurai bride can be sent away simply by 'three and a half lines' if they in any way offend the groom's family. And they don't have the protection of their own funds."

Kazu nodded apprehensively.

Although Kazu seemed uncertain about her impending marriage, Rie was gratified that the plan for selecting Fumi's husband was going smoothly.

The summer of 1853 was consumed in frantic activity: visits by lacquerware dealers, silk merchants from Nishijin in Kyoto, long sessions poring over designs and hues, and sittings for fittings by kimono seamstresses.

"I don't have your sense of taste in these matters," Rie told her cousin Sunao, whom she had invited to stay with her for several days during the selections of kimono and patterns.

The house remained in a continual flutter with daily visits by wedding specialists. Early morning calls of *"gomen kudasai"* at the entrance to the office and house did not end until dusk. Fumi and Kazu were continually suspended between excitement over the impending marriages and apprehension about what lay in store for them with strangers for husbands.

"Be strong," Rie said to them one evening when they lingered at the dinner table. "Always remember that you come from the House of Omura. Just as you have been trained to uphold the honor of our house in your behavior, so also when you are married you will uphold the honor of the Nagata house, Kazu. And Fumi will remain in this house until she and her husband leave in a branch house. This will no longer be your home, Kazu. When you marry, your name will be removed from the Omura register and entered in the Nagata register." Rie paused and looked from one intent face to the other, sorry to see the sadness there. "So no matter what your husband or mother does, you know you must endure. Even I have had to endure often, though I was born in this house and had no mother-in-law here."

As Rie looked at the tense expressions on both faces she recalled her mother's words on the eve of her marriage to Jihei. She hesitated, then repeated the words to her daughters: "Sometimes, a woman must 'kill the self' in order to survive. What this means is that we women can never behave selfishly. We must never lose sight of the welfare and interests of the house. These are our reasons for being. When you have children you will understand these things better. But you have understood what I have taught you. These things are the key to your survival and also to contentment in life, the satisfaction of knowing that you have done your duty and done your best for your house." Rie stopped speaking and smiled inwardly at each anxious expression.

Fumi and Kazu had not taken their eyes from Rie's face as she talked. She thought she detected a pout on Teru's face as she listened with her sisters. Rie poured tea for her daughters. She glanced at Kazu's expression of earnest concern. Fumi leaned against her mother, as if for assurance. Rie glanced at Teru. Why was it that Rie always felt a hint of insolence in Teru? Was it because she was O-Toki's daughter, or was it only her imagination? Teru's meetings with Goro were a nagging worry. Rie had done her best to prepare them, even to the point of making certain that O-Yuki handed them all an illustrated booklet of advice to brides, supposedly without Rie's knowledge. Still, Teru's conversations with

Goro were a festering concern, and yet she couldn't marry all three daughters at the same time. Jihei's death had already delayed the others.

"Now, get some rest, girls. I have confidence you will do well in your new homes." Rie rose and touched the arm of each daughter. With a touch of melancholy, she watched the girls walk down the corridor whispering, their arms tightly intertwined.

The wedding kimonos for Fumi and Kazu were similar but not identical: the finest white silk with Chinese red lining that could be glimpsed each time the bride took a small pigeon-toed step. The obis were white brocade patterned subtly with plum, pine, and bamboo. Rie made certain that the expenditures for Fumi's wedding was a bit larger, though not so much as to be overtly noticeable.

"I don't want to impose the cost of two wedding gifts in one year for Omura weddings on many brewers or friends, so I'm dividing the guest lists," Rie said to Sunao.

"Then the girls' weddings will be smaller than Yoshi's, won't they?" Sunao asked.

"Oh, yes. His was more important. And Fumi's will be too. Remember, I told you I want to adopt a husband for her."

"How could I forget?" Sunao replied. "I'm looking forward to it. People won't know what to make of it, will they?" She laughed, her plump face dimpled. "It isn't as if you didn't have a son. What an enigma you are sometimes, Rie."

Rie smiled, took out her comb and then reinserted it. She looked at her cousin. "I'm so grateful to you, Sunao, for taking the time to help me. I just don't have your taste in kimonos. And I value your company."

"I enjoy doing it. I always enjoy working with fabrics."

Fumi's wedding was a grand affair, and nearly all brewers in Kobe were invited, including Saburo and his wife, at whom Rie stole surreptitious glances from time to time while he did the same. Rie was able to glance at Saburo just as he looked at her, and they shared the briefest of smiles before both looking at Fumi. Rie realized that Saburo knew Fumi was his daughter; she felt warmed and smiled inwardly.

He would have noticed that the shape of Fumi's face echoed his.

Fumi and Eitaro of the Ikeda family behaved with such propriety. Yoshi gave the speeches on behalf of the house and did a most creditable job. By now the servants were all experienced in serving large numbers of guests and caused Rie no concern.

Despite Yoshi's obvious displeasure that Fumi and her husband would remain in the house while Eitaro was being trained to assume the burdens of head of a branch family, Rie was pleased by the addition. So far things were going as planned. It was almost too good to be true. Fumi and her husband were given a room just below Yoshi and Tama's. The house was becoming a continual hub of activity, and Tama was assuming some of the household responsibilities so that Rie was able to spend more time in the office on business matters.

Kazu's wedding went as planned, a respectable affair with what everyone said was a well-trained bride. Kazu, Rie was gratified to note, kept her eyes modestly downcast during the entire ceremony and the long laudatory speeches at the reception. Kazu was now a member of the Nagata family and no longer Rie's responsibility.

At the reception Sunao turned to Rie. "Did you hear that, Rie?" Sunao asked, leaning over in a whisper. "Mrs. Akita said she had never seen such a subtle shade of apricot."

Rie squeezed Sunao's hand. "Good. You chose well."

At both weddings Rie's glance lingered on Saburo Kato and she felt the old feeling of longing, of regret that their time together had been so brief, all those years ago. Rie was nevertheless able to exchange special smiles with Saburo as she nodded to three handsome sons who accompanied their parents. Without wishing to appear too obvious Rie asked Mrs. Kato for the names of her three sons.

"They are Hiro'ichi, Jirobei, and Isamu," she replied, smiling. "Jirobei and Hiro'ichi are already married."

"*Ah,* is that so?" Rie said with a proper bow and smile. Mrs. Kato had given her exactly the information she wanted. She looked closely at the youngest son and decided to make careful inquiries of Mrs. Nakano. In all these years Rie had cherished the notion that perhaps Kazu or Teru might marry a son of Saburo.

That night as she combed her hair she smiled at her reflection in the mirror. Only Teru and Sei remained. She hoped to get her married to Isamu, thereby linking her family with the family of Saburo Kato forever.

Over the next few months Rie spoke with Mrs. Nakano again, and began the negotiations that would lead to the fruition of a cherished dream. Rie made certain that Teru realized what a prize she would have as her husband.

A cold relentless rain was pelting the roofs of the Omura compound. It was nearly midnight, the hour of the tiger. Teru rolled out of her futon and slipped out of the room and along the corridor to the door to the compound area. She pulled her cloak tightly around her head and ran across to the cooper's shed.

"Goro, are you there?" she said in a loud whisper.

"Over here." He loomed out of the black mist and took hold of Teru's arm. "Come, let's go around to the other side of the shed where it's drier and there's no danger of being seen."

The two slapped through the puddles holding hands, around to the back of the shed.

"Goro, Mother is insisting that I marry that Isamu Kato. The o-miai was three days ago. I can't marry him. I won't!" She clung to Goro and choked out her words.

Goro put his arms around her and held her tightly.

"I know." He rubbed her back.

"I want to be with you. I'd rather die than marry that self-important prig," she moaned.

"What can we do? My parents are already arranging my marriage too."

"There's one way we can be together, Goro. Forever." She gazed into Goro's eyes.

Goro's eyes fixed hungrily on Teru's face. "What do you mean?"

Her voice took on a strangely calm cadence. "You know what they did in the Chikamatsu dramas? I've seen it at Bunraku."

"You mean . . . you mean *shinju*, lovers' suicide?" Goro stuttered out the word.

"Yes! Yes! That way we can be together forever! They can't stop us!"

Goro moved his hand up and down Teru's back. "But . . . could you do that, Teru? Could I?"

"We would do it together, Goro. Give each other the courage. We can go to the beach at night, the way the lovers did in the Chikamatsu play."

Goro looked down at Teru's eager, beautiful face and took it in his hands. He kissed her, for the first time, lingering at the taste of her lips.

Teru pressed her body against Goro's insistently.

He put his hands on Teru's shoulders and moved back to look into her face. "We'd better consider carefully, Teru. Plan in detail and make certain that we have the courage to succeed."

"I'm certain," said Teru, her voice sharp, almost metallic. "The life Mother has chosen for me has no meaning. I can't live that way. A brief time with you, however brief, is better than a whole lifetime with that Kato person. We would be together, Goro, really together." She clung to him fiercely.

"I can see how strong you are, Teru. You have the strength of a tiger, at the hour of the tiger." He smiled briefly. He felt his need for her growing, felt the pressure in his groin.

"The wedding is set for three weeks from now," Teru said. "We can meet here a week from tonight, and be ready to go to the beach." She reached her arms around Goro's neck and kissed him on the mouth. "Be strong, Goro. We'll be together forever." She turned and ran back to the house.

Chapter 29

"Only two weeks until Teru's marriage. It will be a relief, won't it, O-Natsu," Rie said, "to have her wedding out of the way? Teru has been such a worry, with her geisha's ways."

O-Natsu nodded.

Rie was glad she had never informed either Kazu or Teru that she was not their birth mother, and that neither O-Yumi nor O-Toki had been invited to the weddings of their daughters. The real parentage of the two girls was not common knowledge among Kobe brewers, though O-Natsu said there were rumors.

"What does it really matter, O-Natsu?" Rie said. "The children of mistresses are often recognized, taken in by reputable houses. What matters is that I have raised them as members of the house. They really are Omura daughters."

O-Natsu refrained from pointing out that while this was true of geisha sons, it was most unusual to recognize geisha daughters.

Exactly one week had elapsed since Teru's midnight tryst with Goro. The hour of the tiger approached. Several times during the week Teru had gone into the garden or stopped in front of the Butsudan when she found it necessary to be alone with her thoughts, with her fateful decision. She knew it was her resolve more than Goro's willingness that would enable them to act out their plan. She did not want to weaken at the last minute.

Teru pushed out of her futon and reached under it for the white obi sash she had hidden there only hours earlier. She thrust it into her kimono sleeve and moved quietly along the corridor to the door to the compound. She slid the shoji open slowly and looked out into the courtyard. The night was clear and cloudless. She decided against taking her cloak. What difference would the chill of November make? Besides, Goro would warm her. She looked toward the shed and could just make out his silhouette in the moonlight. She glanced back at the house as she emerged from it, this house where she had been taught endurance, discipline, and obedience, those virtues so prized by her mother. Well, Fumi, the perfect daughter and sister, was welcome to them.

She moved quickly to Goro, embraced him without speaking. She looked into his tense, sensitive face and kissed him.

He pressed against her, his arms holding her tightly. "Teru, Teru," he moaned hoarsely.

She looked into his eyes. "Let's not hesitate. We'll be strong, won't we?"

Goro nodded, his eyes locked with hers.

They walked out of the back side of the compound onto the moonlit road, took the road to the ocean and walked in silence, arms entwined, careful to avoid chance meetings with anyone. When they reached the shore they stopped, looked into each other's eyes, and embraced. Teru took Goro's hand and led him toward the narrow sandy strip at the water's edge. They sat on the sand and gazed at each other. Goro moved his hand over the front of Teru's kimono until he found the opening. Teru opened her kimono with both hands and lay back on the sand.

"Now, Goro, and forever," she said. She closed her eyes as Goro moved over her.

They did not count the passing of the time of their passion.

Finally, Goro moved away from her. "Yes, we were meant to be together," he said, looking down into her face.

"We will always have each other, Goro."

They lay on the sand in each other's arms until Teru noticed the first glimmer of dawn lightening the sky. She sat up and took from her sleeve the long white obi tie. She drew her knees up and tied them loosely together with one end of the white strip, so that she would not be discovered with her legs apart, later.

Goro watched intently.

"Here, Goro, tie the other end around your leg, not so tightly that you can't walk."

He fumbled with the tie. "This way?" he asked as he twined the strip.

"Yes. We can wait until it's nearly light before we enter the water." She took Goro's hand.

"No regrets, Teru?" he asked in a deep, half-muffled voice.

She faced him, her body pressed against his. "No regrets, Goro."

They embraced and stood. For several minutes neither spoke nor moved. Then she took his hand. "Shall we go now?"

They embraced again, then took small, halting steps into the water. Neither knew how to swim. Teru shuddered and gasped at the shock of the cold waves lapping at their feet, their legs, their bodies.

"We can't stop, Goro," Teru said, sobbing.

They walked hand in hand into the sea, waves washing over them. Teru coughed and sputtered, and further on twisted and turned in agony beside her beloved.

Gradually, they began to sink beneath the waves, Teru's hair floating on the surface of the water above her, then nothing, only the muffled sound of water.

"Mother! Mother! Teru's gone! I can't find her anywhere!" Fumi cried as she ran into Rie's room.

"What do you mean, she's gone?" Rie demanded. "She can't be gone. She's getting married in two weeks." Rie frowned, walked purposefully into the corridor and stepped into the girls' room. She looked into the empty room, then walked to the bathroom and looked in. At the kitchen door she stopped.

"O-Yuki, where's Teru? Have you seen her this morning?"

"*Uh* . . . no, I haven't." O-Yuki looked from Rie to Fumi, who was wringing her hands behind her mother.

"Well, search the house, O-Yuki." Rie paused, suddenly apprehensive. "And go to the cooper's shed. See if Goro is there and anyone has seen her."

O-Yuki turned and ran down the corridor and out to the courtyard.

Rie bit her lip and quickly poured herself a cup of tea, then turned to Fumi. "Did Teru say anything to you last night?"

"Nothing special, Mother. Just good night, as usual."

"*Humph!* Something was not usual at all. Go and have your breakfast, Fumi," she said sharply.

When she was gone, Rie stood in the kitchen sipping tea impatiently. She heard the shoji to the courtyard open and O-Yuki's voice call, "Oku-san! Oku-san! The cooper says Goro is gone too!"

Rie gasped and slammed down her cup. "Horrible! I should have known. She was still O-Toki's daughter, not mine, in spite of everything I did."

Rie turned and walked rapidly through the courtyard and to the inner office, where Yoshitaro and Kinnosuke were going over an order.

"Yoshi! Kinno! Teru and Goro have run away together. And the wedding only two weeks away."

"No!" Yoshitaro said. "How could she . . . they?"

"What shall we do?" She walked back and forth, frowning. "Yoshi, remove her name from the koseki, today!" she ordered.

"I'll go out, Oku-san," Kinnosuke said, "and see what I can learn. They haven't simply vanished into thin air. They can't have gone far. Someone must have seen them." He rose and left the office.

Rie started to speak to Yoshitaro about Teru, but stopped herself. Yoshi was also O-Toki's child. Why complain to him about O-Toki and Teru? She turned and walked along the corridor and out into the garden, past her rock. She paced back and forth on the cold gray stones. What could she do to preserve the name of the house? What could she say to the Katos? And what a disaster to her long-cherished dream. After several minutes she returned to the office, where Tama had joined Yoshitaro.

"I don't know what to say to the Katos, Yoshi," Rie said. She fidgeted with her comb. Her hope of a family bond with Saburo's family was destroyed, adding to her despair.

"Maybe when we know where they have gone we'll know what to say," Tama said, looking up at Rie. "Here, Mother, have some tea. You haven't even had your breakfast."

"I can't eat now, Tama," Rie said. She sat at the table and looked at Tama. "I should have known. I should have guessed," she repeated.

"Don't blame yourself, Mother," Tama said.

"It's not your fault," Yoshitaro said. "She was always strong willed and unpredictable."

The door to the outer office opened and Kinnosuke entered, out of breath. He bowed.

"Their bodies have been found in the water, down by the

harbor," he sputtered. "They were tied together." He looked down and bowed again. "I'm very sorry."

Dead. Rie gasped, her face in her hands.

Yoshitaro and Tama both groaned.

Rie forced back tears as she raised her head. "Yoshi and Tama. You must go to the Katos. Tell them Teru has had an accident, has been killed. Don't mention Goro. Apologize abjectly. And Kinno, go to Goro's father and give him whatever is necessary to hush this up. He may not want it known either. And take care of the cremations, will you? We can't have anyone talking about this. Nothing is to be said. Her name will never be mentioned in this house again."

Chapter 30

Two or three months had elapsed since Teru's death, and the house had a hushed air about it that felt suffocating. Rie fanned herself as she looked down at the words of sympathy penned by Saburo himself. Tender words that touched her heart and brought tears to her eyes, words that she would cherish forever. She tucked the letter neatly into the folds of her obi, wanting it close to her always. He had also sent a specially arranged ikebana exactly like the one they had so admired at the flower festival all those years ago. She smiled through the tears, feelings of gratitude welling up inside her.

With a sigh, she turned her attention to Tama, who now cooked rice to perfection, always rose first and retired last in the family. Rie could find no fault with her hard-working dedication to Yoshitaro and to the house. But Tama showed no sign of becoming pregnant. Rie hesitated to mention it to Tama, recalling her own years of frustration at not bearing an heir. Still, it was imperative that Yoshitaro have an heir.

She was also concerned about Yoshi's attitude toward Tama. Yoshi showed no sign of any affection toward his wife, and seemed oblivious to his duty to provide an heir.

One evening as Rie was closing her shutters and preparing for the night she heard O-Natsu's voice beyond the shoji.

"Yes, come in, O-Natsu," Rie said. "Sit down."

Rie turned expectantly toward O-Natsu, whose cheeks were no longer plump or apple-red and whose hair was thinning.

"I know you have been concerned that Tama has not borne an heir," O-Natsu began.

"Yes, O-Natsu. And I have hesitated to mention it to Tama. You understand."

"Yes, I remember well. And I believe this generation is about to repeat. . . ." O-Natsu paused.

Rie caught her breath. "No! You don't mean . . . ?"

"Yes, I'm afraid so," O-Natsu said before Rie could finish her question. "I have learned that a young geisha at the Sawaraya is pregnant, the geisha whom Yoshitaro visits. Her name is O-Sada." O-Natsu bowed. "I thought you would want to know."

"Yes, O-Natsu. I refuse to have another generation of a geisha's child, a geisha's bloodline, in this house!" Rie turned her comb over and over in her hands, took out her fan, and banged it on the table.

O-Natsu looked down at her chapped, work-worn hands. "I believe the child is due in about three months."

Rie sighed deeply. "Thank you, O-Natsu. I don't believe we need to mention it to Tama. I'll speak to Yoshi about this, about his obligation."

O-Natsu wished Rie good night and left.

Rie turned back to her dressing table and combed out her long, thick hair. What a disgusting twist of fate. Maybe it was not just fate. Maybe Yoshi was deliberately staying away from Tama, refusing to sleep with her. Would a geisha's bloodline never cease to flow in the Omura House? What a calamity that Tama had not become pregnant, just as she herself had not until it was too late.

Several evenings later Rie saw her opportunity to speak with Yoshi at the dinner table when the others had left.

She glanced at him and saw that he was about to leave. "Yoshi, we need to talk. I am concerned that Tama has not yet become pregnant."

"She will never become pregnant," he said with a smug air about him.

Rie frowned. "What do you mean, never? In my case it took a while, but how do you know she will *never* become pregnant?"

Yoshi rose. "It will not happen because she will not have the opportunity."

"Sit! You have not been excused. What do you mean by suggesting that she will not have the opportunity? Do you think you can refuse your duty to this house? Impossible! You were adopted as heir, and you must provide a successor."

Yoshi paused in the doorway. "We will have an heir. I have a daughter already."

"I know about your disgraceful philandering at the Sawaraya. And that geisha has had a child. But we will not bring her into this house as we did you."

"Then there will be no heir, no successor," Yoshi said, and walked from the room.

As Yoshitaro went about the business of the day, he recalled with pleasure his visit to O-Sada when she had told him she was pregnant with his child. She had smiled as she watched his face. He had been so enthusiastic, had embraced her.

"My wife has not become pregnant in three years," he told her.

"Perhaps you have given me a better chance than your wife," she had replied, a mysterious glint in her eyes.

He guessed that Rie would eventually relent and want to bring O-Sada's baby into the house, but he dreaded breaking the news to Tama. He knew Rie would do it, if asked, relieving him of the duty. Still, he felt a twinge of guilt, a bit of sadness for Tama, who had worked so faithfully for the house.

Several months had passed and Rie still hadn't relented and let Yoshitaro bring O-Sada's child into the household. Tired of fighting with his mother over the child, he determined to pay O-Sada a visit. He knew it would be an awkward meeting, painful for O-Sada, yet he could not postpone it.

Faced with the prospect of having no heir for the main house, Rie had no choice but to agree to Yoshi's request to bring in Ume, distasteful though the prospect of another geisha's child in the house was.

O-Sada did not attempt to conceal her tears as she nursed her baby. As he watched, Yoshitaro recalled the earlier conversation, the far happier occasion of his previous visit.

He put a hand on O-Sada's arm to calm her. "But Ume will have a good life, O-Sada. She will have every advantage in the Omura House. And a good marriage."

"Yes," she sobbed. "I know, but I don't want to give her up." She stopped and put the baby to her shoulder.

"Be reasonable, O-Sada," Yoshitaro said, leaning into her. "What life can you give her? And you know caring for you will always be my responsibility."

"Yes, it's true," she said softly. "I don't want her to grow up here, like me. O-Toki has told me she had a daughter besides you, and there was another from the Kitaya, all adopted into the Omura House."

Yoshi stiffened.

She put a hand to her mouth. "I thought you knew about Teru and Kazu."

He shook his head brusquely, eyes downcast. Once again his

mother, if he could even call her that, had lied to him. He could never forgive her. Three children. He had been told the girls were adopted relatives from the country. No wonder she favored Fumi and Sei, who were no doubt her own.

"It was very hard for her to lose them that way. That's why she is always so happy when you visit. She is proud of you." She sniffed. "But I can't bear the thought that I won't be able to watch Ume grow up and marry."

"I'll tell you about her whenever I come. And I'll do my best to arrange that you can see her sometimes, especially when she marries. But that's twenty years away, so don't worry about it now. I promise she will have the best possible life."

O-Sada sighed and wiped at her tears with her sleeve.

"Come," Yoshitaro urged. "O-Yuki is waiting in the ricksha outside."

O-Sada rose holding the baby, picked up a large furoshiki with the baby's clothes, and shuffled out after Yoshitaro. He took the furoshiki, put an arm around O-Sada, then released her and handed her an envelope. She bowed and handed Ume to O-Yuki, then leaned over to kiss the baby a last time before bowing again to Yoshitaro. He watched from the ricksha as O-Sada turned and stumbled back to the entrance, hands over her face.

Rie looked at Tama. The rest of the family had left the dinner table and they were alone.

"I'm sure you are aware, Tama, that the most important duty of the wife of the house head is to produce an heir. You know, the samurai say a bride is a borrowed womb."

Tama sat opposite Rie, eyes downcast. Rie could see that she was twisting her hands in her lap.

Tama bowed. "I am sorry to have disappointed you."

"Well, it can't be helped." Rie sighed. She had not planned to share her own experience with Tama, but it seemed appropriate now. "You know, Tama, the same thing happened to me when I married. My parents adopted your husband because I had no child for several years after I married."

Tama looked up, her eyes widening. "Oh, I didn't know it happened that way."

"Yes, Yoshitaro is my husband's son by a mistress."

Tama caught her breath. "Oh!" was all she could manage.

Rie felt a measure of sympathy for the girl, knowing how such words stung, how they burrowed beneath the skin to leave pain in its wake. But it was kinder to tell her than to have her find out as Rie had—through gossip on the streets. "Yes, a mistress at the Sawaraya, a geisha. Now Yoshi has insisted on bringing in his daughter from the same establishment, though I have been opposed to it. I cannot prevent it, since we do require an heir, a successor to the main house. Yoshi is house head so I may not be able to prevent this, though I have been trying to stop his plan. I have not succeeded. We will have to bring this child in."

Tama's hands flew to her face. Then she bowed, and ran from the room. Rie could hear her crying as she hurried toward the stairs.

Rie closed her eyes, feeling spent by the encounter and bad for Tama. She was about to take a well-needed rest when she heard a ricksha, and walked toward the entrance, fearing what she would find there.

When Yoshi returned to the house with Ume, Rie and Tama both greeted the baby reluctantly. From the moment Ume came into the house Yoshitaro protected her. He looked in on her in the nursery night and morning, often picking her up, even carrying her into the office to show to Kinnosuke.

"Oh yes," Kinnosuke said, grasping a tiny waving hand. "I can see that she is your daughter." Kinnosuke smiled at the gurgling baby.

"I hope she doesn't grow up to look like me," Yoshitaro said, gazing down at her. "I'd rather she took after her mother," he said softly.

"Well, no matter whom she looks like she'll be very important to the next generation in the house. She'll have an adopted husband, as your mother did. Unless you have a son, of course," Kinnosuke added quickly. "But I'll see that she gets the same training you did," he said, patting the baby.

"Good. And by the way, congratulations! I hear that you have had a second son," Yoshitaro said with a touch of envy in his voice. "I hope Nobu is doing well."

Kinnosuke bowed. "She is thriving, thanks to you. Both of our sons are healthy, and Toru is growing fast. Nearly six. He'll soon be going out as apprentice somewhere, to eat someone else's rice. We can't have him grow up idle or spoiled."

"You'll send him out so young?" Yoshitaro asked.

"Have you forgotten that you were helping me here when you were five?"

"I haven't forgotten, Kinno-san. Yes, I would be grateful if you would have a hand in Ume's training."

As Rie eavesdropped on the conversation she realized she felt nothing for Ume but annoyance that the child was now installed as Yoshi's heir. And now she would be the probable wife of Yoshi's successor, another adopted husband.

"That she has no Omura blood is really regrettable," Rie said to O-Natsu, later that day, the only one in the house to whom she could speak so frankly. Ume was granddaughter of Jihei and daughter of Yoshi. O-Toki's bloodline was still polluting the house. "But she will be trained to become a true daughter of the Omura House, totally dedicated to our traditions," Rie added, "and she must never be told of her Sawaraya origins. Every hint of it must be expunged from her character." A fleeting memory of Teru flashed through her mind and she flinched.

Seisaboro was now twenty-one and Rie could no longer delay

arranging his marriage. She again turned to Mrs. Nakano, this time to find a bride from a brewing family, so that Seisaburo and his bride could establish a new branch family. Yet even as the plans progressed, Yoshi appeared withdrawn like his father had been, and turned more and more to Kinnosuke, avoiding Rie whenever possible. Well, it couldn't be helped. The house came above the individual. She had learned it, and he must learn it too.

The Yamada family were respected brewers and had a daughter of the right age. Rie was satisfied at the prospect of a link with another major brewing house in Nada. She smiled. How proud her father would be. She would inform him when she burned incense at the Butsudan in the morning.

"Must I?" Sei said, when his mother told him of Mari, the Yamada daughter.

"Yes, Sei, and she is quite pretty as well as being from a highly respected family." Rie took out her comb, paused, then replaced it smartly. How well Mrs. Nakano's daughter-in-law had turned out to be as a go-between after old Mrs. Nakano had retired. She had trained her successor well.

One evening, as Rie was preparing for the night, she sat before her dressing table combing her hair and musing. The face of the family was continually changing. The only child still at home, once Sei was gone, would be Yoshitaro, but already the next generation was beginning with Ume. And Tama. Rie still thought of her as a new member, though a permanent one, although one who had failed a major duty. To be fair, it was Yoshi who had failed.

"I have no intention of sending you back because you have not borne a child," Rie assured Tama one evening. "I know that some samurai families simply hand a bride 'three and a half lines' and dismiss her if she fails to bear an heir. But we are not samurai, and even if we didn't have Ume I would not do that."

Tama held Ume and appeared to be trying to develop affection for the baby, as she bowed and murmured her gratitude.

Rie continued combing her hair, slowly gazing at each graying strand. Now Eitaro was in the house, not actually a house member, but he came to the office each day and worked right alongside Yoshi and Sei. Rie noticed that Eitaro and Seisaburo had formed a close bond from the start, a friendship. Yoshitaro, though, seemed to keep his distance from Eitaro, insofar as possible in the office. Perhaps when Eitaro finished his apprenticeship in the house and was set up in his own branch, Yoshitaro's attitude might change, or would it only become worse?

One morning Rie lit an incense stick in the Butsudan and clapped her hands to attract the attention of the gods, the spirits of her parents. Then she turned toward the tokonoma alcove and began arranging three stalks of yellow chrysanthemums in a shallow black vase.

"Mother, where are you?" Fumi's voice floated in from the corridor.

"In here, Fumi," Rie answered.

Fumi glided into the room and joined Rie in front of the tokonoma.

Rie glanced at her daughter's glowing complexion. "It's good to see you, dear. And you're looking so well, so happy," the last almost a question. "I'm glad we found you a house so close by. It's not really as if you've left, is it?"

"It's very convenient for Eitaro. I know he appreciates being close by. And, you know, I don't think he objected to becoming a mukoyoshi."

Rie smiled. "Why should he? We're a house everyone respects. He'll have his own branch soon. And he seems to be working well with Kinno, and especially with Sei." Rie did not mention Yoshitaro, whose moods had become blacker over the years since his father had died. "It will be good for the future of the house.

And speaking of Sei, his marriage will really work out well, don't you think? But you know, it will be hard, being so indebted to the Nakanos after so many weddings."

Fumi reached for a chrysanthemum stalk and pulled it from the vase. "You don't mind, Mother?" Fumi began to rearrange the flowers.

"No, dear. You've always been better at ikebana than I."

Rie sat back on her heels and watched Fumi arrange the flowers, and rearrange them.

Fumi rose abruptly. "I want to see Ume, Mother. I'll bring her," she said as she left the room.

She returned a few minutes later carrying the baby, bouncing her up and down in time to a nursery rhyme she began to hum. The baby gurgled and Fumi hugged her, then put her on the tatami between herself and Rie.

Rie reached over and took her on her lap.

"It seems good to have a baby in the house again, doesn't it, Mother?"

Rie forced a smile.

"Of course you always seem so engrossed in the brewery you probably haven't had time to bond with the baby."

Rie rocked the baby. "The family and the brewery are equally important to me, Fumi. They are really one and the same. And I am the senior member here, have been for some time."

Rie began to sing a folk tune to Ume, who chortled loudly.

Fumi reached for a tea tray on the table and poured a cup for her mother. She pushed the cup toward Rie, and reached for Ume.

"Have some tea, Mother. I really came for a reason this morning."

Rie reached for the teacup, glancing at Fumi. "What is it, dear?"

Fumi paused before answering. "I'm pregnant. I'm going to

have a baby." Fumi smiled and leaned back to watch her mother's reaction.

Rie's face lit up. "Wonderful! Are you certain? When is it due?"

"I think in five and half months, Mother."

"And how do you feel? Are you all right? Be careful of your diet, won't you?"

"As you can see, Mother, I'm quite healthy." Fumi laughed.

"That's marvelous, Fumi. Then your baby won't be much younger than Ume. And I hope and pray it's a boy."

"Now, Mother, why would you hope for a boy? You've always told us merchant houses prefer girl babies, so they can find the best mukoyoshi around. But I'm sure you have some reason, some ulterior motive." Fumi laughed and Rie joined in, hand over her mouth. She leaned back and looked at Fumi but did not reply to her question.

Chapter 31

Seisaburo's marriage to Mari Yamada of the East Nada brewing family in April 1858, was totally satisfactory to Rie. The wedding also marked the establishment of the southern branch of the Omura House with Seisaburo as head, and of the northern branch under the headship of Eitaro. Rie could barely conceal her pride from the guests gathered in the reception hall. Yoshitaro presided, and Rie had to admit that he needed to be the one to perform this function. She could not make public the fact that she still held the seal without causing Yoshi to lose face among the other brewers who were his peers, but she knew it still rankled.

"It went very well, don't you think, Tama?" Rie asked in the office the day after the wedding.

"Well enough, Mother," Tama said in measured tones. Rie was pleased whenever she caught Tama listening outside the office door, learning what she could of the business, as Rie herself had done growing up.

"And Kinno-san, how are we doing about buying and selling kuras? We have nine brewing now, don't we, counting Eitaro's and Sei's?"

"That's right. We've been able to turn over one every three or four months recently. It may be a seasonal thing, but we're still the only ones doing it. And we're making a good profit at it." He smiled and bowed.

"Good. What are the other brewers saying in the association?" Rie asked, looking at Eitaro and turning her comb over in her hand.

"I think they're amazed, Mother, and perhaps a bit envious too. I heard some of them talking at the last meeting. And Saburo Kato came up to me and remarked about Kinno's ability. They've all noticed."

Rie felt a sudden warmth at the mention of Saburo Kato.

Kinnosuke bowed to Rie. "Thanks to your training, I've learned the importance of timing."

Never one to let Rie enjoy her successes, Yoshi said, "But Mother, Father always cautioned about going too far in advance of the others. You know the old saying about the peg that stands up. Soon you will attract the attention of the wrong person who may not like that we are so successful, more successful than any other house. It might actually turn out to be an embarrassment."

"Yoshi is right," said Kinnosuke. "And you know, Oku-san, I see a lot of political changes now. The loyalists are speaking out against the Bakufu. And the shogunal edicts can't be enforced. The whole samurai class is indebted to the merchants and the structure is collapsing. However, I believe these problems offer new opportunities for us." Kinnosuke leaned forward with his folded hands on the table and looked at Rie.

"Well, what are you suggesting, Kinno? Could we expand our markets somehow?"

He blinked rapidly. "Perhaps with sales in Edo continuing to expand, we could consider opening new routes to markets farther north and south."

Rie took out her fan and held it suspended. "You mean Tohoku and Shikoku, or as far south as Kyushu?"

"I think both directions," Kinnosuke replied.

"But the northerners are so fond of their local sake," Yoshitaro said. "They're loyal to their brands. They're always boasting that their sake is best. It would be hard to break in there."

"That's true, Yoshi," Rie said. "But we don't want to stagnate, or get complacent about our success." Rie paused to give herself time to overcome her irritation. Yoshi was sounding a bit too much like Jihei for her taste. "And since our Edo market is secure, why don't we set up an office there, study the situation? Could you take the time to go to Edo and do that?" Rie asked, tapping her fan on the table and looking at Kinnosuke.

He nodded after each of Rie's sentences. "We have good connections in Nihonbashi. Yes, I'd like to go before other brewers get the idea."

"Especially Yamaguchi. Then leave as soon as you can, Kinno-san." Rie fanned herself rapidly, then replaced her fan in her obi, avoiding the growing resentment she saw in Yoshi's eyes.

Rie called Eitaro over to hear Kinnosuke's report on his trip to Edo. Yoshitaro wanted Seisaburo to be present as well. Rie wondered if Yoshitaro wanted to reduce Eitaro's voice in the discussion. It seemed, no matter the topic, Yoshi was always reluctant to include Eitaro. In any case, Seisaburo's presence in any matter affecting a major decision was welcome. Rie paused before speaking to look around the table at these four grown men, all of whom she had trained: her own son, Fumi's adopted husband, O-Toki's son, and her chief clerk.

She straightened in her seat. "Well, Kinno-san, what did you learn in Edo?"

He bowed to Rie and Yoshitaro. "Everything is changing there. The Bakufu grows weaker by the day. They say the Satsuma and Choshu samurai are on the move, rallying around the Emperor in Kyoto. The loyalists are gaining strength as the Bakufu weakens. The whole structure seems on the verge of collapse."

"*Ho!*" Eitaro and Seisaburo exclaimed almost in unison.

Kinnosuke took a deep breath and continued. "But besides the Bakufu's weakness, some barbarian ships arrived near Yokohama some months ago. The barbarians demanded that the shogun open the country, allow their ships to land and barbarians to live on our shores. They say these were strange ships; they belched forth black smoke."

"Black smoke? And not on fire?" Seisaburo asked.

Yoshitaro frowned. "How could barbarians make such demands of the shogun?"

"Who knows what will happen now?" Kinnosuke said. "But I doubt the Bakufu can survive this crisis: with their own weakness and the loyalist movement in the south, and this added blow by the barbarians. The Bakufu tried to put them off, but I'm told the ships came back with more demands. Now the shogun is forced to open some ports to the barbarians."

"Really, Kinno!" Rie exclaimed. "What will all this mean for brewers?" she asked, rapidly tapping her fan on the table.

"It's hard to say. The situation is changing so fast. But for one thing kabu controls have become a meaningless formality. We can buy as many as we want now from brewers who are going under."

"Then this is the time we should buy more, isn't that so?" Eitaro asked. He rubbed his ink stick on the inkstone, pushed it between himself and Seisaburo, and took a brush from his sleeve.

"Yes," Seisaburo said, "so long as we're certain of our distribution routes and markets."

"That's a big question, isn't it, with this political instability?" Yoshitaro asked, looking at his mother.

Rie turned instead to Kinnosuke. "All right, Kinno-san. Watch the political situation, everyone . . . but Kinno-san and Yoshi, you can coordinate the kabu purchases for the main house with those of Sei and Eitaro. And don't forget to watch Yamaguchi." She fanned herself rapidly.

Eitaro and Seisaburo dipped their brushes into the prepared ink and began making notes.

"And what about finding an agent in Edo?" Rie asked. "Was there too much confusion to do anything?"

Kinnosuke bowed again, blinked and nodded. "No, actually it was a good time to be there. I found a man to be our agent in Nihonbashi. Yoshioka is his name. I checked his references with friends. He knows most of the big wholesalers there, and distributors too along the northern and southern routes out of the city. Keeps his eye on the whole situation. I think we were lucky to get him."

Rie nodded. "Well done, Kinno-san," she said.

Yoshitaro leaned forward. "I think it might be wise to send one of our clerks to work with him, act as our permanent liaison. We'll need to watch the situation closely."

Rie nodded. "Good thinking, Yoshi. Yes, we need to keep close contact there, especially now. Has Yamaguchi set up an Edo office yet?" Rie was relieved to be able to agree with Yoshi, for once.

"Not yet. I should go to Edo again in a few weeks to see how Yoshioka is doing and what is happening in Edo," Kinnosuke said. "I can choose a man to go along and be based there. I discussed the question of northern versus southern routes with

Yoshioka. He thinks a southern move would be more strategic now, especially in view of Satsuma and Choshu power along that route."

Rie nodded and looked around the room again at the four men.

At the dinner table one evening Yoshitaro took Ume on his lap. "Ume is three now, Mother. I want Tama to take her out for *shichi-go-san*." A day all children aged seven, five and three looked forward to, when they dressed in their finest for the outing. During the day they enjoyed special treats and played their favorite games.

"I've bought Ume a new red kimono for the occasion," Tama said, smiling at Ume.

"Red kimono, red kimono," Ume cried, waving her hands.

Rie looked at Tama. *Too bad there wouldn't be a chance to get together with Kazu,* she thought, with Kazu's Kimi turning seven this year. She quickly dismissed the thought. Kazu was no longer part of the Omura House, no longer her responsibility, and the thought of Kazu always elicited painful memories of Teru.

"Hirokichi isn't three yet," Rie said. "His birthday is still four months away, but I don't think he'd like to be left out."

"It wouldn't really be suitable for him to join Ume, Mother," Yoshitaro said. "You know how important the birthday is for this celebration."

He no doubt wanted above all to protect Ume, but did he want to keep Hirokichi away from the house, too? Rie glanced at Yoshitaro and noticed that he was chewing on a chopstick. *Better than pulling at his eyebrows,* she thought.

When the special day arrived, Tama brought Ume dressed in her bright new kimono with matching ribbons in her hair into the office in the morning to greet Rie and Yoshitaro.

"Oh, don't you look pretty!" Rie exclaimed. "And where

are you taking her?" She looked at Tama, also wearing a dress kimono.

"We're going to the temple. I know they'll have sweets for the children today."

Ume began to jump and cry, "Sweets! Ume wants sweets!"

Rie took Ume's hand. "You can have sweet bean soup when you come home."

Yoshitaro walked over to Ume and Tama. "Take her through the main office so Kinnosuke can see her," he said. "She's old enough to begin visiting."

Tama bowed and took Ume by the hand. Rie and Yoshitaro both watched as they walked toward the outer office.

"It's good she's such a happy child," Rie said.

"Not only happy, she's also bright and pretty," Yoshitaro said.

Rie smiled. There was no need to tell Yoshi her plans for Ume yet.

Chapter 32

"Oku-san," Kinnosuke said to Rie one morning, "Seisaburo has something he wants us to see. He particularly asked that you come too. He says it's going to transform brewing." He blinked rapidly.

Rie looked up quickly. "Transform brewing? What could that be?" She took out her fan from her obi and held it as if to fan herself, but stopped and looked at Kinnosuke.

"I'm not sure. I think his clerk said it has something to do with polishing rice."

"Well, let's go over this afternoon, Kinno-san. Have you told Yoshi?"

"Yes. He's eager to go."

"I want Eitaro to go too. Have someone go and ask him to meet us here after lunch. We'll all go together." She fanned herself. Not surprising that Seisaburo had made a discovery. Already he was well respected in the Brewers Association.

Kinnosuke bowed. "I'll have a horse and carriage waiting. It's a long ride to Nishinomiya."

Horse and carriage was a new mode of transport, available to families who could afford it.

Rie enjoyed the ride in the covered black carriage with horse and coachman, a luxury she had recently adopted that now seemed a necessity. With it came the rare chance to visit her son. She leaned forward to look at the looming wooden brewery buildings as they passed, street after street of towering brown structures, apprentices pulling carts piled high with bags of rice or sake barrels, couriers dashing back and forth on their errands. How wonderful to be outside, to feel the pulse of activity that animated her world. And today there was the special excitement about what awaited them at Seisaburo's brewery. She clutched at the side of the carriage.

Seisaburo was waiting at the main entrance to greet them. Rie was pleased at his invitation.

He bowed. "Welcome. I'm glad you could come, Mother. Please come this way."

He led them into his outer office where several clerks in indigo jackets and leggings stood in a row bowing to greet the head of the main house and his mother.

Seisaburo stood as tea was served. "I have exciting news for you. I have discovered something quite astonishing: a new and far faster and more efficient way of polishing rice. I want to show it to you. Mother, you will be able to observe it too, because we cook and polish the rice outside the main kura, next to our storeroom."

Rie took out her fan without opening it. All four visitors leaned forward expectantly.

"First I'll explain it to you, then we can see it in operation. It's a machine that uses steam power rather than a waterwheel to polish rice. I suspect that eventually steam power will completely replace the waterwheel for polishing."

"Steam power!" Yoshitaro exclaimed.

"How does it work?" Eitaro asked.

Rie rested her fan under her chin, eyes riveted on her son, who spoke so confidently.

"We use coal to generate the steam power," Seisaburo began. He opened a large drawing on the table and pointed as he spoke. "Here, you can see the process. The heat from burning coal boils water in a tank. This produces steam that expands and creates pressure that forces pistons to move the arm that comes down on the polishing area." He looked around the table at his relatives and Kinnosuke.

"And all this comes from burning coal?" Kinnosuke asked.

"Yes. Coal is the source."

"And how much faster or more efficient is this engine than the waterwheel?" Eitaro asked.

"We can polish forty times as much rice as the waterwheel does in the same amount of time."

The men gasped.

Rie placed both hands on the table. "Forty times! Just imagine!" she exclaimed.

"How did you learn about these steam engines, Sei?" Yoshitaro asked.

"Steam power was being used by those barbarian ships that came to Yokohama a few years ago. I went to Osaka some months ago and saw one of the steam engines in operation. I thought we might apply it to rice polishing, so I studied it carefully and tried to reconstruct it here. It seems to be working well." He smiled proudly.

"Brilliant, Sei! Brilliant!" Rie cried. "And you did this all on your own." She beamed. "Now . . . we'll need a supply of coal, won't we?"

"You're right, Mother." Seisaburo nodded. "We'll need to start a coal plant of our own. I've begun negotiations."

"Kinno-san, Yoshi, study Sei's machine so we can build one of our own. You too, Eitaro," Rie said.

"You can model it after mine, Mother," Seisaburo agreed.

"Make sure you learn how it works," Rie told the others. "Come, let's see it." Rie patted Seisaburo's arm and smiled at him. "This will put us way ahead of Yamaguchi."

Seisaburo led the way through the storage area to the new rice polisher.

Rie could not be more proud of Sei.

Rie had Kinnosuke and her sons carefully study the revolutionary steam-powered rice polisher to adopt it immediately for the main house. Within three months of their visit to Seisaburo it was operating. The Omura enterprise thus became the first brewing house in Japan to use steam power for polishing rice.

"And I'm sure everyone will want to adopt it. But meantime it gives us a big advantage, very big." Kinnosuke worked rapidly with the abacus as he talked. "It looks as if we may jump from fifth to third place this year."

"*Ah*, is that so?" Rie rose and began to pace up and down in the office, hands clasped behind her in imitation of her father. "And I remember my father being so pleased when we climbed from number nine to number eight. But you know, Kinno-san, I have always felt Seisaburo would do something remarkable, even though I shouldn't say it, as his mother."

Just then, Yoshitaro entered the office. The moment Rie saw his face she knew he had heard their conversation. And he wasn't happy.

Rie turned to Yoshitaro one evening after dinner. "Yoshi, please bring me the ledger of donations to the temple. It's in that tansu behind you," she said. "It's time for our annual donation."

"Yes, Mother." Yoshitaro paused. "I was going to mention it to you anyway. We've been approached by the head priest.

They're in financial trouble and ask that we double our donation this year." He scratched his chin and looked at Rie.

"Double it?" Rie frowned. "What kind of financial trouble?"

"I believe they had a fire in the old part of the main building. They were lucky to be able to save the rest." He looked at Rie.

"Well, I hope our death records weren't destroyed. But double our donation? That seems too much, don't you think? We should discuss it with Kinno tomorrow."

"We don't have to decide tonight."

Yoshitaro reached for his teacup and took a sip, then picked up the teapot and held it toward Rie.

Rie sipped, then set the cup down on the black lacquer tray. She thought of the evenings she had spent thus with her father. Now she was the parent, not the child, and the relationship was far less peaceful than hers with her father.

"Yoshi," she said abruptly, "this year we will not make a donation to the temple." She took out her comb and fingered it.

"But Mother," Yoshitaro frowned, "we have given to the temple every year, for generations. You know they do the annual memorials for Father and Grandfather, and they care for our graves. How can we refuse?"

"I haven't finished, Yoshi. I'm not suggesting that we give them nothing." She looked at Yoshitaro's perplexed expression and smiled brightly, not revealing the rest of her plan.

"Then what . . . ?" he blurted out.

"What I suggest is that we give it to them, but as a loan at the going rate." She reinserted her comb, a satisfied look on her face.

"A loan, Mother? But we can't give the temple a loan. No one does that. Anyway, what would they use as collateral? What if they couldn't pay the interest, or repay the loan?"

"They have collateral, Yoshi, a great deal of it. They have land, extensive holdings."

"You mean . . . ?"

"Yes, Yoshi, they'll put up collateral, like anyone else who takes a loan. Land can never lose its value."

"I . . . I've never heard of anyone doing this, Mother," he stammered. "I wonder if the temple wouldn't object, refuse the loan?"

"If they need money badly they'll accept it, Yoshi, even as a loan. Where else would they get such a sum? We've been their chief source of funds for many years. They depend on us."

"Well, let's discuss it with Kinnosuke in the morning, shall we?" Yoshitaro said nervously.

"Of course," Rie agreed. "And we should send word to the priest to have him come and meet with you and Kinno."

"You seem confident that Kinnosuke will go along with this idea, Mother."

"Kinno and I almost always agree in a question of business, Yoshi. We think alike," Rie replied without hesitation.

"And he probably wouldn't dare oppose you when you're determined," Yoshitaro murmured.

Yoshitaro hurried to the office the next morning to discuss his mother's proposal with Kinnosuke before she appeared.

"Your mother's judgment in business matters is usually infallible, Yoshi. I have never known her to be mistaken in a major decision," he said.

And yet Yoshitaro could read the tension in the pallor of the other man's face and the set of his jaw. He couldn't openly oppose Rie, Yoshi knew, but for once it was apparent that he wanted to, something he had never done before. If word got out about what she planned to do, it could ruin them. Why was his mother so headstrong?

As if reading his thoughts, Kinnosuke said, "Loaning to the temple may be unprecedented, but she is correct that the temple is dependent on us financially, has been for many years."

"Then you think we should offer a loan in the amount they want?" Yoshitaro asked, his mouth dropping open.

Kinnosuke paused before answering. "I hesitate to oppose her on this, Yoshi. But I agree with you, it makes one uneasy."

"Won't it affect our reputation if it gets out among other brewers?" Yoshitaro persisted.

"It might." Kinnosuke sucked in his breath. "First of all there's no guarantee that the priests will accept the loan. But if they do I doubt they'll make it public. We certainly wouldn't. And this is really a family decision, so I won't say anything, unless your mother insists."

Once again, his mother was getting her way on everything. Yoshitaro sighed. "All right, Kinno-san. Let's see what happens when the priest arrives."

Several days later the two chief priests from the family temple in Kyoto arrived at the main entrance to White Tiger, where Yoshitaro and Kinnosuke awaited them. The senior of them was a rotund man with a large shaved head and heavy jowls, his status apparent in his bearing. The second priest was smaller, with a nervous squint and hands that seemed in continual motion. The priests bowed to Kinnosuke and Yoshitaro, though not as low as Yoshitaro and Kinnosuke. The priest's composure reflected his usual role as communicant of the deities and dispenser of their benison rather than his present mission as supplicant. And as, both were senior in age as well as being priests, Yoshitaro's and Kinnosuke's respectful posture was only natural.

"We are honored to have your presence in our humble establishment," Yoshitaro said. "Please come this way." He ushered the black-robed figures into the inner office and motioned them to be seated. O-Natsu had been instructed to serve the tea, her advanced age more appropriate to the rank of the priests. Rie had asked her to linger over the tea in the room, hoping to overhear some of the conversation and report back to her.

"We are sorry to trouble you with our request," the elder priest began. "We have had an unusually difficult time this year, particularly after the fire, followed by the drought that hit our region these past two years. We beg your consideration." Both priests bowed. The junior of the two did not speak beyond the usual courtesies during the visit.

Yoshitaro reached to adjust his collar. "We understand your position. We are willing to offer you the total amount—" The two men looked at each other and smiled. "—but as a loan, at the usual terms of interest and collateral." He bowed.

The senior priest's left eye twitched. "A *loan*? I see." He closed his eyes and exhaled, arms folded over his ample stomach. His eyes remained closed, his face as impassive as a Buddha.

For several minutes no one spoke.

Yoshitaro rose. "We will leave you alone." He signaled Kinnosuke to follow him from the room.

Several minutes later Yoshitaro heard the elder priest cough. Yoshitaro and Kinnosuke returned to the room and seated themselves opposite the priests again. All four men bowed.

O-Natsu came in with more tea.

"We will be pleased to accept the terms of your offer," the elder priest said and bowed, eyes nearly closed.

Yoshitaro brought an envelope from his sleeve and pushed it across the table to the priest. The visit was concluded.

O-Natsu shuffled as fast as she could to Rie's room. "Oku-san," she whispered at the door.

"Come in," Rie said impatiently.

"The priests have accepted the loan," O-Natsu announced with a triumphant smile.

Rie blew a sigh of relief and took out her small pipe. "Good." She nodded. Why was it that she had a nagging uneasy feeling about the transaction?

O-Natsu coughed.

"Yes, O-Natsu?"

O-Natsu bowed, in a nervous gesture.

"What is it?"

"I don't believe they were happy about it."

As Rie knelt before the Butsudan altar one morning to pay her customary respects to the ancestors, she wondered if she had done the right thing, giving the temple a loan instead of paying double donation, as requested. A nagging worry made her feel unseasonably warm. She placed the rice bowl and sake cup before her parents' name tablets, then set a stick of incense in the small metal censer and lit the taper. No, it was the right thing to do. She was certain her father would have approved. She bowed, holding her hands together, aware as she did so of another person in the room behind her. She turned.

"Oh, good morning, Yoshi."

"Good morning, Mother." Yoshitaro bowed slightly, and went to one side of the room to slide open a cupboard door. He began riffling through the contents.

"Where is the set of Hina Matsuri dolls, Mother? I thought they were kept here."

Rie turned back to the Butsudan and busied herself. "Oh, I gave them to Fumi, Yoshi. You know, she wanted the old set the girls had when they were children."

"Well, we need a set for Ume now. We can't let March third go by without a set. We don't want to deprive her on Girls' Day, do we?" He closed the cupboard.

"Yes, Yoshi, you're right," Rie agreed. "The main house needs a set. Tama will see to it, won't she?"

That evening Rie and Yoshitaro lingered at the table while Tama began clearing the dishes away. She glanced at Yoshitaro and nodded.

"Mother, I've asked Tama to order a full set of dolls for Girls' Day next week."

"Fine, Yoshi," Rie agreed. She fingered her comb, and rested her hands in her lap. "And I would like to invite Fumi to bring Mie when we set the dolls out. She's already two, and otherwise Ume will be alone."

Yoshitaro said nothing, but Rie noticed he glanced toward Tama who had reentered the room. Rie marked his silence, typical when Fumi's family was mentioned.

"Let's get the finest set available, Tama," Rie said. "And I'll ask Fumi to bring Mie on the third." Rie glanced at Yoshitaro out of the corner of her eye, but his face was impassive.

The set of dolls that arrived a few days later at the Omura household was truly impressive: fifteen dolls in their ancient court costume with a five-tiered display stand covered with a red velvet cloth. The emperor and empress stood on the top tier, the emperor to the left of the empress. The court ladies and banquet trays and dishes occupied the second tier. Below them were arrayed the ministers, musicians, and lower officials. Also displayed were a miniature chest of drawers, a hibachi, a dinner table set, bowls, a dressing table, musical instruments and a palanquin in which the Imperial couple rode, all in miniature.

"Wonderful workmanship, isn't it, Tama?" Rie said, examining each piece closely.

"I'll include the peach blossoms tomorrow, Mother," Tama said, "for the feminine traits."

"Oh, by all means," Rie said with a wry smile. "Yes, mildness, peacefulness, and softness."

"Ume is so excited," Tama added.

Rie had been happy at the birth of Fumi's daughter, another child to add to the future of White Tiger. "It will be wonderful to have Ume and Mie celebrate together," Rie said.

Girls' Day, the day Ume and Mie awaited breathlessly, arrived. Both girls danced and waved their arms in front of the display.

Rie took her granddaughters by the hand and sat with them.

"Be careful Ume, Mie. You don't want to touch the dolls.

Let's sit quietly and look at them. And O-Natsu has a special treat for you today."

Fumi and Tama sat behind their daughters, whose eyes were riveted on the dolls.

Fumi reached over and touched the back of Ume's pink brocade obi. "What a beautiful obi," she said to Tama. *And so expensive,* she thought, but did not add.

Tama bowed slightly and looked down.

Fumi turned back to the doll display. "It's a really fine set, Mother," she said. "Better than the one we had when we were young, isn't it?"

Rie wondered if Fumi resented anything given to Ume, but she had never favored Ume over Hiro and was trying to balance things in the family. "Yes, well, we are a larger house now, aren't we, with two branch houses," Rie said with a glance at Fumi's face.

O-Natsu slid open the shoji. "The meal is ready, Oku-san," she said, and quickly disappeared toward the kitchen.

The dining table was laden with special foods for the day, also called the Peach Festival. Girls' Day was meant to signify happy marriage as well as to foster the feminine virtues. Sushi, pink and white mochi, and beautifully decorated candies adorned the table. Ume and Mie squealed in delight.

Following the luncheon, Rie drew the two small girls to her side and began to tell them folktales. She looked at her two granddaughters, both happy, bright children, but neither of whom figured prominently in her plans for the future of the main house.

Just then, Rie heard a firecracker go off somewhere in the distance and started. She had an uneasy feeling about the samurai unrest. She drew the children closer, forced a reassuring smile and said, "Now, where were we?"

Chapter 33

One evening in 1863 the shoji to the office opened abruptly and Eitaro rushed in, panting.

"Eitaro, what brings you here?" Rie said before he could catch his breath.

"Samurai, Mother! They're roaming the streets tonight!"

Rie jumped up. "Samurai? In the streets?" She gasped. She knew the shoguns, daimyo, and samurai were all indigent, unable to pay their debts, and that many ronin, masterless samurai, were on the loose, but this was the first time they had entered their neighborhood.

"Board up all the doors!" she ordered. "Everyone! Quickly!"

Eitaro, Kinnosuke, and three clerks ran to the doors of the kura, house, and office.

Rie turned to Eitaro. "Where's Yoshi?"

Eitaro frowned. "He left earlier this evening. Shall I go after him?"

"No, stay here. It's too dangerous out there. Let's hope he has the sense to return."

As Kinnosuke slid the latch into place at the door near the number one kura, shouting erupted in the street outside. The sound of footsteps running toward the entrance mingled with cries and sounds of scuffling.

"It's the samurai! They're in our street!" Kinnosuke cried.

A guttural voice roared "Rice! Give me rice!"

"Get out! We're hardworking merchants!"

"That's Yoshi's voice! Open the door! Quickly!" Rie cried.

Kinnosuke and Eitaro fumbled with the latch.

A shout, followed by a chilling scream, pierced the air as the door slid open. Yoshitaro lurched through the door and sprawled across the threshold, blood soaking through his kimono.

Rie took in the huge figure of a samurai that loomed at the door, disheveled matted hair and beard covering his face except for his wild bloodshot eyes. Torn dirty breeches and jacket half fell off as he raised his sword in both hands.

"Rice! Give me rice and gold!" he growled in a hoarse guttural grunt.

Rie stood in his path, her heart pounding. "Step back! You'll get nothing until you sheath your sword," she shouted.

He staggered and made two attempts to insert his sword in its scabbard before he succeeded.

"Kinno-san, bring a bag of rice!" she ordered. "Eitaro, help Yoshi and call Tama," she shouted to a clerk.

Glancing down at the pool of blood spreading out from under Yoshitaro's sleeve, Rie knelt quickly, undid her obi and opened Yoshitaro's kimono. Blood oozed from a slash across his upper arm. She hurriedly tied her obi above the wound and yanked it tight until the bleeding stopped.

Tama came running through the corridor. She glanced at her husband, then at the samurai and screamed.

"Bring some cloths," Rie ordered, "and a pan of hot water, Tama."

Kinnosuke dashed in with a bag of rice.

Rie stood. "Give it to him!" she said with a thrusting gesture.

Kinnosuke nodded and heaved the heavy bag at the samurai, who staggered and fell backward to the ground. Kinnosuke and Eitaro quickly bolted the latch again and knelt to examine Yoshitaro. He was groaning, his eyes closed.

They heard the samurai's slurred swearing and grunting as he lumbered off down the road.

"Yoshi has lost a lot of blood," Eitaro said.

Rie leaned over. "We'll send for the herbalist as soon as it's safe for someone to go out," she said.

Tama returned with a pan of hot water and cloths to bathe Yoshitaro's wound.

"Oh, my leg," he cried.

Tama and Eitaro turned him over.

"His leg is bleeding," she cried.

A deep wound gaped in the back of his thigh.

"Bind it quickly above the wound," Rie said sharply. "Eitaro, help her tighten the binding."

Eitaro pulled the cloth tight until Yoshitaro cried out in pain. Rie placed a hand on his chest and looked closely at his face while Tama cradled his head.

"The street is quiet now," Kinnosuke said, blinking rapidly as he leaned over Yoshitaro. "I'll go for the herbalist."

Rie nodded. She turned and walked toward the office, a hand on Eitaro's arm. "I suppose he was at the Sawaraya again. At a time like this! Is it going to kill him as it did his father?" she scolded.

"I don't think his life is in danger, Mother. It is a bad wound, though, the leg wound."

"These samurai parasites are completely lawless," Rie said.

"The shoguns can't keep them under control, neither can the daimyo. We'll have to keep a careful watch now. And we need to get together with our neighborhood association. Eitaro, you'd better get home and check on your family."

Yoshitaro lay on his futon for several weeks, despondent and weakened by loss of blood. Tama remained at his side day and night, encouraging him to eat or to drink tea, and the Chinese herbalist came daily with poultices and potions.

"His arm is healing well, but his leg looks bad," he told Tama in the corridor one day. "It is turning purple. I believe we will have to remove it to save his life."

Tama's hands flew to her face and she ran to Rie's room.

"Mother! Come! The herbalist says my husband may lose his leg!" Tears streamed down her face.

Rie rose, took Tama's arm, and propelled her firmly toward the ground-floor room Yoshitaro had taken over. "We'll see," she said.

The herbalist was still standing in the corridor clutching his herb pouch in both hands, looking anxious. "It's true, I'm afraid, Oku-san." He bowed. "It may be necessary, to save his life, and the sooner the better for him. It would be dangerous to leave him as he is."

"Then go ahead, tomorrow if necessary." Rie frowned.

"We'll come for him in the morning, then."

"Eitaro and Kinnosuke will accompany him," Rie said.

That evening Rie sat with Tama, who held five-year-old Ume in her arms.

Rie looked at the two. "Well, Tama, I guess this means there will be no more children from the Sawaraya. Yoshi will not be able to go around at night, or in the daytime either for that matter. The burden of work on Kinnosuke will be much heavier." She sighed.

Tama looked down without speaking.

Yoshitaro continued to languish in his old room on the ground floor. His spirits flagged. O-Sada ghosted through his dreams at night and even his daytime reveries. He despaired of ever seeing her again. Tama came in to sit with him at her needlework when she was not busy elsewhere.

"Try these prawns, your favorite," Tama said one evening, holding the delicacy toward his mouth with chopsticks.

Yoshitaro shook his head and turned away.

"Tama, I know you have tried hard to rouse Yoshi from his lethargy," Rie said one evening. "It's such a worry. We miss him in the office. I wonder. . . ." Rie paused and looked at the comb she was revolving in her hand. "I think you should come into the office and work with me a bit each day while Yoshi is mending. We don't know when he will be able to resume his work. You can begin to take some of the responsibility in the office. One day you and Yoshi will be responsible for everything." Rie was confident in Tama's ability and her eagerness to learn the business.

"I know." Tama nodded.

"Beyond your usual responsibilities, Tama, I want you to become more familiar with the business side of things. Kinno and I can use some help, especially with Yoshi out of the office these past weeks."

Tama nodded again. "I'll do my best," she said.

Rie detected Tama's interest. Good.

"Please make time to come to the office tomorrow, won't you?" Rie replaced her comb.

Kinnosuke visited Yoshitaro in his room with business questions that required decisions but was unable to rouse him from his torpor. Kinnosuke found Rie in the office and spoke to her about it. "He shows no interest in anything, Oku-san. I know he has suffered a great shock and is not able to get around. But I fear what may happen if he doesn't make some effort. And it's his will he has lost, not his ability."

Rie nodded slowly. "I know, Kinno-san. You're right. I've been considering just what to say."

Moments later she rose and walked slowly to Yoshitaro's room, her head bowed and a hand resting against her face. She slid open the shoji and looked toward the futon where Yoshitaro lay with his eyes closed. Glad that he was alone, she knelt beside the futon and placed her hand on his arm.

"Yoshi," she said softly.

He opened his eyes and looked at her dully.

"Yoshi, you cannot continue this way. You are still head of the house," she said quietly but firmly. "You must get up and perform your duties. The responsibility for the brewery and family rests with you. Tama and Ume are upset that you are lying here, not moving. We all are. Please sit up."

She reached over and placed a backrest behind him.

Yoshitaro struggled to raise himself with his arms and leaned back.

"But how can I manage? How will I get around?"

Rie looked at his face, grown lean and pallid. "Kinno is having some crutches made for you," she said. "He'll bring them to you this afternoon. You need to practice on them. One of the clerks will help you. It may take time, but you'll get used to them."

Yoshitaro sighed and reached for a glass of water. He mumbled inaudibly.

"Please, Yoshi, remember who you are." Rie flourished her comb and replaced it forcefully. "Show the Omura spirit!" she said, her voice rising.

Yoshitaro looked at her without speaking.

Rie bowed. "We rely on you," she said as she glanced back at the recumbent figure and left the room.

Chapter 34

"Yoshi, come on," Rie said as he hobbled slowly toward the office on his new crutches, for the first time without assistance. "Let's go to visit Sei again. Kinno says he has another surprise for us."

"I don't know if I—"

"Yes, of course you can," Rie said before he could finish his sentence. "Kinno is going with us. He's calling a ricksha."

Rie walked past Yoshitaro to the office and signaled Kinnosuke to have a ricksha brought to the entrance. Yoshitaro struggled painfully to the door.

"Very good!" Kinnosuke exclaimed. "You see, you can manage alone. It's just a matter of balance and confidence. Come. The ricksha is here."

Yoshitaro inched along to the main entrance behind Rie and Kinnosuke.

"Here, first sit on this step," Kinnosuke said. "Then use your arms to boost yourself up to the seat. You need to strengthen your arm muscles to bear your body weight. Some exercises will help. Here."

Kinnosuke helped Yoshitaro heave himself up to the seat.

"See, you can do it, Yoshi," Rie said, patting his shoulder. "Now relax and enjoy the ride."

The ricksha rumbled off over the cobblestones. Yoshitaro clung to the ricksha with both hands to balance himself as they bumped along.

"I'm looking forward to seeing Sei's new baby," Rie said.

"Is that the surprise?" Yoshitaro asked.

Rie laughed. "Oh no, we've known that the baby was expected for some time. I have a feeling it's something more to do with brewing. You know how clever he is. Steam power has made such a difference in rice polishing. Other brewers are all beginning to use it."

Rie and Kinnosuke commented on each brewery as they passed the long line of breweries strung in a necklace along the coastal road as far as the eye could see.

"Look at that, Kinno and Yoshi. Hirabayashi has added another kura this year."

"Yes, we need to pay special attention to them now," Kinnosuke replied.

"*Ah,* there's sake in the air today, isn't there, Yoshi? The best of perfumes, I always say. It makes one feel alive, doesn't it?" She smiled at Yoshitaro and was pleased to see him soften.

The ricksha turned a corner and Seisaburo's massive kura loomed before them.

"What is that, Mother, next to Sei's three kura?"

They gazed at the huge red structure made of something other than wood.

"I wonder, Yoshi," Rie replied. "Well, here's Sei."

Seisaburo emerged at the entrance and bowed. "Welcome, Mother. And how are you, Yoshi?"

He put out a hand to help Yoshitaro down from the ricksha.

"Come, Kinnosuke, all of you. I want to show you my new kura."

"A new kura, is it?" Rie asked as they followed Seisaburo into the courtyard. There before them towered a building the size of all kura. But it was unlike any other.

"What have you done here, Sei?" Rie asked.

Kinnosuke was already touching the walls and examining them closely. Yoshitaro leaned against the structure and turned to look at it.

"It's made of brick, you see," Seisaburo explained. "It's the same size, but the bricks make it much easier to control the temperature. And I have a strong feeling it will reduce the danger of spoilage. Everything else is the same. You can taste some of the sake from this kura." He motioned Kinnosuke and Yoshitaro to enter while he stood outside with his mother.

Kinnosuke and Yoshitaro stepped through the kura door and disappeared inside.

"If it's as you say, that it's easier to control the temperature, then we should also be building brick kura, shouldn't we? But what about the cost, Sei? Please go over that in detail with Kinno and Yoshi, won't you?"

"Certainly, Mother. Actually, the cost of building with brick is not all that different from lumber." He smiled.

"Sei, have you made another discovery that will change the way we brew, or at least the buildings we brew in?" Rie put a hand on her son's arm and a smile illumined his face. "Now, you go and give Kinno and Yoshi the details. I'm going to see your baby."

"Yes, have tea with Mari, Mother. She's expecting you. She's eager to show you the baby."

"As I am to see him." Rie paused and smiled again. "And Sei, you know your grandfather would be very proud of you." Rie turned to enter the house and hummed an old folk tune as she walked. At the front entrance she called out, "Mari, I'm here."

The day after their visit to Seisaburo's house Rie bustled into the office to talk with Kinnosuke and Yoshitaro.

She settled herself at the low table and took out her fan. "What do you think, Kinno, Yoshi? Should we build a brick kura?"

"No question about it, Oku-san. Of course we can discuss it with Toji. But I think we should not only build one or two, but we should consider converting to brick kura exclusively. Seisaburo convinced me that they are more efficient, and also safer than wooden kura. Not as susceptible to fire."

Yoshitaro bit his lip. "But what would we do with our wooden kura, Kinno? It would be expensive to change. We can't abandon them."

"We wouldn't need to convert all at once. We could rent out some of them at first, and demolish others and rebuild on the same spot. I think we can adopt a schedule for gradual conversion, one or two kura each season. That seems to be Sei's plan too."

Rie looked at Kinnosuke and tapped her fan on the table. "Good, Kinno-san. Let's begin this summer and get one brick kura ready for the start of the season. One or maybe two." She paused and looked down at the fan, opening it and turning it over in her hands.

Yoshitaro leaned forward. "Why don't we buy the old Nakanishi property in the next street? Since he died they aren't brewing now, are they? One reason they have failed is that they were never willing to take even the smallest risk."

Rie smiled. "Good, Yoshi. I don't think his widow is going to continue. And their daughter is too young for a mukoyoshi."

Rie turned her fan over and placed it on the table deliberately. "Then see what you can do about purchasing the property, Kinno-san. Those buildings are so old they'd have to be rebuilt anyway. We can build our first two brick kura there, and start with them in the autumn."

Kinnosuke nodded.

"And I want Eitaro to visit Sei too. He should start to convert."

Rie closed her fan smartly and tapped the table.

Some weeks later Rie walked into the garden to try to catch a little afternoon breeze. She reached a handkerchief from her sleeve and wiped the perspiration from her face. The cicadas were in full voice, a summer symphony. She sat on her rock and gazed at the koi in the pond. They were growing so big. The old orange-and-black grandfather koi had been there since her father's time, a venerable fish.

She scratched her chin. What was it Eitaro had said about the Choshu radicals, the loyalist samurai? They had gone so far as to bombard English ships passing through the straits of Shimonoseki. The shoguns had retaliated, joined by Satsuma and Aizu forces in a punitive expedition against Choshu. Choshu samurai had been driven out of the imperial capital in Kyoto. But wait. Eitaro said the Choshu loyalists were at it again, that was it. They were still attacking the barbarian ships, against Bakufu policy. All this political, even military, unrest—these Choshu radicals rampaging around brandishing their swords—this was bound to affect business, especially this close to Kyoto. She fanned herself rapidly, rose, and walked back inside. She would ask Eitaro to join them this evening.

Later, after dinner, Eitaro sat with Rie and Yoshitaro while Tama cleared away the dishes. Rie poured chilled sake of the top grade for Eitaro and tea for Yoshitaro, then held out her cup.

"Just one, Eitaro," she said and sipped slowly. "What's this I hear about Choshu? Tell me what you know." She looked first at Yoshitaro, then at Eitaro.

"Everyone was talking about it at the Brewers Association meeting yesterday," Yoshitaro began. "There's much unrest in Choshu and Satsuma, and it's affecting Kyoto."

Eitaro pushed his hair back from his face. "Choshu is still firing on barbarian ships, the English ships at Shimonoseki. And all this talk of 'Revere the Emperor; expel the barbarians' has support in the south. It's dangerous. The Bakufu has had to sign agreements with the barbarians. They say the barbarians can't be kept out, what with their black ships and guns. And Choshu has been buying up these guns and cannons, using them against the English."

Yoshitaro put both hands on the table and looked down. "But the southern fiefs are so powerful, and I hear Satsuma won't help the Bakufu again. You know, the Satsuma and Choshu forces want to end the shogunate. 'Revere the Emperor, expel the barbarians' is their slogan. That's what they're fighting about. There's a Tosa samurai trying to bring Satsuma and Choshu together, and I hear he's having some success. Satsuma and Choshu, with the support of some samurai from Tosa and Hizen, may change the whole picture."

"No doubt about it, a Sat-Cho alliance could mean the end of the Bakufu," Eitaro said slowly.

Rie handled her cup. "You don't mean it, Eitaro," she said. "What would happen if the Tokugawa shogunate collapses?" she asked looking from her son to her son-in-law.

"We don't know yet, Mother," Yoshitaro said. "Things are so uncertain everywhere, both in Edo and Kyoto."

"Was Sei at the meeting yesterday?" Rie asked.

"Yes, and he spoke up, said he thought Satsuma and Choshu might well be the future center of political power," Yoshitaro said.

"Just imagine!" Rie exclaimed. "What an exciting time to be alive!"

"Exciting, yes, but so unstable, Mother," Yoshitaro said. "And who knows what it bodes for us brewers."

Rie turned to him. "We'll survive, Yoshi. Just remember how many generations have been brewing here through all kinds of crises." She sat back on her heels and inserted her comb. "The key is to keep our wits about us. And try to keep up with everything that's happening in Kyoto and Edo."

Rie sat alone at the dining table one evening after Yoshitaro had left. Tama was in the kitchen working.

"Excuse me," O-Natsu's voice wafted in softly.

"Yes, O-Natsu, come in," Rie replied. She looked at the face of her old servant, now white haired, her step halting. Rie indicated a zabuton at the table.

"What is it, O-Natsu?"

"Well, Oku-san, this is difficult to say." She paused, looked down, and cleared her throat.

Rie looked at her sharply. There was no possibility of another geisha's child.

"I know how loyal Kinnosuke has always been to you and Yoshitaro. He is the most important person to the business."

"Yes, of course, O-Natsu." Rie rested the tip of her fan on her chin. She did not take her eyes off O-Natsu's face.

"Well, it's Nobu, his wife."

Rie frowned. "What about Nobu?"

"She has spoken to someone at the Yamaguchi's, saying you have shown favoritism toward Fumi and Hirokichi, over Yoshitaro and Ume." O-Natsu bowed low and looked at her hands.

Rie placed her fan on the table deliberately. Had she shown favoritism? She must admit, she had. Still, everyone knew that loyalty could never be in question; moreover if Nobu spoke of matters internal to White Tiger at Yamaguchi's, serious damage could result. Yamaguchi had shown that he was continually on the alert to defeat White Tiger.

"Are you certain about this, O-Natsu? This is not some idle rumor?"

"I am afraid it is not a rumor, Oku-san. I have known the person who told me for many years. She is a very close friend, and she would not speak ill of you."

"I see. Thank you, O-Natsu. You have always kept me informed in matters of importance. You are as valuable to me as Kinnosuke." Rie bowed.

"I am so sorry," O-Natsu said as she bowed and left the room.

Rie put both hands to her face and sighed. She would have to ponder what O-Natsu said. It would not do to take any rash action.

The next morning Rie stopped to caress the cypress support, then walked into the garden early, before anyone else was stirring in the house. She wiped the dew off her rock with her handkerchief and sat. She looked over at the koi swimming lazily in the pond. How many decisions affecting the house had she made over the years sitting on this very rock? She rested a hand on her chin and looked down at the gray stepping stones that wound a sinuous pattern through the garden and around the pond.

Kinnosuke was the single most important person to the work of White Tiger, after herself and Toji. She had often thanked the gods for sending him to White Tiger as a young boy, just as she had silently congratulated herself for promoting him in the office. His work was crucial to the success of White Tiger and to its status in the brewing world.

Still, it went without saying that loyalty to the house was absolute. Kinnosuke must have given Nobu the impression that she, Rie, was showing partiality to Fumi and Eitaro and their son, Hirokichi. Hiro was now a precocious child of ten, a few months younger than Ume. But Ume, as Yoshitaro's only child, was Kinnosuke's favorite. He always carried sweets in his sleeve, and Ume ran into the office each morning to greet him, holding out her hand as part of her ritual.

"Good morning, Banto-sama," Yoshitaro had trained her to say. And somehow, during these brief morning visits of Ume's, she began to absorb bits of information about the work of the brewery. And because Rie wanted Hirokichi to learn the work of the main house as well as his branch, she often invited him to the office. But had Kinno noticed some subtle difference in her attitude toward Yoshi and Eitaro, and had he spoken to Nobu about it? But for Nobu to speak to someone at Yamaguchi's was unconscionable disloyalty. Rie stirred uneasily on her rock. She sat there, her heart heavy with what was to come. Was there another option? Another way to proceed? She stared into the distance for the answers, thought of her mother and father. Her promise to her father. *Oh, Kinno,* she thought, the weight of what must be done pressing on her chest. *I am sorry.* She stood and walked slowly back into the house. She would wait until the end of the day, until everyone but Kinnosuke had left. Then she would do what she must.

Chapter 35

Rie opened the shoji and walked into the inner office in the early evening. Kinnosuke still sat at his table working with the abacus and ledgers after the others had left. He looked up quizzically and bowed.

She looked at him, dear Kinno-san, and took a deep, fortifying breath. How she hated to hurt him. She wished she could leave him unaware for just a moment longer, but she could not. *Oh Kinno,* she thought. Rie stood holding her fan below her obi with both hands and for a moment said nothing.

"Kinno-san," she began. "Would you come into the parlor please?"

Kinnosuke blinked. "The parlor, Oku-san?"

"Yes, please."

Rie turned, opened the shoji, and walked along the corridor. She heard Kinnosuke's slippers slapping after her. She took two zabuton from a stack at the side of the room and set them in front of the Butsudan, where the spirits of the ancestors attended. She arranged her kimono carefully under her as she sat and indicated a zabuton facing her. She inhaled deeply and paused.

Kinnosuke sat, bowed, and kept his eyes lowered to the tatami.

"Kinn-san, you know how I have valued your work at White Tiger all these many years."

He bowed.

"And your loyalty."

He bowed lower, twice.

"Loyalty can never be called into question. It is absolute." His head was bowed too low to reveal any expression.

"Of course," he murmured.

"Unfortunately it has come to my attention that Nobu has been speaking ill of this house to people at Yamaguchi's. It is disloyal, a dishonor for the house. Speaking to our chief rival about our house cannot be tolerated."

A choked, gasping sound came from Kinnosuke, his head dropping still lower.

"You realize, Kinno-san, that this is a dishonor we cannot abide."

Again Kinnosuke choked and gasped, unable to speak.

"You must divorce Nobu," Rie said abruptly. She hated to break his heart, loyal Kinno, yet what else could she do?

"Divorce?" Kinnosuke huffed and looked up, his face white.

"There is no choice," Rie said. She wished such a drastic measure weren't necessary. But it was.

Kinnosuke stammered. "She is . . . she is the mother of my two sons, and my daughter." His eyes blinked and his breath came in rapid gasps.

"Divorce her!" Rie repeated sharply, her heart tightening in her chest. Oh, Kinno-san.

Kinnosuke squeezed his eyes shut to try to contain his tears. His fists clenched on his lap. He began to bow repeatedly.

"I am sorry. I am sorry. I have no words to apologize." He repeated the refrain over and over as he bowed.

Rie stood. "I am sorry too, Kinno-san. So sorry. It is most unfortunate," she said as she rose, walked to the shoji, and left Kinnosuke shaking and bowing in front of the Butsudan. Yet she couldn't help but wonder if she'd done the right thing.

The next morning Yoshi hobbled rapidly into the dining room where Rie was still drinking her tea. "What do you think you have done, Mother, telling Kinno to divorce his wife, and talking about honor? How can you do this, to the person who has helped you achieve what White Tiger has become?" he said, pacing back and forth in front of her. "Questioning his loyalty, indeed! Have *you* no sense of loyalty? Have *you* no concern for anything other than the house? The house is all I hear, nothing about the people in it." Yoshi was gasping for breath.

"Calm down, Yoshi. Kinno knows about loyalty very well. I have not accused him of disloyalty. But his wife, Nobu, has been talking against us at Yamaguchi's. That is something we can't tolerate, and at the very house that has caused us so much grief. It cannot be excused. It is regrettable to cause Kinno unhappiness, but he is well aware of what affects the interests of the house. We can't compromise on this." Rie sighed.

Yoshi stalked from the room and walked to the office. Kinnosuke was seated at his table, head on his hands.

"Oh, Kinno-san . . . I understand that Mother has ordered you to divorce Nobu."

"It is true." He raised his head, tears in his eyes.

"I'm very sorry. You have been happily married so long, and you have your three children. . . ."

Kinnosuke hung his head but said nothing.

"You know, Kinno-san, ever since I was a child I've felt closer to you than to Mother. She can be tyrannical at times. *You* were the one who really raised me, who took pains to teach me. I shall always be grateful to you."

Kinnosuke bowed. "Thank you. As a child you were always so eager to learn. Of course my debt to your mother who gave me this opportunity and trained me is heavy. Her sense of timing in business is without equal. I have learned much from her and can never repay my debt." He bowed again.

"Perhaps you and I can work even more closely together in the future, support each other," Yoshitaro said.

"My loyalty has always been to the Omura House. That is why the charge of my wife's disloyalty is so painful to me. I wonder if I should resign." He looked querulously at Yoshitaro.

"Certainly not! That would serve no purpose, and I'm certain that Mother would not accept it. It would leave us weakened. We have no one to replace you. Your efforts are crucial to our success. I have no question about your loyalty. I cannot work without you."

Kinnosuke bowed low. "Thank you for your confidence. Then I shall remain with you." He bowed to the floor.

"Thank you, Kinno-san. You have my sympathy in this difficult time. Please let me know if there is anything I can do to help."

Yoshitaro put his hand on Kinnosuke's shoulder and shook his head.

Kikuji Yamaguchi sat at his worktable, leaning backward and forward, backward and forward, belching frequently.

He called his chief clerk Yusuke to his table. "We can do something to stop Omura now. You know, their young Master was wounded in a samurai attack, lost his leg. Kinnosuke is overworked. He can't watch everything."

"That's so," Yusuke said, scratching his bald head. "What do you suggest?"

"We can get control of some of their shipping contracts now that they have less sake to ship. They won't be expecting it."

Yusuke sucked in his breath and closed his eyes. "I see. . . ."

Yamaguchi looked at his aging clerk, face grown lean, shoulders hunched. Was he losing his aggressive push? "Get to the port tomorrow, first thing," Yamaguchi ordered. "Make sure you get the Omura shipping contracts."

Yusuke bowed. "Certainly."

"I'm going over to see Fumi," Rie announced loudly as she took up her parasol and walked out the entrance to the office where Yoshitaro and Kinnosuke were working. Yoshitaro nodded curtly. What little gains she had made with him after the amputation had disappeared after her decree that Kinnosuke divorce his wife. She could only hope that this too would pass. She had done the right thing. The necessary thing. And yes, for the house. The house was the point.

Rie had called Seisaburo to Fumi and Eitaro's. She wanted to talk to her children without having Yoshitaro present, and Fumi offered the best pretext. It would be the first time she had undertaken a family discussion of a problem in the house without involving Yoshitaro.

Rie twirled her parasol and listened to the sound of her wooden geta on the cobblestones and the raucous voice of the tofu man going house to house with his cartload of bean cake.

"I'm here." The bell on the slatted gate tinkled as she slid it open and hurried to the entrance.

"Come in, Mother." Fumi gave a quick bow.

"And here's my precious grandchild," Rie said, patting the head of Hirokichi's sister, Mie, who peered around her mother at her grandmother.

"Sei is already here," Fumi said. "They're in the parlor." She placed slippers on the floor in front of her mother and led the way to the room she had decorated with a special ikebana arrangement for her mother's visit.

Eitaro stood and took Rie's arm. "Please have a seat, Mother." He bowed and indicated a zabuton backing to the tokonoma alcove.

"And how are you, Sei?" Rie asked her son. "What new surprise have you for us today?" She smiled.

"I think it's you who has the surprise today, Mother. Eitaro tells me that you ordered Kinnosuke to divorce his wife."

Rie flushed at the accusation. "I just didn't see any alternative, when I learned that she had been speaking ill of Fumi and Hiro at Yamaguchi's. It was a dishonor, and worse, disloyal."

"What exactly did she say, Mother?" Eitaro asked.

Fumi moved closer to her mother.

"According to O-Natsu's friend, she accused me of favoritism to you and Hiro, over Yoshi and Ume." Rie frowned, at the same time feeling a twinge of guilt.

Eitaro pursed his lips and looked at his hands on the table.

Fumi leaned toward Rie. "And has he divorced Nobu?"

"He did so, of course," Rie replied, feeling a deep regret. "She has left."

"I hope it won't affect Kinno's work," Seisaburo said.

"I doubt it," Rie replied. "You know how close he has always been to Yoshi, and Yoshi is totally dependent on him since his accident. Kinno has been extremely attentive to Yoshi lately, even more than usual. Yoshi has particularly urged him to stay, and they have always been so close."

"Well, I hope it doesn't create a problem for you. Will it be uncomfortable for you to work with him now?" Eitaro asked.

Rie fingered the teacup in front of her. "I'm convinced his support of Yoshi won't waver." She hoped her words didn't reflect a hint of doubt.

"What about his children?" Fumi asked.

"They're still with their father, at least the two sons are," Rie said. "I think Nobu may have taken the daughter with her."

Fumi frowned and hugged Mie.

Rie took out her comb and twirled it in both hands. "It's unfortunate, but it's not a disaster. We mustn't let it paralyze us. This is an exciting time, with so many new opportunities. We need to move in new directions, not be stalled over something that's past." She did not mean to sound cold. She simply had to refocus them away from the personal and onto business. "There's a bigger problem. Now it seems that Yamaguchi has captured our shipping contracts with three of our shippers. We have to do something."

Seisaburo leaned forward. "Well, I've been thinking about shipping anyway. We have to negotiate our charters every winter."

"That's so," Rie agreed.

"Wouldn't it be better if we had more control over shipping?"

"Of course. And now with Yamaguchi's move it's a crisis. Could we buy ships of our own?" Rie asked, taking out her fan.

Sei glanced at his mother. "Buy ships? No brewer has done it yet, which might give us a real advantage, to be independent of the charter agents." He looked at his mother, then Eitaro.

"There's still the question of the loaders, the stevedores," Eitaro said, "but as shippers we'd definitely have more control over costs."

Rie lit up at the news. "Well, what are the risks? What will the long-range effects be? This is something new. We need to think of what would happen if we lost a ship in a storm."

"We're so diversified, Mother, as you have always urged, that I think we would survive the loss of a ship," Eitaro said.

"Then that's decided. Now I have to persuade Yoshi and Kinno," she said, frowning and tapping her chin with her fan.

"Of course Kinno has always looked ahead. It may not be a problem. Why borrow trouble, Father always said."

Eitaro cleared his throat. "I was thinking. Could we start wholesaling? We have good sources of Yamada Nishiki rice. This would give us extra funds we could use for buying a ship or two."

"We have no choice about ships. We have to counter Yamaguchi's move," Rie said. "It's true that wholesaling is more traditional, but also the dealers and routes are entrenched. With ships we won't have that kind of opposition, at least from other brewers. None of them has gone into buying ships."

"Ships are the key to our biggest markets," Seisaburo urged. "And we have stayed ahead because of our willingness to innovate and take risks."

"I'll go back and talk to Kinno and Yoshi. Give them something to think about besides Nobu."

A few weeks later Yoshitaro hobbled into the number one kura on his new crutches. It was his first venture there since he lost his leg. It was winter, brewing was in full swing, and the kurabito were hurrying from one part of the compound to another. Yoshitaro paused to rest against the wall near the entrance.

"*Ah*, Master. How good to see you again. We were all so concerned."

Yoshitaro looked around. It was Toji, bowing repeatedly, his ruddy face beaming. "Do you wish to, *ah* . . . may I help you?" He glanced at Yoshitaro's one leg, then looked down and bowed.

"Thank you, Toji-san. I'll manage. I just want to look at the filter."

Yoshitaro hopped toward the boat-shaped wooden press where the final stage of brewing took place, the residue of lees filtered out from the brew to leave the liquid clear and nearly colorless. Minutes later two kurabito stopped to bow and ask if he needed help. He shook his head and murmured, "No, thank

you." *They're obviously embarrassed,* he thought. He felt an angry
flush move from his neck toward his forehead. And the missing
leg still pained so that he often bit his lip. The slash of the samurai sword across the back of his thigh was still agony. He leaned
against the filter, his crutches resting against it, grateful that the
two kurabito had gone elsewhere.

If these men, people he had worked with for years and knew
him so well, could not bear to look at him on his crutches, how
would he ever face O-Sada? How would she be able to look at
the stump, the remnant of his leg? It was so grotesque that he
himself could barely stand to look at it. Tama had tried to keep
from wincing when she had to change the dressing, but Yoshitaro
could sense her distaste. Kinno had been so supportive, a real
savior. And his mother treated him as if nothing had happened.
He was still Kinzaemon XI of the Omura House, she kept reminding him.

It would be too painful to go again to the Sawaraya. It was
possible that O-Toki and O-Sada would welcome him again.
They probably would, but it would not be the same. He was
still O-Sada's patron and O-Toki's natural son and benefactor.
He would not forget their financial needs. They would probably pity him, but pity was not what he craved when he went
to the Sawaraya. It was easy to understand why his father had
gone there so often over the years. There they accepted a man as
he was, made him feel important, even attractive. Attractive. He
could never be considered so again. The Sawaraya was the only
place a man could totally relax. But nothing could induce him to
go back now. How he would survive without those visits, without
O-Sada's soft ways, he could not imagine.

As for children, he had no wish to approach Tama. There was
no need for further exploration of a possible pregnancy. That
meant that Ume, the miracle of O-Sada's love, would be his
only child and would represent the next generation. Like Rie,

she would one day have an adopted husband. The history of the house would repeat itself. Yoshitaro reached for his crutches to return to the office. He must make sure that Ume became the focus of attention, not only his own and Kinnosuke's, but also his mother's.

Chapter 36

As Rie walked toward the kitchen one morning she heard excited voices in the inner office. She hurried along the corridor and opened the shoji.

Kinnosuke glanced toward Rie and said, his thin voice higher than usual, "The loyalists have won, Oku-san. It's happened, just as Seisaburo predicted."

Yoshitaro struggled on his crutches to move closer to his mother. "They say there was fighting in the streets of Kyoto between Sat-Cho samurai and Bakufu forces," he said. "Now they're saying the shogun has relinquished power to the emperor, and the emperor has gone to Edo with his court."

Rie hooked her thumbs in her obi and looked at Yoshitaro, then at Kinnosuke. "Well! The end of the Tokugawa shoguns! I never thought I would see the day. What does this mean for us, I wonder?"

"Too soon to tell, but we've got to be on guard," Kinnosuke

said. "There's going to be an emergency meeting of the Brewers Association this afternoon."

"Make sure Eitaro and Seisaburo know, Yoshi," Rie said, feeling a sense of urgency.

"We'll all go," Yoshitaro said.

Rie tapped her fan on the table. "I want to know everything that's discussed. In detail."

Yoshitaro dipped his head in acknowledgment. "Don't worry, Mother. We'll give you a full report."

Rie spent the rest of the day in agitated activity. She followed O-Natsu and the maids around the house, at one point grabbing the feather duster from O-Yuki and flourishing it furiously in the parlor at each item in the Butsudan and tokonoma. Early in the afternoon she bustled out to the compound, tied back her sleeves, and attacked the barrels with a brush. Then she hurried back into the inner office, took the ledgers onto a worktable, and turned pages, following columns of figures with her fingers. "Don't overlook anything," she muttered to herself. She sat there long after all the clerks had left, unaware of the time until O-Natsu called her to dinner.

"They're still not back, O-Natsu. I don't feel hungry."

O-Natsu set bowls of steaming miso soup and rice in front of Rie. "But you must eat something. They're sure to return soon."

Rie picked up the soup bowl and sipped, then plucked out some tofu with her chopsticks.

She paused. Yes, there was the sound of the outer shoji being opened, the stamping of geta-clad feet on the earthen floor of the entryway, and voices—Yoshitaro's, Kinnosuke's, and Eitaro's too.

Rie rose quickly and hurried to the entrance. "Welcome home! Come and tell me what happened. You must be hungry."

The men gathered around the dinner table and, hoisting up their kimonos to sit cross-legged, cleared their throats.

"I'm glad you've come too, Eitaro," Rie said.

O-Yuki brought in more rice and miso, with small dishes of mountain vegetables, mackerel, pickles, green tea, and sake.

Rie looked at each man then turned to Yoshitaro. "Tell me!" she said.

"Mother, there's a lot to tell and there's nothing to tell. It's really too soon to say what's going to happen in Edo. Until we know the situation there we won't know how it will affect us. All we know for certain is that everything is changing in Edo and elsewhere."

"It took so long just to learn that?" Rie asked sharply.

Kinnosuke blinked several times, his thin face twitching. "What we do know for certain, Oku-san, is that we will continue brewing for the rest of the season, just as if nothing had happened. Of course something has happened, but as Yoshi said, we don't yet know what the effects will be."

"What took so long today, Mother," Eitaro explained, "is that people were discussing various possible outcomes in Edo. But without real knowledge of what's happening it was only speculation. I spoke with Sei and he thinks we should go to Edo, now, at least one of us, to see what we can learn. We need to talk to Yoshioka and the man you sent there, Suganuma. I think that's the best we can do for now." Eitaro turned to the dishes in front of him.

Yoshitaro put down his chopsticks. "What seems certain is that Satsuma and Choshu are in control there now, supporting the emperor. And they've got some samurai from Hizen and Tosa with them. The shogun has retired, without a major battle, just some skirmishes in Aizu and the south. Those samurai were mostly bluster and swagger anyway, attacking unarmed individuals," he added, looking down.

"Yes, Yoshi," Rie said. She reached over and put a hand on his arm. "Well, they haven't stopped you, have they?" She picked up a teapot and poured for him.

* * *

Several weeks later Rie stepped into the corridor and caught sight of Yoshitaro hopping rapidly toward the office. She marveled at how adept he had become at getting around on crutches. She was on the verge of complimenting him when she stopped herself. Better not to call attention to his disability, since he himself seemed to be accepting it. At least he no longer complained, and he had stepped back into his role as house head. She followed him into the office, where several clerks were talking excitedly.

"Oku-san, and Master," Kinnosuke spoke up. "It seems there's been a public proclamation by the new government. It's posted outside the old Bakufu commissioners' office. We need to know what it says. I think I'd better go." He blinked several times.

"Yoshi and I will accompany you, Kinno-san. I'm anxious to know too. Send for a ricksha."

Spring had come and gone and with it the kurabito who returned to their farms in Tamba. The end of season celebration had been held, and the kura buildings were quiet. Sales had been brisk following the hanging of the leaf ball at the front entrance. It was the time of year when only the office clerks remained busy.

As the ricksha drew up to the entrance a second ricksha arrived with Eitaro seated in it.

"I see you had the same idea, Mother," he said. "Come, ride with me." He reached a hand out to help Rie up.

"Good. Yoshi will ride with Kinno."

The streets exploded with life, ricksha and carts clogging the narrow lanes, all headed in the same direction. Excitement was in the air as ricksha runners raced for position in the line of traffic. Rie sat back, her arm resting on the side, enjoying the crowds and the sea breeze against her face. She was pleased that her enjoyment had not diminished with age.

The monsoon rains had not begun, and she was grateful for the light wind from across the harbor. She always paused to look at the cask ships anchored there, some on dry dock having their sails or hulls repaired.

As the rickshas neared the main intersection, they jammed every possible space, making it impossible to move.

"We'll walk from here," Eitaro said. He helped Rie down, made sure that Kinnosuke and Yoshitaro were behind them, and signaled the rickshas to wait.

"Can you make it, Mother?" Yoshitaro asked.

"Yes, Yoshi. How about you? Do you want to wait in the ricksha? There's such a crowd."

"Maybe you'd better wait here, Master," Kinnosuke said.

"No, I want to see the proclamation," Yoshitaro insisted.

As Rie and Eitaro elbowed their way toward the front, Rie could hear men shouting as they read. Yes, they were nearly all men, most of them merchants and townsmen, by their clothing. No samurai were in evidence. Then over at the edge of the crowd Rie spotted a samurai still wearing his swords, his face and head covered by a huge straw hat to avoid recognition.

"He must be embarrassed to appear in this crowd," Eitaro said.

Several inches taller than Rie, Eitaro was able to read the proclamation. He held Rie's elbow as he read. "It proclaims 'the Restoration of the Emperor,' and the emperor and the new era are both named 'Meiji.' Just a minute. There's also a Charter Oath, it says. Let me see if I can read it." He edged closer, Rie clinging behind him. She looked around, trying to catch sight of Kinnosuke and Yoshitaro.

"I don't see them anywhere," she said, frowning.

"There are five articles in the Oath, Eitaro read: '(1) Deliberative assemblies shall be widely established and all state affairs decided by public discussion. (2) All classes, high and low, shall unite in actively carrying out the administration of affairs of state.

(3) The common people, no less than the civil and military officials, shall be allowed to pursue whatever calling they choose. (4) Evil customs of the past shall be abandoned and everything shall be based on the just laws of Heaven and Earth. (5) Knowledge shall be sought throughout the world so as to invigorate the foundations of imperial rule.' That's the end. Well, we still have to know what it all means, don't we?" he said.

"Try to remember those five points, Eitaro. We'll need to talk them over and try to understand what they mean. We need to find Yoshi and Kinno now." She turned.

They squeezed back against the encroaching mob. Rie stumbled, shoved by an insistent plebeian. Eitaro caught her as she was about to fall.

"Oh, there's Yoshi." Just as she spoke an enormous figure looming ahead pushed against Yoshitaro, causing him to fall to the ground.

"What do you think you're doing here, with your one leg?" roared the man.

"It's Yamaguchi," Rie said. She looked at him as he swaggered away. "Bully!" she shouted. "We'll get him for this," she mumbled. "Yoshi, are you hurt?" she asked, taking his arm. Kinnosuke had already helped him up.

"Well, I nearly fell too, Yoshi," Rie said.

Yoshitaro shook himself. "I'm all right."

"It was hard for anyone to stand," Rie said. "Come, let's go home."

"Edo is no longer Edo, Mother. It's now called Tokyo," Tama said one morning at breakfast.

"Ah, Eastern Capital," Rie said.

"So many things happening there," Yoshitaro said. "All these new notions from America and Europe: banks, railroads, constitutions, political parties, a parliament, a new army and navy, a new solar calendar. It's amazing! One thing I heard Kinno talk about might be useful to us."

"What's that, Yoshi?" Rie asked.

"He said it's a new form of economic organization the government is supporting. It's called a joint stock company."

"What is that exactly, Yoshi?" Rie asked.

"He said it's a way of spreading the risk among a group of investors," Yoshitaro said.

"We need to learn more about it, then, don't we?" Rie asked.

Later, in the office, Kinnosuke spoke with Rie. "One thing is certain, there are no more kabu shares," he said. "We can produce as much sake as we want with what rice we can procure. No more government controls. The new government has its hands full doing other things." He blinked rapidly and sucked in his breath.

"But doesn't this mean that everyone else can also brew as much as they want, including anyone who has never brewed before?" Yoshitaro asked.

"True," Kinnosuke agreed, "but we have an advantage. We're number three. New brewers just starting out won't be able to compete."

"It seems one key to competing now is to buy as much rice as we can," Rie said, tapping her fan on the table. "So, Kinno-san and Yoshi, shouldn't we send to our suppliers immediately? Offer a slightly higher price, just over the going price, to ensure the largest supply." Rie looked at Eitaro, who had entered the office.

"I think you're right, Mother," he said. "I'm going to move in that direction too."

Eitaro always seemed to grasp the importance of timing faster than Yoshitaro.

Rie broached with Kinnosuke and Yoshitaro the idea of purchasing ships, the suggestion she had already discussed with Eitaro and Seisaburo.

"Since Yamaguchi has taken over most of our shipping contracts we need to buy ships, as soon as possible."

"We don't have a choice, do we?" Kinnosuke said. "It will take negotiation. No brewer has done it, but that doesn't mean it can't be done." He blinked.

"You know the shippers, don't you, Kinno-san?" Rie asked.

"Several." Kinnosuke nodded. "There's a medium-sized shipper in port who's in difficulty, I hear. The head of the house died last month and the succession is in dispute. They may be willing to put one or two ships up for sale."

"Then this is the time to approach them, isn't it?" Rie said.

"It looks as if we should move now," Yoshitaro agreed.

"And there's another possibility," Rie began and took out her fan. "It would mean competition, but I was wondering if we might do some rice wholesaling, as Sei suggested? We have excellent sources now, really more than we need, even with our new kura. It would give us more influence over the price of rice and enable us to expand future production. What do you think, Kinno-san?"

"As you say, there's a lot of competition with the already established routes."

"We could make gradual inquiries. I know it would take some time. I don't expect we could do it all this year, but what about for next year's harvest?"

"We can try, yes," Kinnosuke nodded and blinked.

Rie smiled and poured tea for the two men. Yamaguchi had made it easy to obtain their agreement on buying cask ships. Rie hoped to catch Yamaguchi off guard.

A few months later Rie wanted to visit Seisaburo again, this time alone, without Yoshitaro or even Eitaro. When it came right down to it, Seisaburo was becoming her most trusted business ally, apart from Kinnosuke. His entrepreneurial skill was without peer. Confident though Rie was in her choice of Eitaro, she knew Seisaburo had the edge when it came to innovation. Rie left through the kitchen door, telling only O-Natsu where she was going. She smiled at the sense of adventure finding her own rickshaw gave her, a simple enough act but not part of her daily routine. Seisaburo was not expecting her, but she trusted to luck that she would find him there.

She left the ricksha at the entrance and entered the gate whose tinkling bell announced her presence. Seisaburo's wife, Mari, greeted her with a bow and a smile.

"Welcome! What a pleasant surprise. And you came all this way alone?" She placed slippers at the edge of the hall platform for Rie.

"Oh, yes. Is Sei in the office?" Rie asked without polite preliminaries.

"I am afraid he has gone to our other kura. He should be back by noon, though," Mari said, nodding.

"I wonder if your banto, Hirano-san, would mind if I talked with him?"

"I am certain he would be honored to speak with my husband's mother from the main house. Please wait here a moment." Mari indicated a seat in the parlor near the tokonoma.

Rie sat at the lacquer table. A maid bustled in with tea, but Rie only nodded.

Mari returned, breathlessly solicitous. "Please come this way, Mother," she said. She led the way along the earthen corridor to the office.

Seisaburo's chief clerk, Hirano, bowed low to Rie. "What an honor to see the mistress of the main house here, Oku-san," he said. Mari excused herself and left Rie alone with the ample, heavy-browed chief clerk.

Rie bowed slightly. "Actually, I had hoped to speak with my

son about a rather delicate matter, but as I know you are his loyal banto. . ."

"Is there something I can do to help?" Hirano asked.

Rie looked at him, this sturdy, experienced man in his forties. She herself had advised Seisaburo about hiring him when Sei began his branch house operation, and Hirano was aware of his obligation to her.

"Well, Hirano-san, I have been thinking. Wouldn't it be a good idea to have one of your clerks come to work at the main house for a while? We could send you one of ours in exchange. It would be a good experience for both boys and make our house ties stronger. Having an apprentice eat someone else's rice works both ways, doesn't it?" She did not mention that she hoped to find an apprentice she could keep as Kinnosuke's future successor.

She smiled and looked around the office at three young clerks working there. Her eye rested on a boy she judged to be the right age, about fourteen, a well-built boy, with a businesslike air about him.

"What about that boy over there? A good worker?" she asked.

"*Ah,* he is my son. Yes, I have been training him, grooming him myself." He bowed. "He has been helping your son."

Rie nodded. "Would you be willing to part with him for a year? Of course you would still be dealing with him on a regular basis, and you would have one of our clerks in exchange." Rie kept her eye on the boy and became more persuasive as she watched him.

Hirano bowed. "I would be honored to have my son work in the main house for a year."

"What is his name?" Rie asked.

"Buntaro. He is thirteen years old, soon fourteen."

"The right age. Good. I'll wait until my son returns. We can formalize the arrangement if it is agreeable to everyone. I'll send you a most able clerk in exchange."

Rie bowed and returned to the house to wait. Mari brought in more tea, then excused herself to take care of her children. "My husband will be back soon, I am sure," she said.

Rie nodded. She hoped Seisaburo would not object to her selection of Buntaro as Kinnosuke's apprentice. Kinnosuke and Yoshitaro might be another matter.

Chapter 37

 A few days later Rie caught Yoshitaro alone at the dinner table.

"You know, Yoshi," she began slowly, "it might be a good idea to begin thinking about selecting the apprentice who will become Kinno's successor."

"There's no hurry about it, is there? He's still young and we have several clerks about the right age. We could start grooming one of them. No lack of talent or training."

Rie took out her fan, then put it down and poured tea for Yoshitaro.

"That's true, Yoshi. But you know, there's something else to consider. She paused and looked pensively at her fan. "You know what they always say about having a son or apprentice 'eat someone else's rice' so they don't become spoiled or complacent, so they learn other ways of doing things."

"What are you getting at?" Yoshi chewed on a toothpick.

"Well, I wonder if it might not be mutually advantageous for us to take an apprentice from one of our branches, either from Eitaro or from Sei, and send them one of ours in exchange for a year?"

"I suppose it's a possibility. I'd prefer one of Sei's, if you put it that way."

"All right," Rie nodded, pleased that he had so readily acquiesced to her plan. She knew Yoshi would prefer Sei's apprentice to anyone from Fumi's house. "And I wouldn't object to the idea of promoting a clerk from Sei's to be Kinno's successor eventually, if he works out well."

"But what would our clerks think if they were passed over by one of Sei's? And I'm not sure Kinno would agree. Haven't we caused him enough trouble, forcing him to divorce Nobu?"

"You can persuade him, Yoshi. I know you can. And he'll see the wisdom of it. Just think of all the improvements Sei has made in brewing. Having a future banto trained by Sei will enhance our business in the future. It's bound to. It will make our tie with Sei's branch even stronger. You need to be looking toward the future, Yoshi. Kinno may be young now, but he won't last forever. Neither will I." She paused to smooth her hair self-consciously. "We can try him out, see how he works. We don't need to make a decision about Kinno's successor until he has worked here a year or so and proven himself. No need to mention that plan to Kinno yet."

Yoshitaro nodded but frowned, his mouth a study in negativity. "You are very persuasive, Mother."

"You can be too, Yoshi, especially with Kinno. He values your opinion above everyone else's. And after all, you have the final say in any decision."

Yoshitaro raised his eyebrows slightly but said nothing.

* * *

The emperor's birthday, a holiday, meant that Fumi was bringing her family for a visit. Emperor Meiji, a child of thirteen at the time of the Restoration in 1868, was now only seventeen. Everyone knew it was the samurai loyalists from Satsuma and Choshu, not the child emperor, who had transformed the country from an isolated feudal regime to something resembling a modern nation-state.

"How good it is to see you all." Rie held out her arms to Hirokichi. Whenever he came to the main house for training, he followed Buntaro around, the new clerk from Seisaburo's branch. Buntaro was now installed as a permanent clerk in the office, and even Kinnosuke had agreed that he be promoted to number one apprentice. Rie smiled whenever she saw Hirokichi and Buntaro together. It repeated the pattern of Yoshitaro and Kinnosuke years earlier, a bond to be fostered.

"And Mie, come here, my dear." Rie put an arm around Mie, who sat down next to her. "Hiro too." Rie handed both children some candies from her sleeve.

"Hiro, you've grown so. How old are you now?"

"I'm eleven, Grandmother. My birthday was three months ago."

"Don't tell me I forgot such an important event! How neglectful of me. So you're the same age as Ume, aren't you, dear?" Rie smiled at Ume and Hirokichi.

"I'm nearly twelve, Grandmother," Ume said, frowning at Hirokichi.

"You're all growing up so fast I can't keep up with you," Rie said laughing. She indicated a plate of cakes to Tama, who passed them and poured tea.

"Hiro is very busy these days, Mother," Eitaro said. "Besides his apprenticeship here he spends time with me the first thing each morning. We go into the kura to check everything."

Rie glanced at Eitaro and thought how good it was for Fumi that her husband was not only capable but also attractive, with his sharply chiseled features and agreeable manner.

"My, is that so?" Rie said. "And how do you like that, Hiro?"

"It smells wonderful in the kura, Grandmother. I like to watch the bubbles grow with the yeast, and the koji room is so warm on cold mornings. It's too bad you can't go into the kura, Grandmother." Hirokichi tossed a ball jauntily as he talked. "Ume can't either," he said, with a superior glance at his cousin.

Ume pouted and stuck her tongue out at Hiro.

"That's right, Hiro. We women can never enter the kura. It's for the safety of the sake. We are taught never to cross the threshold. And our sake has only gone bad once," Rie said.

"Did you enter the kura that time, Grandmother, and make it go sour?" Hirokichi asked.

All the adults laughed, including Rie. Then she thought of Jihei's treachery, and her smile vanished, her mood darkened.

"No, I didn't cause it, Hiro," she said.

Rie leaned over toward Fumi. "I knew Hiro would be a bright child, even before he was born," she said softly, not wanting Hiro to become conceited.

Tama looked at Rie and leaned forward. "And Ume has started scouring the barrels, Mother. She's so thorough. Toji is very pleased with her." Tama, like Yoshi, was always eager to protect Ume. It was a shift since Tama's anguish when Ume was adopted in.

"Yes," Rie said. "That's what I used to do when I was young, Ume." She glanced at Ume. "Your mother did too. It's good to see these traditions carried on by the grandchildren."

"How is Buntaro working out, Mother?" Eitaro asked.

"He's an excellent worker, excellent. And we've promoted him now to Kinno's number one apprentice. Sei is so far away that I'm glad we have this tie. Not like you, close by so that we can talk every day. You know Kinno worked in the kitchen at first. I found him there boiling rice."

"Is that so?" Eitaro said. "I didn't know. So he rose from rice boiler to head clerk?" He nodded appreciatively.

"And Buntaro shows the same promise as Kinno. That's what really pleases me," Rie said. "I'm glad his father and Sei didn't insist that he go back, though I know they miss him." Rie realized that Sei and Buntaro's father were deeply disappointed to lose Buntaro.

"There's a problem with the loan to the temple, Mother," Yoshitaro said in the office one morning.

"Yes," Kinnosuke agreed, worry lines making him appear older than his years. "It was a five-year loan, and they are not able to pay the interest. They haven't paid for the last four months." He looked from Rie to Yoshitaro.

"I see," Rie said. She tapped the table with her fan.

"The priest came from Kyoto yesterday afternoon. He said, correctly, that the principle and interest have reached a total of fifteen thousand yen. They cannot pay the interest on it. He was quite distressed," Yoshitaro said, watching his mother.

"I was afraid that might happen when they asked for such a big loan," Kinnosuke said.

"Yes, it was not totally unexpected," Rie said, although she had hoped it would never come to this. "Now we will have to treat them like any other borrower. Accept some of their collateral." She reached over for the ledger book in front of Kinnosuke.

Yoshitaro frowned. "You mean . . . take the temple's land?" he asked, wide-eyed with shock.

"They have quite a lot of good mountain land that they don't need, and the demand for our wood and coal is increasing. We use a lot ourselves. So many are using steam power now. With the extra money we earn, we can make a larger donation so that they won't be greatly affected, and won't lose face by being unable to repay the loan."

Yoshitaro smoothed the hair back from his face to reveal a gathering storm, and asked, "How can we do this to our family temple? Our ancestral records and graves are there. This would be a huge blot on our reputation. It just isn't done, to take collateral from a temple, any more than it is to loan to them."

"Yoshi, this is a new era. It calls for bold measures if we are to keep up with the times and stay ahead of the competition. We can't cling to old attitudes."

"I didn't like it when we made the loan, but this is even worse," Yoshitaro said, leaning on his crutches. He frowned. "I'm afraid when word of this gets around it will be bad for our business. We'll be criticized. More than that, think of the bad karma that will accrue from taking temple land, taking advantage of the family temple. You can't go against the gods and priests."

Rie sighed. Although she understood his worries, even agreed, it was too late to be timid. It would only make matters worse. Instead, they needed to make the best out of a bad situation. Yoshitaro was at times so obviously Jihei's son, not hers. "Yoshi, don't be fainthearted," she said. "Your father was that way too. Our markets are not only secure, they are expanding. And I doubt others will come to know of this. And as I said earlier, we can make added donations to the temple with our earnings. What do you think, Kinno-san?"

Kinnosuke spoke rapidly. "As the temple is more a family matter, I don't feel I can offer an opinion. The decision is up to you, and the Master. But if you really want my opinion, I think Yoshi may be right."

"We should consult with Sei and Eitaro," Yoshitaro said, taking advantage of Kinnosuke's evasion.

"I am sure they would support me," Rie said.

Yoshitaro stomped around on his crutches. "Well, this is something I refuse to do. And *I* would be the one who would have to inform the priest, not you."

"Business is business, Yoshi!" Rie countered, standing in front of him so he could not escape her. "We often have to do things we do not enjoy. Yes, it's your responsibility as house head. You'll have to go to Kyoto tomorrow. Kinno can go with you and take care of the financial details."

Kinnosuke bowed, but she could see the tension in his face.

Rie knew that if she didn't do something quickly, Yoshi's anger would soon spill over. She touched his arm, but he merely pulled away.

"There's no need to take all their mountain land," Rie said, trying a more conciliatory approach. "This won't change our relationship. I doubt they'll want to publicize these arrangements any more than they did the loan, and in the end, this will help the temple, which is in desperate straits financially and is dependent on the house for support."

"Aren't we all," said Yoshi coldly, staring her boldly in the eye.

Rie ignored the challenge, and instead inserted her fan in her obi, rose, and left the office.

As Rie was preparing for bed that evening, thinking of Yoshi and Kinno's opposition to taking temple land, and even loaning to the temple, her father's words of warning came to her. "You know what they say about the peg that sticks up. It gets pounded down." How many times had she heard this? Competition in business could not be avoided. But had she allowed her zeal for making White Tiger number one to cause her to stray too far from tradition, to get too far ahead of her competitors? Did she detect some resentment in the behavior not only of Yamaguchi but other brewers as well? Moreover, it was known among brewers that she, a woman, was making decisions for White Tiger, not Yoshi. She was venturing into many areas reserved for men.

These troubling thoughts coursed through her again and again. How she missed her father and his unerring good judgment.

Rie needed a walk in the garden one morning several weeks later, a chance to take stock of all that had happened in the family and business. She stepped out and felt herself bending, as if under a great weight of worries. She straightened as her geta crunched against the carefully swept gray pebbles. She brushed her hand across her favorite rock and sat. Yoshi had not come around as she had hoped. Instead he had remained sullen, aloof. She sighed. At least her children were married now, all gone. A major part of her responsibility had been discharged. Only with Yoshi and Teru had she failed; Teru still a wound that festered. Now she could focus fully on the business side, though it had never been far from her thoughts, even when the children were present. The temple's mountain land was a valuable addition to the Omura holdings, forested mountain land necessary for coal production and sales. She wished Yoshi and Kinnosuke could understand that.

She gazed at the koi pond and looked for the old fish, the grandfather fish that had inhabited the pond so many years. There he was, still lazing at the far side. As she watched, two red maple leaves circled dizzily down and touched the surface just above him. The koi swished into action and carried the leaves on its back to the center of the pond. She gazed, eyes half closed, and saw a ship, a cask ship carrying barrels of sake to Tokyo, the newly named capital.

The Omura ships now numbered six, and other brewers had followed their lead in purchasing ships of their own. Perhaps it was time to take another step in the shipping venture that had proven so successful. It was a matter of organization, a business issue, a way of deploying resources most efficiently. Kinno would offer some suggestion. His loyalty had really not wavered after divorcing Nobu and now with the tension around the temple, had it? And he had become so protective of Ume, just as he had always been of Yoshi. Surely Kinno would welcome a new move that could propel White Tiger to the forefront in yet another area. Other brewers watched him with great interest and followed his lead in each step he took.

Now with Seisaburo's vision added to her own, Kinno's dedication to the house could only strengthen. How gratifying that Sei was her son, though it was regrettable that his special talents were not shared by Yoshi, who tried so hard to live up to his role as house head. "At least our sake will not kill him as it did his father," Rie mused.

She stirred on the rock, brushed off her kimono, and walked back through the corridor to the office. She lowered herself to the table where Yoshitaro sat.

"Good morning, Yoshi," she said. "Where is Kinno?"

"I believe in the outer office, Mother," he said stiffly. "Shall I get—?" Yoshitaro stopped, unable to raise himself easily.

"Don't worry, Yoshi. I'll call him," Rie said, wishing that they could bridge the gap that seemed to have divided them since the argument over the loan to the priests.

When Kinnosuke joined them, he and Yoshitaro looked expectantly at Rie.

"Our shipping is going well with our six ships now, isn't it, Kinno-san?"

Kinnosuke nodded. "Quite well, yes. That side of the business has a potential to expand, it seems certain," he said, looking at Yoshitaro as he spoke.

"Just what I was thinking," said Rie, her excitement mounting. "Now what was it you were saying recently about this new form of business organization? Was it called joint stock?"

"That's right. A joint stock company is organized among several stockholders, owners, as a way of spreading the risk. They say it is useful in new ventures," Kinnosuke replied. He looked at Rie quizzically.

"Well, Kinno, do you think our shipping has reached the stage where we could form our own shipping company, perhaps using this new form? Wouldn't it give us still better control over shipping and labor?"

Kinnosuke scratched his head and sucked in his breath. "We were the first to purchase our own ships. I see no reason why we can't be the first to form our own shipping company." He nodded.

Yoshitaro looked back and forth at his mother and Kinnosuke, then just shook his head.

Chapter 38

Several years had elapsed since White Tiger organized the first brewery-owned shipping company, and in the interim everyone in the Omura household had grown older. Ume was twenty and Hirokichi nearly as old. Yoshitaro was forty-four, and Rie had already passed sixty-five and entered the second cycle of life on the Chinese calendar, still vigorous and intent on keeping ahead of the competition.

Rie, ever watchful of Hirokichi, could not have been more pleased at what she saw. While some might view him as spoiled by Rie and Fumi, for Rie he embodied the innovative spirit of the new Meiji era. A jaunty confidence and optimism radiated from the clean regular planes of his face. He was an attractive young man, liked by everyone and especially popular among the brewers. Now that he was nearly of age, he worked regularly with his father and was a less frequent visitor to the main house. Rie's hopes for the future were materializing in Hirokichi. Her father would be proud to know she would pass the mantle on to his grandson. And if this new joint stock company was successful, the Omura House might finally be number one, just as she had promised him. She smiled, but then with a twinge of guilt her thoughts turned to Ume.

Ume, only child of the main house, was now a beautiful, amiable young woman the age of marriage. While just a hint of Yoshitaro's nose and unruly hair suggested itself, Ume could be considered attractive and of above-average intelligence.

The fortunes of White Tiger were definitely on the rise, yet something nagged at the back of Rie's mind, made her uneasy. She couldn't quite put her finger on it.

Several evenings later the family was at dinner. Tama had brought in the rice and other dishes, and Ume was pouring tea.

"I wanted to speak to you about Ume, Mother," Yoshi said. "Kinnosuke and I are both pleased with the way she has developed. I feel we should be able to select an appropriate mukoyoshi for her soon, someone like Father."

Not like Jihei, Rie thought, but was careful to keep her face a mask. "Yes, Yoshi." She smiled. "I've been giving it some thought too, now that she's nearly twenty. There are several acceptable prospects."

Yoshitaro started to speak again, but began coughing and put a handkerchief to his mouth. He doubled over and could not stop his racking cough. Rie looked at him sharply. Was it her imagination, or had he lost weight?

"He has developed a bad cough lately, Mother," Tama said with a worried glance at Yoshitaro. "Sometimes it keeps him awake at night." She did not mention that it must have also kept her awake, worrying, but Rie could see it in the sallow shadows beneath her eyes.

"Have you called the herbalist, Tama?" Rie asked.

"I'll do that tomorrow early," she replied. "Ume, bring more tea for your father."

Ume rose and left the room.

Rie ate without speaking. That was it, the nagging worry. Yoshitaro had never completely regained his health and spirits since he lost his leg. He had resumed his duties well enough, but lacking the edge of his former enthusiasm. Rie was certain Kinnosuke was aware of it and equally certain that he was protecting Yoshi, helping him out in his work to avoid any unwanted questions. This cough would bear watching.

Glancing at Yoshitaro, his food still untouched, Rie said, "You must eat something, Yoshi."

He took up his chopsticks and picked at his rice. "I'm all right. Don't worry."

Some months later Rie walked into the inner office and found Kinnosuke and Yoshitaro engrossed in conversation at the worktable. Buntaro had joined them.

"Come, Mother," Yoshitaro said. "Buntaro has some interesting information."

"Yes?" Rie smiled at the well-muscled young clerk and seated herself next to Yoshitaro.

"You remember those black ships, the steam-powered ships that appeared at Yokohama with the Americans some years ago?" Kinnosuke asked, blinking rapidly as he spoke.

"Oh, yes," Rie said. "Sei told us about them. Everyone was so frightened by them at first."

"Well," Kinnosuke continued, "Buntaro was at the port yesterday. He says one of these ships has anchored there, and another is expected today."

"What is their cargo? And who owns them?" Rie asked sharply. She turned to Buntaro and took out her fan.

He bowed. "They say they are owned by the English and are chartered to a company in Tokyo. Apparently they have brought some of the new foreign goods to sell here in Kobe."

"Foreign goods." Rie paused and looked at Kinnosuke. "Well,

we in Kobe have always welcomed Chinese goods, so these foreigners will find a profitable market here. And that means they may be looking for cargo to take back to Tokyo, doesn't it?"

Kinnosuke straightened and sucked in his breath. "That's just what I was thinking, Oku-san. They're much faster than our cask ships, and of course larger and safer. It looks as if they may make our ships obsolete. And it may not take long."

"We should get to the port today, Kinno-san, you and Buntaro-san. Make some of our barrels available immediately, some that we marked for local sales, or some that were scheduled for one of our cask ships."

Kinnosuke bowed twice. "Yes, I believe we'll have to plan how to convert. It will be difficult, costly at first. Our cask crews will need to be trained too."

"See if you can get some of the crew from one of our ships placed on one of the steamships as apprentices, Kinno-san. The important thing is to act now, without losing time." She turned to Buntaro. "Your information was crucial, Buntaro-san. Thank you." She nodded, almost a bow.

He bowed smartly and looked pleased.

She turned to Yoshitaro who was leaning forward intently, trying hard to suppress a cough.

"Yoshi, try to organize this, can you? Kinno and Buntaro can do the legwork . . . but you need to coordinate the operation here." Rie knew she was perfectly capable of organizing, but she hoped to restore Yoshi's energy. She looked at Yoshitaro's pallid face and hoped the challenge would spark some of his old enthusiasm. She toyed with her obi, eyes flashing. "This is wonderfully exciting, isn't it, Yoshi? I feel it's the most important opportunity we've had in years. It may change the way sake is marketed everywhere." She placed a hand on Yoshitaro's shoulder and smiled.

He coughed and bent over, his hands over his mouth.

Kinnosuke and Buntaro both rose and began talking animatedly about their visit to the port. Buntaro darted out to the kura to see about readying some barrels. As Rie left the office every clerk had been alerted and was going into action on Kinnosuke's orders. She tapped her fan on her hand as she walked out, her thoughts on Yoshi rather than business.

One evening Rie sat at her dressing table in the second-floor room she had taken over after Yoshitaro's accident. She fanned out a handful of her long thinning hair and saw that white strands had begun to spread beyond the hair at her temples. She combed and re-combed her hair attempting to conceal this proof of aging. At her last birthday she'd turned sixty-six, and she found it hard to realize that she was older than her father had been when he died. She felt no lessening of energy, no crippling rheumatism or the chilblains most people her age, including O-Natsu, complained of when the damp chill of winter settled in. The most she could say was that the cold energized her, spurred her to an extra burst of activity she always associated with the brewing season. Her health was exceptional; her spirits buoyed each year by the progress of the rice through the fermentation in the kura, so closely was her inner being bound to brewing. She knew it had been the same with her father, but she had never sensed the same intimate connection in either Jihei or Yoshitaro. Watching Hirokichi closely, she thought she could detect in him signs of a sixth sense, an almost physical bond with brewing. Could this somehow be her biological legacy through Fumi? She combed slowly, and paused, her comb in midair as she heard footsteps on the stairs.

"Excuse me, Grandmother," a soft voice wafted through the shoji.

"Oh, come in, dear," answered Rie.

Ume opened the shoji and bowed.

"I've brought you some tea to warm you before you sleep," she said and knelt beside Rie to set the tray down.

Rie looked at her and smiled at the only grandchild of the main house. Ume was always so cheerful, eager to please, and a good worker. Rie looked at the large black eyes, startling against so pale a complexion. She does have a kind of beauty, Rie thought. It was unfortunate that she was not really an Omura daughter.

Ume leaned gracefully to pour tea for her grandmother.

"Ume, now that you are twenty we must think of your marriage, mustn't we?"

Ume looked down at the teapot and bowed.

"Has your mother spoken to you about it?" Rie asked.

"She said something about finding a mukoyishi, Grandmother, but nothing definite."

"Of course there is no hurry, dear. But you are of the age."

Ume looked up quizzically, her dark eyes reflecting an air of mystery in the flickering lamplight.

"We have no lack of prospects, dear. You know we are a major house, and your marriage will be a big event in Kobe."

Rie looked at Ume. This beautiful, conscientious granddaughter tried so hard to please and yet Rie had never been able to accept her as she had Fumi and Sei. She could never know that she was a geisha's daughter and granddaughter. There had been a time when Rie considered bringing Hirokichi in as Ume's adopted husband, since both had been trained in the main house. That was what Yoshitaro expected and Kinnosuke assumed. But for Rie, Ume was ineligible by bloodline to marry the next house head.

Rie had been powerless to keep Yoshitaro, proof of Jihei's philandering, or to prevent Ume, Yoshi's child by another geisha, from entering the house. Now there were grandchildren eminently qualified to succeed, and free of O-Toki's or any other geisha's bloodline, most eligibly Hirokichi. Rie still safeguarded the official seal and refused to give it to Yoshi. Rie's power in the house had grown over the years, and Yoshitaro, weakened by accident and illness, would have to struggle for his goal to have Ume and a husband succeed.

Rie knew in her heart that she had never been able to warm to Yoshitaro as she had to Fumi and Seisaburo. Still, aware of this difference, she had always sought to be fair to Yoshitaro who, though he had not performed brilliantly, had proven an able house head, far more capable than his father. He had shown strength of character, refusing to follow his father's destructive path. Instead, he had been struck by samurai violence, and now by disease.

Rie looked again at Ume's face, the lamplight glowing across her black eyes and striking features. Rie paused and pushed her long hair behind her shoulders.

"We don't need to decide your marriage yet, dear. We can keep it to ourselves for now. This will be our secret, the two of us, all right?"

Rie smiled at Ume and tried to fathom her feelings.

"I guess so," Ume said. She bowed and picked up the tea tray.

"Good night, dear. Sleep well," Rie said, and turned back to her dressing table.

Chapter 39

Rie opened the shutters of her upstairs room early one morning, then thrust her hands into her sleeves and shivered. A chill wind was soughing down from Mt. Rokko. Ice crystals glistened and wove a gossamer web on the trees and shrubs of the garden. The faint pink plum blossom buds peering between the leaves and lacy crystals reminded her that it was already February. Why was it that the older one grew, the faster time passed? At sixty-seven she must be nearing the end of her allotted time, a life already longer than most. She was making preparations. Each morning she reported to the ancestors at the Butsudan, whether or not Tama had set out the rice and wine. And each evening before going to sleep she sat quietly for several minutes, reviewing in her mind what she had done for the house during the day. That way there would be no major miscalculations when the time came to join the ancestors. Hadn't her father done something similar when he sat alone in contemplation each evening? This was a comforting thought.

She dressed quickly, put on her padded winter wrap and tapped down the stairs to the kitchen, where she picked up a pair of clippers. At the door to the garden she slipped into wooden geta and foraged out into the icy scene. A chill mist enveloped the garden, and Rie hurried to the plum tree. Rain lashed at her eyes when she reached up and clipped two blossom-laden sprigs. Back in the warmth of the kitchen, she arranged the stalks in a low celadon vase. In the parlor fresh incense burned before the name tablets, proof that Tama had preceded her. She placed the vase carefully before the scroll hanging in the tokonoma alcove, and moved on her knees to the Butsudan.

She lit a second incense stick, then clasped her hands before her face and closed her eyes.

"Father, Hirokichi will do. He will be best for the house," she whispered.

Rie sat in the garden late one afternoon musing about Buntaro's startling information about the black ships, the steamships that had entered Kobe port. All the changes she had witnessed in her lifetime in the brewing and selling of sake flashed through her mind: the discovery of pure Shrine Water that granted divine assistance to brewers near Nishinomiya; the discovery by her own son of steam power to replace the waterwheel rice polishers; the development of kura of brick construction, also by Seisaburo; and now the steamships she and Kinnosuke both knew would replace the cask ships and transform forever the way sake was transported to major markets. And her father had told her of advances before her time, most notably the replacement of the foot treadle by the waterwheel for polishing rice. The dizzying pace of change before her eyes was proof of Japan's progress since the coming of the Western barbarians, just as the Satsuma and Choshu leaders had promised for this new era called Meiji, "Enlightened Rule."

Rie silently thanked the gods that she had been able to grasp the significance of each of these developments almost at the moment of its appearance. Her father and Kin had always praised her sense of timing. Yes, it was true. This did give her an advantage over other brewers, even the sales-oriented Nada brewers. These new steamships were just the latest example. And Kinnosuke had immediately grasped the importance of each step. That White Tiger was at this very moment sending the first barrels of sake by steamship to Tokyo gave Rie a sense of elation, a feeling she knew was central to her life as a brewer.

Brewers as a group were well known for their attachment to tradition, for doing things as they had always done. This conservatism was natural. Brewing sake was the oldest, the primal, business in Japan. In the earliest stories of creation the first mythical hero, Yamato Takeru, had ordered eight barrels of sake for the eight-headed demon, and when the ogre was far gone in his cups, the hero had wielded his sword to slice off the monster's eight heads. All Japanese knew that in every town and village throughout the land the sake brewers were the most honored and respected of inhabitants. Their pride in brewing was legendary. It must be some quirk of fate that granted her this special sense of the importance of timing in this ancient and honored profession.

As these thoughts ran through her mind she inhaled deeply and caught the whiff of salt air pushing inland off the ocean. She smiled. Wouldn't it be wonderful if Hirokichi or Buntaro fashioned a miniature model of one of the new steamships? It would be something to put in the parlor, perhaps even in the tokonoma next to the Butsudan. Her father would appreciate it.

The Meiji government issued new regulations delimiting the amount of rice that could be used for brewing sake, and it was therefore imperative that all brewers attend the association meeting. Yoshitaro, Kinnosuke, Eitaro, Seisaburo, and Hirokichi all would attend. During the first two decades of the Meiji era, the government, preoccupied with so many dramatic innovations, had not gotten around to placing controls on brewing. Now every brewer in Nada and Nishinomiya, in fact throughout the country, was concerned to know what the new directives would be. Each association would be assigned an allotment, and limitations on individual brewers would be determined by the Brewers Associations, those close to local conditions. The Nada meeting was doubly important because the president was to be elected as well. Rie felt that Seisaburo had a chance, though at thirty-nine he might be considered young for the position. Still, as head of an Omura branch and with his reputation as one of the region's most successful brewers, Rie felt he could not be ruled out.

"Yoshi, you and Eitaro must support Seisaburo for the presidency," she said, excited by the prospect. She went to the door and saw Yoshitaro and Kinnosuke off for the meeting. "It is so unreasonable that I can't go too," she muttered under her breath as the ricksha pulled off into the street.

Rie invited Seisaburo and Eitaro to return to the main house for dinner after the meeting. She ordered special delicacies for the occasion. The intervening hours passed slowly, interminably. She tried her hand at some needlework to help pass the time in the late afternoon, but soon set it down impatiently. She could still hear her mother's voice after all these years: "Try to be more careful with your stitches, Rie. They're a bit irregular." She looked at them and saw that they still were. A rueful smile played around her lips.

Several hours later Rie heard rickshas and voices of the men returning. She hurried to the door to greet them and quickly surveyed their faces before focusing on Yoshitaro, who stood closest to her.

"It's all right, Mother," he said. "Sei was elected vice president. Kato is president. Yamaguchi was defeated. I could see that he was angry. He had tried to line up votes."

"Good! *Huh!* Yamaguchi's still angry that we got access to Shrine Water, after all these years," she said. "Still, it's good that you're vice president, Sei. I am so proud of you. President next time, yes? Come. Dinner is ready."

Thrilled for her son and for the business and house, Rie led the way into the dining room and motioned the men to be seated. Kinnosuke was included as well, since the dinner was also in the nature of a family business council. O-Yuki brought in tea and three flasks of warmed sake with cups, and the men began pouring for each other, loosening their kimonos.

"Sei had some support, Mother," Eitaro began, "but Kato is senior."

Rie remembered Saburo's elder brother, and was pleased that the Kato family had captured the prestigious position, as Sei's predecessor.

"It's only natural," Seisaburo said. "At my age I didn't really expect to be elected."

"But after Kato's term is up, you'll be next, won't you?" Rie nodded confidently as she spoke.

"Possibly so. By that time I'll be in my forties. But I think Kato will be in for several years. And the new system will be in place by the time I take over."

Rie nodded and turned to Kinnosuke. "What about the new regulations? How will they affect us?"

He rested his chopsticks on his rice bowl. "It's as we thought. The individual allotments will be made by the association, a bit like the old kabu system. It won't be a great hardship. The allotments will be made according to past production, and since ours has been rising steadily we'll be all right, with even an allowance for a bit of expansion."

Rie put down her cup and nodded. Her heart gave a small flutter, something it had begun recently. She ignored it. "Good. Good."

She asked Eitaro to remain behind after the others had left the table. Recently, she had begun to feel her age and knew that it was imperative that she find a successor soon.

She took her fan from her obi and placed it on the table before her. "You know, Eitaro, that the reason I have encouraged Hirokichi all along, had him spend time here with Kinnosuke and Buntaro and, of course, Yoshi, is that I envisioned bringing him into the main house as Yoshi's successor."

Eitaro bowed correctly. "That is what Fumi has led me to believe. A great honor and opportunity it will be for him, and for us." He bowed again. "It will also be a chance for us to choose Mie's mukoyoshi."

Rie glanced at Eitaro's clean-planed face and turned her fan over several times. "So I'll have Fumi bring him over in a few days. Now that his twenty-first birthday is approaching we can begin preparations."

"I'll mention it to Fumi but of course not to Hiro," he said. He stood, bowed low, and bade Rie good night.

A few days later Rie sent a request for Fumi and Hirokichi to come to the main house. She met them at the entrance and ushered them into the parlor, where a low lacquer table stood in front of the tokonoma. O-Yuki brought in tea.

"How are you, Mother?" Fumi asked.

"As well as can be expected at my age."

Hirokichi smiled. "You seem very healthy, Grandmother."

"Thank you, Hiro. Yes, I can't complain. And speaking of age, now that you are of age, Hiro, we can plan for your future, your marriage in particular."

"That's true, Mother," Fumi nodded, without indicating that she knew what was coming.

"We need to settle your marriage, Hiro. You know that White Tiger is now number three in all Japan."

"I know, Grandmother," Hirokichi said. "It's impressive."

"We have plans for a great future for you." Rie paused and took out her fan. She toyed with it in her lap. "Yes," she continued. "There is a concern for the succession to the main house. You have been trained carefully, and your parents and I feel it is time to find a bride. You will succeed to the main house, Hiro, at the time of your marriage to a bride of our choice." Rie sat back, satisfied, and glanced at Hirokichi.

He stiffened, his neck and shoulder muscles visibly tensing. He looked down and bowed toward Rie.

"You do me great honor, Grandmother. But I am not ready to marry yet."

"Well, then, in a year, Hiro," Fumi said, frowning.

Hirokichi looked straight ahead. "I cannot marry a bride I do not choose," he said. He bowed again, looking down.

Rie frowned and tapped her fan on the table. "You realize, Hiro, that you have a heavy obligation to the main house. Frankly, you have been trained to succeed. Kinnosuke, and my son too, have taken great care in your training. Now it is only fitting that you marry a bride selected by the main house."

"But I cannot," Hirokichi said, frowning.

Rie stared at her grandson, unaccustomed as she was to such open defiance.

"There is no such thing as *cannot* where obligation to the house is concerned. No question, Hiro." Rie's voice rose sharply.

Hirokichi stood and bowed. "I am very sorry, Grandmother and Mother. But this is something I can never do." He bowed again, turned, and left the room.

Stunned, Rie tapped her fan sharply on the table. "Fumi, it is your responsibility, yours and Eitaro's, to persuade him. It has been our plan, our goal, ever since he was born."

Fumi bowed. "We will do our best, Mother. But you know how stubborn he is. He has been since he was a baby."

Rie knew all about stubborn. "And he has so much talent,

apart from his training. Maybe Kinnosuke or Buntaro could talk to him."

Fumi shook her head. "If he won't listen to you and me, I doubt there's anything Kinnosuke or Buntaro could say that would sway him. And he knows Kinnosuke has always favored Ume."

"Perhaps we've spoiled him, Fumi, as your only son and the eldest boy in his generation. Sei's son is too young still. Yes, I'm afraid I have spoiled him." Rie's mouth turned down at the corners and her whole being seemed to sag. "Well, you and Eitaro will have to persuade him. There is just no alternative."

Chapter 40

Two years had elapsed since Rie first broached the subject of marriage with Hirokichi, but he remained stubbornly opposed. He and Ume were nearly twenty-three and still unmarried. The situation could not be allowed to continue. Moreover, Yoshitaro's health was declining dramatically.

Rie hurried to see Fumi and Eitaro one morning to try to end the crisis.

"I'm sorry, Mother, but there's nothing more we can do to persuade Hiro," Fumi moaned. "We've tried everything, but he's adamant." She squirmed uncomfortably.

Rie leaned forward, her voice rising higher than normal. "This is unheard of. It's one thing to be stubborn, but to continue to defy the main house is an outrage. We can't tolerate it. Ume must be married now. She's nearly twenty-three, and we've been approached by several families. We can't postpone her marriage any longer." She looked at Eitaro, then back at Fumi.

"I have no way to apologize adequately, Mother," Eitaro said.

"We have done our best for the past two years. We have failed." He bowed abjectly.

"And Mother, this has created so much tension in our house. Hiro doesn't stay at home in the evening. He has taken to staying away more and more."

Rie pursed her lips. "People will think there is something wrong with Ume if she doesn't marry soon. It's such a worry. And with Yoshi's poor health we must settle the succession. I just don't know what to do. And of course Yoshi expects Ume to succeed with a mukoyoshi."

Fumi put a hand on her chin. "The trouble is, Mother, there is someone else he wants to marry."

Rie thought of Saburo, young and handsome, his brown eyes so caring. Then of Jihei. She understood more than anyone would ever guess. But what must be, must be. "Since when do personal wishes enter where marriage is concerned? The house is what matters," Rie tapped her fan on the table.

"Well, you know how Hiro has always been, Mother," Fumi said. "How can we change his character now? He knows he is the eldest and most capable of his generation. You have said so yourself. That's why he is so confident."

"I intended for him to be twelfth house head, but now I don't know. Kinnosuke always called him Botchan, and it's true, he is spoiled. Well, who is this girl he wants to marry?" Rie put down her fan and looked at Fumi.

"I'm not exactly sure, but I'm afraid she may be a geisha," Fumi said, looking down.

"A geisha! Marry a geisha! Preposterous! No Omura man is going to marry a geisha. Patronizing one is bad enough. Marrying one is out of the question. I won't hear of it." She scowled, the corners of her mouth turned down.

"So we've told him, Mother," Eitaro said. "He surely would not have our blessing for such a marriage. We would have to consider disinheriting him. I doubt he would go through with it under those conditions. But the trouble is I'm not sure." He rubbed his nose slowly.

"What a dilemma! And what shall we do about Ume? People are talking," Rie said.

And that night, she lay awake, tossing and turning.

The next morning Rie hurried purposefully into the office after a hasty breakfast. She was glad to find Yoshitaro alone and sat down opposite him.

"Good morning, Yoshi." She smiled at him.

Yoshitaro looked up, his face thinner and paler than ever.

"Where is Kinno?" she asked.

"In the outer office filling orders," he said, his voice rasping. He coughed, a handkerchief to his mouth.

"You know, Yoshi, we can't delay Ume's marriage any longer." Rie twirled her fan on the table.

"I know, Mother." He coughed again, and Rie noticed spots of blood on his handkerchief. He wiped his mouth and struggled to speak. "We've been approached by three families now. Which do you favor?" he asked.

"Of course Hiro was our choice, but he is still being stubborn. Eitaro is threatening to disinherit him if he marries that geisha he told Fumi about." Rie paused and looked down at her fan. "There's only one way out, Yoshi."

He put his handkerchief on his lap. "What's that?" he asked, eyebrows raised.

"Ume will have to marry one of the three, probably the Kuniyoshi son, and establish a branch house. And Hiro will succeed you. We will give him the succession if he agrees not to marry the geisha."

Yoshitaro's hands clenched on his lap. "You mean, force Ume out of the main house? Mother, we can't do that!" His heavy brows drew together in a deep frown. He coughed uncontrollably.

Rie sighed heavily. She cared for Ume, yet what else could be done? She heard a rustling beyond the door to the outer office and guessed that Kinnosuke was listening. "It's not what we hoped for, but it's the only way out of this impasse, Yoshi. Ume will be set up in a branch. We'll be generous with her, and I think Kuniyoshi is the best of the three. He'll do well by us and by her." She squared her shoulders, then poured a cup of tea and pushed it across the table to Yoshitaro. "You must take better care of your health, Yoshi. Have you seen the herbalist lately?"

"Yesterday," he replied abruptly, then bent over and continued coughing.

Rie looked in alarm at the crimson spreading in his handkerchief until it was nearly soaked. She stood abruptly and rushed to the kitchen. Tama looked up, startled.

"Quickly, Tama. Take some damp towels to Yoshi in the office. He's coughing so badly."

Tama reached for towels, dampened two in a basin, and ran to the office, Rie behind her.

Tama knelt quickly and began wiping Yoshitaro's face.

He pushed her hand away. "Don't get so excited, Mother. I've been taking the medicine regularly. But I can't agree to sending Ume out of the main house. It's her birthright." He glared at Rie.

She knelt at the table again.

"Yoshi, dear," she said more gently, "please be reasonable. It's not something I want to do."

"Why not set Hirokichi up as a branch? Or just have him inherit Eitaro's?" Yoshitaro said.

"I've told you, Yoshi, that I think this is the only way to prevent him from a disgraceful marriage that would dishonor the house. And you know how clever he is, Yoshi. He could build White Tiger to the number one position."

"I can't agree." He bent over and coughed again. "I will only allow it if you promise to disinherit Hiro if he refuses a bride the house chooses." He looked down glumly. "And it will make Kinno very unhappy to see Ume sent out. He counts on her to succeed. We both do."

"Yes, you're right, Yoshi." She paused. "But he isn't a member of the house. This is the way it has to be." *The way it has to be.* How many times had she had to say those words over the years? She put both hands to her face, then rose and left the office.

Three weeks later Rie called a full family council at the main house: Yoshitaro, Tama, and Ume; Fumi, Eitaro, Hirokichi, and Mie; and Seisaburo, Mari, and their children, Masako and Nobuo. Rie took greater care than usual in dressing for the morning meeting in the parlor. Zabuton were arranged around two tables placed together. Yoshitaro sat at the head of the table with Rie at his left, Tama on his right.

Rie and Yoshitaro greeted family members as they arrived at the main entrance. Tama set out the best kutani teacups.

Rie had discussed with Yoshitaro what to say. They were finally in agreement. Well, reluctant agreement.

"Welcome to all of you," he began, bowing and glancing around the table. "As you know, we have been discussing the question of succession to the main house and the marriages of Ume and Hirokichi. We have sought your guidance in these matters for these past two years and more."

As he completed each sentence, Rie and Tama both bowed slightly. O-Yuki brought in teapots and poured for everyone.

"Now, as a result of these discussions we have been able to arrive at solutions that will be acceptable to all." He coughed, his handkerchief over his mouth. Beads of sweat formed on his brow.

"First, Ume will marry the Kuniyoshi second son and establish a branch. We have decided to agree to the o-miai meeting and the wedding soon after."

Rie glanced at Ume but could see no sign of emotion on her face. Ume had brought tea to her grandmother several evenings earlier, as had become her habit.

"Sit down, dear," Rie had said. "There is something I would like to discuss with you."

Ume had poured tea and listened attentively.

"I know that two years ago, when I mentioned my hope that you would marry Hirokichi, I could see that you were not enthusiastic, though I knew you would do as we thought best."

Ume had bowed and nodded.

"Now, that marriage does not seem possible," Rie said, picking up her teacup.

Ume's eyes had widened. "Oh?" she said quizzically.

"Yes, dear, we feel the Kuniyoshi son will be the best husband for you. You know, the family has approached us and waited for over a year. So now we have decided to set you up in a nearby branch house, with the Kuniyoshi son as your adopted husband."

Ume had looked down abruptly. "A bunke, a branch house?" she asked in a small voice. "Not here in the main house?"

"No, dear. You will receive a generous sum to begin your own branch. We believe you will do well with the Kuniyoshi son. He is the best of the three, now four, that have approached us. And I believe you will prefer him to Hirokichi. He has become a most stubborn person. He would be difficult to live with."

Ume had looked thoughtful, but said nothing other than good night to her grandmother when she left the room.

Rie had asked Eitaro not to reveal the decision to Hirokichi before the family council met. She did not want to give him another chance to protest. A decision announced at the family council would be final. Now, as she looked out at the familiar faces of the council she made her next proclamation.

"And second," Yoshitaro continued, "Hirokichi will succeed

me to the main house, but only on condition that he marry a bride of our choice."

Rie glanced at Hirokichi and saw him frown darkly and look down.

"In the event that he refuses to marry the bride we select, he will be disinherited, removed from the koseki register." Yoshitaro covered his mouth and glanced at Hirokichi.

Hirokichi pouted, grunting loudly, his frown deepening.

"We will begin negotiations now for Ume's wedding. Following her wedding, discussions regarding selection of Hirokichi's bride will commence." By this time sweat was pouring down Yoshitaro's face. He wiped his face with his handkerchief and began to cough.

Tama bowed. "Please have some tea and *casutera* cakes." She passed two plates of the new Western-style cakes around the table.

The formal part of the meeting was concluded, and family members began to shift on their zabuton. Some began to sip their tea and make polite conversation.

Hirokichi rose abruptly and left the room. The shoji leading out the front entrance slammed shut, the bell clanging loudly.

Later the same afternoon, as soon as she could free herself from duties in the main house, Rie hurried to Fumi's.

"Oh, Mother," Fumi said as she greeted Rie at the entrance. "I'm not sure Hiro will agree. Eitaro is worried too."

Eitaro joined Rie and Fumi in the parlor. "What Hiro said, Mother, is that if he can't marry O-Fusa he will remain unmarried. He wants to succeed to the main house, but he will remain single."

Rie frowned. Unheard of! What a stubborn young man. "We can't have a bachelor as house head. Being head of such an important house, any house for that matter, is the work of two people, a couple, and an heir is essential as successor," Rie said.

Eitaro bowed. "Hiro says the house has always taken in the children of geishas, so there will be no problem of lack of heirs," Eitaro said. He bowed and excused himself to return to the office.

"Hiro is too clever," Rie said, her mind working. "And he goes too far."

"Well, Mother, he believes he is meeting most of Yoshi's conditions if he does not marry O-Fusa. And actually, our main purpose was to prevent that marriage," Fumi said. "So however cunning it appears, don't we have to agree to let him succeed?" she asked.

"He has agreed to only part of the conditions, Fumi," Rie said. "Until he agrees to the rest he will not succeed. Yoshi will back me in this, I am certain."

Mother and daughter sat in an uncomfortable silence.

Chapter 41

Ume was married to the Kuniyoshi son as Rie wished, and Yoshitaro had not been able to prevent it. He was very angry about it, Rie knew. The couple was well endowed with facilities and capital to establish their branch house in Nada. Yoshitaro, though he had not seen O-Sada since his accident, managed to arrange for her to be among those who served at the reception, so that she could see her daughter married. Rie was too preoccupied with the guests to take more than a cursory notice of the exceptionally beautiful woman working among the servants at the reception.

Kinnosuke had made it clear he was disconsolate, shocked beyond belief that his protégée, Yoshitaro's only child, should be denied succession, shunted off to a branch family. The assumptions and hopes on which Kinnosuke had based his life work he saw dashed in a single stroke by "Rie and her spoiled daughter and even more spoiled grandson," according to a conversation that Rie had the misfortune to overhear between him and Yoshitaro.

"I must retire now," he announced to Rie and Yoshitaro. His head was bowed and his shoulders tensed.

Rie gasped and leaned toward the spare figure of the chief clerk she had handpicked and trained from childhood. "We know you are unhappy that Ume is no longer in the main house. But Kinno-san, there was no other way to stop Hirokichi from dishonoring the house. This was the only solution. It wasn't what we wanted." She paused and placed both hands on the table. "You know how we value your work. White Tiger would not have reached the number two position without you. Please reconsider, Kinno-san. Please. We cannot do without you." She bowed low. She looked up and saw tears beginning in Yoshitaro's eyes.

Yoshi coughed and sputtered as he tried to speak. "Kinnosuke, you have been my teacher since I was a child, as long as I can remember." He stopped to cough again, and put his handkerchief in his lap. "As you know, my health has not been the best of late. I entreat you, stay on at least until the end of this brewing season. I cannot manage without you." His words trailed off in a hoarse rasping sound.

Rie put her hand to her mouth and bowed, eyes lowered. She did not fail to note that Kinnosuke also bowed as low as possible.

Kinnosuke struggled, a catch in his throat. "*Ah*, Master," he began, and stopped, overcome. "It pains me to see you in such a sad situation, with your ill health, and losing your heir." He paused again and blinked to hold back tears. "I will do as you say. I will stay until the end of this brewing season. Then I must ask you to allow me to retire. I believe Buntaro is capable of taking over."

"Buntaro is capable and well trained, thanks to you, Kinno-san," Yoshitaro said. "But you can never be replaced at White Tiger."

Rie could not speak. She wrung her hands, then bowed, rose quickly, and left Kinnosuke and Yoshitaro looking at each other. As she passed the wooden support she paused and slowly caressed it.

Kinnosuke remained until the end of the season as he had promised, Yoshitaro with him almost constantly. At the same time Buntaro gradually worked more closely with both men, who were grooming him to assume all of Kinnosuke's many duties.

Yoshitaro insisted that Kinnosuke be given a special sayonara dinner. Rie had already planned to give him a handsome pension, and a dinner helped assuage some of her guilt over removing Ume and causing Kinno to retire. Even Yoshitaro was surprised at the size of the pension, an amount so large that when it became known among Nada brewers it caused a minor sensation. Rie wanted it known publicly that the gratitude of the Omura House for his long and loyal service was unbounded. She spared no expense for the dinner, a formal family affair.

Kinnosuke sat at Yoshitaro's left at the occasion, which featured the finest Kobe sashimi and the new foreign import, beef, in a mixture called sukiyaki. Kinnosuke tasted it but turned instead to the sashimi. Beef, a strange unfamiliar flavor, was no doubt as unpalatable to him as it was to Rie.

Yoshitaro attempted a speech after the meal. He spoke from his zabuton, as it was impossible for him to rise or stand easily.

"It is with great regret that White Tiger and the House of Omura bid you farewell," he began with a bow from the waist. "Your outstanding, long, and loyal service to our house is without precedent in all of Nada and has made White Tiger what it is today." Choked with emotion, he bowed several times, tears streaming unchecked down his face.

Watching Kinnosuke and Yoshitaro throughout his halting speech, Rie felt a tightening in her throat. What would the future bring to White Tiger without this extraordinary man? Would she live to regret what she had done the past few months?

Kinnosuke, never garrulous, managed only a few perfunctory words. He bowed and blinked repeatedly. "I owe everything to you, Master, and to Oku-san." He bowed to Yoshitaro and Rie and stopped speaking.

The future of White Tiger was in one sense not greatly different from what it had been. Kinnosuke and Rie had imbued all the clerks in the office and men in the kura with a fierce pride in their sake and a canny business sense. Buntaro proved a talented successor to Kinnosuke, with the same sense of timing and eye to the future. In another sense Rie's concern at Kinnosuke's departure was well founded. She watched Yoshitaro closely and was saddened to see a gradual loss of nerve, a lassitude slowly begin to erode what energy he had regained following his accident. Kinnosuke had been largely responsible for Yoshitaro's resumption of duties after the loss of his leg, Kinnosuke who had been intimately connected with Yoshitaro during his entire working life. The departure of Kinnosuke left Yoshitaro with an emptiness, a dark void that could not be filled. It was obvious that his health was suffering, and as the months passed the physical decline became increasingly apparent. He rarely smiled.

Rie spoke to Tama one morning in the dining room after Yoshitaro had gone to the office.

"I am so worried about Yoshi, Tama. I'm afraid Kinnosuke's retirement was a blow he may not recover from." She sighed and looked at Tama.

"Yes, I know," Tama said. "He seems worse than after the accident. It is his spirit as much as his body that I worry about."

Rie looked at Tama and thought how rare it was to see her smile these days. "And if something should happen to him, with

Hiro still refusing to marry, our succession would be a critical problem," Rie said.

"Hasn't Hiro had two or three o-miais?" Tama asked.

"Oh, more than that, Tama. He has refused them all. Fumi is at her wit's end. And now he is twenty-four. What a worry!" Rie tapped her fan on the table. "I know you have been spending more time in the office, Tama, ever since Yoshi's accident. And now with Ume gone you will be freer to do even more. Isn't it quiet here without Ume?" Rie smiled briefly. She did not really feel like smiling about Ume's departure, but wanted to improve Tama's mood. "Well, we need to try to encourage Yoshi."

"Yes, we must," Tama said. "I'm glad that we have Buntaro."

"But Buntaro is so recent. He was never that close to Yoshi. It was completely different with Kinno." Rie sighed again. "Come, let's see how Yoshi is doing."

Hirokichi's refusal to marry any of the women the younger Mrs. Nakano and other go-betweens brought to o-miai meetings was causing the Omura House great embarrassment and threatened to become a minor scandal. It was not his association with O-Fusa that caused raised eyebrows. Most men who could afford it patronized one or more geisha. But that he was promised succession to the great Omura House and despite that, continued to reject all prospective brides was a violation of all standards of propriety.

Yoshitaro was furious, Rie was irate, and Fumi railed helplessly.

"It's already four years since we sent Ume out, Mother," Yoshitaro complained. "We should have kept her here with her husband as successor, and we would still have Kinnosuke with us. Hirokichi is nothing but trouble for the main house." He coughed, then straightened and pushed his hair back from his face. He scowled. "I never thought Hiro was a good choice. He doesn't deserve to succeed," he said.

"It's too late now, Yoshi," Rie said. "We'll have to make the best of it. I have a feeling he'll come around if we find the right bride."

"There is no right bride for him. How about bringing in Seisaburo's son?" Yoshitaro asked.

"Nobuo is still too young, Yoshi. He's not eighteen yet. It's true that he has had the best training. But we don't want to think of his marriage yet."

Yoshitaro coughed uncontrollably. Rie left the office and went to the garden to try to recover her peace of mind. She sat on her rock to meditate, to try to collect her thoughts. Just then the door to the kitchen corridor opened and Fumi appeared.

"Mother, may I speak with you?" Fumi asked.

"In a minute, Fumi." Rie racked her brain, implored the gods for help in finding a solution to the problem that had plagued the house for so long. Fumi's distress was more than she could deal with at the moment. And Yoshitaro's anger was damaging his health even further. She sighed, rubbed her throbbing temples, and reluctantly rose to go in.

"Oh, Mother, I need to talk to you," Fumi said again as soon as she saw Rie.

"I know. Come, let's go to the parlor. Would you bring us some tea please, O-Yuki," Rie said as she passed the kitchen.

Rie and Fumi sat at the low lacquer table near the tokonoma.

"What shall we do, Mother?" Fumi asked.

"Fumi, I thought you had come with some good news or a new idea," Rie said, frowning.

"No, there's no sign of hope. So many o-miais and Hiro has refused them all. And my husband wants to disinherit Hiro. We can't even do anything about Mie's marriage with this hanging over us." Fumi rested her chin on her hand and leaned toward her mother.

"We can't delay Mie's marriage any longer. Hiro's stubbornness is all over Nada now and it won't help Mie to find a husband, whether or not he succeeds to the main house."

Fumi pouted. "It's just not fair to Mie. I've told Hiro so."

"Complaining will not help us or change his character, Fumi. We need to think of a way out. Hiro is very talented when he puts his mind to his work. I'm still confident about that. I can't support disinheriting him. But five years is too long. We must act now."

Chapter 42

Three months after Rie's conversation with Fumi a worse crisis threatened the house. Yoshitaro's health took a sudden drastic turn. One night he hemorrhaged; blood soaked his futon faster than Tama could contain it. Rie sent for the herbalist urgently in the middle of the night, but Yoshitaro was beyond help. Rie put her hand on Yoshitaro's face and neck, and rested her other hand on his. Tama rocked back and forth in distress, covering her face. Before morning Yoshitaro's last rasping breath failed. Rie and Tama sat on either side of his futon, aghast.

When morning finally dawned, alerted family members gathered from the branch houses: Ume and her husband, Eitaro and Fumi with Hirokichi and Mie, and Seisaburo and Mari with their two children.

Rie had no chance to be alone with her emotions before having to greet her children and their families.

"Well," she said deliberately, as they sat around her in the parlor, "we all knew his health was failing, but we didn't expect the end so soon." She glanced at Ume and saw her dabbing at her tears. "And now we are a house without a head." She looked pointedly at Hirokichi. "We are in an untenable position. We will plan to have the memorial service five days from now. Eitaro and Sei, please make the arrangements. Then we will need to take steps about the succession." Rie bowed to her sons and Tama. Rie glanced briefly at Fumi and saw that she was weeping. Hirokichi sat as if made of stone.

In the days before the funeral Rie felt her age and the flutter in her heart had increased with the added stress. She had witnessed the deaths of too many house heads: her father, her adopted husband, and now her adopted son. It was too soon after Kinno's retirement. And it was not the natural order for one's children to predecease one. Lack of a successor was a crisis of major proportions.

The funeral was as large as Jihei's had been. Most of the Kobe and Nishinomiya brewers came. But who should make the formal greetings in the absence of a house head? Rie was tempted to ask Eitaro to make the announcements, but because of Hirokichi's intransigence, she turned instead to Seisaburo.

On the day of the memorial service Rie thought her son looked quite distinguished as he stood at the head of the room filled with black-clad mourners. She scanned the room quickly until her glance rested on a hunched figure in the corner. It was Kinnosuke. Not far away was Saburo, the man who had given her Fumi. The man who had seen her through every crisis, if from a distance. Rie felt a catch in her throat.

"We thank you all for coming today to remember the head of the Omura House." Seisaburo's resonant voice filled the room. "He has joined the ancestors suddenly. In this difficult moment for the house we are especially grateful for your continued cooperation and support," he continued.

When Seisaburo finished his speech, sake was served down the lines of seated mourners. Next to Tama, Rie sat straight-backed, eyes downcast, with neither the need nor ability to speak. She left Tama, Eitaro, and Seisaburo to greet the departing guests. Even to speak to Saburo seemed too great an effort on this painful night.

The next morning Rie found it difficult to rise at her usual hour. She heard Tama stirring downstairs but could not summon the energy to join her in the kitchen. Well, I am seventy-four, she told herself, and Tama is capable of supervising the household. She turned over on her futon, but a disturbing thought invaded her consciousness. Yoshitaro's sudden demise had left the house without a head. To be sure, business would not stop; she herself had possession of the Omura family seal, the seal that made official any decision or document. Still, she must be up. She threw off the futon, and as she slowly rose heard her knee joints crack. She dressed, slapped down the stairs to the kitchen, and asked O-Yuki for a cup of tea. She sipped slowly, then went to the parlor and peered in. Tama was seated before the Butsudan, incense smoke curling around her bowed head.

Rie turned without speaking and went into the wintry garden. It was March, not a time to linger, but she needed the solitude. She thought about Hirokichi's continued recalcitrance, and tried to dismiss him from her thoughts. He had not shown that he was deserving of the headship yet. She brooded and glanced at the ripples the koi caused on the pond's surface. She paced slowly the length of the garden and back, hands thrust into the sleeves of her padded kimono, her gaze focused on the cold gray stone steps. It was way too late now to recall Ume and her husband to the main house. Soon it would be time to prepare for the end of season celebration, but it would be briefer than usual. Her thoughts rested on Tama, Yoshitaro's steadfast, hardworking widow; Tama, who had worked at her side uncomplaining all these years. Rie nodded and murmured softly, "Yes."

She turned and walked back through the house to the parlor, where Tama still knelt arranging thin reeds and grasses in a black vase.

"*Ah*, Tama," Rie said, joining her before the Butsudan. "How are you this morning, after such a difficult ordeal?"

"Good morning, Mother, and you?"

"Well, I have been thinking, Tama." Rie lit an incense stick and pushed it deeper into the ash mixture.

"You know we cannot exist without a successor to Yoshi."

"I know," Tama nodded, pausing with a stem in her hand to look at Rie.

"I have decided because of Hirokichi's stubborn opposition to have you succeed for the three years allowed."

Tama's eyes widened. "Is it possible for a woman?"

Rie smiled. "Yes, with the approval of the local officials a woman can succeed for three years. It's in the regulations of the association, though it doesn't often happen."

Tama bowed deeply. "I wonder if I would be capable."

Rie took out her fan. "I have watched you work here for over twenty-five years. You have worked as hard and capably as anyone. I am here to support you. Only remember that it will be necessary for you to speak at some formal occasions. You can practice. And spend more time with Buntaro now."

"I will do my utmost for the house, Mother." Tama bowed deeply, her forehead touching the tatami.

"I know," Rie said softly. "You always have."

Tama's investiture as successor to the headship of the house coincided with the end of season celebration. The celebration was more modest than usual, appropriate to the recent death of the house head and the temporary succession by a woman. Seisaburo made the announcement that his aunt was succeeding to the headship for three years.

Tama's words of acceptance were brief. "We are grateful you have taken the trouble to join us today to celebrate the end of brewing for the season. We humbly request your continued co-operation with the House of Omura." Tama's face reddened with the effort of speaking in front of Nada's important brewers for the first time. "We thank you and ask that you enjoy some of our sake." She then walked among the guests, bowing graciously and greeting them as she had seen Yoshitaro do. It was not common for women of the house to be present at the end of brewing celebration, but this occasion was unusual, a woman becoming house head.

Rie smiled as she watched. Some things a woman could do as well as a man, even better. She looked over at Tama and a shiver of apprehension shook her. Could a woman be house head for longer than the allowed three years? It had never happened before.

Late one evening Buntaro went on an errand to the number one kura. Brewing was finished for the season, and the workers had returned to their farms for the summer. The interior of the kura was completely dark. He tried to focus and moved along the line of barrels, his hand touching each one as he moved. Silence. Only the dull echo of his geta on the earthen floor. He paused. What was that sound? He sensed a presence somewhere in the kura. He listened, did not move. There it was again. Was it the sound of footsteps? Who could it be? The kurabito had all left. The clerks were gone for the night. He crept farther along the line of barrels toward the wall. He paused and looked both ways, peering into the murky darkness. There it was again, the sound. He turned abruptly toward the right and saw something move, a figure.

"Who's there?" he cried.

The person began to run toward the door.

Buntaro raced down another aisle and reached the door just as the intruder came around the corner and nearly collided with Buntaro.

In a series of rapid thrusts Buntaro slammed his knee into the man's groin, banged his knee against his chin, and twisted the man around, pinning his arms behind him. Holding the intruder to the ground with his knees and arms with one hand, with the other hand Buntaro pulled the man's head back by the hair. "What are you doing here? Sent by Yusuke, from Yamaguchi, weren't you?" Buntaro said gruffly. He recognized Yusuke's apprentice, Hachirobei, a slight young man about his own age.

Hachirobei gasped for breath but said nothing.

"Speak!" Buntaro commanded.

Still the culprit made no reply.

Buntaro moved his knees to pin Hachirobei's arms, freeing both hands to encircle his neck.

"Answer now, or you'll never talk again."

Buntaro tightened his grip.

Hachirobei's eyes bulged. He gasped and choked.

"Ready to talk?"

A slight nod of the head.

Buntaro loosened his hold slightly. "Well?"

Hachirobei coughed. "I . . . I was . . . looking for your recipe."

"*Ha!* Another of Yamaguchi's tricks."

Buntaro let go of Hachirobei. He scrambled to his feet, and as he turned toward the door, Buntaro gave him a swift kick.

"Out, rat!" he shouted into the night. "The Brewers Association will hear of this," Buntaro muttered as he walked out of the kura toward the office.

***

O-Natsu, though older than Rie and long since retired, still came to the house each day to sit a few hours, often in the old nursery, long since empty of children. She had no other family, never having married. Rie found her presence comforting, and since the pace of her own life was slowing, her steps often took her to the nursery of an afternoon. There the two white-haired women would take from their obis their long tiny pipes and reminisce. One would say something, and the other would nod and exhale a thin white wisp. Rie knew that a stranger looking in would not guess that one was mistress, the other servant, so easy was their companionship. The wisdom and plain common sense of O-Natsu Rie found nowhere else.

The days and months of Tama's headship passed, and White Tiger prospered.

"Tama," Rie said to her daughter-in-law one morning, "our shipping business is prospering beyond our expectations. I have an idea for something new."

Tama looked at her mother-in-law and marveled at this woman whose face wrinkled around the eyes now and whose voice occasionally cracked, but whose mind was still the most agile she had known. "What is it, Mother?"

"Buntaro says there are rumblings of trouble with China now. He thinks there may be a military confrontation."

"Yes, I heard him say something about it. He sounded very concerned."

"I want Buntaro to go to the port and buy two of those English steamships, ships that can transport troops. Of course he will negotiate a good price."

"Oh?"

"Then," Rie continued, "we can charter the ships to the government at a good fee. The government will need ships if it transports troops to the continent." Rie tapped the table with her fan. "The English have the best steamships. Then when the fighting has ended we can sell the ships and make a good profit." Rie smiled, sitting straight-backed, her eyes sparkling.

"How clever you are, Mother. Yes, it is a good idea. We should discuss it with Buntaro today."

"He has become even more aggressive than Kinnosuke was, don't you think, Tama?"

"Yes, he does keep up with the pace of the times."

"Come, let's go and speak with him." Rie rose slowly, taking Tama's arm as she did so.

Chapter 43

Buntaro hurried to Kobe port soon after Rie and Tama spoke with him about purchasing two English ships and chartering them to the government. As he walked along the wharf he encountered two clerks from another brewery sauntering along, speaking in guttural, gruff voices. They eyed him suspiciously.

"Where to, Buntaro?" one asked.

Buntaro said only hello.

"On a secret mission for the Omura House?" the second said impudently.

"That Omura woman must be possessed by the fox spirit. That's the only explanation for her craftiness," the first clerk said. They both guffawed.

Cheeky fellows, Buntaro thought, and hastened away from them. He was well aware that he was watched wherever he went by curious, even jealous, clerks. It was the price of success. White Tiger's prosperity was legendary, and Buntaro sometimes wondered if being so far ahead of most other brewers didn't have its drawbacks. Was it appropriate to succeed in the competition when one's competitors viewed it as being at their expense? He dismissed these thoughts as he approached the office of the English ship owners. Honest success was the measure of any business negotiation or decision, as his father and Kinnosuke had always taught him. He squared his broad shoulders and walked through the door of the shipping office.

Fumi came through the kitchen corridor door calling for Rie. "Where is she?" Fumi asked O-Yuki, who was working in the kitchen.

"I think she's upstairs in her room," O-Yuki said.

"Not feeling well?" Fumi persisted.

"I'm not sure. Maybe she's just resting."

Fumi padded quickly upstairs to her mother's room and opened the shoji.

"Mother, are you all right?" Fumi asked.

"Oh, come in, Fumi," Rie replied, feeling a little nostalgic after Yoshi's death. It had hit her harder than she'd ever thought possible. Or maybe she was just recognizing her own mortality. "She sat at a small table rummaging through a large lacquer box. "I'm fine, Fumi. I was just looking through some of your grandmother's things. I'm sorry you never knew her."

"So am I, Mother," Fumi said. She sat next to her mother and dabbed perspiration from her face.

"What's the matter, dear? You seem upset," Rie asked.

"The same old problem, Mother. It's just that the longer we postpone the marriage, the worse it gets. Mrs. Nakano is at her wit's end. Forty-five o-miais! Can you imagine? And Hiro has had his twenty-seventh birthday. Some people are saying there's something wrong with him." Fumi fanned herself vigorously.

"There's nothing wrong. Nothing that more discipline wouldn't cure," Rie said, holding up a gold-threaded obi tie. "Here, dear, I'd like you to have this. It was your grandmother's favorite. Please don't show it to Tama. I'll give her another one."

Fumi held the gold tie up to examine it. "Lovely, Mother, thank you. I'll cherish it." She thrust it into her sleeve.

"I've been meaning to tell you, Fumi, that I'm going to talk to Hiro soon. I'll make it plain to him: either he accepts a bride or he will be disinherited. Perhaps I'll send for him tomorrow." Rie continued to sort through the items in the box, unwrapping and refolding each carefully.

"Well, I suppose it has come to that." Fumi stopped fanning herself and bit a fingernail. "It's a good thing we didn't wait for Mie to be married. She'd be way overage for marriage now." Fumi looked at her mother. "Have you been feeling well lately, Mother?"

"Well enough for over eighty, Fumi. But I have to admit, the stairs are becoming harder for me and my heart flutters some-times. I'm thinking of moving back to my old room downstairs. It's closer to the garden too. Come, let's go down and have some tea. Tama will join us. She's working in the office."

Fumi helped her mother up and they descended the stairs to the parlor.

"Would you call Tama, please? And have O-Yuki bring us tea."

Fumi returned with Tama, followed by O-Yuki carrying a tea tray.

Tama knelt, bowed, and smiled. "Buntaro is back from the port, Mother. He managed to purchase one of the two large English steamships."

Rie beamed and nodded. All her plans were falling into place. Why then did she have a touch of melancholy? "And he was so skillful and quick to catch that Yamaguchi thief. Yamaguchi will suffer for it. He won't have thought of buying steamships."

"Yes. I think Buntaro is already planning his Tokyo trip," Tama said. "One of the ships is docked at Yokohama. The other is here in Kobe. He said he wants to go to Tokyo by ship and buy the other there."

"*Ah!*" Rie sighed, feeling her age. "If I were younger I would like to make the trip too. Imagine going to Edo . . . Tokyo, by a steamship! I was going to say maybe you could go, Tama, but we need you here, to settle the matter of Hiro finally. I'm going to talk with him tomorrow. Of course you are more than capable of acting as house head, Tama. But we're over the time limit now, and the officials are asking embarrassing questions, you know."

Tama poured tea for her mother-in-law and sister-in-law.

The following day Hirokichi, whom Rie had summoned to the main house, approached the door to the parlor where Rie waited for him. He bowed stiffly.

"Good afternoon, Grandmother," he said in a deep, resonant voice.

"Hiro, come and sit by the Butsudan with me," Rie said. She patted a zabuton next to her.

"You know, Hiro," she said looking directly at him, "I selected you to succeed your uncle soon after you were born. And when you were younger you justified my choice. But in recent years you have changed. Your commitment to the house is flawed, Hiro. Think about what this means for your life, your future." She paused and leaned forward intently. "Do you understand?"

Hirokichi bowed, his somber expression unwavering. "I will think about it, Grandmother."

"You have had ample time to think about it, Hiro," she said sharply. "I want you to understand the consequences of your continued refusal. We can brook no further delay." She looked at his still bowed head.

He nodded.

"I want to see you again one week from today, Hiro. I expect you to decide to accept your responsibility by then."

One week later Hirokichi appeared at the parlor door at the same hour of the afternoon. He bowed and entered. She prayed that he'd had a change of heart. If not, she would have to play her hidden card.

"Come, Hiro," Rie said. "Sit. Have you decided?" She looked at him intently.

Hirokichi bowed when he was seated. "I will find a bride, Grandmother."

"One the house can accept?" Rie took out her fan and toyed with it.

"I believe so," he said. "In fact, I have found her."

"Really?" Rie's voice rose. "You mean you have found a bride by yourself, without our go-between? What are you talking about? No such thing!" She opened her fan and fanned rapidly.

"Yes, Grandmother. I have found her."

Rie noted a slight smile on her grandson's face and felt a rising anger that her grandson could be so smug.

"But you cannot select your own bride. Remember, the condition was that you marry a bride of our choice. Before I ask who she is, are you certain she will be suitable, acceptable to the main house?"

"Quite certain, yes." He bowed.

"And who might she be, then?"

"Naoko Fujiwara." Hirokichi raised his head and smiled broadly.

Rie put her fan over her mouth to stifle a gasp. "What? A girl from the Kyoto nobility? Where did you get such an idea, Hiro?" She leaned forward. "Have you met her? What makes you think her family would allow her to marry a brewer?" Rie dropped her fan and leaned forward, her hands pressed against the tatami.

"I was introduced to her at a Kabuki performance a few months ago, Grandmother. She is third daughter in her house. I believe she wishes to marry me and that her father will allow it."

"What makes you so certain that she would or could marry you, Hiro?" Rie picked up her fan, her hands resting on the table.

"I am confident about it, Grandmother. I have seen her several times at Bunraku, and we have had some opportunity to talk. She has already spoken with her father. I met him also at a Bunraku performance."

"*Humph!* Too much confidence is as unattractive as too little, Hiro. Well, if her house agrees, it will be the first time a brewer has ever married a bride from the nobility." Rie pursed her lips and looked critically at her grandson.

"Well, isn't that what you have always taught us, Grandmother? That White Tiger should be first in everything?"

Rie quickly picked up her fan, brought it to her face and burst into a peal of laughter. Here, after all, was a grandson fit to succeed to the headship of the house and to honor her father's memory.

"All right, Hiro. If in fact her parents agree, you have my blessing. Yes, I think it will be a master stroke, a good beginning for you as successor." She smiled. "Tama has had the position for five, nearly six years, twice as long as generally permitted. Now we can go ahead with the formal arrangements for the wedding and your succession as well. Of course her family will be responsible for the wedding arrangements." Rie put a hand to her hair. "Won't Mrs. Nakano be surprised, for we should give her the honor of sitting as go-between after all she has done for us. All of Nada will take notice." Rie straightened and smiled at her grandson. "And here, Hiro." She reached into her obi and handed the house seal to Hiro. She thought of Yoshi, the fight they'd had over this very seal, and felt a flash of regret. It was a bittersweet moment. One she would not soon forget.

Chapter 44

The wedding reception of Hirokichi and his Fujiwara bride was a glittering event that astounded all of Kansai. The wedding was not only the event of the year; it also marked the investiture of Hirokichi as Kinzaemon XIII. The bride's Kyoto family and friends, exquisitely attired and impeccably mannered, nearly filled the reception hall, with less room for the Omuras and other brewers. Everyone knew the Kyoto nobility had more status than wealth, and that the Omura House was one of Japan's wealthiest brewing families. The marriage was a mutually advantageous union, such as had been happening between families of the samurai and merchant classes. But this was a first, a union between a brewing family and a family of the old nobility. Rie felt awed that her house was now allied in marriage with the ancient Fujiwara house, and yet at the same time, she couldn't help but feel that an era was ending and a new one beginning. She saw in both Naoko, the bride, and the bride's mother, a hint of her own mother's aristocratic features and distinctive nose. If only her parents had lived to see this day.

The entire house and especially the upstairs room was cleaned and readied for the bridal couple. Rie hoped Naoko would learn to feel at home with the customs of the Omura House, but she left to Tama the instructing of the bride. That Naoko's family did not brew was overshadowed for Rie by the anticipation that Naoko's aristocratic Fujiwara blood would benefit the house. Hirokichi by his marriage could gain access to exclusive levels of society about which Rie had only the vaguest knowledge. And although it brought her pride, it also brought home the fact that life would soon be different. Times were changing, customs were changing, and shortly, an era would be ending, the mantle passed to a new generation, one with nobility running through its veins. The geisha's bloodline banished from the house at last. Still, she did not wish her grandson to feel inferior to his noble bride.

"Don't forget, Hiro," Rie told him a few days before the wedding, her head held proudly, "sake brewing is as ancient as the nobility, perhaps even older. In every town and village sake brewers are the most respected people. We have always been the producers, we merchants. The samurai were parasites, and the nobility also lived on what the merchants produced. They still do."

After the wedding, while Hirokichi fell comfortably into the work of the main house with Buntaro, Rie saw that Naoko felt awkward, thrust suddenly into a working family. Rie was certain that Tama would treat Naoko with fairness, even compassion, but the responsibility of instructing Naoko was a daunting one.

"I wonder if she will ever be able to do the work we have done, Tama?" Rie lamented as the two women sat drinking tea one evening in Rie's room.

Tama raised her eyebrows. "I don't know, Mother. Her background is so different, and she is not accustomed to hard work.

She has been trained in the polite arts. She does very well with ikebana, and I have seen some of her fine needlework. And you know she has brought her koto with her."

"That won't go very far in the brewery, will it?" Rie said sharply, then softened her tone. "Well, it's a good thing that all the women in the house know what to do without being told by Naoko. I doubt that the house will suffer, at least while we are alive. I wonder in what new direction Hiro and his bride may take White Tiger?" She paused and took out her small pipe, once again feeling the winds of change stirring.

Rie hated to admit that she was feeling her age, her legs and knees less agile, her vision losing clarity. She worked consciously to keep her back straight, not bent from years of bending and bowing as with other women her age. She went to the office less often now, but expected Tama and Hirokichi to come to her to report on problems and decisions, whether important or minor matters. She felt comfortable with having given the seal to Hiro, but a sense of loss, too. It meant her own road would soon be coming to an end.

One morning Tama came to Rie's room before noon and called at the door, "Mother, may I come in?"

"Of course, Tama." She looked at her daughter-in-law, now graying at the temples, her plain face somehow a reminder of her faithfulness.

"There's good news, Mother," Tama said brightly.

"Is that so?"

"Buntaro is back from Tokyo. He says the war with China is over. He and Hiro think the time has come to sell the two ships we chartered to the government."

"Good, Tama. Yes, I'm glad both Buntaro and Hiro know about timing, and you too. Yes," Rie said, and reached for Tama's hand to help her rise. "I'll go to the office with you. I want to see about the price."

Tama stepped aside so that Rie could precede her slowly down the corridor to the office. When Rie entered, clerks working in the room stopped to bow low and leave the office.

"Good morning, Grandmother," Hirokichi said with a bow.

"How good to see you in the office," Buntaro said.

"What's this I hear about the war being over, Buntaro-san? Is it really true?" Rie asked.

"Yes, I arrived in Tokyo just a few days after the fighting stopped. It's given our shipping a boost, but I'm glad it's over," Buntaro replied.

"I know it's time to sell now; the sooner the better," Hirokichi said.

"Just so, Hiro," Rie nodded.

"So Buntaro and I are going to Tokyo tomorrow. I'm fairly certain the government will want to buy back the two ships they used for transporting troops."

Rie nodded. "We've owned them just a bit over two years, and they were indispensable to the government during the war." Rie paused. "Ask at least sixty percent more than we paid for them. Then if they want to bargain, don't go below thirty percent more," she said.

"Yes." Hirokichi nodded. "That's about what Buntaro and I were thinking."

"Yes, do go tomorrow, Hiro-chan," Rie said. She nodded to Buntaro and her grandson and left the office. She shuffled slowly along the corridor, thankful that the fortunes of White Tiger rested in the hands of the two aggressive, forward-looking young men in the main office. That Naoko was not familiar with the requirements of a brewer's wife was perhaps less important in the long run. Naoko was gradually becoming accustomed to what was surely a more frugal, less luxurious lifestyle, wasn't she? She paused at the pillar and rested her head against it.

The same afternoon Rie went down the corridor to the nursery. She wanted O-Natsu's company. There were times when it was so satisfying.

Rie slid open the shoji.

Old O-Natsu looked up. "*Ah,* is it you, Oku-san? Good. Good." She nodded, tried unsuccessfully to rise, and moved a zabuton over toward Rie.

Rie sat and moved toward the teapot on the table. She reached for two cups and poured.

"*Heh, heh,*" O-Natsu chuckled. "Good for the house, this new bride, isn't she?"

"There are some advantages to having a Fujiwara bride." Rie nodded and sipped her tea. "What makes you say so?"

"Pregnant already, I think," O-Natsu said.

"What? Has someone said something?" Rie glanced up quickly.

"No need," O-Natsu said, nodding. "Just look at the eyes. I had a glimpse at them this morning in the kitchen." Her smile revealed several toothless gaps.

"Well, O-Natsu, I'll make certain. And it isn't that I doubt you. You have always been the first in the house to learn of a pregnancy, haven't you?" Rie laughed, her hand over her mouth, a reflex even in O-Natsu's company.

That night as she sat before her dressing table combing her long white hair Rie mused. Having Hirokichi and his Fujiwara bride as successors was far better than if Ume had married Hirokichi. Now the bloodline of O-Toki and Jihei and the influence of the Sawaraya were finally gone from the house. Rie's revenge against Jihei was complete. Naoko's baby would have none of O-Toki's blood. The bloodline of the main house would be pure, even enhanced by the Fujiwara infusion. Rie nodded and smiled at herself in the mirror. "Yes, Hiro, you are good for the house," she muttered. How proud her father would be when she reported at the Butsudan.

Hirokichi and Buntaro returned from Tokyo elated by their

success in selling the two ships at a handsome profit. It was not White Tiger's only success since Hirokichi had become house head.

Hirokichi came to Rie's room one morning looking unusually jaunty and elated.

"What is it, Hiro-chan?" she asked as soon as he entered the room.

"We've made it, Grandmother! White Tiger is now number one! It was announced at the Brewers Association last night." He grinned, his well-muscled arms akimbo.

She gasped. This was the day she had striven for ever since that day at the well, when she had lost the heir, had shirked her duty. Rie looked at Hirokichi, and bowed several times. She quickly took a handkerchief from her sleeve and dabbed at tears that threatened to overflow.

"*Ah,* Hiro-chan. What I have worked for all my life. . . ." She paused and held up a bony hand. "Come, give me a hand. I must go to the Butsudan."

"Yes, Grandmother, I'll accompany you."

Rie hobbled slowly to the parlor on the arm of her grandson pausing briefly to touch the aged column. She removed her slippers and shuffled to the Butsudan in her tabi. Hirokichi placed a zabuton in front of the altar. Rie knelt slowly, clapped her hands and closed her eyes.

Hirokichi pulled up a cushion and sat quietly next to his grandmother. When she opened her eyes and turned to him he said, "I have more news for you, Grandmother. Naoko is going to have a baby in a few months."

Rie nodded and smiled. "Good."

"We would like your permission to build a house at the side of the compound here." He pointed toward the vacant area beyond the old well.

"A new house, Hiro? You don't want to live here with me?"

Rie queried, frowning. A vague disappointment settled in her bones. She had worked so hard, only to see the children scatter to the four winds.

"Oh, it isn't that, Grandmother. But Naoko has seen some of the new Western-style houses in the city. She thinks it would reflect the spirit of the new era and enhance the reputation of our house."

"I see." Rie was silent for several minutes. Hirokichi waited. "Well, Hiro, you have done well. And it may be that Naoko will help you advance our status even more. I have never opposed doing something new. Yes, you may build it. I wonder what it will look like."

"You will see, Grandmother, you will see."

Two months later the purple-robed priest came to bless the site for building Hirokichi's house. Rie watched him shake his white paper wand just as he did for the opening of the brewing season.

The house Hirokichi built was unlike anything Rie had seen. She watched from the parlor when the shutters were opened in the morning as the structure took shape, each of two stories fronted by a railed veranda behind which were arched doors. Built along Western lines and inspired by pictures Naoko had seen, its two-story frame dwarfed the old main house in style if not in height.

"I wonder why they are covering the wood with white," Tama said to Rie one day as they sat together and watched the builders put the final touches on the house.

"It must be what Naoko saw in those foreign picture books," Rie said. "Well, Hiro wanted something new, and that is what they have. The baby will be born in the new house." She nodded slowly. "Everything changes," she said, and took out her tiny pipe.

Hirokichi moved into the grand new home in time for the birth of the baby, a girl born auspiciously on New Year's Day. Rie and Tama celebrated the doubly felicitous occasion with Hirokichi beside them. All the branch families came to pay their respects to Rie and Hirokichi at the old main house. Even Ume and her husband appeared. Rie felt a great contentment descend on her as she looked around the room at Fumi and Seisaburo and their children, and a great sadness as well, knowing that life has a cycle: spring, summer, autumn, winter. She turned to Hirokichi and reached for him to pour her a cup of congratulatory New Year's wine.

"You know, Hiro, I'm happy it's a girl. It will be good for the house," she said, smiling at the old adage until her eyes disappeared.

"I hope she will grow up to be like you, Grandmother."

Rie smiled and bowed. He had deeply pleased her. "I'm anxious to see her," she said.

Two weeks later Naoko came to the door carrying the baby. Rie and Tama exclaimed over the tiny struggling infant and ushered Naoko into the parlor.

"Please, sit here in front of the Butsudan," Rie said. "Tama, bring a zabuton."

When Naoko was seated she held the baby out to Rie, who reached for her gingerly.

"We have named her Hana, Grandmother, after your mother."

"*Ah,*" Rie said, and bowed over the baby, tears starting in her eyes.

"I want to invite you and Aunt Tama and Mother Fumi to our house, Grandmother," Naoko said. "The day after tomorrow please come in the afternoon. I will play my koto for you."

When Naoko left with the baby, Rie turned to Tama. "Well, I guess now I need a special invitation to visit my grandson in his new house," she said, pride mingled with a poignant sense of herself as a person passed by with the changing times. Then she shuffled off to her room.

Chapter 45

Rie and Tama could still see workmen coming and going, making last minute changes to the elegant new home in the compound and house servants bustling in to help Naoko. Rie enjoyed the activity vicariously from the vantage point of the parlor shutters that were opened to the courtyard.

Fumi arrived in the afternoon to join Rie and Tama for the much anticipated visit.

"I haven't seen the inside of the house yet, Fumi, only what you see from here," Rie said.

"Nor have I, Mother. Come, let's go over."

Fumi and Tama took Rie's arms and helped her across the courtyard.

A servant greeted them at the large arched doorway and ushered them into the parlor, a room unlike any the three had seen before.

"Mistress will be with you presently. Please be seated," she said, and left the room.

The women looked around for zabuton.

"I thought it was finished," Fumi whispered.

"Where are the tatami?" Tama asked. "Just bare wood. And I don't see any zabuton."

"What are those things with the long legs?" Rie asked, looking at square wooden pieces with backs and padded cushions.

The women were still standing, looking around in puzzled bewilderment when Naoko entered exquisitely attired in a pale blue kimono, smiling and bowing.

"Oh, I'm sorry to keep you waiting, Grandmother," she bowed. She hurried to Rie's side. "Please be seated," she said, holding Rie's arm. "This is a Western-style chair, Grandmother. Can you sit in it?" She helped Rie into the chair, where Rie sat uncomfortably, her feet dangling above the floor.

"And Mother, Aunt Tama, please take a seat. I am so honored that you were able to visit today," she said in her politely soaring voice.

The maidservant entered and placed tea and cakes on small, high wooden tables next to the chairs. Rie noted that the cakes were from the Kadatoya in Kyoto.

"How is the baby today?" Fumi asked.

"She is fine and healthy, thanks to you," Naoko said. "I'll bring her here after I have played. She is napping just now. Please help yourselves." She indicated the cakes on the tables.

The long koto sat on a mat on the wooden floor, a zabuton facing it.

Naoko seated herself gracefully and leaned forward. She placed bone picks on her fingers and paused, her hands resting lightly on the thirteen strings.

The visitors fixed their eyes on Naoko, a vision of elegant aristocratic beauty as her fingers began to dance over the strings. The liquid tones of the koto filled the room with a mellifluous familiar melody. Naoko's fingers raced faster and faster until the three older women were mesmerized.

Well, Rie mused as she listened, her family never had the leisure for these refinements. They had only heard the koto or samisen when they went to a concert, so infrequently. If they had a chance to squeeze in anything but brewery work they tried to teach the kurabito to read and write a bit. *I guess the Omura House is going to become something very different now.* She sighed, feeling yet again that life was changing, and with it would come an end of an era.

Naoko played another selection before turning to Rie. "I don't want to tire you, Grandmother," she said.

"Oh, I am enjoying your music, Naoko. We have never had the opportunity to hear the koto in the house before. Thank you." Rie nodded. "And Naoko, please tell us what that large black box with the black-and-white teeth is." Rie pointed to a piece of furniture standing against the far wall.

"Oh, that is called a piano, Grandmother. Come, I'll show it to you."

The women approached the piano cautiously. Naoko played a scale and a few chords. "When Hana is old enough she will have lessons on the piano," Naoko said in her lilting voice. She rose from the stool. "I'll bring Hana now. Excuse me," she said, and disappeared through a doorway.

Naoko returned carrying the infant wrapped in a white lace-trimmed garment, a white bonnet on her head. The three older women surrounded Naoko, exclaiming and reaching for the baby's waving fists.

"*Ah,*" Rie said, her gaze on the lovely baby girl. "My first great-grandchild. I am so pleased that you have named her Hana."

"Yes, my husband thought you would be. He was particular about choosing her name." Naoko bowed.

When the visit was over the women walked back toward the old main house. Before they reached the entrance, Hirokichi walked rapidly toward them. "Grandmother, Mother, have you heard?"

"*Eh* . . . what is it, Hiro?" Rie asked.

Hirokichi took Rie's arm. "We reported Buntaro's discovery of Yamaguchi's treachery at the last Brewers Association meeting, you know."

"Oh?"

"They say Yamaguchi committed suicide yesterday."

Rie stopped and looked at her grandson, her heart fluttering suddenly, and yet she was surprised at how little satisfaction the news gave her. "*Ah* . . . so that is how he ended?" She paused. "Then I must tell my father. He would want to know." She bowed slightly to Hirokichi and continued into the parlor, where she knelt in front of the Butsudan, Tama and Fumi behind her. Rie bowed and was silent for a few moments. Then she turned and asked Tama to bring tea.

The three women sipped slowly.

Tama leaned forward. "I could never get used to that kind of furniture and that hard floor. Don't they have tatami? I didn't know if I should ask."

"I wonder," Rie said. "Well, Fumi did you ever think the day would come when you had to wait for a special invitation to visit your son's house?"

Fumi shook her head and smiled with a hint of pride. "It's a new age, Mother. Who knows what new things Hiro will introduce?"

"I am thankful he is house head now and that my time will soon end. He has raised White Tiger to number one," Rie said. "That is enough."

"We were already well on the way, Mother, weren't we?" Tama said firmly.

Rie laughed softly, her fan over her face. "Yes, Tama, well on the way."

That night as Rie sat in her room alone the thought came to her that she herself wished to select the characters for her tombstone. She took out inkstone, brush, and rice paper from her black lacquer writing box inlaid with mother of pearl. She poured a few drops of water onto the inkstone from a miniature iron pot, and rubbed the inkstick back and forth until the ink was of proper consistency. She dipped the tip of the brush into the ink, held the brush over the rice paper, and paused. She wrote "spring blossom" a few times. Then she dipped the brush again and wrote "autumn reverie" twice. Next she wrote "tranquil water." She sighed and dipped the brush again, the pain that Toichi's death had caused her all those years ago receding with the last word written. She wrote the characters for "first sake," then smiled and set the brush down on the inkstone.

She went back to her dressing table and picked up her comb. "First sake," she said to herself and smiled until her eyes were nearly slits.

Rie heard Fumi's voice in the corridor one morning.

"Fumi? Come in, dear."

Fumi opened the shoji to her mother's room. She sat and faced Rie.

"How nice to see you." Rie smiled. "Have a cup of tea, dear."

Fumi inclined her head, as though noticing for the first time how her mother had aged and become mellowed, without the hard edge she'd once had. "Mother, Eitaro and Sei want to have a family gathering to celebrate your eighty-eighth birthday."

"Oh, dear, let's not talk about my birthday." Rie shook her head, her lips pressed firmly together.

"But Mother, your eighty-eighth is so important. You know

you always told us how important it is because the numbers resemble the character for rice. We must celebrate."

Rie broke into a wrinkled smile. "Oh yes, that is true, dear. All right."

"Wonderful! It will be doubly special because Hiro has a surprise for the occasion."

"*Ah,* Hiro often has surprises for us, doesn't he? I wonder what it is this time."

"You will see, Mother." Fumi sipped tea with Rie for a few minutes, then excused herself, saying the celebration would be in time for her birthday, two weeks hence.

The entire family assembled for Rie's important birthday. All the children and grandchildren: Sei and Mari and their children, Fumi and Eitaro with Mie and her husband, even Ume and her family and Kazu and her family had been called for the event. Rie touched her special hair ornament—the one Saburo had given her—and smiled.

The maids had removed the shoji in the main room and set out many lacquer tables in rows, as for a wedding reception or end of year celebration.

Hiro brought in a man carrying several large pieces of equipment. "This is Mr. Akita, Grandmother. He is going to take a picture of you, your likeness. This is a new invention that has come into the country recently. Your picture will then remain for all future generations of the family to see and enjoy."

"My picture? What an idea. I don't really want people to see what I look like now, Hiro-chan." She tried to adjust her hair, to arrange herself in a more presentable way. She sat absolutely straight as Mr. Akita set up his equipment with the tripod and black cover.

"You look beautiful, Grandmother. And I want us to toast you on your birthday." He raised a cup and all the family followed suit, with cries of "Happy Birthday, Grandmother."

Rie looked around at her assembled family and bowed, trying her best to conceal her tears. All the family was present, though Kin, Kinnosuke, and Buntaro were also part of what she had worked all her life to achieve. White Tiger was now the largest sake empire in all the land.

Rie's days and months passed quietly, often in her room or in the nursery with O-Natsu, sometimes in the parlor in front of the Butsudan, occasionally making her way slowly down the hall to the office to speak with Hirokichi and Buntaro.

One day Rie hobbled out into the courtyard and paused at the huge barrels where she had spent so many vigorous hours. She glanced toward the dark door of the kura and inhaled her favorite scent, the yeasty aroma of brewing sake. Then her gaze rested on the old well, and for a moment she could almost imagine Toichi there. She had done what she had set out to do and taken a small step toward redemption in the process. But now, looking back, she knew that redemption wasn't enough. What her father had given her was so much more than what she could have ever given him in return. He had given her a rich sense of tradition, and now she was passing that tradition on to Hirokichi.

With that, Rie walked deliberately into the main house and into the front room where she carefully placed a zabuton directly before the altar, then sat so that she faced it. The morning light was glancing in through the open shutters. She reached for an incense stick, lit it, and placed the small vase in front of her father's name tablet. Smoke swirled up around her head and curled toward her mother's name tablet. The image of her mother's face came to her, the delicate outlines of Hana's chin and patrician Kyoto nose. She sat motionless for several minutes, and heard her mother's voice call ever so faintly, "Rie."

Rie jumped, startled. She strained to listen but could not hear the voice call again. She looked again at the Butsudan. There they all were, the name tablets of the generations of Omuras: her

father, Kinzaemon IX; Jihei, Kinzaemon X; Yoshitaro, Kinzaemon XI; Tama, still alive, who intervened in the chain but whose
name as a woman would not figure in the formal succession,
though she had been intermediary as number XII. And finally
there would someday be Hirokichi, who had married a Fujiwara
bride from the nobility and succeeded as Kinzaemon XIII.

Rie's eyes filled as she was overcome with memories of so many
generations, so many deaths. She glanced out the open shutters into the courtyard where the sunlight was filtering past the
old well. A pang of grief shook her. Her eyes moved on toward
the barrels. There beside a barrel heaved on its side was a bent,
white-haired figure in a worn, indigo-dyed kimono. Who was it?
She leaned closer to the open shutter and peered out. It was O-
Natsu, surely it was O-Natsu. Wasn't she holding someone by the
hand? Rie caught her breath. Yes, it was Hirokichi's two-year-old
daughter, Hana, Rie's mother's namesake.

What was it the country women in the south said? Rie remembered hearing the ancient folktale from O-Natsu. A woman
should not live to see her great-grandchild. Food was too scarce
in those poor farming districts. So a son took his old mother on
his back when her great-grandchild was born, took her up to a
mountaintop and left her there to die.

Rie smiled and allowed a tear to run down her cheek at the
painful thought. There was no one to see. How fortunate that
she was Rie, daughter of Kinzaemon IX, widow of Kinzaemon
X, mother, yes mother, of Kinzaemon XI, and grandmother of
Kinzaemon XIII of the House of Omura, and now White Tiger
was number one in all Japan. She sat perfectly straight before the
Butsudan, inhaled the yeasty aroma and smiled.

Acknowledgments

I am indebted to many individuals who offered suggestions, encouragement, inspiration, and technical assistance during the writing of this novel. My agent, Natasha Kern, said, "I'm the perfect agent for your book," and, in fact, was. Editors Carol Craig and Carrie Feron believed in the book from its inception and guided it with unerring vision through to completion.

A host of friends offered continual support, among them Paul Wood, Sue Riford, and Pat Palmer on Maui; in Boulder, members of my writing group—Thora Chinnery, Diana Vari, Carol Dow, and Sherri Jennings—as well as other friends: Hua-ling Hu, Takeko and Art Sakakura, Keiko Beer, Billie Corrigan, Sherry Oaks, Jody Berman, Faye Kleeman, Polly Christensen, Mariko Sumida (Honolulu), and Kitty Felion (Erie, Pennsylvania). I am immensely grateful to them, as well as to Masami Yabune in Japan and also to those who helped me through the idiosyncracies of computers: Sherry Oaks, Nancy Fritch, and Polly Christensen.

I was fortunate to have guidance and information on the history of the sake industry, Japan's most ancient industry, from two leading authorities, Professor Manabu Yunoki of Kwansei Gakuin University and Professor Sakurai of Chiba University.

The book would never have been written without the many brewers who shared stories of their families, their brewing traditions, and the technology of the brewing process. As I traveled from Akita, Niigata, and Fukushima in the north to Kyushu in the south, brewers were more generous of their time and hospitality than I could have hoped. In some cases I was a guest for a week at a time and had an opportunity to observe brewing at each stage and to explore the inner recesses of the architecture of house and kura. I was given lectures on brewing by brewmasters, I tasted enticing grades and varieties, and was wined and dined along with brewers at ceremonies celebrating both the start and end of the brewing season. Out of respect for traditions of brewing houses I do not here identify individual brewers who have been so kind and helpful. It is my hope they will realize the depth of my gratitude.

This is a work of fiction. While certain incidents are based on historical events and eras, the characters depicted are products of the author's imagination.

Joyce Chapman Lebra
Boulder, Colorado
2008

A+

AUTHOR
INSIGHTS,
EXTRAS, &
MORE...

FROM
**JOYCE
LEBRA**
AND
AVON A

Note to Readers

Imagine yourself near Kobe, Japan, in the year 1830, a time when the feudal Tokugawa shoguns are on the verge of collapse. The real economic strength of Japan is in the hands of the prosperous merchant class, the chonin, and among them sake brewers are the most powerful. As you bounce along the coastal road in your ricksha you see rows of towering brown wooden structures, the kura, where sake is being brewed. You pull your cloak tighter around your throat against the icy wind blasting down from Mt. Rokko, for it is winter, the height of the brewing season.

Pull up to the entrance of one of the breweries where the noren hanging over the door announces the name of the brand. As you stoop under the noren and enter the main office you are assailed by a pungent yeasty aroma, the scent of sake, that pervades the room and beyond into the house itself. This enterprise is also the house; the two are one and the same. Beyond the outer office and the inner one are the rooms where the family lives. Clerks are scurrying back and forth waiting on customers and dealing with suppliers of the koji mold and yeast used in brewing. If you listen carefully you can hear the singing of the kurabito, the brewery workers, a rhythmic tune matching their tasks as they work.

This is a man's world in a male-dominated society. Brewing is a masculine occupation. Women, even senior members of the house, are not allowed to enter the kura for fear of pollution. Even to step near the entrance is to court danger. The entire process of brewing is surrounded with purification rituals. Sake is the most ancient and honored industry in the land; none can be married or buried without sake being imbibed.

The one exception, a niche in this all-male structure, comes with the birth of a baby girl in a large merchant family. You will hear the midwife announce loudly, "It's a girl, so the house will prosper!" And you know this to be true, since with only a girl child, the house can, when the time comes, adopt a husband for the daughter, a husband who has proven himself the ablest clerk around. As house head he will then propel the house and enterprise to success. This is what usually happens. In those rare cases where, due to a miscalculation and despite careful investigation by the marriage go-between, the husband proves to be a disappointment, the door to this androcentric structure can be pushed open a crack, and the house daughter can, if she is capable, step into the role and power of a house head, acting behind the scenes.

A century and a half later when I was visiting during one of my many trips to Japan, I became fascinated by the intertwining of enterprise and family in traditional businesses. I briefly explored five businesses until I realized that the sake industry was Japan's most ancient, and was also extremely familial and traditional. These features made it irresistible to me as a historian. I then spent many months visiting breweries ranging from Akita and Niigata in the north to Kyushu in the south. I benefited from the gracious hospitality and willingness of brewers to share family traditions and information about brewing technology. More than once I enjoyed a brewer's hospitality for days at a time.

I then considered the prospect of house daughters in brewing families. While exploring this possibility I encountered one example of a woman who had been so successful that it seemed she was an embarrassment to her descendants, who were extremely reluctant to speak about her. A sociologist pointed out to me that I was "storming the family castle," that the details of a family's history are often too intimate, too private, to share with outsiders. This only whetted my interest further. The only alternative, then, was to write fiction, to imagine the life of such a woman. This woman became Rie.

Joyce Chapman Lebra
Boulder, Colorado
2008

Discussion Questions for Readers' Clubs

1. Were you surprised by how powerful sake brewers were in the eighteenth and nineteenth centuries?

2. Why was this house happy to have a daughter as an only child?

3. Was Jihei a typical mukoyoshi, adopted husband/househead?

4. What challenges did Rie face as a woman? What advantages did she have as house daughter?

5. Why was Rie so unhappy to have Yoshitaro adopted as househead and heir? Would you be?

6. Do you think arranged marriages worked at the time?

7. Why were people so surprised Rie wanted to adopt a mukoyoshi for Fumi?

8. Some Americans have asked, why didn't Rie have the nerve to sneak into the kura when no one was looking? What do you think?

9. What would have happened had Rie been discovered during her assignation with Saburo? What would have happened to Saburo?

10. What was your reaction when Rie demanded that Kinno divorce Nobu?

JOYCE LEBRA, a recognized authority on the cultures of Japan, India, and Asia/Pacific women, is professor emerita of Colorado University. She lived in Japan many years and authored twelve nonfiction books.

Joyce Lebra